# LARGER THAN LIFE

"Entertaining and sophisticated."

—*Marie Claire*

"Parks has scored another surefire hit with *Larger Than Life.* . . . Expect to see it peeking out of handbags near you soon."

—*Heat*

"A *Bridget Jones* meets motherhood scenario . . . fun and funny."

—*Booklist*

"Entertaining and humorous."

—*Library Journal*

# PLAYING AWAY

"Compulsively addictive!"

—*Elle*

"An affecting first novel . . . a cheeky first-person narrative. . . . A balanced exploration of the rules of marriage."

—*Kirkus Reviews*

"*Playing Away* is a very edgy book. It's also wickedly funny and very sexy."

—*Publishers Weekly*

D0061750

# STILL
# THINKING
# *of* YOU

## *Adele Parks*

New York   London   Toronto   Sydney

DOWNTOWN PRESS, published by Pocket Books
1230 Avenue of the Americas
New York, NY 10020

Originally published in Great Britain in 2004 by Penguin Books

Library of Congress Cataloging-in-Publication Data is available.

ISBN-13: 978-0-7434-9650-6
ISBN-10:    0-7434-9650-7

This Downtown Press trade paperback edition December 2006

10   9   8   7   6   5   4   3   2   1

DOWNTOWN PRESS and colophon are trademarks of Simon & Schuster, Inc.

Manufactured in the United States of America

For information regarding special discounts for bulk purchases, please contact Simon & Schuster Special Sales at 1-800-456-6798 or business@simonandschuster.com.

For my mum and dad

# ACKNOWLEDGMENTS

Thank you to Amy Pierpont and the team at Downtown Press, and to Louise Moore, and the entire team at Penguin, for continuing to make my dreams come true. You are all such a warm, committed and enthusiastic gang.

Thank you, Jonny Geller, Deborah Schneider and Carol Jackson, who are outstanding agents and friends.

Thank you to the staff at Hôtel des Dromonts in Avoriaz, all of whom ensured that research had never been so pleasurable! Particular thanks to Mehdi Dehmane, assistant manager, who was amazingly patient, helpful and hospitable. Your pride in des Dromonts is completely justified, and I only hope that I have done justice to this stunning hotel.

Thank you to Christelle Lacombe, manager at Avoriaz Tourist Office, for your time and expertise.

Thank you to all the lovely readers who have sent me emails and letters, and all the lovely readers who haven't written, but have bought my books. Without you this whole process would be pointless.

Thanks to my family and friends, who continue to overwhelm me with their support and love.

And thanks to Jim. Oh, for lots of things: for teaching me to snowboard and giving me marvellous insight into "boy thinking" and for wearing T-shirts to tell people to buy my books, for believing in me, caring for me and loving me. You make my days joyful.

# STILL THINKING *of* YOU

# 1

## *Rich and Tash*

It was so easy. Falling in love had, after all, been so easy.
Rich had never been convinced that he had the knack for loving. Sex, yeah, positively expert, but loving? He'd had a sneaky suspicion that "falling in love" was something that happened only to people in movies or to the weak-minded. Or maybe he'd been born without the necessary gene that enabled a healthy, happy, two-way loving thing because he used to find it impossible to imagine wanting to share everything from your sock drawer to your life. His parents were still together, yeah, but they seemed to exist side by side in a state of bored tolerance rather than in perpetual bliss. His mother filled her time with concerns about neighbors' hysterectomies, and his father's chief concern was his golf handicap. Rich doubted that they had ever been young and in love. It wasn't exactly inspiring.

When his mates said that they'd found a girl they wanted to marry, he'd assumed that the desire was one largely driven by practicalities. Clearly some people liked the company, or the laundry service, or the security of being a double-income family. It wasn't that he wanted to be callous. In fact, the reverse was true. He'd always wanted to believe that there was something chemical—no, something magical—that dictated with whom you spent your life. He always wanted to believe that there was a soul mate out there somewhere. But he'd given the mysterious "falling in love" dozens of opportunities and thirty-three years to take hold; it never had.

Until Tash.

They'd been right. All those people that used to say stuff like "You know when you know." Those starry-eyed blokes who stuttered their way through speeches at wedding receptions, earnestly trying to communicate their passion and their willingness to subdue themselves to a bigger force than their reason. They'd been right. Falling in love did make everything lucid, bright and simple. And yet at the same time it was the most mysterious, exotic and different experience of Rich's life. An irresistible contradiction.

He loved her, and she loved him. They were lovers. Rich wondered how many people across, say, London—no, make it bigger than that—say, Britain. How many people were at this precise second telling one another they loved each other? And how many of them meant it as much as he did?

Because he did mean it. He meant it all the time. Not just when they were having sex. He loved her smile; it was broad and frequent. She had fat lips; clearly they were blow-job lips, which was an advantage, but he also admired them because they were happy lips. He loved her laugh; it was low and throaty, like a smoker's laugh, even though she didn't smoke. He loved her thoughts and how frequently and openly she expressed them, and how she insisted on bringing everything back to a personal level. He used to hate the type of person who, during a really sensible discussion of whether U.S. and British troops ought to be deployed to some far-flung place, would pipe up to say, "Well, all I know is it's wrong because my next-door neighbor is in the army and he may see action." That sort of argument used to irritate his intellectual mind. But now he realized that everything *was* personal at some level; everything was simply about whom you cared for. Tash was right. She was also right to want to drink Fair Trade coffee and use Body Shop products. All that girlie stuff was good.

He loved her body. He loved the smell of her hair. He was fascinated by the things that made her angry, and thrilled by the things in which she delighted. He loved the vulnerable curve in the nape of her neck and the way she shivered when he kissed her there. He loved her cum.


Tash finished cleaning her teeth. She put her toothbrush back in the cup and smiled at her reflection. That was her toothbrush, in a cup, in Rich's flat. Although they'd only been seeing each other for just shy of two months, she had a toothbrush in his flat, and that felt good. Unlike Rich, Tash had never wondered if she'd find true love. She'd expected to. Her parents had been happily married for forty years. Even now she might walk into their kitchen and find them kissing. Not full-on kisses obviously—that would be damaging—but affectionate, closed-mouth kisses. Her brother and his partner had two robust, amusing, boisterous boys. They laughed and argued in what Tash considered to be the correct proportions. Love had never been a secret to her. It was easy; it was natural. It was everywhere. She'd been in a number of long and short and virtually split-second relationships, but the dumping or being dumped had always been relatively painless. She'd never cried about anyone for longer than a week.

Tash had a few very close friends with whom she happily shared the contents of her head and heart on a regular basis and a larger number of more casual mates with whom she was happy to have a drink. She was sporty and therefore fit in the health sense and in the leave-men-panting sense. She liked painting (people with hobbies are happier). She had a dog (people with pets are said to live longer). Tash believed in natural justice; she thought there was definitely something in horoscopes; she wished people of all religions could live together peacefully; and she was sure the God whom she believed in would allow unbaptized babies as well as decent nonbelievers into heaven. She thought there might be something in reincarnation; she'd never had her tarot cards read, but didn't scoff at those who had; she had a monthly direct debit to the National Society for the Prevention of Cruelty to Children (NSPCC); she didn't care whether people held their knives and forks correctly or incorrectly; she recycled her bottles at Sainsbury's; she was a vegetarian, but she wore leather shoes. She had always expected to find true love.

She just hadn't expected it to be this good.

Tash hadn't been able to imagine feeling this excited yet this content. This happy and yet this terrified. This amazed and this amazing.

It was another almost uncomfortably hot night, so Tash pulled the covers off the bed and climbed in next to Rich.

She started to move her hands across Rich's chest and unapologetically down, toward his crotch. It didn't surprise her that he was semierect; they both existed in a state of almost permanent arousal. Rich ran his hands over her lithe body, enjoying again the sensation of her tight ass and tiny, firm tits. He already knew that he wanted to marry this girl. He wanted this beautiful, sexy woman to be his forever, and he wanted it so much it sometimes hurt him. Get that. Richard Tyler, philanderer extraordinaire, was so much in love it actually hurt him.

Of course, in the past he had told other women he loved them—it was expedient.

They kissed with their eyes open. It used to freak him when he opened his eyes midkiss to find her sapphire blues staring right back at him, but now he always kept his eyes open, too. Tash had explained that she thought it was more honest. She'd kissed plenty of men whom she wanted to shut out, but she wanted to drink up Rich, every ounce of him. It was as though she sucked in his soul through her stare, and she poured back her heart.

"How are we going to keep it this good?" asked Rich in a whisper.

Tash broke away from the kiss and stared at Rich. "God, you are a funny one. It's not difficult," she laughed.

"It is. Staying in love *is* difficult. There's no point pretending anything else. Tash, how are we going to keep it this amazing, this real and exhilarating?" Rich felt panicked. He could not imagine recovering if he lost her now.

Tash instinctively knew this was not a moment to laugh off Rich's fears. "I think it's down to honesty, baby. No secrets, no lies, just one hundred percent respect and honesty. It's such a simple rule. If we follow it, we can't go wrong."

Rich thought about it for a moment. Could it really be that easy? He ran through a number of scenarios of possible fatal blows to a relationship and tested them against Tash's rule. No secrets, no lies, just 100 percent respect and honesty. It would be impossible for either of them to have an affair if they stuck to the rule (something he had to admit he had been prone to in the past). It would be impossible for the relationship to be eaten up by paranoia or jealousy (God, if he could have a penny for every time some girl lost the plot by torturing herself with unnecessary suspicions). If they respected one another, they were unlikely to fall out about the split of domestic duties, hogging the TV remote or either one spending too much time with their mates (he meant him spending too much time with his mates—girls were rarely accused of this crime).

Maybe it could be easy.

In their cocoon that smelled of sex and oozed with warmth and affection, Rich could not imagine how anything could ever go wrong. Tash was a genius. Tash held the secret formula to a happy ever after. Tash *was* his happy ever after.

"Tash?"

"Yes?"

"Will you marry me?"

"Yes, Rich, I'd love to."

# 2

## *Meeting and Greeting*

For the first two months of their relationship, Rich and Tash did the thing that lovers usually do—i.e., stay in bed, only resurfacing for food, condoms and work when it was absolutely unavoidable. After Rich proposed, they were no more inclined to get up, but they found themselves talking more and screwing ever so slightly less. Remarkably, they both enjoyed this stage just as much as the first stage. The more they talked, the more they found they had in common and the more deeply in love they fell.

"I've always wanted to play a musical instrument. Preferably the guitar," said Rich.

"Me, too!" Tash giggled at the thought that they shared the same secret ambition. "After the wedding we should take lessons."

"We can put guitars on our wedding list," laughed Rich. "You're happy, right? Moving into Islington, into my flat?" Rich loved his flat. It had an enormous fridge, TV, shower and bed. He didn't waste any time considering the rest of the fixtures, fittings or furniture, and he almost reveled in being a cliché.

"I've always liked Islington, although I do think we should put detergent on the wedding list, too," replied Tash, who already had plans for a new sofa (squishy with lots of cushions) and new bed linen, and to repaint the entire place—to eradicate all traces of beige.

They both wanted children. A boy and a girl would be ideal, but of course they agreed that the health, not the sex, of the baby was the most important thing. Two years' time was a good point to start trying for a family; neither of them was in a particular rush. They both loved snowboarding, breakfast in New York diners, George Orwell, football, Frank Sinatra and Marmite. Neither had joined the mile-high club, but both wanted to. They talked about everything: their families, their work, their homes, their dreams, their fears and their friends. Rich had met Tash's three best mates, within weeks of their first date. Although they'd all been slightly the worse for wear after a night on the town, Tash reasoned that at least he'd got the measure of them. Rich talked about his great bunch of mates from college.

"I've known Jason, Mia, Kate, Ted and Lloyd as a man and as a boy," he boasted. Technically, he had known them as a man and as a young man, but he wasn't inclined to describe it that way. It didn't sound as catchy, and Rich liked to sound catchy. They'd met aged eighteen and, here they were, still firm friends at age thirty-three. "We've seen one another through exams, first jobs, first loves, marriage and births."

"Tell me about them."

"Well, Jase, he's my best buddy, I guess. He is one of the most charismatic men in London. A huge and very successful flirt." Rich smiled. He enjoyed his mate's success with women almost as much as he enjoyed his own. "He's massive in the advertising world. His reputation stretches across the Atlantic. You'll love him," Rich stated confidently. "Ted comes from a very wealthy family. Lewis-Ponsonby."

Rich's voice went up at the end of the sentence, indicating that Tash ought to recognize it. She shrugged, indicating that she didn't. In fact, seconds after the name was mentioned, she couldn't even remember it; that sort of stuff never stuck in her mind. "They are in Debrett's. He can trace his family as far back as the court of King George the Second," added Rich. "Ted probably doesn't have to work. He could live off his family's wealth, but he decided to make his own fortune as a trader. Don't you think that's impressive?"

"I think it's sensible. An idle life would be mind-blowingly dull."

"Suppose . . . and Ted is phenomenally intelligent. Kate's father is the chairman of Bristol University, and she's frighteningly bright, too. She could easily have followed her father into a career in academia, but chose to make a career in the City like Ted until she got pregnant, and now she's a full-time mum."

"How did she take to the change?"

"Oh, she's cool with that decision as she always wanted to recreate the traditional family upbringing that she enjoyed, and besides which she's just the perfect mum. I couldn't imagine a better one."

"Why's that, then?" Tash asked, grinning, already curious at what Rich thought made a good mum.

"God, the stuff she knows, she's just fabulous, like she really loves them."

"Naturally," laughed Tash. "Mums tend to."

"Ted and Kate married aged twenty-three and are still totally into one another. Can you believe that in this day and age?"

"Yes, I can, actually," said Tash, laughing more. It was obvious that Rich was still battling with his innate cynicism. "What about Mia?"

"Mia was the most wanted woman in college, a total beauty and also extremely intelligent. Both Kate and Mia are fascinating women. You'll love them. They'll love you."

Tash beamed, sure that they would all love each other. How could she not love them? From these descriptions it was obvious that she was about to meet some of the most amazing people in the United Kingdom. Which was fantastic. If not a little intimidating.

"They are a great bunch of pals," added Rich, almost to himself.

"And Lloyd?"

"Oh, he's divorced." Rich shrugged, and took a slurp of his coffee.

"What else? There's got to be more to the man than that."

Rich thought for a moment.

"At college he was the most focused of us all. Always seemed to know where he was going and how he'd get there. He wrote these sort of life plans, you know, things he had to achieve before he was twenty-one, then twenty-five, then thirty."

"What sorts of things?"

"All sorts. Places he wanted to visit, where he wanted to live, rungs on the ladder which he wanted to climb."

"Incredible."

"He always wanted to join the civil service."

"Incredible," repeated Tash, but this time she spluttered into her coffee.

"He's not just a paper pusher. He's involved with all sorts of important stuff."

"Like what?"

"I'm not sure if I really know," admitted Rich with an apologetic grin. He shrugged, and added, "I don't think divorcing Sophie was on the list."


The gang and Rich had history.

Tash and Rich didn't have much history, but they were now looking forward to their future, so Tash was desperate to meet these people who were important to Rich, and she wanted them to become important to her, too. She had found Rich's descriptions of his mates a little inadequate, more thumbnail sketches, really. But men never gave the sort of detail women liked. She didn't care about the things he told her—the professions of their fathers and where they lived—she wanted to understand the essence of these people. She filled in the details with wishful thinking. She expected that the guys would be like Rich (although not as cute), they'd be charming and clever and funny and sporty. And she imagined that Kate and Mia would be like huge treasure chests—not only would they have interesting nuggets of information on Rich, but Tash just knew that she'd have two brand-new best friends as well.

Rich decided to throw a dinner party to get everyone together and to celebrate their engagement. Despite his friends agreeing that it was a "fabulous idea" and that they "couldn't wait to meet Tash" and were "almost breathless with anticipation," it took six weeks to coordinate calendars and finally fix a date that was mutually convenient. Tash didn't understand the problem; when her friends wanted to get together they just did so. They shopped or played CDs and drank tea together. They didn't have to coordinate calendars, nor did they do anything elaborate in terms of catering. Usually they'd order takeout; often they'd make do with a packet of Kit Kats. Still, people did things differently, and she was cool with that. Life would be dull if everyone were the same. After all, it was exciting and out of the ordinary, throwing a proper dinner party with napkins and three courses, and separate wineglasses for red and white wine. And while Tash was a little bit daunted by the fact that she felt like her mum, as she arranged flowers and put shiny black olives into a little bowl, she took comfort in the fact that Rich was acting like her dad. He'd spent the afternoon washing his car, and now he was decanting red wine to allow it to breathe. Tash wasn't fond of olives; she didn't really believe anyone was. It was her secret belief that people trained themselves to like olives because they were supposed to be sophisticated. Olives were the thirty-something equivalent to learning to smoke or having your ears pierced. So she bought a multipack of Walkers crisps from the garage, just in case.

Tash took great pains in selecting her outfit for the dinner party; after all, it was sort of her engagement party. She'd dismissed the idea of keeping on her old pair of jeans and a T-shirt, the outfit she'd normally slob about in on a Saturday night, as Rich had spent nearly 200 quid in Tesco and a further fifty in Majestic Wine. This evening wasn't a slob-out type of affair.

It had been a very warm day and Tash was feeling 100 percent summer, so she changed into a floaty, floral dress and painted her toenails a pretty pink to match. She looked in the mirror in Rich's bathroom. Typical boy, he didn't have a full-length mirror anywhere in his house, so she had to stand on the loo seat to get a half-decent view.

The dress didn't work.

She looked like she was about to meet her boyfriend's parents, not his mates. In fact, contrary to general expectations, when she had met Rich's parents the whole event had been no big deal. They'd all met up for supper straight from work one night. Tash couldn't even remember what she had worn. She just remembered having a good laugh and Mrs. Tyler getting tipsy on Baileys.

Both Mr. and Mrs. Tyler had fallen over themselves to be nice to their daughter-in-law-to-be. For a start, she was easy to like, and secondly, they were delighted that Rich had finally decided to settle down. Frankly, Tash could have had two heads and they'd still have believed that she was the best thing since the invention of the can opener. They thought this because—despite their son's scathing dismissal of their relationship—they considered themselves very lucky and they wanted Rich to be as lucky. Neither were they the type to talk openly about their feelings all the time; it wasn't done in their day. But they knew that they loved one another deeply, and their greatest wish was for Rich to find someone he could grow old with, someone who would take an interest in his golf handicap (however feigned), someone with a good heart who would worry about neighbors' operations (however gory). They thought Tash fitted the bill nicely.

Tash tried on another outfit. Tight black trousers and a crimson and purple Diesel top. She knew that Rich loved her in this getup. And she wasn't daft; she knew why. The trousers clung to her backside, and the top was designed so that you had to go without a bra. Which Tash could pull off with her tiny 32A boobs—it was one of the rare occasions that small breasts were an advantage. She repainted her toes with a ruby varnish—twice because she was shaking the first time and made a real mess of them—and she carefully applied her makeup. She was ready. She checked her reflection. Cool. She looked good.

God, it was like a first date.

Tash wouldn't have liked to admit it, but she was desperate for Rich's friends to like her. It really, really mattered. Odd, because as a rule Tash wasn't one for external endorsements. She liked herself. Of course, she occasionally looked at her waistline and had a fleeting concern that she could pinch more than an inch, but generally her confidence only plummeted at certain times of the month. Then she would wonder just what could be done with her hair, and why her face shone like her mother's prized and frequently polished dining table. On the whole, however, she was happy with the way she felt about herself and the world in which she lived. Crucially, she was happy before she met Rich, and now she was delirious.

Maybe that's what was making her so nervous.

Tash walked downstairs and found Rich in the kitchen. He had his back to her, as he was chopping vegetables. She saw at once that he hadn't changed and was still in his jeans and T-shirt from earlier in the day. Bugger, maybe she'd gone over the top. Rich turned to her.

"Wow, you look stunning, babe," he said, as he pulled her toward him and started to kiss her. He broke off. "Are you wearing lipstick?"

"Yes."

"Oh."

"Shouldn't I be?"

"Well, it's up to you, babe. Of course, you look great with full makeup and everything. I was just wondering if I've ever seen either Kate or Mia in lipstick." He paused, and shrugged. "I just don't want you to feel overdressed, you know, out of place or anything."

Tash grabbed a bit of paper towel and started to rub off her lipstick. She became impatient with herself. This was ridiculous. Rich liked her in makeup. He'd often said so. More important, she liked herself in makeup.

"Well, I won't feel out of place, with or without my scarlet lipstick. I just thought I'd make an effort. We are throwing this dinner to celebrate our engagement," she muttered, peeved with Rich for his implicit criticism, and even more peeved with herself for taking notice.

"Yeah, and you look great, babe. God, if we were going to a bar, you'd turn heads."

"But you don't like what I'm wearing to meet your friends?"

"No, I'm not saying that. You look very glamorous."

It didn't sound like a compliment. In fact, this sounded like a disagreement. Their first. Tash wondered if she had time to nip upstairs and put on her jeans again. The bell rang. Clearly she didn't.

# 3

# *Introducing Kate and Ted*

First to arrive were Kate and Ted. Tash was relieved to see that they had both made an effort and that they had dressed up, too, and she was only a little disappointed to note that Kate and Ted's interpretation of "dressed up" was shirt and chinos for him, shirt and chinos and pearl stud earrings for her.

Still.

Kate and Ted both looked older than Tash had expected. If she'd seen them on the street she would have put them at late thirties or early forties. They were both rotund and, while Kate was quite short and Ted rather tall, they looked like one another. It wasn't just that they were sporting the same outfit. They both had mid-brown hair (although Ted's was streaked with gray and Kate's was clearly streaked at an expensive hairdresser's—with auburn), and they both had brown eyes and rosy cheeks. They looked wholesome.

Tash beamed and was prepared to be impressed and to be impressive. She took a deep breath and tried to stay calm. It wasn't easy. She'd known Rich for three and a half months now and hadn't felt calm since they met. She'd felt exhilarated, alive, indestructible, purposeful, sexy—just bloody fantastic. It wasn't easy to stay calm.

"Ted, Kate, this is Tash. Ted is a trader, Kate is a full-time mother and, well . . . Tash is my fiancée," said Rich, shyly.

Everyone laughed; the introductions were silly, as they all knew that much about one another, at least. Kate handed Rich a couple of bottles of wine and Tash a large box of Belgian chocolates.

"Wow, that's so generous of you."

"Well, you've probably been in the kitchen all day, right?" said Kate.

"No, to be honest I haven't. I can only make so-so goulash and curries. Rich has done all the cooking."

"Oh," said Kate, and then she shrugged at Rich. "Bad luck."

"I'm not handing over the chocs, though. Possession's nine-tenths of the law." Tash grinned.

"Actually, it's not," said Ted. "I studied law at college, and that's a common misconception."

"Oh." Tash paused. "Well, OK, I'll share them." She laughed quite heartily at her own joke, but she was the only one who did so, as Rich had scuttled off to pour some gin and tonics. Kate and Ted stood, smiling politely; Tash realized she was supposed to offer them a seat.

"God, sit down. Don't stand on ceremony for me. You must have visited Rich's flat more often than I have. It goes without saying to make yourselves at home. Kick back; take off your shoes," offered Tash. She was, as usual, barefooted. Ted and Kate sat down on the settee. Neither of them took off their shoes, but they did hold hands, which Tash thought was sweet.

"Unusually hot weather we're having this year, aren't we?" said Ted.

"Terrible for the gardens," added Kate. "They're parched. Do you garden much, Tash?"

"No," Tash confessed. "I live in a second-floor flat, so I don't have a garden."

"No garden!" Kate and Ted chorused. They looked shocked. Tash reran the conversation mentally. Had she just offered to show her new Brazilian wax? Clearly she had made a terrible faux pas.

"I have a rubber plant," she offered.

"I can't believe we are here on time, can you, Ted?" asked Kate.

"It is unusual," confirmed Ted.

"We've finally found a reliable babysitter. She actually turns up when she says she will."

"Oh, that's good." Tash smiled. Kate knew that Tash wouldn't have a clue just how good it was, so she pushed her point home.

"It's taken seven years."

"Bloody hell. So, give me details. Names of your kids, ages? Rich was useless when I asked him," said Tash.

"Really? You surprise me. He is, after all, Elliot's godfather," commented Kate.

Tash blushed. She knew she'd put her foot in it. "Well, you know what men are like," she mumbled.

"Our *children* are called Fleur, Elliot and Aurora. I really don't like the term 'kids,' except if we are talking about baby goats. They are seven, five and two." Kate smiled at the thought of her offspring.

"Wow! I hadn't expected your kids, er, children, to be so old. That means you were having babies when I was just twenty." The words were out before Tash noticed that they could be taken to be rude. Bugger. "I mean, I knew you were Rich's age. If I'd thought about it, you are easily old enough to have a seven-year-old." Bugger. "I just meant you don't look it," she hurried on, in an attempt to cover the gaffe, but gave up under Kate's cool, calm stare.

"You should look forward to your thirties, Natasha. They are great years," said Kate evenly.

"Oh, I do, I do. I can't wait to get old." Bugger. Bugger. Bugger. Tash fell silent. It seemed safest. No one said anything for a while, and the room was hushed except for the whirr of brains searching for polite topics of conversation.

"So, what do you do, Tash?" asked Ted, trotting out the usual London opener.

"I'm a retail merchandiser, which is just a posh name for a window dresser."

"Really?"

"Yes."

"That must be nice."

"Yes." Tash thought for a while, then added, "I work freelance, but have regular contracts with two or three pretty prestigious outlets. I love it. It's creative and flexible. I like being my own boss." Tash wished she'd shut up and wondered why she was suddenly justifying her existence. She sounded like Miss England bidding for the judges' approval.

"Being your own boss must be very nice," said Ted. "I envy you."

"Yeah, well, earning millions must be very nice, too. I envy you," laughed Tash. Neither Kate nor Ted joined in with her laughter. Instead they looked embarrassed. "God, sorry, I didn't mean to be crass. I was just joking," explained Tash. "I don't envy you. I earn a decent-enough wage. Not that I'm saying your life isn't enviable. I mean, it is. . . ." Tash gave up digging.

"Don't ask me what I did before the children were born," said Kate. "I hate that question. It implies that whatever I did before was more important and defining than bringing up children. Which I resent."

"Absolutely," said Tash. It was a good point, if a little forcefully made.

The small talk became minuscule, then disappeared altogether. The silence stretched, and felt like a couple of weeks to Tash. She wished Rich would hurry back with the drinks; suddenly she had a really keen thirst. Tash used all her mental energy to will the doorbell to ring again.

Which it did. She almost ran to answer it.

# 4

# *Introducing Jason and Mia*

S o, you must be the gorgeous Natasha. I can see why you lured Rich away from bachelorhood," said Jason, beaming. "I'm Jason, but the gang calls me Scaley. You can, too, if you want."

"OK, and you should call me Tash." She grinned. She wondered if Jason's nickname was something to do with his acne-pockmarked skin or whether maybe he could swim like a fish.

"As in Scalectrix," he explained, as though reading her mind, which she sincerely hoped he couldn't. "I like fast cars and gadgets and stuff."

"Mostly, he likes fast women," interrupted Rich, who was suddenly at Tash's side. "How are you, buddy?" The boys gave each other a manly, back-slapping hug, and Tash "Aahhhed" to herself. She always found guys hugging guys heartwarming. It was probably the reason she had so many gay friends.

Tash immediately liked Jason. He burst into the sitting room and dramatically lifted the atmosphere. There were no more lulls in conversation, just plenty of chat and laughter. Jason was reputedly a massive hit with the women, and Tash understood why this would be the case. He was not in the slightest bit good-looking, as Tash had expected—he was very short, eyes a bit close together, poor skin—although he *was* totally charismatic, as Rich had promised. He was fun, sharp and confident, and he seemed to have an unlimited supply of gripping anecdotes. She liked his delight in his life, his work and his flat—a flat that was crammed with big-boy gadgets. He didn't seem to take himself—or, for that matter, anyone else—at all seriously.

"Mia's late as usual, I suppose?" asked Jason, pausing after amusing everyone with a story about presenting to a new client who, unfortunately for Jason, turned out also to be an old lay. It was clear that Scaley was good at laughing at himself, which guaranteed that no one else ever laughed at him, only with him. "Rude girl, that Mia," commented Jason with a playful wink. "Have you had the pleasure yet, Tash?"

"No."

"Should be interesting."

Before Tash had a chance to digest Jason's comment, the doorbell rang, and she went to answer it.

"Hi. Mia, right?" Tash beamed at the woman who stood at the door.

Tash and Mia swept their eyes up and down one another, quickly appraising. Mia was wearing jeans and a T-shirt. She *was* wearing makeup, but it was the sort of makeup that men didn't notice—powder, lip gloss, a bit of mascara. Her hair was glossy and cut into a style that somehow carried an expensive price tag. Her nails were manicured, but painted with a clear finish, no color. She was a large girl—not fat, just broad and tall. There was something Amazonian about her. She had big brown eyes that showed she was fun, clever and, if necessary, cunning. Her skin was creamy, flawless. A good-looking girl, definitely. More "well put together," more "makes the most of herself," as Tash's mum would say, than "total beauty," as Rich had said. But lovely all the same.

Mia spotted Rich, who was behind Tash, and her face split into the broadest Julia Roberts–style smile. Mia's loveliness was immediately further enhanced by sexy loose lips framing straight white teeth. Ah, thought Tash, got you. Mia was the college goer. Men often confused that with "total beauty."

"Richie, my Action Man," Mia cried, "how are you?" Mia swept past Tash without so much as a nod. "I've brought you a bottle of Merlot, your favorite and mine. Aren't I clever?" She hugged Rich, and plonked a huge kiss on each cheek.

Mia walked straight into the sitting room. "Don't get up," she instructed, as she bent to kiss the air that swirled around Kate, then Ted. "Ms. Monopoly, Big Ted, you two look absolutely amazing." Her grin spread and was genuine. "We all have ancient nicknames," she added, presumably to Tash, although she didn't look at her as she spoke. "Games and toys. Don't worry if you don't pick them up; they are *very* private. Don't feel you have to use them."

Tash was relieved to hear that. She couldn't imagine calling Ted "Big Ted" and, while it was clear that Kate wasn't a fish-and-chips sort of girl, it sounded a bit rude to call her Ms. Monopoly.

"Scaley Jase, have you been waiting for me?"

"All my life," beamed Jason.

Mia couldn't harness her grin. She found it difficult to disguise the fact that she liked to flirt with him. They'd dated for nearly three years in college. If quizzed, they'd both dismiss the "ancient history" as "totally juvenile," yet neither had ever dated anyone else for longer than three months since. Mia flopped into the chair Tash had been sitting in, and picked up Ted's sparkling water. She took a huge glug, then announced, "Big Ted, water is a big girl's wimp of a drink. You should be ashamed. I thought it was G & T."

"I'm driving."

"Would you prefer a G & T, or something else?" asked Rich.

"No, I'm on a health kick. This suits me." Rich poured another drink for Ted. "I'm exhausted. I've been on a ten-mile bike ride this afternoon. Well, I'm not going to let my fitness levels drop," announced Mia.

"Mia did the London marathon, in April," explained Rich. "She made an incredible time, three hours thirty-five." Tash smiled and nodded. "This is Tash," added Rich, as he put an arm around her. Tash felt her skin melt comfortably into his.

"I guessed. Hello. Have you done the marathon?" asked Mia.

"God, no, never appealed to me. I prefer flinging my body around an aerobics studio to keep fit."

"Really? You've done it, haven't you, Rich?"

"Yeah, it was hell. I did it in 2000."

"And Kate and Ted did it in 1998. The first time I did it, didn't you? I've done it three times now. I'm addicted. Lloyd did it way back in 1994, didn't he?"

"Yes, and again in 2001 with me," said Jason. "Jesus, I thought I'd die."

"Never appealed to you, though, hey, Natasha?" said Mia.

"No," confirmed Tash.

"Well, it's not for everyone. It takes a lot of commitment; it's a lot of hard work. Shall we eat?"

# 5

## *Polite Small Talk*

Things didn't turn out exactly as Tash had hoped. The tuna steaks were seared to the right side of blue, the chocolate soufflé rose to the required height and the Brie was served at room temperature, as she knew was tastiest. Yet despite all this, something stopped the evening from being a success. For a start, Tash was disappointed that Lloyd wasn't there. She'd wanted to meet the entire gang. Tash had quizzed Rich as to why Lloyd was not there, and he had muttered something about Lloyd's calendar being chock-ablock, but during the evening it transpired that Lloyd hadn't actually been invited. Everyone agreed that this was best; he wasn't himself since he split up from Sophie.

"He's not a particularly amusing guest at the moment," commented Jason.

"Surely that's when our friends need us the most," said Tash, "when they are feeling crap?"

No one answered, but they swapped looks which suggested that they all knew more on the subject than Tash, and Tash conceded that they possibly did.

Kate changed the subject by asking, "Has anyone seen Freddie Walker recently?"

"Funnily enough, I had lunch with him just the other day," said Mia. "He's terrific; doing very well. Managing partner at his firm, you know."

"What is it that his firm does exactly?"

"Oh, I'm not sure, *exactly*. Something in the media. Very glamorous. He's done terrifically well." Everyone nodded their agreement.

"Have you heard from Miles Beaumount?" asked Ted.

"Yes, I met him at the Beeb about a month ago. Some business we're talking through together," said Jason, but he didn't expand.

"We had Clara and Marcus over for dinner on the eighth," said Kate.

"Are they well?" asked Rich.

"Yes, great," confirmed Kate and Ted in unison. "Expecting their second."

Tash stayed silent. She didn't know any of the people who were being mentioned, and none of Rich's gang knew her friends, so it seemed pointless mentioning them. Nor did Tash join in when Ted asked her if she knew the statistics behind gun crime in the London area. She had nothing much to say on Kate's topic either, namely that, in her opinion, some Tibetans had lost patience with the Dalai Lama's message of peace. When Mia asked her whether she agreed that Sir Ludovic Kennedy was a bigot, she was stumped. She didn't know who he was. She mentally scanned her memory to see if his name was tucked away anywhere. Had he been mentioned in her history A level? Was he a dictator, a theologist? It transpired that he was a broadcaster with views about gay TV kisses. She hadn't read Robin Cook's diaries, which the former cabinet minister had kept in the run-up to the war in the Gulf. She thought such exposés were sophisticated kiss-and-tells and quite undignified. Instead of saying so, she just said that she preferred reading novels. Tash could have kicked herself. She knew that she hadn't come across as clued up on anything important. She wanted to be a credit to Rich, but feared that she was behaving like a high-interest overdraft.

Kate noticed Tash was being left out and said, "Let's talk about something else. We are clearly boring Tash." She smiled. "Tash is a retail merchandiser, you know, Mia. She's very interested in clothes."

"Fascinating," said Mia, but she appeared disinterested. "I don't know much about clothes, I'm afraid. I never really have time to follow fashions."

Mia wasn't particularly trendy, but nor was she unfashionable. Enjoying clothes had been considered frivolous when Mia studied for a degree at college, and it was then that Mia made up her mind on personal grooming and many, many other important matters. As an undergraduate, Mia soon learned that girls who expected men to pay for drinks, girls wearing makeup or girls caring about beautiful shoes were all seen as signs of patriarchal domination. Mia did not want to be dominated by the patriarch. She reacted by sleeping with men she didn't care for and not with the ones she thought she might care for; this behavior made her feel, if not powerful, then certainly less vulnerable. Mia never admitted, especially not to herself, how much she envied women who let men buy their dinner or those who got excited about a new lip gloss or somehow just knew what length skirt was a "must have" each season.

Mia wore a lot of black because it slimmed down her thighs, and no one ever looked inappropriate in black. She considered shopping a chore. It promised all manner of wonders and delivered only disappointment. Mia bought whatever her personal shopper in Selfridges told her to buy (her personal shopper was inspired by the very windows that Tash dressed—both women would have been disgruntled if they'd known). Taking the advice of a personal shopper was far easier than trailing endlessly up and down high streets, forging through crowds of silly teenagers. Her personal shopper ensured that she had an outfit for every occasion and, while her outfits rarely earned Mia notice, they at least never caused her any embarrassment. Some people could get it so wrong.

As someone who had never bothered to develop an individual style, getting it wrong was something Mia avoided.

"What did you study at college that led to such a career?" asked Ted.

"English," replied Tash.

"Where?"

"Brighton."

"How old are you, Natasha?" asked Mia.

"Twenty-seven."

"Where is your family from?" asked Kate.

"Salford, just outside Manchester."

"Is your father in textiles?"

"No, he was an engineer. He's retired now." Tash was confused. She felt as though she were being interviewed for a job, and she shifted uncomfortably in her seat. She wanted Rich to rescue her, which was odd because up until that moment she'd never believed in knights in shining armor, but then, she'd never come across fire-breathing dragons before either.

Jason played Sir Lancelot. "Are you planning on having babies, and if so will you have mine?" he asked, laughing. "Leave her alone, poor girl."

"Is this a Jamie Oliver recipe?" Kate asked Rich, changing the subject. Having found out what they needed to know, they didn't direct another comment at Tash for the remainder of the evening.

# 6

## *Mia's Bomb*

Kate and Ted left just before midnight, as they didn't want to irritate their new babysitter by returning too late. Mia and Jason stayed for another hour, only stumbling out into the warm summer night after Jason, Tash and Rich had drained every bottle they could find, bar the cooking sherry. Abstemious Mia had looked on with distaste, although in truth she was more envious than repulsed.

"Isn't this the type of night that makes you want to stay up and watch the sunrise?" Jason asked, flinging his arms wide. He spun around on the path, nearly losing his footing and slipping onto the road. "Life is fucking fantastic. Fucking electric. Fucking bright and sparkly, and so fucking full of love, isn't it? Who'd have thought it? Old Rich, ready to settle down."

Mia glared and didn't answer. Even if she had drunk the cooking sherry, she was unlikely to have agreed.

"Tash seemed a totally cool honey," commented Jason. "Don't you think?"

"She didn't have much to say for herself," replied Mia with a cold honesty she reserved for her old friends.

"Great legs."

"For God's sake, Scaley, do you ever think with anything other than your penis?"

"Not if I can help it." Jason grinned, ignoring Mia's irritation. "Listen, I'm going on to a private club that I've just been given membership to. It's up in Soho. Do you want to come?" He was sure if he could only get a glass or two down Mia, then she would relax a little and perhaps become more of her old self.

"What, and hang out with a whole load of inarticulate drunks instead of just one inarticulate drunk? No thank you, Scaley."

"It will be fun," said Jason, with persistence. Mia threw him a look which expressed her doubt. She spotted a cab about twenty meters up the road. Thankfully, it was for hire. She shot up her arm. "Call me when you sober up. We can discuss the plans for the stag."

"What will you have to do with the stag?"

"I'll probably have to organize it. You can't be trusted." Mia saw Jason's look of puzzlement. "Why shouldn't I organize it?"

"Er, because you haven't got a penis, and even if you had, you wouldn't think with it," laughed Jase. "Left to you, we'll spend the afternoon Jimmy Choo shopping."

"I loathe shopping."

"You don't know the first thing about strip joints."

"That's why the Internet was invented," argued Mia. "I am one of his best friends. I don't like you implying that I'm not the right person for the job of arranging a stag do simply on the grounds of my gender." Mia hopped into the cab. "I would offer you a lift, Scaley, but I can't risk you puking in the cab. Good night."

Mia flung herself back on the seat and barked her address at the cabbie.

"Nice night, luv?" he asked.

"Not really," she said as she snapped closed the partition, making it clear that she didn't want to talk. Why should she have to chat to the cabdriver? She was paying for a service; she didn't need another new best friend. Besides, his views were bound to be ill-informed and bigoted, derived from tabloid press. She could do without them.

Mia slipped off her shoes and massaged her feet against one another. She rubbed her eyes and nose.

What was wrong with her?

Recently, in the past six months or so, she had been consumed by overwhelming feelings of anger, resentment and, she might as well admit it—at least to herself—jealousy. Tonight had been torture. Rich had always been a confirmed bachelor. She'd thought they'd be company for one another as they edged their way toward old age. Now look at him. He was gaga. And over what? A very ordinary girl that he'd known for about five minutes. It wasn't that Mia wanted Rich in the way Tash did, but she knew well enough that a married friend was a lost friend. She would have to kiss goodbye to those weekend breaks that she, Rich and Jase took from time to time. There was no way that Rich would still be her date for corporate events now that he was about to turn all pipe and slippers on her. She resented the fact that, from today onward, any confidences she shared with Rich would automatically be shared with Tash, too. Tash wasn't her friend.

But it wasn't just Rich's engagement that had upset her.

Recently, whenever she looked around, *everyone* seemed to have it better than she. Of course, Ted and Kate had it all; everyone other than the Beckhams had reason to envy *them*. They were very happy, extremely rich and, most desirable of all, they had three children. OK, Jason wasn't sorted in the same way, but he didn't seem to want much more from his life than regular, uncomplicated lays. His ambitions were easy to fulfill. Even Lloyd seemed better off than she. His marriage might have broken down, but he was with someone else now and he was at least a father. Christ, her life really must be crap if she was jealous of a sex addict and a weekend dad.

She hadn't always felt like this. She used to think that she had it all. In fact, she used to think she *was* it all. She was born into a fiercely intellectual but still loving family. She had an older brother and an older sister whom her parents exerted most of their parental expectations upon, and therefore she was left pretty much to her own devices. She was encouraged and praised in both her sporting and academic achievements; she'd secured a place at one of the best universities in the country to read French and economics. Her big breasts and grin had seized her numerous admirers. Her first-class degree had guaranteed her a job in the fast track of the Foreign Office.

Yet.

Mia might have a Ph.D. and an important job in the Foreign Office, but that didn't keep her warm at night, did it?

Her biological clock was more of a biological time bomb, about to violently shatter if she couldn't force a solution soon. If she had to pinpoint one thing that she most resented about Tash, it was not her flippancy, her inability to look at the serious issues in life or her insistence on concerning herself with insubstantial matter such as heel heights. It was not her beauty or even her success in finding a man to marry.

It was her youth.

Tash was six years younger. Six years. And she was in a relationship, about to get married. Right now, when Mia was deafened by her biological clock ticktocking toward midnight, all she wanted was a bit more time.

For several months now it seemed that everywhere Mia looked she saw nothing but pregnant women, or women with babies or tiny children. Of course, that was life, and all around her people were living. Life was teeming out of every school gate, every play park. Life was springing and zooming and buzzing in every skip, hop and jump that she saw countless children execute. Life was radiating from their sticky hands and faces as they devoured ice cream on street corners and in buggies. She saw life in tantrums and spats and squabbles.

It took every ounce of restraint for the normally steely Mia not to cry at the sight of a bawling baby. She felt compelled to pick them up and hush and comfort them. It was only the fear of being arrested that restrained her. It was physically impossible for her to walk past a heavily pregnant woman. It was embarrassing. She found herself talking to all manner of pikey mums-to-be, striking up inane conversations about the weather or the efficiency of supermarket checkout queues, just so she could ask the question "So, how long have you to go?" Then perhaps she'd be invited to feel the baby kick, and as she reached out to stroke their blooming bumps she wanted to implode with awe.

And jealousy.

Mia sighed. She was a self-confessed control freak. She cycled to work because she couldn't handle the anxiety of dealing with late trains, let alone the idea that someone else was in the driver's seat. A few years ago she had experimented with growing her own vegetables. She'd gone so far as to put her name down on the council waiting list for an allotment because she could not tolerate the thought of eating food that someone else had grown or, more specifically, eating food that someone else had doused in pesticides. As it happened, she wasn't particularly green-fingered and would probably have starved if she hadn't found a small, local, organic greengrocer whom she vigorously bossed and cross-examined as to all his methods of production. Mia liked to know when and where the consumer durables she bought were made, what her boss and her employees had written in her appraisals (however painful), how much her friends earned, ate and exercised. She liked to know who was having sex with whom, and how often, and how good it was. She did her best to influence all of the above, but the one thing she couldn't control was time. She longed to turn back the clock, but she could not.

There was a time when Mia had been much more relaxed. When she had thrown parties and had not felt the need to calculate the number of canapés and glasses of alcohol per head, nor the cost of said canapés and alcohol, let alone the projected cost of broken glasses. At college she had a reputation for throwing the wildest parties. They were not planned several weeks in advance. They were spontaneous events, conjured up in response to the question "What shall we do tonight?"

Mia settled back in the cab and couldn't help but smile at the memory. As soon as she offered to throw open her room for a bash (well, hers and Kate's room, technically), then it was all hands on deck. Kate was always in charge of catering, which in those days amounted to little more than a speedy trip to Tesco's to buy a cartful of crisps and garlic bread. Jase and Rich would run around campus spreading the word and inviting all and sundry. Ted and Lloyd would move furniture, dragging the beds out of the way to create room for a makeshift dance floor, and Mia would buy the booze. She always bought crates of beer and a vast number of bottles of wine. Obviously some people would bring liter bottles of screw-top wine, but Mia liked to provide her guests with something that cost at least a few quid a bottle. She'd insist that she wouldn't clean her toilet with most of the cheap wine proffered, but in fact she was simply generous, something she didn't feel needed talking about.

She must have thrown a dozen or more similar parties in the four years she was at college. Every one of them was a monumental success. Friendship and fun and difficult-to-define comfortable familiarity had drifted through each event. Everyone had oozed such uncomplicated optimism and unfettered enthusiasm for life. They had a real belief in the brilliance of their futures.

Mia closed her eyes, telling herself it was because she was tired and not because she was trying to blink back tears. She acknowledged with a profound irritation that she had found parts of this evening a strain. She was aware that she no longer found it easy to be entirely relaxed with the old gang. She no longer thought it was a natural state of affairs if they all knew everything there was to know about one another, which was at once a disappointment to her and also a direct result of her own actions. She had not confided her longing for a baby to anyone. At college the gang had forged their way through well-mannered small talk, progressed to intimate revelations, moved on to huge debate and finally completed the circle so that their conversations relaxed into an almost continuous discussion on the story line of *Neighbours*. Now, they seemed to have regressed back to the small talk, only it was no longer always well mannered.

Mia gave up the line of thought. It was too depressing. Instead she started to run through the list of names she liked for babies. It was her favorite game.

# 7

## *Clearing Up*

Tash reminded herself that these people meant a lot to Rich, and Rich meant everything to her. Yet she couldn't help breathing a sigh of relief when they finally left her to the washing up at 1 a.m.

"They really liked you," said Rich, as he slipped his arms around Tash's waist and breathed in the smell of her hair. She was concentrating on the washing up, so didn't turn to face him.

"You think so, hey?" she asked, not absolutely convinced. Yes, Jason liked her. That was clear. She had legs, breasts and a vagina; he wasn't going to dislike her. He borderline fancied her, which was ideal. They could gently flirt, knowing it would never go anywhere, and he could ask her for advice on women. Not that he seemed to need it, if the anecdotes that he relayed tonight were anything to go by. And he clearly adored Rich. She could trust him not to tie a naked Rich to a lamppost the night before their wedding.

Ted and Kate were quite unlike any of Tash's friends. They seemed genuinely excited that they had managed to book tickets for the Khachaturian Centenary Concert with the Philharmonic Orchestra, George Pehlivanian conducting. Apparently it was mid-October's must-see. But they were not interested when Tash generously offered her spare tickets for the Robbie Williams concert at Knebworth, which was probably just as well because her old mates would sell their grandmother's souls to secure tickets and would not appreciate her giving them away to her new friends. Their conversation had been fiercely intellectual, as Rich had promised. But rather than being stimulated, as Tash had expected, she was paralyzed. She knew she'd come across as dim, which was infuriating. Still, there was plenty of time for her to drop into conversation that she had actually read Salman Rushdie's *The Satanic Verses* and James Joyce's *Ulysses.* She hoped that one day they'd be friends enough for her to admit that she hadn't actually enjoyed either book.

But Mia.

"Absolutely, they loved you," enthused Rich, interrupting Tash's thoughts and ignoring the nuances of the evening.

"Well, why wouldn't they? I'm very nice."

"Mia even made up a nickname for you, a rare honor. Come on, leave the washing up. I'll do it in the morning."

Tash peeled off the rubber gloves and allowed Rich to lead her by the hand up the stairs.

"Have you ever slept with Mia?" asked Tash, as they undressed and slipped between the sheets.

"Yeah, a long time ago. Just once." Telling Tash about old lovers was easy. Their pledge to be totally honest with one another demanded a level of trust and an expectation of clear-headed responses.

"That explains a lot," stated Tash simply, as she fought a yawn.

"It wasn't an exclusive club."

"What do you mean?"

"Well, obviously there was Jason. They used to be an item, but she's slept with Ted, too."

"Ted?"

"Yeah."

"Blimey."

"I'm not sure Kate knows that."

"No, I don't suppose she does." Tash rolled on top of Rich and started to kiss his chest; he stroked her back. "What was Mia's nickname, then?" she asked between kisses.

"Bridge, as in the game. Very complex."

"Given what you've just told me I'd have had her down as Poker."

Rich laughed, and moved closer to kiss Tash. They kissed for a very long time. Slowly exploring each other's mouth, tongue and lips as if for the first time, not for the thousandth. Tash took hold of Rich's hard penis and guided it inside her. Gently, she rode him, and they made love very quietly, very carefully. When Rich came, Tash lay exactly where she was until it became uncomfortable. Then she rolled off him, and they lay side by side, Rich spooned around Tash.

"How many people have you slept with, Rich?" asked Tash curiously. "Do you keep count?"

"I have a number, but I couldn't put a name to every one."

"That's awful," said Tash, as she playfully hit him. "How insensitive. So, go on, how many?"

"I can't tell you that."

"You have to." She giggled. Rich leaned close to her ear and whispered the number.

"No!" she yelled, feigning shock and horror.

"What? What should I have said? What's the right number?"

"I'm teasing you. The correct number is the real number, however many or few that may be. I mean, what's the right scenario? Would I have preferred it if you'd slept with fewer women and had had longer relationships? Or would it have been better if there had been lots more, but you'd never cared for anyone at all before me? I don't know. It doesn't matter. Everyone has a history."

"Oh, yeah?" Rich smiled. "I thought you were a virgin when we met," he joked.

"Right," laughed Tash.

Eventually, their breathing slowed, and they were seconds away from a peaceful, slightly drunken sleep when Tash thought to ask, "By the way, what nickname did Mia give me?"

"Didn't I say?"

"No."

"She called you Barbie, as in—"

"Barbie doll."

Rich fell asleep, and Tash was left wondering whether the nickname could be interpreted as anything other than a declaration of war.

# 8

## *Lloyd*

I t was late October, but still startlingly warm. The leaves on the trees had turned red and were starting to fall. A warm, honey light dripped through the gaps left between the branches and rested on a blanket of horse chestnuts and color that lay on the ground. The majority of Londoners took advantage of the mild autumn. They sat in cafés drinking smoothies and refusing to don jackets. They laughed and joked. They hung on to summer and ignored the displays of Halloween pumpkins that had crept into the window of every shop.

Not Mia.

Mia was also fighting time, but not simply because she wanted to lazily loll in cafés. She didn't like wasting precious hours simply having fun. Since Action Man and Barbie Babe had announced their engagement, Mia had been planning and plotting and scheming to find a way to turn their situation into one that was advantageous for her. It might be Barbie Babe's wedding, but Mia was trying for something even higher. Mia wanted a baby. Nothing was more important than that.

Mia rummaged around her bag for the small makeup mirror that she thought might be hiding in there. She sighed, briefly disappointed by her reflection. She ran her fingers through her hair— it was too short. She hated it. However, she was almost thirty-four and had come to accept that hating her haircut was part of her hairdressing experience, as intrinsic as the ugly nylon gowns and the luxurious head massage. She would hate it intensely for twenty-four hours, then she would forget it until she needed it cut again. She'd love it for the week between booking her next appointment and attending her next appointment. She used to think that this showed her insecurity, but she now chose to believe that it showed she was a perfectionist.

She fumbled for her mobile phone and searched for Lloyd's number. She rang it and was surprised to find that it was out of use; it had been a while since they were in touch. Mia called his ex-wife, Sophie, to secure his new mobile number; she'd provided it, but not much else by way of conversation, and was barely civil in response to Mia's question about how little Joanna was faring—"Extremely well, thank you." Sophie had never had any social graces, thought Mia.

Mia dialed Lloyd's new number, and he picked up after just two rings.

"Checkers, it's me."

Lloyd knew immediately that it was Mia on the line, even though he hadn't heard her voice for nearly six months. No one else still used this nickname from college. He wished Mia wouldn't. He'd never liked it. Checkers was the less cerebral little brother of chess and the nickname had never seemed like a compliment. Apparently Mia had chosen it because, as she said, "Lloyd *appeared* very black and white, and you could guarantee he was always one move ahead." He'd never been sure what she meant by that, although she had made her proclamation with a big smile, as though she were being nice. He supposed that she meant he was a great planner. And he was. Or at least had been. Nowadays it seemed hard enough to put one foot in front of another, let alone plan years ahead as he had always prided himself.

"Checkers, how the devil are you?" she screeched. "You have been on my mind for so long now. I've been meaning to call. Meant to almost every day. Have you heard Action Man's news?"

"He called last week, actually, to say that he's finally taking the plunge. But he was rushing to a meeting so we didn't get a chance to talk at any length. Great news. Tell me, what do you know about Natasha? I like her name."

"Do you?"

"Is she Russian?"

"Hardly, she's from Manchester. I think her parents must be a bit pretentious."

"What's she like?"

"I've only met her a couple of times."

"And?" Lloyd knew Mia well enough to know that she always made her mind up about people instantly. She'd then declare a great fondness—or, more often, a damning condemnation—then she would hastily add that it was unfair to judge a book by its cover, and that she was reserving judgment until she got to know the subject better. In reality, no one got a second chance after a first impression.

"She's slim."

"And?"

"Blonde."

"And?"

"Tall."

"As tall as you? Do you see eye to eye?" Lloyd chuckled at his own wit. Mia chose not to answer. "Is she clever, funny, what? Give me details," demanded Lloyd.

"It's always hard to say when someone is marrying one of your oldest friends, isn't it? I'm not sure I can be objective. I mean, who is good enough for your best friend? I don't know much about her. She went to a very ordinary university, one of those that's really a poly, so she's no genius."

Lloyd wondered whether going to an ancient university was the best thing that had ever happened to Mia. It seemed to be the only thing she ever measured anyone by. Lloyd decided to move the conversation along.

"Rich told me that they are taking off to the Alps to get married, just the two of them, and that they are planning to pull a couple of witnesses off the slopes. Sounds cool." Lloyd was thinking about his own very big and very formal wedding, several years earlier. He hadn't thought it was possible to argue about the thickness of the card of an invitation, but apparently it was. "I think they've made a wise move having a no-fuss wedding."

"Do you?" Mia wasn't so sure. She'd hoped for a big bash, where everybody got drunk and sentimental. As it wasn't to be, she had concocted an alternative plan. "Listen, it's just a quick call to run through the details of the stag weekend." Mia hoped she sounded breezy and efficient, rather than tense and a little desperate.

"Rich never mentioned a stag weekend."

"It's a surprise. I'm arranging a stag holiday for Action Man."

"*You* are?"

"I am one of his best friends, even if I am a woman," said Mia, hotly irritated. She'd met with the same surprise not only from Jase, but also Ted, so she was particularly alive to any implied criticism. "I thought that you, Action Man, Scaley and Big Ted and I could all go away for a couple of days, just like old times. I'm planning something wild in Dublin."

"You and four guys?"

"I suppose Kate might tag along, but we often did that at college."

"And you're thirty-three and still unmarried, I just don't understand it," joked Lloyd.

"Ha-fucking-ha," snapped Mia. She was stung because she'd had the same thought herself, a thousand times. "So how does the second weekend of November sound?" Mia took a deep breath. She hoped she sounded nonchalant. She had been living on a knife edge for the past few months. She'd planned everything so carefully. The timing of the stag do had to coincide with her cycle and, of course, getting Scaley Jase on the trip was paramount, but she had to give the necessary attention to the demands of everyone's calendars.

Yes, she'd considered sperm banks; she'd investigated them quite thoroughly. Rationally, she knew that one could trust the medical notes that read "6 foot 2 inches, MENSA member, with blue eyes and no medical conditions," but how could you be 100 percent sure? Mia constantly had visions of the Elephant Man, without the IQ and with more congenital deficiencies. Besides, the cost of artificial insemination was extraordinary, and she had to start watching the pennies now. She was unlikely to be flush after she had the baby and gave up work.

She had considered getting pregnant via a one-night stand, but there was always the danger of the unknown there, too. A guy might seem like a rational, intelligent, pleasant enough guy while he's eating pizza, but what's to say that in reality he's not an ax-wielding psycho? And if she took the time to get to know the one-night stand, then that, too, would lead to all sorts of complications. By definition it was no longer a one-night stand if she actually knew the guy. It would be a relationship. The donor might suddenly decide he was in love with her (men that she wasn't particularly attracted to were always doing that). Then he might decide that he wanted to help bring up the baby.

There was no chance of that with Jason.

Mia couldn't see a baby in Jason's flat. Imagine the sticky fingerprints on his vertical Bang & Olufsen hi-fi. He had the one with the option to play one of six CDs. He loved that hi-fi because when the phone rang he was able to change the CD from Kylie Minogue to a moody lounge track, just in case it was a woman calling and he wanted to impress. He had no idea how entirely Austin Powers he appeared to the outside world. He usually picked something like *Hôtel Costes* to play. Even though he lamented that

it wasn't as hip as it had been in 2001 when he stayed at Costes
and actually met Stéphane Pompougnac, sat and drank with him,
talked about what inspired his mixes. He'd confided in Mia that
the *Costes* CDs "had become mass market, a victim of their own
success, but they were still good tunes." She'd replied curtly that it
was a shame that he'd have to abandon it now and find something
more cutting edge as the likes of Ted and Kate played it as background music at their dinner parties.

Imagine the baby pressing all the buttons on his Cosmo dual-
band GSM phone and messing up the oh-so-considered (and contrived) message that Jason had recorded. Apparently the phone
had an integral data-fax—whatever that meant. Mia had no idea,
however often Jason explained it. You could buy software to allow
video conferencing; Jason intended to do so. Naturally there was
no handset. The phone cost the average guy's month's salary, but
he wasn't an average guy and he earned way more than an average
salary. Anyway, the phone hadn't really cost him a penny as the
advertising agency where he worked had paid for it. They deemed
it a necessary accessory for their newly appointed creative director
of Q&A. It was worth every penny because Jason was able to hold
one woman as he talked to another if the occasion arose—and it
sometimes did.

Mia smiled to herself. She knew Jason well enough to know
that he was genetically perfect father material in every way—and
a total vacuum emotionally. Exactly what she wanted.

Now all that was left for Mia to do was to tie up loose ends
such as inviting Lloyd along to the stag do. She wanted to give all
her old college friends the impression that the only thing that
concerned her was that Action Man have a great time. There were
bound to be questions after the trip, when she conceived. It was
essential that the pregnancy appear absolutely accidental. No one
must guess how she'd schemed for the event. Arranging the trip
had involved all her negotiation skills, her cunning, her discretion

and her determination. Providing Checkers could make that weekend, however, she thought it was in the bag.

"Fantastic. Count me in," said Lloyd, although he was thinking he ought to check with Greta first to see if she had anything on the calendar that he needed to be involved with.

"Cool," said Mia. "I wondered if you'd have to check with Greta."

"No, no, no problem there," assured Lloyd. He hoped that he sounded like a man that successfully managed his relationship with his girlfriend. A man that had found balance and attained intimacy, while avoiding intrusion. "There won't be any argument. Greta doesn't do arguments." His ex-wife, Sophie, had been the queen there. Greta, on the other hand, sulked. Lloyd didn't think it was necessary to add these choice pieces of info.


This wedding was good news for Lloyd. He hadn't heard from the gang for such a long time. It would be good to catch up with all the guys and spend some real quality time with them. Sure, they texted one another reasonably regularly. Sure, they called occasionally, and they even made plans to meet for dinner or to go away together for a weekend from time to time. Invariably, though, those plans were canceled at the last moment. Everyone worked so hard. People had come to expect a cancellation because of a meeting running late or a sudden and urgent request to put a report together for 8 a.m. the following day. He was possibly the worst culprit of all for last-minute cancellations.

Sophie used to grumble about that all the time. She used to say that he ruined her social life. He never understood that. Why, if he had to work late, couldn't she go along to Kate and Ted's without him? When he used to ask her that she would reply that she'd rather spend an evening with her own friends, and then he'd ask, "Well, why don't you?" She'd always argued that she never planned to see her own friends because they always had plans to see his, plans that he always canceled at the last minute.

He could replay these rows word for word. She must have plenty of time to spend with her own friends now. She never understood just how demanding his work was. Bitch. At least Greta got that about him. She knew that he, and what he did, was important.

Lloyd thought it was peculiarly poignant that the gang used to call him Checkers because everything in his life was black and white, and he was always a step ahead of the crowd. Since he and Sophie split up, everything was a blurred, indistinguishable mass of grays. He felt he was way off track. If life was a race, he was falling behind.

Sophie had kicked Lloyd out of his home one year, one month, two weeks ago. She'd shouted that he was useless, neglectful and hurtful. She'd yelled that she was sick of trying to win his attention, let alone his approval. She'd cried she was exhausted, sick of doing everything for the baby on her own, while still trying to keep her own career afloat. He'd pointed out that things were easier for her in her career than they were for him in his because she worked at home and for herself. She argued that this just made things scarier; there was no such thing as a day off. She'd also argued that she was the biggest breadwinner and therefore what she did was important. She never actually said *more* important, but she thought it. He knew she thought it.

For fuck's sake, she organized parties.

It was supposed to be a little part-time something-to-do job that would fit around their future family. Who would have thought that the vol-au-vent-eating population was so greedy? There seemed to be a party every night, which left Sophie little time to support Lloyd in his career. She knew that was what he expected of her. They'd talked about it at the beginning of their relationship, way back when. A civil servant needed a wife who supported him, not one with her own career. When he'd argued this, Sophie had said, "I have two words for you, Lloyd: 'Cherie Blair.'" Very funny. The last two words she'd flung at him were not as considered.

Soon, it wasn't just the staff and catering that Sophie organized, but the flowers and photographers. In some cases she helped the hostess to find the perfect outfit. The company grew so fast and efficiently that she was able to franchise the name and take a cut of four more companies doing the same thing in different areas of London. In her third year, Sophie made a profit of over £170,000. Just for throwing parties. It didn't seem right.

There was no way that Lloyd would ever earn that much in his field. Civil servants earned next to nothing. While he missed the money that Sophie had earned, he didn't miss the fact that Sophie earned it. Greta didn't earn much, but she worked as a research assistant in his department, so she saw that what Lloyd did was important. He was involved in real issues—management of funding in retirement homes for the elderly, the overhaul in the nursery voucher system, for example. Sometimes, he paper-shuffled and argued about a change in the days that the garbage men collected the trash, but everyone had to start somewhere. Greta saw he was powerful, authoritative and significant. Greta knew that she didn't buy a big share of voice in their relationship, and it suited them both.

Lloyd didn't regret his affair with Greta. He didn't even regret Sophie finding out. Most of the time, he thought he was much better off without Sophie. Greta was younger, better groomed, more accommodating. Bigger breasts. She came from a wealthy Austrian family. As she was foreign, any miscommunication could easily be dismissed as a language barrier.

Rather than a heart barrier.

He preferred the sulking to the rows. Greta was less work than Sophie. Lloyd constantly reminded himself that he was in a better position now that he was a man with a girlfriend rather than a man with a wife. So why did he continue to make these constant comparisons?

Lloyd sighed. Why did he feel perpetually tired? He wondered if he should be taking a vitamin supplement. He'd have to ask Sophie . . . No, he meant Greta.

"Well, I just wanted to touch base. I have to go now. My taxi is just pulling in at the Indian Embassy. I have a meeting there. I'll be in touch. I have your email address. I can't wait. It's going to be so exciting," said Mia, interrupting Lloyd's thoughts. "All the old gang back together. My oldest and bestest friends." Mia liked to give all her friends the title "best," or "old," or both. She hoped that it gave the impression that she was a nice person, even though she, and even her oldest and bestest friends, often had occasion to doubt that this was the case. She *was* a clever, funny, sexy, extremely bitchy person, but, then, that was often better than being nice in the circles in which she mixed.

"Absolutely," agreed Lloyd, but he wasn't sure if Mia heard, as she'd already rung off.

# 9

# *Tash's Reaction to the Dublin Trip*

No. Absolutely not."

"Why not?" asked Rich, somewhat surprised by Tash's response.

Tash hesitated. She wasn't sure *why* she did not like the idea of Rich and his friends going away for a stag weekend to Dublin, but she didn't, not one bit.

"Don't you trust me?" asked Rich. After all, he had told her about that time he'd done a stripper, for a bet, at some debauched stag weekend or other. It was a complicated male ego thing that Tash didn't get, but she hadn't seemed at all concerned about the incident either. In fact, she'd been pleasantly curious. Her questions had been agreeably erotic. She'd just commented that no one should be defined by their work and had been a bit bra-burning brigade about Rich going on about bedding a stripper rather than noticing the woman for herself.

"Of course I do," said Tash, raising an eyebrow and a grin.

"So, what is it?"

Tash wasn't sure she could articulate her objections to the trip. Was it that Mia was going along? Was it that the gang would be building more memories, memories from which she would be excluded? Was it that her hen party was destined to be a much lower key affair? Her friends didn't earn the type of salaries that made rushing off for party weekends a viable option. They'd be opening a few (admittedly, quite a few) bottles at someone's flat and, by way of celebration, to distinguish the evening from numerous other Friday nights, they'd order pizza *and* garlic bread.

"It will cost a fortune. Do we have that type of money to squander just before the wedding?" Tash's speciality was squandering money—that was why she didn't have any form of savings. Rich knew this and consequently looked baffled. "The boarding trip to the Alps isn't going to be cheap," she added.

"Damn right, it isn't," said Rich. "It's our wedding, and I'm not planning on cutting any corners. It may be a small wedding, but it's still the biggest day of my life." Rich put his arms around Tash and drew her toward him. "We can afford it, baby," he assured her.

"My brother's girlfriend, Celia, is expecting her baby that weekend." Tash knew she was now grasping at straws.

Rich looked stunned. "I'm not birthing partner material," he pointed out. "I'm sure that event can go ahead with or without me. I'll toast the baby in Dublin."

Tash searched around for another objection. "But it seems silly if more people go to the stag party than the actual wedding," she insisted. Tash didn't actually believe this either. She'd never placed too much importance on etiquette, conventions, customs or rules. These traditional measures—which kept most people motivated, law abiding and supported—were unimportant to Tash. She followed her gut, worked with her instincts and, while she had little interest in deliberately shocking or rebelling, she had never seen a need to conform either. She wasn't intending to be willfully dishonest, she was just finding it surprisingly difficult to be entirely honest with herself.

"Maybe that's the answer," said Rich. He beamed at Tash. "You genius. You've just given me a great idea." He kissed her forehead.

"What?"

"Instead of having a stag party I'll invite the gang along to the boarding trip, and you can invite some of your friends, too. It will be great fun. Mia talked about all the cool stuff we used to do."

"The good old days," interrupted Tash.

"Exactly." Rich grinned, not catching the sarcasm in his fiancée's voice. "And I have to admit that she did paint an irresistible picture."

"I bet she did," deadpanned Tash.

"She reminded me about how close we all used to be. Work and stuff gets in the way as you get older. We don't catch up as often as we ought, but she pointed out that my wedding had to be marked somehow."

"Our wedding," said Tash tetchily.

"Of course, of course," assured Rich. He looked at Tash, and tried to gauge her reaction. Tash tried to hold her face in a neutral expression. Tash definitely wanted to stick to the original plan of stealing away alone. But weddings did funny things to people. Normally, she was an intelligent, independent woman who pretty much did her own thing, and she was more than comfortable with that. She had not thought it necessary to marry in a white dress, in a church, in front of all her friends and family. The wedding, and, more important, the marriage that followed the wedding, was just about Tash and Rich. It was all about Tash and Rich.

She also accepted, however, that weddings came loaded with expectation, tradition and a probability that you'd never get away with doing exactly what you wanted.

"But if you really want to stick to the original plan, I'll do whatever *you* want, whatever makes *you* happy. We could still keep it to the two of us and a couple of witnesses, if that's *really* what you want," said Rich.

Tash wished that she could hide from the excitement in Rich's eyes at the prospect of his friends joining them, but she couldn't. She couldn't be so selfish as to deprive him of his big day, standing up in front of his friends who all meant so much to him.

And next to nothing to her.

"OK," she said. And she must have said it with more enthusiasm than she felt because Rich looked delighted.

# 10

## *NFI and RSVP*

Tash felt miserable as she crossed the final name off her list of friends and family that she'd invited to the wedding. Really, thoroughly, inconsolably miserable. No one could make it. Not a soul. Tash couldn't understand her disappointment. She'd *wanted* a very tiny wedding and had not been worried whether her friends and family would see her become Mrs. Tyler. But now—now when she'd invited nearly a dozen people, now when they had turned down her kind invitation—now she desperately wanted someone from her side to be at the ceremony.

Tash caught her breath and felt instantly guilty for thinking in terms of "sides." It wasn't a battle; it wasn't even a football match. There were no sides. It was just that all of the guests Rich had invited had said yes, that they would love to come to the wedding, and none of the guests Tash had invited had been able to.

Her parents had been bitterly disappointed that she and Rich had chosen to marry on the slopes. Neither of them had ever been on skis in their lives. The most adventurous holiday they'd ever had was taking the caravan to France, on a ferry. They were insisting on throwing a party on their return. Rich and Tash had agreed because they realized it wouldn't have made any difference if they'd disagreed; Mrs. Richardson had already invited about forty close friends, family and neighbors. Few of whom Tash would recognize in a lineup. Tash had given in to the inevitable. Her brother and Celia were extremely regretful that they couldn't join Tash and

Rich on the slopes. They both enjoyed boarding, but Tash could see that it was impossible so soon after the birth of baby number three. Celia magnanimously suggested that Tash's brother go without her, and he magnanimously turned down the opportunity. He couldn't leave Celia behind to manage three kids under the age of four.

Her pal George was a single parent and also had to say no because she couldn't find child care for a week. Mandy, David, Eliza and Greg all apologized, but pointed out that January was not a good month to try to go on holiday because their plastic was pushed to the limit after Christmas. They promised, however, to show up at the party. And her best friend in the whole wide world, Emma—her dead cert, her final hope, who had sworn that nothing would keep her away from Tash's wedding—had just called to say that she'd broken her leg and wouldn't be able to make it after all.

Tash had found it extremely difficult to be sympathetic. She put the phone back in the cradle just as Rich opened the door to the flat.

"Hello, gorgeous. How has your day been?" Rich asked the question, but didn't give Tash time to answer before he bore down on her. His lips pushed against hers, and his hand was already weaving its way up under her sweatshirt, searching for her nipples. Tash impatiently pushed him away. "What's wrong?" he asked. He knew it wasn't his greeting. Normally Tash liked him coming in and jumping her bones. In fact, generally she defied stereotype and insisted on being just as randy as he was. "Are my hands cold?" Rich rubbed his hands together.

"No," sighed Tash. "Well, yes, it's December; you're freezing. But that's not a problem. Emma has just been on the phone and she's had an accident at work, fallen off a ladder and broken her leg."

"Oh, poor thing," said Rich. "Is she a window cleaner?"

"No," Tash snapped impatiently. "She's an administrative assistant. She was fixing a blind in her boss's office."

"I bet that's not in her job description. She'll be able to claim compensation."

"You are missing the point, Rich," said Tash crossly. "She won't be able to make it to the wedding. That means no one is coming from my side." Tash corrected herself, "None of the guests I've invited can make it. Not one."

"Oh, I am sorry, Tash. That's a bummer." Rich walked through to the kitchen to put the kettle on to make Tash a cup of tea, then he thought better of it and opened the fridge to hunt out a bottle of wine. Tash was clearly very disappointed.

"Still, look on the bright side. All my gang can make it, and what's mine is yours. There are plenty of friends to go around." He smiled as he passed her a glass of wine. Tash accepted the wine, but not the words of consolation.

Over the past few months, Tash had spent more time in the gang's company. Ted and Jase were decent enough guys. Ted was a little dull and Jase a little blasé, but Tash was aware that it seemed churlish to grumble that one of Rich's friends was overly earnest and the other not earnest enough. Tash had yet to meet Lloyd— she wondered if he would fall somewhere in the middle of the earnest stakes. But Tash wanted a girlfriend on the holiday. Someone she could giggle with, swap lipsticks with, someone who would stay up until the early hours to discuss the meaning of life. Tash knew that neither Kate nor Mia could offer that.

She and Kate had settled into a polite acquaintance. Not a friendship, exactly, but the early strands of one, maybe. But it had not been easy. Whenever they spent time together, Tash found herself struggling for topics of conversation they could share. Tash had very little interest in school league scores, while Kate had none in the pop charts. Tash did not have access to the waiting list for Harrow or St. Paul's School, so could not do any favors for Kate. Kate was not a member of any of London's trendy nightclubs, so could not save Tash from having to queue or plead with bouncers.

Tash found Kate overly serious and sensible to the point of boring. And she was aware that Kate probably found her rather frivolous and perky to the point of giddy. Still, Kate was easier to like
than Mia, but then Tash suspected that Attila the Hun would have
been easier to like than Mia. Mia was cold and self-consciously
clever. It seemed that she had taken an instant dislike to Tash and
that she'd nurtured the dislike into something much stronger.
Tash was disconcerted that Kate still called her Natasha and not
the more familiar Tash that all her friends used, but then Mia
called her "Barbie Babe."

"Is Lloyd bringing his girlfriend?" Tash asked. Maybe Greta
would be an ally, she thought hopefully. She took a huge slurp of
wine and mentally chastised herself for again using vocab more
suited to a war room. Maybe Greta would be a *friend*.

"I didn't actually invite Greta," admitted Rich. He loosened
his tie and sat on the sofa with Tash. He started to massage her
feet with one hand, holding his wine in the other.

"You didn't?"

"No. I've never met her. None of us has. If Lloyd wants her to
come along he only has to ask, but he hasn't asked. I'm not sure
how serious he is about her. If he was very serious, then he'd have
made the effort to introduce her to the gang."

It felt like another blow. Tash pulled her feet away from Rich
and tucked them under a cushion out of reach. It was a silly and
pointless gesture, as she'd been enjoying the massage, and it wasn't
Rich's fault that her friends weren't coming to the wedding—but
it was his fault that his were.

They fell into a silence that Tash thought was uncomfortable
and Rich didn't notice. "Why did you ask if Emma was a window
cleaner?" asked Tash suddenly.

"Well, you said that she'd fallen off a ladder at work, and the
first association I made was a window cleaner."

"Are any of your friends window cleaners?"

"Of course not."

"Then is it likely that my friends are?" Tash seethed.

"Well, your friends have more varied careers," said Rich. "All my friends are lawyers or doctors or management consultants. Yours are musicians, designers or writers." In fact, a number of Tash's friends were still waiting for their big break and therefore technically waitresses, temps or unemployed. Rich chose not to spell this out explicitly. He picked up a copy of the *Evening Standard* that Tash had discarded earlier, turning to the TV listings and starting to scan read.

"My friends might not be as—" Tash wanted to say "dull," but chose "predictable" instead. Both she and Rich knew the difference in vocab was indiscernible. "My friends might not be as predictable in their career choices as your friends are, but their careers are still important."

"I never said they weren't," pointed out Rich reasonably. The very reasonableness of his tone further irritated Tash.

"You were being derogatory asking if Emma is a window cleaner."

"I did not say anything derogatory about window cleaning as a career choice, and if any of your friends had chosen that line of work—which they haven't, I note—but if they had, then I would simply ask if they could do mine for less than thirty quid, which is what I currently pay and I consider to be a rip-off."

Rich's reasonableness had slipped into sarcasm. Tash felt frustration and disappointment bubble over into ill-focused anger. She was surprised to acknowledge that she was hunting out a row. It would have been fortuitous if a telemarketer had called at that moment. Tash would have found a certain amount of satisfaction bawling down the telephone that, no, she wasn't interested in health insurance, replacement windows or completing a survey on her grocery-buying habits. But the phone stayed silent, so Tash chose to pick a row a little closer to home.

"So you'd be comfortable with my friends working for you?"

"And you'd be *un*comfortable with that?" Rich finally lowered the newspaper and met Tash's eye. He'd encountered enough women to identify misdirected anger when he saw it. He also knew that this type of anger could be as fatal as the more justified and honed variety.

"Fuck you, Rich," spat Tash. She was stunned to hear the words come out of her mouth. She rarely lost her temper and had never lost it with Rich. She loved Rich. Totally loved him. And this was not his fault or his problem. If she could have, she would have swallowed back the words, but that was never possible. She waited for Rich's reaction.

"No, I'm going to fuck you," he said, and then he leapt on Tash. He started to pour kisses on her face, her hands, her head, her body, anywhere he could make contact. Tash shrieked with laughter and relief that Rich had chosen to ride out the tide of her fit of anger. Her bad mood instantly vanished. She giggled, twisted and turned, and pretended that she didn't want to be drenched in his kisses, but they both knew that she now lived to be soused in his love. And he in hers.

Slowly, slowly, Rich found a way to every inch of her body. He kissed her crossness away and sealed in reassurance. They discarded their clothes with ease and confidence, willingly exposing their bodies to one another and anticipating the great pleasures that were to come. Tash kissed Rich, too, and she stroked, sucked and licked him. When his cock was in her mouth she felt overwhelmed with the love she felt. As he moaned, slithered and shook, she began to feel ashamed of her earlier displays of irrational anger and her suppressed jealousy of his friends. Because it was when he slipped his glacial fingers inside her and touched her hot, drenched flesh that she was able to identify and admit that it *was* jealousy that she felt. She was envious and intimidated by their shared past. Yet at that moment when she dripped cum on to his hands—

a piercing release that left her quivering and begging for him to climb inside her—at that moment she knew that no one had ever been so close to Rich, no one had ever shared so much.

As Rich climbed on top of Tash, he took a moment to admire her. He'd slid inside many beautiful women in his time, but never, ever had his thrusts brought him such untold delight. He adored making her happy. He loved the glazed, half-crazed look he brought to her usually serene face as he pushed, grabbed and pulled at her. She yelped with pleasure and desire, and begged him not to stop, even though her hair was wet with sweat and stuck to her back, her tits were wet with his kisses and her thighs were wet with her own cum. When it was impossible for him to hold back a second more, he exploded in her. Showering her with confidence and contentment. Rich collapsed inelegantly on top of Tash and stayed, paralyzed, until his breathing calmed.

For some moments there was silence between them. Tash listened to the sounds of the house. The printer, fridge and Play-Station quietly droned. The clock in the hall ticked softly, and Tash could hear the radio she'd left on in the bedroom. She could just make out that it was the latest boy band crooning their latest predictable but palatable tune. She believed it was a cert as the Christmas number one.

"What are you thinking, Tash?" asked Rich.

"I was wondering what will be number one when we get married and what music we'll dance to at our fortieth wedding anniversary. What were you thinking?"

"I was thinking that we should row more often if the making up is always that good," said Rich, and beneath him he felt Tash giggle.

# 11

## *Ted's Baby Sister, Jayne*

"Ted, it's your sister."

Kate handed Ted the phone and silently prayed it wasn't trouble, while preparing herself for the fact that it almost certainly was. Jayne never rang unless she was in trouble and, most specifically, in need of bailing out. Money, or a lift home at three in the morning because she was so drunk she couldn't hail a cab, or someone to feed her cats, or someone to call her boss because she was pulling a sickie. Kate didn't usually mind. That's what families were for, helping one another. But sometimes it was just a little bit frustrating that Jayne was always the one being helped. Jayne was thirty, for goodness' sake, not sixteen. It was time she stood on her own two feet. Kate and Ted had three children of their own. She didn't have space for a fourth. Jayne consumed a black hole of time and emotional energy.

Kate took a deep breath.

She ought to be more charitable. In reality she had nothing to be sore about. Kate's life was the type of life that invariably inspired jealousy. She had met the love of her life when she was eighteen and married him when she was twenty-three. She had been saved from the awful bed-hopping that just about all her friends seemed to have endured. There were no regrets in Kate and Ted's marriage. No past encounters that seemed more attractive; no current flirtations that seemed more alluring. She had not settled for her husband, like so many brides seemed to, desperate for security, sacrificing passion. Kate had felt passionate about Ted and even now, fifteen years after their first encounter, she still thought he was the best man to walk the planet. The best for her. They had three beautiful, healthy, happy children. Her husband earned a telephone number as a salary, which afforded them a very privileged lifestyle. Kate's life was perfect. It really was, and telling herself so was not an exercise in convincing herself all was perfect. It was more a case of reminding herself.

Kate felt ashamed that she'd had mean thoughts about her sister-in-law. It wasn't Jayne's fault that she wasn't as sorted as Kate was. Kate actually blamed her parents-in-law. They had brought Ted up with a stiff upper lip that was so well developed that he was in danger of getting lockjaw, and yet they had spoiled and indulged Jayne throughout her life. They expected nothing from her except a "good marriage," by which they meant a family name as old as their own and a bank account which was rather more substantial than their own. Ted's family was in the difficult position of being formerly moneyed. Everyone assumed they were still loaded, but the extent of their ready cash was not great anymore. Most of their dwindling income from their land went on maintaining the enormous family home. The rest was lavished on Jayne, who was showered with anything she wanted and everything she could possibly imagine needing, except the word *no.* The family's excessive indulgence had left her helpless, whereas Ted found it almost impossible to ask for help. It made Kate cross.

Kate sighed. She recognized that few people knew what they wanted out of life and therefore very few people knew when to call themselves happy or even lucky. As old-fashioned as it sounded, maybe what Jayne needed was a good man. Not necessarily a wealthy one, but a kind and decent man. Not that it seemed likely. She never seemed to hang on to the same chap for more than five minutes, which was odd because she was extremely pretty and intelligent, and one of the best flirts Kate had ever known.

Kate listened to Ted's sympathetic tones, and she started to piece together their conversation from the half she could hear. She did this while she gathered things together that needed to go into the day bag. They really didn't have time for this now. The cab would be here soon. It was a good job that she'd checked their ski kit last night and that their cases were full, just waiting for her to add the last-minute toiletries.

It was clear that Jayne had fallen out with yet another boyfriend. Kate couldn't even remember the latest one's name. She'd given up feigning even a polite interest. Had Ted packed his toothbrush? No, it didn't appear so. Kate went to the bathroom cabinet and scrabbled around until she found a spare toothbrush, deodorant, shaving gel and razors. She knew if she didn't check these things it would be her finding a chemist to buy replacements when they got to France. Where were the euros that they'd brought back from Barcelona last weekend? In the drawer where they kept their passports, probably. Kate dashed down two flights of stairs, found the euros and the passports, plus Ted's sunglasses, then rushed back upstairs to their bedroom. Ted was still on the phone.

For goodness' sake, Ted. She wished he'd get a move on. They had such a lot to do. Going away for a weeklong break took at least four weeks to organize, at least it seemed that way to Kate. She had to pack for the kids who were spending the weekend with Ted's parents. She had to leave copious notes of instructions regarding food preferences, medical conditions, school runs, extracurricular activities and other invites from which Fleur, Elliot and Aurora benefited. Her mother had kindly offered to move into their house from Sunday teatime for the rest of the week. It was best for the children to be in their own home; their schedules ought not to be upset just because Kate and Ted were having a week away.

A week away without the children. Kate felt a confusing mixture of emotions, something between ecstatic and terrified. She and Ted hadn't been on holiday alone together for more than seven years. Imagine, they could go to restaurants that didn't serve food in colorful cardboard boxes. They could stay out late at night, without having to worry about interrupting sleep patterns. They could have sex at any time of the day.

They could have sex.

And it would be so much fun going away with the old college crowd. Mia, Rich, Jason and Lloyd. They'd had such good times together. Never a dull moment, always laughing and joking. Of course, they'd studied, too, but that wasn't what it had been about. It had been about that sense of possibility. Future. Kate could feel eighteen again.

And yet.

She caught sight of a pile of discarded children's clothes next to the wash basket (not-quite-in-the-wash basket—her constant nagging hadn't achieved that goal). The clothes were grubby, sticky, soiled with food and mud and child sweat. Kate felt her heart contract with love. Suddenly she didn't want to leave them. She didn't want to go skiing at all. She'd much rather stay with the children, ensure that the correct shoes or Wellington boots went on the right feet every morning, that hats and scarves were duly donned. It was simple and safe and comforting.

However many notes she wrote, however competent her mother was, it still felt as though she was abandoning the children. Kate didn't think couples ought to have children if their sole raison d'être then became getting away from them. She had friends that didn't work, but still had au pairs to do the washing and cleaning, and nannies to do the loving. Not Kate. Kate prided herself on the fact that *she* had brought her children up, not hired help, even though they could easily have afforded an army of nannies, baby-sitters, after-school carers and au pairs. Personally, Kate found the concept obscene.

Although obviously she could see the attraction. Of course she could, especially on a particularly grueling day when London traffic jams conspired to make her late for dropping the children off at school. "Hurry, Mummy. I'll be in trouble," the panicked Fleur would cry. Kate would pray that the traffic started to roll again before poor Fleur worked herself into an inconsolable state. Such a sensitive child, plagued with asthma and allergies. Kate could appreciate that hired help might ease the days when Fleur and Elliot did arrive at school on time, but had the wrong kit packed in their bags—a recorder instead of a French vocabulary book, football boots instead of tennis shoes—social disgrace. No doubt a nanny would have made things easier on days when Aurora had suffered from cutting her teeth, or now when she was battling with the frustration of being a "terrible two." If only Kate's toddlers were terrible for a single year—that hadn't been her experience. On days when the children fought, squealed and bickered their way through breakfast to teatime, and finally landed as exhausted, resentful little bundles into their beds and cots—on days like that Kate could clearly see the attraction of a nanny.

Maybe Ted was right and a holiday would do her good.

She checked the clock on the bedroom wall. They'd be late if they weren't careful.

"Oh dear," said Ted as he reemerged from the hall and into the bedroom.

"What is it?" Kate only just resisted adding "now."

"Jayne's split up with her latest chap."

"Oh, thought as much. What was his name again?"

"Rob, or Rod, or Bob. I lose track."

Kate put her arms around her husband and hugged him. She marveled at how alike they were. She wasn't the only one who was fed up with the constant SOS signals that came from Jayne. Poor old Ted, the eternal big bruv. It wasn't an easy role to be cast in, not when he had a female version of Peter Pan as his sister. Kate suddenly felt sorry for him.

"She'll get over it."

"No doubt. But this time she is acting pretty scarily. She seemed really agitated and unhappy. A bit desperate. She asked if she could come away with us to Rich's wedding. I can't even remember mentioning the wedding to her."

Kate wondered if Ted truly lived on another planet. "She's talked of nothing else for weeks," muttered Kate. She zipped up the day bag and turned back to Ted expectantly; she was ready. She sighed inwardly when she noticed that Ted still needed to change his shirt. He had egg from breakfast on the left-hand side pocket. She'd told him about that three times. Ted looked worried. She knew that Jayne could be extremely manipulative. The chances were that she didn't even care about this split with Bob, or Rob, or Rod, or whomever; she simply fancied a holiday. It was obvious to Kate that Jayne had been angling for an invite for a while. She was always trying to muscle in on their crowd, forever inviting herself to parties and even intimate dinners. Kate wished she'd find some friends of her own. Ted would have a terrible time now if they went without her. He'd spend all his time worrying about her.

"Jayne kept insisting that a week on the slopes was just what she needed. Hedonistic fun, she said. I told her that it was terrible form inviting oneself somewhere, especially to a wedding party, but she was most insistent. Said she couldn't face being on her own. I told her it was impossible. That we were setting off any minute now, but—"

Reluctantly, Kate suggested, "Maybe she could come with us."

"Do you think so?" Ted looked eager; this was clearly what he wanted to hear.

"Rich and Natasha are very laid-back. They probably wouldn't mind if one more person joined the party. It'll even up the numbers a bit again. There are only three girls, and there are four chaps.

The only one of Natasha's friends that did accept the invite had an accident and had to pull out." Kate had already told Ted this, but through experience she knew she'd probably have to tell him another two times before he computed the information. "In fact, isn't Jason single at the moment?"

Kate was warming, already hatching a plot. Ted understood it immediately, but was unsure as to whether he thought it was a good one. Was Jason a suitable beau for his little sister? Jason was a bit of a scoundrel, which made for very entertaining anecdotes, but his sister . . .

"I'll call Natasha and see if I can clear it. Jayne's met Mia and all the boys quite a few times, hasn't she? She works in the same company as Rich, doesn't she?"

"Yes. But it's a big place. I don't think they've actually come across one another at work. Neither of them has ever said so."

"My point is she has things in common. She'll fit in."

"Do you think it will be OK?" Ted tried to put thoughts of Jason out of his head; surely Jayne wouldn't look at him anyway. She did sound very upset; he wouldn't be comfortable leaving her at home. Oh shit. This was the last thing he needed. As if he didn't have enough to worry about.

"I'll call Natasha right now," Kate said, with more enthusiasm than she felt. She didn't really want Jayne on the trip, but as Jayne always got what she wanted, Kate might as well bend to the inevitability of the situation now. If she and Ted argued, they'd be late.

Besides, it wasn't just Jayne who needed a holiday; Ted definitely needed a holiday, too. He had been acting oddly recently. No, *oddly* was too strong a word—*differently* was probably a fairer description. It was nothing Kate could put her finger on. He was as kind and generous as ever. Perhaps not quite so attentive, just a tiny bit distracted. It wasn't that he was working harder than usual. In fact, he really seemed to be making an effort to get home at a reasonable hour of late.

There had been a time before Aurora was conceived when Kate had resented the ridiculous hours he worked. He was a trader, for God's sake. Didn't the markets ever close? Apparently, yes, but when they did Ted had to schmooze clients at fancy restaurants and casinos until the early hours. She'd done it herself once upon a time, which probably made standing on the sidelines harder to stomach. When he'd suggested they go in for a third child she'd, rather unusually, let out a yell. "What's the point when you don't see the two you have?"

She'd cried and shouted and reasoned that the children missed him, that she missed him, that bringing them up on her own was overwhelming, and it did feel as though she were bringing them up on her own. In those days she was lucky if he made it home before ten. Even then he'd sometimes come home, eat his supper (without looking up from his plate), then retire to his study to "finish off some paperwork." Things had been much better since Aurora was born. Kate was sorry she'd had to make a fuss, put her foot down, but she was glad she had. Recently Ted had made it home by six or six-thirty. He'd found balance. He'd reprioritized. He'd had a word with his boss, and his boss had been very gracious about the situation and agreed that work wasn't everything.

So he couldn't be stressed at work.

Kate felt a slight pang of guilt and apprehension that she didn't know what was worrying her husband. She didn't have time to think about this now. They really were going to be late. Perhaps miss the plane if a decision wasn't made.

"She skis, doesn't she?" asked Kate.

"Snowboards, actually," confirmed Ted.

Naturally, thought Kate. No doubt Jayne thought skiing was passé in comparison to the far edgier sport of snowboarding. Kate walked back onto the landing. She picked up the phone and started to punch the buttons of Natasha's number. Kate sighed, and wished she'd been born the type of woman other people took care of. Rather than the more prosaic role in which she'd been cast, the one who looked after the organization.

# 12

## *Departures*

The departure lounge at Heathrow Terminal 1 was a represen-tative snapshot of Britain at that moment, insomuch as it was full of pasty, post-Christmas, lardy people who had clearly eaten and drunk too much, partied too hard and slept too little in the previous month. The airport was bursting with people who defi-nitely needed to visit spas and slopes to shake off their Christmas excess. Clusters of family groups sulked and snarled at one an-other, while shop sound systems piped out jolly jingles, still prom-ising winter wonderlands, even though it was the end of January. The reality of Christmas (dry turkey and ill-advised, drunken fumbling with colleagues at office parties) was far from the fantasy (snow-covered mountains and hot chocolate by an open fire) and this fact was never more clear than in late January. No amount of bright new scarves and woolly hats or new warm coats not yet ru-ined by the dry cleaners could disguise that.

The bridal party, however, provided a contrast.

The gang had arranged to meet up outside WH Smith's, so that they could check in together and secure seats next to one another on the flight. Their mood was entirely school trip. Yes, the bridal party cut a definite dash through the noise and chaos of the departure lounge. They were all fit, wealthy, confident and, if not young, then certainly young enough. They may have indulged in ill-advised, drunken fumbling with colleagues at office parties like the rest of the population. They may have been subjected to dry turkey and one too many mince pies, but you would never know it. Their smiles were broad, their laughter loud and hearty, their shoes and hair shining. The group of friends parted the crowd as though it were the Red Sea. People turned to stare. It was clear that these were people who knew success, love and luck.

The girls hugged and kissed one another. The boys punched each other's shoulders affectionately. They were not oblivious to the envious stares, but far from being fazed, they languished in the onlookers' envy, and laughed that bit louder than necessary and talked that bit posher than usual.

"Lloyd, good to see you, mate," said Jason, as he held a hand in the air for Lloyd to high-five. Lloyd did so, and tried not to feel self-conscious. "It's been a long time. Far too long."

"I'll second that. Nice to see you again, buddy," said Rich, as he shook Lloyd's hand warmly. Kate and Mia leaned in to hug and air-kiss him, too. Ted smiled shyly from the back of the crowd, and gave a small wave. Lloyd smiled back, relaxing a little. Rich pushed Tash in front of him and introduced her.

God, she was lovely. Rich had done well there. Good luck to them. He knew that Mia thought it was stupid them rushing into a marriage like this—after all, they hadn't known each other for even a year yet. But Lloyd didn't subscribe to that theory. He and Sophie had known each other for two years before they'd become engaged, and then they'd had a sensible twelve-month engagement. And look at how they'd ended up. Lloyd handed his passport to Rich, who had turned his attention to presenting everyone's passports to the girl at the check-in desk. He was ensuring that the air miles were registered on their exec cards.

"Where's your card, babe?" Rich asked Tash.

"Card?"

"Your exec card."

"I don't have one." Tash smiled.

"We'll have to put that right. I'm going to make sure that your life is going to be one long honeymoon."

Tash kissed him affectionately.

Yup, the way Lloyd figured it, Natasha and Rich had as much, and as little, chance as anyone else of making it.

"Hiiiiiii," a woman's voice cut through the chatter. For a moment no one could see to whom it was attached. As the woman with the voice emerged from the back of the check-in queue, it seemed that everyone in the terminal turned to look at her. Her clattering heels silenced the drone of the conveyor belts, escalators, piped music and conversations. She was jaw-dropping.

"You must be Natasha," said the stunning woman. She held out her hand for the bride-to-be to shake. Tash took it, but clearly didn't know whom she was greeting. Kate stepped in.

"That's right, and, Natasha, this is Jayne. We're so grateful that you let her join us. It's such a big favor, thank—" But Kate was cut short as Jayne swept past her and linked arms with Tash.

"Absolutely darling of you," said Jayne.

"Oh, no problem," Tash reassured with a grin. She had been delighted when Kate called to ask if the "wayward little sister could join the party." Tash was certain that a wayward little sister was exactly what the party needed. She'd agreed immediately, without checking with Rich. To Tash's surprise, Rich had been a bit sulky about it. He'd said it was bad-mannered of Jayne to invite herself along, and pointed out that their original idea was to have a very private ceremony. Tash had pointed out that one more person would not make a difference.

"I couldn't possibly have faced another night alone. Can I call you Tash?"

"Well, my friends do." Tash smiled, delighted that she'd clearly made the right call. Jayne was so warm.

"And we are going to be such friends. Now tell me, I want to know all about your plans for the wedding. I love a wedding. Can't get enough of them, darling. And snow, I love snow. And handsome men." She turned and smiled flirtatiously at Rich, Jase and Lloyd. "If there's one thing I love more than weddings or snow, it is a handsome man," she laughed, then in a fake stage whisper added, "Although I couldn't eat a whole one, darling." Jayne grinned and Tash giggled.

Jayne was a delight and a relief. It had taken her just four sentences to adopt Tash's true nickname and insist that Tash would be her *friend.* Tash gratefully surrendered to Jayne's gushing and merriment, and she happily followed her toward the magazine rack.

"Have you got lots of these bridal magazines, Tash darling?" asked Jayne, pointing to the row of mags that showed blushing, demure, seductive and girlie brides by turn beaming from the covers.

"Er, no. We're not having that sort of wedding."

"What sort?"

"Well, big. White. I just mean that I won't be needing advice on seating plans."

"Darling, you are having a white wedding. There'll be snow everywhere. It's the ultimate in romantic," said Jayne, as she reached for a clutch of the mags and headed off to the till.

"I mean, I'm getting married in waterproofs, not organza," Tash pointed out.

"Well, I'll buy these mags for me, then. I love them. My wedding is all planned. Even the groom. Although he hasn't actually agreed to it." Jayne beamed, but Tash noticed her eyes were watering.

The poor girl! Tash hadn't realized that Jayne had been engaged to her ex, or if not actually engaged they must have had an understanding if Jayne had started to plan the wedding. God, how awful. No wonder she was devastated. Tash wondered whether coming on holiday with a bridal party was the best idea for someone who had recently been jilted. Looking through bridal magazines seemed positively masochistic.

"I'm not sure we really need those mags," said Tash. "I don't think they are relevant."

"Darling Tash, don't underplay it too much. It is your big day." Jayne suddenly turned to Tash and stared at her with fierce intent. "You *are* thrilled to be getting married, aren't you? Ecstatic?"

"Of course," Tash assured her. "Ecstatic. Obviously."

"Of course you are thrilled to be marrying Rich. He's absolutely darling."

Tash grinned. After knowing Jayne all of about ten minutes, already she could guess that Jayne described everyone as "absolutely darling."

"And the word on the street is that he's scalding in the sack," whispered Jayne.

Tash laughed. She was pleased—that was just the kind of comment her mates would make. Jayne would make an excellent surrogate best friend in the absence of her real ones.

The women, although both attractive, looked nothing alike and so provided a complementary contrast to one another. Tash was tall, willowy and blonde; Jayne was slight, curvy and dark. They both wore their hair long, the ends of which swayed and brushed up against one another as they walked jauntily toward the till.


Mia watched as Lloyd and Jason circled Jayne and Tash. Jayne had certainly changed since the first time the gang had met her when she came up to college to visit Ted. She was about fifteen, or sixteen at the oldest, when the rest of them were nineteen. Just three years and yet it had seemed such a huge age gap at the time. The undergraduates had thought they were so worldly wise and sophisticated, and that Jayne was just a child. They'd been wrong on both counts.

Back then, she'd been gauche and not quite ugly, but certainly plain. Chubby, bad skin, that sort of thing. Now Jayne wore her chestnut brown hair way past her shoulders. It was cut into layers and had auburn highlights subtly threaded throughout. When the light caught her hair she was swathed in a red halo, more devilish than angelic. She had huge brown eyes that took up most of her face. They were framed by thick, long lashes, which Jayne liked to look from under. There were no signs of her former chubbiness. although she did have large breasts. Her body was trim and toned—it was clear that she was a regular gym visitor. No one could miss the fact that she had full red lips and dazzlingly white teeth, as she had this little habit of nibbling her lower lip, which somehow drew attention to both attributes. She was tiny, probably only five-foot-one or -two; Mia knew she was the type of woman that made men wish they had a coat of armor and a charging white steed.

"I knew that Jayne worked with you, but I hadn't realized that she was a particular friend of yours," Mia said to Rich, with ill-disguised bad humor.

"She's not," admitted Rich uncomfortably. "Peterson Windlooper is massive. I think I've only come across her once or twice. Obviously, I've met her a couple of times socially through Ted, over the years—just like the rest of you guys." He drew Mia close to him and away from Kate and Ted, whispering, "They begged an invite on her behalf. Apparently she's just split up from her boyfriend and she was inconsolable, desperate. Very awkward, obviously. Tash said yes out of politeness. I am as surprised as you are to have her here, believe me." He shrugged.

Lloyd said something, and Jayne threw her head back and let loose squeals of laughter. Mia couldn't believe that Lloyd had *ever* said anything funny enough to warrant such amused appreciation.

"Yeah, she certainly looks depressed," she sniped.

"Jealous, are we?" he teased.

"No. Why should I be jealous?"

"Well, if Jayne hadn't come on the trip, the women were in a minority against the men. And you, my dear Mia, were in a minority of one as the only single woman here."

"Don't be ridiculous. You guys are all ancient history. This is hardly the type of holiday that I'm intending to seduce on," lied Mia. In fact, Rich was absolutely correct in his diagnosis as to why she was irritated by Jayne's presence. That was the problem with old mates, they knew you too well. Mia, however, was not going to admit as much. "I think Jayne is a great girl. I'm pleased she's come along. The more the merrier."

"Right," said Rich, but he raised his eyebrows and grinned, making it clear that he didn't believe her, not for a second.

# 13

## *Jayne's Pain*

Despite her forced gaiety, Jayne was frantic. Devastated. Bewildered. How could he have dumped her so completely, so unceremoniously, so *stupidly?* They made such a great couple. They were so entirely right for each other. She knew that her sister-in-law dismissed her love life as trivial, but Kate didn't have a clue. Kate was so smug; everything was so easy for *her*. She had no idea what it was like *out there*.

But it was tough. Very tough. Jayne was sick of sleeping with dead-eyed strangers, hoping that they could offer her some consolation, a spark of intimacy.

Everyone was always looking for the One. But that was not Jayne's problem. She'd found her One, her man. She knew who she should be with, to whom she belonged, who belonged to her. They had so much in common. They were both into the same type of music, they liked playing the same sports, they both hated period dramas and loved action movies, and they even supported the same football team, for God's sake. Her friends liked him. His friends adored her. They were sizzling in the sack. They were a perfect match.

But he would not commit.

This constant breaking up and making up was beginning to wear pretty thin. At first it was very romantic. The kiss-and-make-up bit was so much fun that Jayne had sometimes provoked a row on purpose, but she hadn't risked that strategy for a long time now. When they were together they had the best times. It was so obvious. So why weren't they together more often?

Jayne had done everything she could think of to try to get some kind of clear commitment out of him. It didn't necessarily have to be a princess-cut diamond, but she was hoping that he'd find room in his chest of drawers for her to keep her scanty panties. She'd played best friend and sex siren. She'd pleaded; she'd sulked; she'd ignored him. She'd hung on his every word. Her friends kept pointing out his lack of response to all forms of cajoling did not bode well. Gently, at first, they'd dropped hints that there were plenty more fish in the sea and that maybe he wasn't the One. They'd pointed out that the other fish were already hooked, and all she had to do was reel one of them in. This was true. But what a depressing fact. Why was it that she never wanted the ones who were besotted with her? Later her friends' hints had become more robust as they insisted that she couldn't hold a gun to his head.

Thank God for this holiday. If she hadn't . . . Oh fuck, it didn't bear thinking about. Her life would have been over. Thank God Kate finally came through and asked for the invite. She wouldn't have liked to do it herself, and she could hardly just turn up, but a holiday was just what she needed. *And* what he needed. This break would do them good. Then he'd see. After a week, he'd see that she was his girl, the one for him. After the week's holiday, well, then they'd start again. She was sure of it.

"I love airports, don't you?" asked Tash, interrupting Jayne's thoughts. Tash beamed. "They are such romantic places."

"Darling, they are awful places; full of tense parents, screaming children, petulant staff and terrorists."

Tash laughed, "Look around you. Airports are full of poignant good-byes and joyful hellos. And shops, really good shops."

Tash was clearly a very happy woman. Her excitement at being a bride-to-be only served to emphasize Jayne's misery. Still, Jayne knew it would not do to wallow. She had too much pride to let her brother's friends know just how completely alone and totally, utterly distraught she really felt. Showing her hand, let alone her heart, was not her style.

Jayne smiled. "I guess I'm spoiled because I travel such a lot with work. I've stopped noticing airports."

"God, I can't imagine stopping noticing Caviar House, although I never buy anything there or any of the other luxury goods stores, come to think of it. But I just love browsing. Most of all I love the general sense of anticipation that hangs in the air. The fact that everyone is going somewhere, doing something important with their day, do you know what I mean?"

Jayne forced a smile and nodded. She did. Her heart was splintered. Ruptured. But putting some distance between herself and London might be the answer. This flight might be the most important one of her life.

"I do know what you mean, darling, but you've run out of time for window-shopping. That was our flight they called. Come on, and don't forget your beanie." Jayne handed Tash her hat. She'd left it on a chair and probably would have lost it.

# 14

## *Up, Up and Away*

Ted noted that Jayne's presence was clearly a welcome one, which was in equal parts a relief and a concern to him. With the exception of Mia, everyone had a soft spot for his baby sister. Mia didn't count. As far as Ted could make out, Mia didn't actively like anyone much these days.

There had been a time when she'd been much more gentle and kind. He remembered it. A time when she was young and naïve, and had slept with all her friends because it was fun and because she was careless. Ted still smiled at the memory. He'd only slept with Mia once, the same as Rich. It had been when Mia adamantly believed that every woman was entitled to explore her sexuality and that it was a crime that sexually active women were seen as sluts, or needy, or hard. That's what she'd said. And the boys weren't going to object as she moved from flirtation to flirtation. Things had changed, of course, when she fell in love with Jason. And changed even more when they fell out of love. Not that she'd ever admit as much.

Jason was clearly Mia's One. And at the time it had seemed that Mia was Jason's. But it was difficult to know what either of them was really thinking nowadays. Now that Mia did sarcasm and Jason did anyone.

Ted remembered that Jason and Mia had fallen in love about the same time as he and Kate had finally found the courage to make public their commitment to each other. Mia had been horrified that Kate and Ted had become engaged so young. She'd yelled at them both that by marrying they were conforming to outmoded standards and that they'd regret it. She'd said that they'd grow up and hate each other, resenting the lost opportunities that each would embody for the other.

But she'd been wrong.

He and Kate were very happy together. He loved Kate and the children so much. It was Mia who was unhappy. Mia and Jason, who had decided that they had to split up even though they loved each other, just in case there was someone out there that they'd love more. Of course, there hadn't been. Mia had started on a life of serial monogamy and went out with a string of young hopefuls that she'd found hopeless. When she hit her late twenties she gave up dating altogether. She married her work and, from time to time, according to Kate, Mia slept with younger men who didn't ask questions and didn't want to stay for breakfast. Proving to everyone else just how alike they were, Jason did the same. He slept with young beauties who hoped he could enhance their career or at least their street cred. And when firm breasts lost their thrill, he started to buy an obscene amount of electrical goods. Jason had two plasma TVs.

Each was as stubborn as the other.

And now it seemed that this holiday was going to cause Mia more pain. It was clear that Ted's fear was founded; Jason saw Jayne as holiday totty and would be making his move on her. His tongue had almost hit the floor when he first caught sight of her. Although he'd never admit as much, Jason liked to think of himself as cool as far as women were concerned. He was used to being pursued. After all, he lived in London, was in his thirties, single, straight and, while he wasn't particularly good-looking, he was tremendously rich. A veritable catch. Lloyd hadn't been much more discreet. It was clear that he found Jayne's presence a bonus because she evened up the numbers, saving him from the humiliation of always being the spare part. Goodness knows why he hadn't brought Greta along. It was well past the time that they should have been introduced. Ted watched, and sighed as both Jason and Lloyd scrambled to sit next to Jayne. Lloyd was the lucky one. He was in seat A1, Jayne in A2. Jason had to content himself with being separated by an aisle. This was somewhat of a relief. At least Lloyd wouldn't have any serious intention to seduce Jayne, not with Greta at home.

Kate and Ted sat in silence. Kate peered over the row of seats in front of her.

"Jayne's fine," Kate reported. "She seems to be getting on very well with Lloyd. I'm sure Natasha and Rich don't mind her joining us. Natasha looked particularly delighted."

"Jolly good," replied Ted.

He knew he was a concern to Kate. She thought he was worrying about Jayne and so had taken it upon herself to worry about Jayne for him. He didn't want to be a worry to her. Oh God, how could he be anything other now? He watched as she knotted her brow into anxious lines that reminded him of an ordnance survey map. Sharing a problem with Kate did not halve it, it spread it. More like double the trouble. And he'd never wanted to cause her any trouble. It had been his ambition to protect her for a lifetime. To swaddle her. That's why it was so difficult to confide in her about his . . . issue. He turned his head away from his wife. He wanted to pretend that he was trying to read over the shoulder of the passenger who sat across the aisle from him. Unfortunately that passenger was reading the blurb on the sick bag. He hoped Kate wouldn't notice.

"She really *is* fine. You have no need to worry about her," insisted Kate. There was just a smidgen of impatience in her voice, barely detectable.

"I'm not worrying about her," replied Ted.

Ted half hoped that Kate would push for more. That she'd ask him if he were worrying about anything else. If she did ask outright, he wouldn't lie to her. But she didn't push. Instead she said, "Did I tell Mother that the cat needs worming?" She didn't wait for an answer, but added, "I'm fraught about Fleur's grade I piano exam on Tuesday. Do you think she'll pass?"

Ted knew Kate thought that this was a terrible time to come away. The kids had just started a new school term. She thought that she should have stayed at home and supported them. It was out of the question that the children take more time off, just after the Christmas holidays, but Ted had firmly believed that they had to accept Rich's invite. They couldn't refuse to come to Rich's wedding, whatever was going on in the real world.

The real world. Oh God, oh God. Ted tried not to think about it. He had become expert in ignoring the burning issue. Instead he picked up Kate's hand, squeezed it hard and then kissed it.

She gave him a broad smile, and leaned over to kiss him on the lips. She was randy. She'd interpreted his gesture as an indication that he was, too.

Well, it wasn't an unreasonable thought. They'd have a nice meal together—one Kate didn't have to cook—and a couple of glasses of wine. Maybe they'd even get in the hot tub together.

Maybe it would lead to sex. He owed her that much. The real luxury of this holiday would be that they'd have time to relax. And *talk*. Ted knew that relaxing and talking were one and the same thing to Kate. Even if she was reading a book she would have to look up from it and tell whomever was in the room what was happening. His idea of relaxation was usually silence. He never said a word when he was reading. Even when he'd finished an article or report—he wasn't one for novels—and Kate asked him what he thought of it, all he would say was "Not bad" or "Quite good." He might suggest that she should read it herself.

But they did need to talk. He knew that. He just didn't know how or where to start. He was expecting a demand from her soon. He was *hoping* for it. If she insisted they "have a talk," it would make things easier for him. Recently she'd often found him in the study or in the garden shed. She'd realized that he wasn't planting or mulching fertilizer, or even reading the newspaper. She'd caught him sitting doing absolutely nothing.

"You have to open it to get anything from it," she'd gently scolded, pointing to the copy of the *Financial Times* lying unopened on his lap. "What are you doing? Dreaming how to make our next million?" And then she'd kiss him on the forehead and ask if he wanted a cup of tea. He'd always agreed to tea so that he hadn't had to answer her more difficult question.

Ted pinched the top of his nose and rubbed his eyes. He'd looked pale when he'd looked in the mirror today. And he knew he looked tired. It was only a matter of time before Kate noticed this, too, and then she'd demand to know why.

He was terrified that she would ask for an explanation and terrified that she wouldn't, in equal proportions. What would he tell her? That he was a coward? A failure? A liar?

There was a time, before the children had been born, when they didn't even need to talk; they had known each other intimately. It used to be unimaginable that Kate wouldn't know what was on her husband's mind or that he would be reticent to tell her anything, everything. When they'd been younger, they used to lie awake all night, too desperate about each other to want to waste time sleeping. In those days they'd known every one of each other's hopes and successes. Odd, then, that now, so many years on, when they had realized their hopes of a three-story house in Holland Park, when they had brought three children into the world—children in good health and in good schools—it was so much harder to even hint at fears and failures. Indeed, it was the fact that their hopes were realized and their successes were abundant that made talking impossible. Ted noticed dandruff on his shoulder. He must ask Kate to buy a bottle of that T-Gel shampoo that he'd seen advertised. There was something about dandruff that made one appear vulnerable. Ted wondered if he could start talking now. Here in the comfy leather seats, where there were no kids to interrupt, no phones, no doorbells. No escape routes.

"I hope your mother can find Elliot's riding hat and crop. I didn't leave a note to say which wardrobe it's in," said Kate.

"I'm sure they'll manage," replied Ted. He then accepted the hot towel from the air stewardess, closed his eyes and pretended to fall asleep.

# 15

## *Flying High*

Lloyd searched for something to say to Jayne. In the departure lounge she had seemed to find him especially amusing, which he found disconcerting. He knew he wasn't *especially* amusing; in fact, he rather suspected that he wasn't very good at small talk. His mother and father were both accountants, and he'd always thought that was explanation enough. Besides, he was one of four boys, so he had grown up in an environment where the standard of conversation rarely reached above grunts. He was particularly bad at talking to attractive girls. Thinking about it, he was an unlikely adulterer. Sophie had made all the moves in their courtship, and indeed Greta had thrown herself at him, too. She'd made her intentions so transparent and laid herself so completely on the line that he'd believed it would be rude to turn her down. He wasn't complaining, and he wasn't trying to duck the responsibility. The truth was he'd hardly believed his luck.

"How did you manage to get a ticket at such late notice?" Lloyd asked Jayne.

"I bought one at the desk." Jayne smiled.

"Isn't that a really expensive way of doing it?"

Jayne shrugged, and grinned. Both were utterly charming gestures and had the effect of making Lloyd feel silly for having brought up the subject of cost. Lloyd flushed. He didn't want to appear to be a cheapskate, yet it fascinated him how wealthy his friends were.

Lloyd calculated that Jayne's disposable income was undoubtedly double his own, and she didn't have child support to pay.

Lloyd was feeling more than slightly self-conscious because he could feel the first quiver of an erection as he watched Jayne bend forward to rummage in the bag at her feet. Her clingy, cropped top rose slightly at the back, her trousers were hipsters and the Calvin Klein tag of her underwear was clearly visible. Lloyd picked up his copy of *Private Eye* and decided to concentrate on the satirical wit rather than Jayne's ass and tits. Such thoughts about Ted's younger sister seemed indecent, an offense against Ted. Not to mention Greta. Oh God, what would Greta say when she found out that Ted's sister had wangled an invite just because Kate and Ted had asked for one?

Greta had been extremely hurt that she hadn't been invited to the wedding. She'd seen the NFI [Not Fucking Invited] as a slight and carped on and on that his friends didn't like her and didn't respect her. She'd complained that they blamed her for the breakup of his marriage and moaned that she didn't like being seen as the scarlet woman. Lloyd hadn't pointed out that, technically, she had been the other woman, so his friends' coolness was perhaps understandable. He liked a quiet life. He didn't like to rock the boat. He'd upturned one family home already; he had no intention of doing so again.

Greta had said that he ought to decline the invitation or that he should call Rich and get him to extend it to include Greta. And maybe Greta had a point. He could see it—after all, she was his girlfriend officially now. Maybe, well, yes, definitely, that's what he ought to have done. But Lloyd hadn't wanted to cause unnecessary problems now that he was finally being included in the old gang again. He knew that Greta would eventually drop the subject, so instead of calling Rich he'd pointed out that Mia and Jason weren't bringing dates. Greta in turn pointed out that Mia and

Jason were once a couple and that if they took a trip down memory lane he was going to feel like a huge fifth wheel. Lloyd had laughed, and commented that he had more chance of getting it on with Mia than Jase, which, in retrospect, wasn't a very clever thing to say to a disgruntled girlfriend. But that was his point, he wasn't very good at talking to women. Lloyd had spent an entire evening assuring Greta that he did not want to get it on with Mia, or anyone else for that matter, and that he didn't even find Mia attractive.

Oh God, Greta would be livid if she knew he was sitting on a plane trying to restrain an erection because Jayne was sitting next to him. Jayne was certainly attractive. Yes, Greta would be furious to discover that Tash and Rich had been welcoming and would undoubtedly have agreed to her joining the party. She would jump to the conclusion that the only reason she wasn't at the wedding was because Lloyd hadn't wanted it enough. Was she right?

A solution popped into his mind almost as quickly as the problem had. Greta didn't have to know that Jayne had joined the party. He'd be careful when taking photos and talking about the trip. He didn't have to lie to Greta, exactly. He could simply avoid talking about the situation. That seemed like a good idea. And right now, he'd have a drink. A whisky. A double, in fact. That seemed like another good idea.

# 16

## *Touchdown*

They arrived at Geneva International Airport, collected their baggage and found their way through the elaborate border control, moving from Switzerland to France by walking a few meters. Kate wanted to telephone home, something about a riding crop.

"Well, old buddy, I never thought you were the bondage type. Forgotten your crop, hey?" said Jason, laughing. He was addressing his comment to Ted, but he managed to take in Jayne at the same time. He winked at her and was delighted that she faced his innuendo full on, without blushing or turning away. Was she flirting with him? At the very least she knew he was flirting with her. Ted ignored him and walked toward the car rental desk.

Jason didn't care. He felt strangely high, genuinely excited. Avoriaz was a beautiful place. Skiing was his favorite pastime. He was on holiday with all his mates. He enjoyed a good wedding because deep down—and he meant very deep—he was a big softie. And to top it all, while holidays always guaranteed a number of opportunities to flirt, it was an added bonus that there was new, remarkably hot skirt available in their group.

Life didn't get any better than this.

"Jason, did you see that pretty blonde in the row behind yours?" Kate asked, teasing him.

He had noticed the honey. She had a good face.

"Yeah, I thought she was cute, but when she fell asleep her mouth fell open." Jason shuddered with mock disgust, a disgust which he actually half felt.

"Even pretty women's jaws go slack when they are sleeping, Jason. It's normal. It's real," snapped Mia.

"Do they? I wouldn't know. I never let pretty women sleep." He grinned. "Look at that!" he yelled excitedly, his attention quickly moving away from the pretty woman on the plane. He picked up a leaflet from the number advertising the bars, hotels and clubs there to tempt the tourists.

"It says here that we could have taken a helicopter to the resort. That's what you should have done, Rich. Only the best for the bride and groom. Don't you agree, Jayne?"

Jason was a pro when it came to flirting, and he knew that it was always a successful ruse to address every comment to the object of your attraction. It made them believe that they were the only person in the world for you; it seemed to help women forget that he was shorter than average.

Jayne smiled a slow—and God, yes, he was certain—sultry smile at him and Rich, and replied, "Absolutely. Rich deserves the best."

"I'm really sorry, I wish I'd known about the helicopter," said Rich apologetically, turning to Tash. She laughed, and kissed him on the lips.

"Don't worry. Traveling on a tandem would seem like the lap of luxury as long as I'm traveling with you."

"I think I'm going to be sick," said Mia, and Jason knew that she wasn't entirely joking.

They'd arranged to hire a huge four-wheel-drive Mitsubishi Shogun. But as Jayne had joined the trip, one extra bod and board made that impossible for everyone to squeeze into.

"We can offer you two Audis instead," said the guy behind the desk at Hertz rental. "It is a slightly more expensive option, a further two hundred euros."

Ted handed over his Amex to pay for the lease of a second car. Jayne flashed her cutest smile and pecked her brother on the cheek.

"I think it would have been more appropriate for her to get out her own plastic, by way of a thank-you. Wouldn't you say?" Mia whispered to Jason.

"Women like Jayne aren't used to paying their way, Mia. Besides, who cares? It's not our business."

They found the cars and broke into two groups. Jayne and Kate piled into the back of one car, while Lloyd and Ted strapped luggage to the roof and tossed up to see who would drive. This left Jason, Mia, Rich and Tash with the second car.

Jason turned to Rich, "You'll have to drive, mate. I had a glass of champagne and two vodkas on the plane."

"No problem." Rich took the keys.

"Scaley! Just because we are women doesn't mean we can't drive, you know. I passed my test when I was seventeen years old, first time, and I've never had so much as a parking ticket," scolded Mia, as she climbed into the back with Jason. In fact, she didn't really fancy trying to negotiate the snowy mountains, especially driving on the wrong side of the road, but she didn't like the assumption that she wasn't up to driving.

Jason rolled his eyes. Sometimes he wished Mia could be just a little less feisty. Why couldn't she be more like Tash, who had sat in the front seat next to Rich and said nothing? Tash was more than happy to concentrate on reading the next chapter of her novel, although Rich had different ideas.

"Forget the novel. You're navigating," he said, as he tossed a map and a grin at Tash. Tash groaned.

"If you can't read maps, we could swap places," said Mia.

"Thanks, but I'll be fine," replied Tash.

"If the translation is unclear, I am fluent in French. I did my—"

"—degree in it. I know. No, really, I'm fine," said Tash a little more firmly.

Jason shook his head in despair. Mia was so competitive. What was she trying to prove? He could barely remember the time when he found her attractive. Barely.

As it happened, Tash navigated them through Geneva, along the A40, past Bonneville, past Cluses and toward Chamonix without a hiccup. The two rental cars with large trunks, snow chains and roof racks headed toward the mountains. The gang felt like intrepid adventurers, but were comfortable in the knowledge that the holiday would be the fun side of exhausting.

"Good service on the flight, don't you think?" asked Jason. He was thinking of the two hard-body air stewardesses, one of whom had slipped her name and mobile telephone number into his jacket pocket.

"It was ace," said Tash. "So exciting. I just love those smart leather seats and the tiny glass bowls of fresh fruit and the little jam pots. Club class is amazing. Unfortunately, I made the ultimate blunder and tried to pay for the champagne."

From the corner of his eye Jason could see Mia smirk. He was determined not to catch her eye and allow her to turn it into a conspiratorial moment, so instead he beamed at Tash.

"You're right, it is cool traveling club," he said. "A real treat."

"Yeah, well, you only get married once," said Rich.

"Sometimes more, Action Man," commented Mia.

Jason finally looked at her, but it was more of a glare than a conspiratorial wink. God, she could be a bitch. He was so well rid of her. He often thought so. OK, he also found it a bit strange that his best mate and partner in crime was now besotted and therefore a walking marshmallow. But Jason liked it. Live and let live, that was his motto.

"What?" asked Mia. "I'm only being realistic. In this day and age, it is a fact that over forty percent of marriages end in divorce. I'm just saying that getting married is not a once-in-a-lifetime experience anymore."

Rich didn't take his eyes off the road; Tash picked up her novel.

"Why don't you just shut up, Mia," whispered Jason.

"I didn't mean anything by it. I was just saying."

"Well, just don't." Then he added in a louder voice, "I love Avoriaz. It's so entirely St. Tropez in the snow."

He'd read that in a Sunday supplement, and the phrase had stuck with him, and while he wasn't entirely certain he understood it, let alone believed it, he was keen to change the subject.

"Isn't it just," agreed Mia, who clearly thought it was a clever comment.

"What?" said Tash, who clearly thought it was a poor one. "I'm thinking young, sexy, hip people walking around in fur bikinis and knee-high boots," she giggled, gently teasing. Jason and Rich laughed, too. "But then it might be for all I know. I've never been to Avoriaz."

"Really?" Mia screeched in disbelief. "I thought everybody who called themselves a skier had been to Avoriaz at least once." She shook her head. "I'd never have believed it. I didn't think I even knew anybody who hadn't been to Avoriaz."

Tash turned around in her seat to face Mia head-on. She was already sick of the jibes. Wasn't Mia's reaction a little over the top? It wasn't as though Tash had confessed to not owning a passport. Mia steadfastly stared out of the car window and watched the countryside whizz by, pretending to be intent on admiring the beauty of long-forgotten farmhouses that were centuries old.

"I'm not a skier, I'm a boarder," Tash stated. She was hoping to sound dignified, but she realized she sounded pathetic.

"I want to try boarding," said Jason, trying to give the impression that he was oblivious to the aggression between the women. It was amazing that Rich seemed to be genuinely so.

"*We* all came to Avoriaz the first winter that we had jobs. Gosh, that will be twelve years ago," continued Mia. "Such a long time.

We've covered some ground, haven't we, Action Man? Hey, Scaley Jase?" Mia squeezed Jason's leg.

"God, that was a fantastic break." Jason smiled. He forgot that he was finding Mia irritating. As he wallowed in the memory, he recalled a sweeter girl.

"I hadn't realized you'd been here before, babe," muttered Tash, turning to Rich.

Rich still didn't take his eyes off the road. He shrugged. "I'd forgotten I had. I can't really remember all the resorts I've been to now. Not after so many snow seasons."

Jason watched Tash and, from his seat behind her, he could see her shoulders sink. She was silent for the rest of the journey. Bloody women. Clearly she was disappointed. No doubt she'd have had this idea that they would be discovering somewhere new together. Now she was sulking that Rich hadn't mentioned that he'd been to Avoriaz before. What did it matter? They were getting married, weren't they? Women! He didn't get them. And no matter how many he had, he still wouldn't get them.

Why did Mia choose to be moody and pushy when he knew she could be lovely when she wanted to be? She could be funny, interesting and kind. Kate used to be a laugh and now she was just dull, forever going on about the National Curriculum and not much else. He really doubted that she ever gave head nowadays. And Tash, who seemed like a really great girl, had suddenly turned sulky and silent just because her boyfriend had visited this holiday resort about a million years ago and forgotten to mention it. Fair enough, Jayne was cute, but experience showed him that he only held this opinion because he barely knew her. Women were good from afar, but far from good up close. Jason had been feeling a bit warm and fuzzy seeing Rich all loved up. He had been playing with the idea of, considering the possibility of, well . . . maybe . . . looking for a girl to date steadily. But, no. Once again he was catapulted back onto the bachelor shelf, and he was glad to be there.

# 17

## *Arriving*

The resort was a car-free zone. The only traffic was horse-drawn sleighs that merrily jingled bells as though they were in a perpetual wonderland. There were no roads, just snow-covered tracks and lots and lots of timber.

The hotel's architecture was funky 1960s at its best, organic, free-flowing and full of interesting nooks and crannies. There were two restaurants run by the famous chef Christophe Leroy. They were both painted red, creating a womblike effect, warm, cozy and safe. There was a bar, a terrace and a library. There were huge, colorful cushions and footstools scattered liberally throughout. Chopped wood was stacked near the open fireplace, and huge pictures of ripe fruit hung on the wall. All the decor was rich and refined, magnificent and modern, and made complete with heavy shimmering fabrics, wood trims and an indefinable but very distinct air of chic. Simply walking into the reception area made it very clear that you were joining an exclusive club.

"Wow, this place is fantastic." Tash smiled. She turned to Rich and landed a large smacker on his lips. He returned her kiss while trying to maintain his grip on their snowboards and other luggage.

"You like it, my lady?" he asked, smiling, happy that she was happy.

"I love it." She smiled back. "It's even funkier in real life than the brochures made it appear. It's easily the best place I've ever stayed in."

"You haven't even seen the bedrooms yet," said Mia. "Just rein in that enthusiasm. The service will undoubtedly be very French."

Tash ignored Mia. Her aura of happiness was impenetrable. The resort and the hotel were better than she could have imagined. The car journey had been hell. Mia simply was not a pleasant woman, at least not to Tash. Tash hoped, but doubted, that the French *chocolat chaud* would warm up Mia. Even if it couldn't, this was her wedding and no one could spoil it. She was sure of that. The wedding was going to be special.

It was going to be perfect.

Rich started to talk to the receptionist in French. He told her that he and his fiancée had a booking for their wedding later in the week, and he clearly enjoyed the fuss that this declaration caused. Like streamers from a party popper, congratulations flowed. The receptionist confirmed that the suite was waiting for them, as were the complimentary champagne, fruit, chocolates and spa products. When Rich had proposed to Tash, they'd agreed that they wanted a quiet wedding. Rich had insisted that he would not enjoy the fuss and the attention getting married would bring. He'd been wrong. It was true that the whole world loved a lover. And he loved being a lover who was loved. And, well, it was all just lovely.

"We are very 'appy to 'ave you all 'ere," said the receptionist. She flashed a broad smile at the gang. "Pleeze let me know if there is anything ah can do to make your stay more pleasure."

Jason smirked, and whispered under his breath, "Sure will, doll." Rich raised his eyebrows in mock reproach and handed over the key to Jason's room.

"Do you think she knows that she is the exact replica of every Englishman's dream of a sexy French woman?" asked Jason.

"Calm down." Tash smiled.

"It's not my fault. Foreign women's accents so do it for me," defended Jason. He shook his head apologetically, as if to suggest that he was remorseful that his adolescent desires still ran unfettered; the truth was, he was proud.

"Don't you like the Queen's pronounced?" asked Jayne, in perfect clipped tones.

Jason grinned, winked and replied, "Yes, posh beauties do it for me, too."

"Don't pay him too much attention," warned Mia. "All women do it for him. He's on a constant quest to prove himself."

"Do you have a small penis?" joked Jayne.

Yeeessssss. She was in the bag. Jason grinned. No woman would make that kind of suggestive comment unless they fancied a bit.

"Enormous, thank you."

Everyone knew this to be the case. Whenever he stayed over at his friends' homes he made a point of walking about in his clingy Y-fronts. Besides which, the enormity of his penis was one of his favorite topics of conversation.

"That's not the problem. It's because he's ugly," sniped Mia, although she regretted it instantly. Why was she being so catty? She didn't think Jase was ugly. She had just wanted to point out that his looks were far from classically handsome, which she suspected was Jayne's type. Mia had always preferred something less orthodox, and she'd always found Scaley very attractive.

"Sadly, no chance of getting lift passes for today," said Rich, turning from the receptionist and interrupting the giggles. "It's too late, and the lifts will be closing in an hour. Kate, Ted, you'll have to pay for an upgrade. I booked everyone superior standard rooms, but there weren't any standard or superior standard rooms spare, so Jayne will have to have yours, while you take something bigger."

Ted studied the discreet leaflet that detailed the prices of the rooms. The next size up was a deluxe. It was an extra thirty euros a night. He shrugged, accepting that he'd have to take the hit because his sister had come on the trip.

"I'm afraid there weren't any deluxe rooms available either. The only spare room was the junior suite." Ted glanced at the price list. The suites were eighty euros more again. He sighed, and signed the receipt.

"I could always bunk in with you and Tash." Jayne grinned.

Rich ignored her comment.

"Oh, mate, all your fantasies come true," joked Jase.

"Don't be ridiculous," snapped Rich. "Tash and I are looking for some privacy, actually."

"Well, it would be my idea of nirvana."

"I suggest everyone goes to their rooms and unpacks, then we'll rendezvous in the bar at, say, six, for cocktails," continued Rich. "Although, I would caution against getting too hammered this evening, not if we want to make the most of the snow tomorrow. Reports forecast a snow dump tonight. We should have several inches of fresh powder to take advantage of first thing in the morning. It would be a crime to miss out because we were nursing hangovers."

"Rendezvous!" shouted Jason, Lloyd, Mia, Kate and Ted in unison.

"Right, Tash, let's go," instructed Rich, who seemed unnaturally tense and therefore had turned into the very model of a modern major general. What was he talking about, "cocktails" and "rendezvous"? Tash had never heard Rich being so officious. He seemed really stressy. She gave a mental shrug. It was nothing. She knew he just wanted the whole trip to be a success and that it was important to him to keep the show on the road. Someone had to be organized.


Mia was wrong, Tash was right. The rooms didn't disappoint— they were stunning. As Rich pushed open their bedroom door, Tash was enveloped in a world of luxury and elegance.

"My God, a video and cable, *and* a hi-fi," she giggled.

Rich struggled with their numerous bags and the cumbersome snowboards and boots.

"Oh my God. Oh my God," said Tash, as she jumped up and down on the giant bed. Rich started to put their passports and traveler's checks into the safe as Tash dashed around the suite.

"Have you seen in here?" she yelled from the bathroom. "There's a hot tub." Rich smiled at Tash's excitement.

"I guess I've gotten a little spoiled with traveling with work. I've forgotten the excitement of searching through the complimentary soap basket."

This was exactly what Tash was doing at that moment.

"That's just what Jayne said about airports. How can you become accustomed to such splendor?" she asked, wide-eyed and incredulous.

"Ah, Jayne, yes," Rich called through to the bathroom. "There's something I need to tell you about Jayne." He should have told her straight away, as soon as Jayne's name came up. It was just a bit of history, no big deal. He would have mentioned it already only none of the others had a clue either. It was awkward.

Tash bounced (because she'd lost the ability to walk calmly) toward the window and pulled back the blinds to admire the view. "Wow!" they chorused.

The snow was falling quite heavily now. Avoriaz was perched on the top of a sheer cliff that plunged more than a thousand feet into a narrow valley below. It was a ski town quite unlike any other in France. The view, a fascinating mix of eerie and spectacular, was breathtaking. The hotel had large windows from which you caught the view of the Alpine setting of all the Portes du Soleil ski areas.

"Can you see how the form of the buildings echoes the sheer faces of brown slate that they sit on?" asked Tash. "When we were driving in I noticed that, from a distance, the staggered heights of the multistory structures, the hotels and apartments, blend perfectly into the topography. They must have designed this place with quite some thought."

Rich stood behind Tash, wrapping his arms around her body and resting his chin on the top of her head. He squeezed her tightly; she made him so proud. It was true, the resort buildings were unobtrusive. He'd noticed that, but he hadn't made the connection between their design and the topography of the mountains. Now that Tash had mentioned it, it was obvious. He loved the things she noticed, the things she said, the way she thought about things. It would surprise Mia, but Rich considered Tash the brightest woman he'd ever met.

"I read about the architect of this hotel. His name's Jacques Labro. And des Dromonts was the very first building constructed in this style, the style that became the distinct Avoriaz style," added Tash. "That was, like, half a century ago. Isn't it cool to think that this hotel set the architectural pace for the entire resort?"

They both fell into a comfortable silence again and watched the snow fall. They were both thinking about the fact that every child learns: no two snowflakes are alike. They were both thinking that this wasn't a surprise. After all, no two people are alike. Neither felt a need to say anything.

After a while Rich said, "You know, it's possible to ski to Switzerland from here."

"We should." Tash smiled.

And that was another amazing thing about Tash, her "can do" attitude. He loved that adventurous spirit in her. He was sure if he came home from work one day and suggested selling everything and moving to Africa or Japan or somewhere, she'd simply say, "What should I pack?"

"Thank you for bringing me to such a stunning place," sighed Tash. "It's beautiful."

"Thank you for agreeing to come and . . ." Rich turned Tash around so she was facing him. "And, most important, thank you for agreeing to be my wife. You've made me happier than I'd ever imagined it was possible to be."

The couple giggled, almost embarrassed at how easily they had fallen into using clichés to describe their love for one another. It was odd to them that they used words other lovers had used because they were sure no one had ever felt as happy as they did now. They started to kiss and all memory of either Jayne or the rendezvous time was forgotten.

# 18

## *Appetites*

It was just nauseating the way Action Man and Barbie Babe insisted on parading their togetherness. Admittedly, they were here in Avoriaz for their wedding, but it was also everyone else's holiday. And Mia, for one, found their constant kissy-kissy ways rather embarrassing. They weren't teenagers, for God's sake, and the last time Mia had been so blatantly loved on she had been nineteen. She and Jason had not been able to keep their hands off one another, but that was hormones, surely.

"I'm ravenous," said Rich, reaching forward to grab a handful of nuts from the plate on the table. Clearly he had post-sex hunger.

"I hope you washed your hands," commented Mia. She smiled so that her remark didn't sound crude.

Rich laughed, and asked if anyone wanted a drink.

"You shouldn't be getting them," said Jason. "It's your wedding gig. Ted, it's your round, isn't it? How about some champagne?"

Ted was known for his generosity, and on this occasion, like all others, he didn't disappoint. He ordered two bottles of Veuve Clicquot and left his Amex behind the bar. Kate smiled smugly, which really irritated Mia. It wasn't as though it were Kate's money being splashed around. She didn't work. She got to stay at home and play with the kids all day. Mia's irritation was almost immediately subdued by shame. In all honesty, she knew that one of the things Kate liked most about her husband earning a tremendous salary was that they could afford to be generous with their friends. Kate firmly believed one of the nicest things about having money was sharing it. Mia shouldn't be mean about her. But sometimes it was hard watching them be so bloody perfect.

"Did you catch up with Louisa and Will over the holidays?" Kate asked Mia.

"We exchanged cards and telephone messages. They're really well. Really, really well by all accounts. Louisa is expecting *again*."

"Is she, my goodness. That's splendid news."

"Absolutely," said Mia, smiling, although she didn't really think so. Louisa and Will had two children. They didn't need a third. It wasn't fair that some people had so much and she had . . . well, it sometimes felt as if she had nothing. "Has anyone heard anything from Helena and Mark?"

"Yep, aha. They're great, too. Just moved into a new house. White Georgian number in Notting Hill," said Jason.

Lloyd let out a low whistle. "That must have cost a bit. What do you think?" He could barely imagine.

"That size, in that area. Have to be close to a million and a half," guessed Rich.

"Really?" Lloyd shook his head.

Louisa and Will, Helena and Mark, Kate and Ted, now Rich and Tash. Mia sighed. It was as if they weren't real people on their own, only half-people. Mia was just Mia, and it felt lonely. Intellectually, she knew it shouldn't. She knew that she was an independent woman with a great job, her own flat, her own car and her own night classes, but she did *feel* lonely. And recently the loneliness outweighed everything else. It outweighed the sense of satisfaction she gained from doing a good job in the office. It outweighed the feeling of wonderful indulgence that came with knowing you could suit yourself when it came to any decision, be it choosing a holiday destination or a toothpaste brand. It outweighed the pride she felt over owning a smart two-bedroom flat in Fulham. The loneliness was all-consuming. Her plan *had* to succeed. She would not, no, could not, go on as was.

"Shall we go eat?" asked Jason.

"Damn fine idea," said Jayne, jumping up enthusiastically.

Mia rolled her eyes in exasperation. She wondered what drugs Jayne took and vaguely wondered if she should take them, too. Jayne had more bounce than a jack-in-the-box on E. Yet she managed to combine her (offensive) optimism and glee at the world with sophistication. How did she manage that? Mia's particular brand of sophistication came directly from her deep cynicism at the world and was articulated through her constant sarcasm. Besides, she couldn't imagine that Jayne ever actually ate anything. It simply wasn't possible to eat and retain an ironing-board-flat stomach. She was just one of those girls who was aware of how attractive a ferocious appetite is in a thin woman. Men somehow associated one appetite with another and assumed she'd be good in bed.

Mia knew all the tricks; she'd played most of them. She'd bet money on the fact that Jayne would order huge quantities of food and insist that everyone else do likewise, but throughout the meal she would always be far too busy being amusing and entertaining to actually take a bite. Besides which, eating destroyed lipstick. Mia glowered at Jayne's thin back as she followed her into the dining room. Jason was falling over himself to be pleasant. He was asking if Jayne could teach him how to board. Clearly he fancied her like mad. This was no surprise to Mia, but it was still a disappointment. Bugger. Jayne's presence could really screw up Mia's plans. She was depending on the fact that Jason would be short of amusement and diversion. How was she supposed to seduce him if he was infatuated with someone else? Bugger, bugger.

If not now, when? Keep calm, stay calm, deep breath, she instructed herself. A good mental attitude is extremely important in these matters, she'd read that. Just as important as folic acid tablets. Mia was not a quitter. Jayne was a nuisance, yes. She was an unforeseen circumstance, yes. But her presence didn't necessarily mean disaster. Maybe Jayne wouldn't fancy Jason. If she rejected him, then Mia could be waiting with open arms to comfort him. OK, it wasn't the most glamorous or romantic notion, but Mia was past all that nonsense. She didn't want Jason to fall in love with her. Just to impregnate her.

She'd simply have to keep her eye on the Jayne situation. Although watching her now, it really seemed as though she fancied Natasha more than she fancied Jason. She was all over the girl. She'd clearly decided that they were one another's new best friends. Jayne had squeezed in between Rich and Tash so that she could "really get to know the beautiful bride." She laughed at everything Tash said, even though most of it was dull trivia about the wedding, and she was forever touching her. Mia watched in amazement as Jayne used her napkin to wipe away a crumb of bread from Tash's lips.

"I love it here," said Jayne. "You've chosen a really beautiful place to get married, Tash. I so admire your taste, darling." Jayne poured some wine for Tash and herself, then clinked glasses. "I do hope nothing goes wrong."

"Why should anything go wrong?" asked Rich.

He looked at Jayne with real anger. Clearly she'd pissed him off by squeezing between him and Tash, and stealing the limelight.

Jayne turned to Rich and batted her eyelashes. Really, she batted them. Mia couldn't believe it. She didn't think anyone did that except in cartoons.

"I'm sure it won't," said Jayne sweetly. "I'm just saying I hope it's all perfect. Little things can go wrong when you are planning a wedding, you know. You might run out of champagne, or maybe the chef can't get some vital ingredients, or the bride breaks a leg boarding." Jayne laughed at Rich's terrified face. "I'm just joking. I'm sure nothing will go wrong. Now, let's eat."

She squeezed Tash's hand, and patted Rich's knee. Then she turned her body so that it was directed toward Tash and started to discuss the menu.

Mia had to admit that together they were both breathtaking. Tash's blonde straight hair fell forward and brushed Jayne's dark curly hair—even Mia thought it was erotic. Rich, Jason and Lloyd were captivated. Only Ted seemed oblivious as he stared off into the middle distance. Planning how to spend his next million, Mia supposed.

# 19

## *Good Times*

The bar was swaying. It was made of Plasticine or Play-Doh or something. Lloyd wasn't sure, but everything was morphing in front of his eyes. It was possible, as Kate had just said, that he was drunk. He couldn't be certain. He tried to count how many drinks he'd had. He'd had a gin and tonic before dinner, a double. Then he'd had about five or six glasses of wine with his food. Well, the conversation was flowing, so the wine was bound to accompany it, or maybe it was the other way around. Then they'd come here to this club and had some beers. Après-ski was met with the same enthusiasm as the action on the piste, so he was not alone in his intense state of inebriation.

The club was moist. The people were sweaty. The floors were swilling with slopped beer, and the walls were damp with condensation created by scores of hot bodies squeezed into one smallish room. There were mounds of discarded clothes under stools and tables which Lloyd kept stumbling over. It was extremely cold outside, so although everyone arrived in several layers, as the alcohol and the music took effect, most people began to strip down to clingy, skimpy T-shirts. Lloyd wasn't complaining. He liked looking at the girls in their cropped tops, grinding and grinning on the dance floor.

Lloyd was a surprisingly good dancer. He enjoyed dancing all the more so because people didn't particularly expect it of him, a thirty-something civil servant. Not that he danced much anymore. Opportunities to strut your funky stuff weren't exactly prolific in the life he'd chosen. It was unlikely that a group of civil servants would decide to hotfoot it down to the Brixton Academy on a Friday night after a particularly grueling week. He was much more likely to relax with a jar of bitter in his local. But the old gang remembered him as a good dancer, and therefore they thought it was natural that he should take to the floor, which made it easier to do so.

Lloyd didn't actually recognize the tunes that were playing. He might have been "with it" once, but he'd stayed the same and "it" had moved on, becoming something different. He'd have liked to hear a bit of early Pulp or Oasis, but luckily the hip-hop tunes were easy to move to and Lloyd was a fast learner. He closely watched the younger dancers and mimicked their moves in a convincing manner. A group of pretty young girls allowed him to dance nearby. They occasionally smiled at him, and he smiled back. At one point he even wiggled hips with a brunette, but he didn't try to take it any further. When the track finished, he scuttled back to the others, making the excuse that he needed a drink. He didn't offer the brunette a drink. She looked disappointed. She would have said yes, but Lloyd preferred leaving the flirtation exactly where it was. He knew the dangers of being overly flattered by a flirtation.

It was bloody fantastic being in a club again. He could dance, he could drink and he could flirt. The alcohol stretched the possibilities—the expectancy, the warmth, the wit. He could pretend he was . . .

What?

Young again?

Still married?

Someone else altogether?

Suddenly Lloyd felt an overwhelming depression swamp him. How was that possible? Only seconds ago he was feeling fifty meters tall, and now he felt flattened like a bulldozed building. He helped himself to a glass of water from the bottle on the table, then fell back into one of the more comfy chairs. He looked around. Tash and Rich were making out. Yup, actually going for it in the club, as though he'd just seduced her. He felt lonely. He missed . . . Well, Greta, he supposed. He missed Greta. Or something. Or someone.

Lloyd could see the brunette he'd been dancing with. She was now grinding hips with a lanky twenty-something. Lloyd disinterestedly watched the new couple fade into the throng. He shivered. His sweat, induced from exerting himself on the dance floor, already felt freezing cold on his hot skin. He felt sick and tired as he recognized that his hangover had already started to kick in. In truth, he wasn't sure he would feel any better if Greta were here. Sometimes he was lonely even when he was with her. They lived a fairly isolated life at the moment. They only ever socialized with people from the office. The people with whom Lloyd saw his future lying. He missed the old gang—they shared a past. He'd held a secret belief that as soon as they were all together again that nagging loneliness which seemed to coat him, invisible but as tangible as a brick wall, would dissolve. He felt nauseated with disappointment that it hadn't.

The dinner had been great fun. The conversation had bounced, leaped and ricocheted around the table. There was no denying it; every one of the old gang was great dinner-party company. Their views were informed and honed. Their ability to express themselves was amusing—in fact, magnetic. They were a great bunch. It never ceased to amaze Lloyd just how many jokes and anecdotes Jason had up his sleeve. He was the only man that Lloyd knew that didn't rely on a small number of faithful jokes, pulling them out time after time on every social occasion. Sadly, most men were oblivious to the audience joining in the punch line, but not Jason. Jason was the guy who started the funny emails.

And Kate and Ted were so eminently pleasant. It was lovely the way Kate asked about his daughter, Joanna. Not many people did that. They assumed he didn't have an interest in her, which was ludicrous. He had split up from Sophie, not his daughter. He'd wished he'd been able to answer Kate's question about whether Joanna was immunized against MMR, though. It wasn't that he didn't take an interest; it was just that Sophie dealt with all the medical side of things. Still, he was sure Kate had been impressed when he had turned the conversation and told her how much he'd spent in Hamley's toy store last month.

He was even beginning to enjoy being called Checkers by Mia again. It did at least show that he belonged.

Rich and Tash seemed very happy. She was certainly lovely to look at.

But their affability and conviviality had not been able to disperse that nagging feeling of aloneness. In fact, oddly, it had somehow served only to make him feel more lost. Lloyd shook his head. That didn't make sense.

It must be the booze.

# 20

## *Hanging on the Telephone*

Lloyd staggered to the loo. Peeing often helped to sober him up as it involved a lot of concentration to avoid getting his shoes wet. He went back into the bar and sat down between the making-out Rich and Tash, and Kate and Ted, who were sitting holding hands but not a conversation. Mia was dancing with a complete stranger, and he couldn't see Jason and Jayne. He assumed they'd gone off together somewhere. He was a quick worker, that Jason. Lloyd didn't know whether to feel envy or pride at his friend. He checked his watch and considered calling Greta, but it was very late and he was very soused. She might not be too happy to hear from him.

But he should. Yes, he should. Lloyd found his jacket on the floor and pushed his arms into the sleeves. He staggered outside without fastening it, which was a mistake as it was subzero outside. He stood under the porch of the doorway into the bar, trying to shelter, but merely annoying the people who were intent on getting inside. He jabbed memory 3. Which was Greta's number.

His direct line to his office was stored in the first memory button, and Sophie still had second place. There was nothing significant about that, he'd argued to Greta. He just hadn't got around to changing the order. It was unnecessary.

Greta picked up the phone after only three rings.

"Gretait'ssme," slurred Lloyd.

Greta, a channel away, rubbed her eyes, sat up in bed and flicked on the bedside lamp.

"What time is it, Lloyd?"

"Ten past two."

It was ten past one in the UK, but Greta didn't mind. When she had been Lloyd's mistress she'd grown used to receiving inconvenient calls, late at night.

"Are you having fun?" she asked brightly.

"Was, but now I miss you and I'm sad."

"Oh, poor boy," giggled Greta, pleased. "How's the snow?" Greta was a good skier herself.

"Oh, it's looking good. Falling as we speak. I'm looking forward to getting out there."

"And how are all your friends? Is it nice to see everyone?" Greta asked politely. She had made her point that she thought it was rude she had been excluded, but the holiday had gone ahead without her. There was no point in harboring any resentment. Or, at least, there was no point in showing any more resentment.

"They're all well. Excellent form."

"You don't feel too much of a fifth wheel being the extra guy?"

Lloyd didn't take the opportunity to say that he was no longer one of seven, but now one of a group of eight. He just mumbled, "I'm fine, just missing you, Grets."

"Lloyd, what are you doing out in the snow? You'll catch your death, darling. Come in at once," shouted Jayne. She was leaning out of a window of the bar, her mouth was almost touching Lloyd's ear. She flashed her widest, most beguiling smile. "You simply must come and save me from Jason." She put her hands around her mouth and yelled in a fake stage whisper, "No one warned me that he was such a charming octopus." She giggled as Jason pulled her back into the bar and firmly closed the window, sealing in the good-time vibe.

"Who was that?" asked Greta. Her tone was colder than the icicles hanging from the rooftops.

"Jayne," replied Lloyd simply. His office life had taught him never to volunteer more information than required.

"Is she there with Jason? Has Jason taken a girlfriend?" she demanded, her sleepy, sultry tones well and truly banished.

"No, no, nothing like that. Jayne is Ted's sister. She's here because—" Lloyd wondered if he could get away with pretending that she wasn't in their party at all, that it was a coincidence and in fact she was skiing with a group of friends. No, probably not. Greta would question him about the group of friends. She'd probably start imagining any amount of untrue and ugly situations. He had to come clean.

"She's here because Ted and Kate backed Rich and Tash into a corner. Jayne needed a holiday. It's all very embarrassing."

"She called you 'darling.'"

"She calls everyone 'darling.' She leads the type of life where everything *is* 'darling.' It doesn't mean anything. Look, Tash and Rich are just being good friends. Jayne's split from her boyfriend and needed cheering up."

"Yes, they are very good friends. I know who to call, then, if ever I split from my boyfriend," said Greta, and then hung up.

Shit.

Lloyd stared at the phone in surprise. He hadn't expected her to take it well, but he hadn't expected her to hang up on him. It wasn't civilized. Bloody women. He supposed he'd have to call her back. After all, that's why women hung up phones, or walked out of restaurants and bars, just to see if you'd follow them. He hit memory 3 again.

"Hello."

The voice was sleepy and surprised, but it was not Greta, it was Sophie's voice. He'd hit the wrong button. Lloyd momentarily considered hanging up, but he knew that Sophie would dial 1471, and then he'd look like a prat for hanging up. Best he bluff it out.

"Hello, Sophie. Happy New Year."

"Don't be ridiculous, Lloyd. It's late January. It's not New Year's," snapped Sophie, recognizing Lloyd's voice in an instant.

"Still never too late to say Happy New Year, is it?"

Sophie sighed. She hated New Year's Eve and never stayed up to welcome the new year in, never had. Her policy was to ignore it. At least to ignore it in a personal sense—professionally it was a big night for her. This year she had had all four of her catering teams at important events. They'd all been great successes and had already led to further recommendations and leads for more work. One of the events was a private party for a TV presenter. The evening had been "Verrrry showbiz, daaarling," and had been covered in one of the gossipy glossies. Sophie admitted that as far as New Year's Eves went, this year hadn't been bad. But she didn't celebrate New Year's. Why couldn't Lloyd remember something as simple as that about her? And, most important, it wasn't bloody New Year's, so why was he calling?

"I wasn't sure if I'd catch you," said Lloyd. "I thought you might be working."

Even soused his voice betrayed a sneer. A sneer that said Sophie working was a problem, a betrayal. He still thought that her having a successful career was a bigger betrayal than him slipping his dick inside his personal assistant. Sophie sighed, and tried to remain patient.

"I don't have to attend quite as many events as I had to in the old days. It's one of the perks of being a boss of an extremely competent staff. Besides, I don't like leaving Joanna with babysitters too often, even if I could find one that was prepared to stay after midnight." Sophie wondered why she was bothering to explain this to him. Why did she always feel that she had to justify herself to him when he no longer meant anything to her?

"Why the call?"

"Just thought I'd see how you are. Oh, and Joanna, of course," drawled Lloyd, trying to sound, if not sober, then at least less drunk than was the case. It was wasted effort. His ex-wife knew him too well. She resisted pointing out that by ringing in the middle of the night he was unlikely to speak to Joanna.

Instead she said, "We're fine, thank you. Presumably you couldn't get hold of Greta. She's probably in some club somewhere where the reception for mobile phones isn't too good. Isn't that what you always used to say to me when I tried to call you at an ungodly hour? When you failed to come home."

Sophie wished that she didn't say these things. She wished that she could stop "having a go," to use the vernacular. But she couldn't. She clearly remembered one particularly painful evening, and she wanted Lloyd to remember it, too. When their daughter had been about eight months old she had woken, screaming, in the middle of the night. It transpired that her temperature was 104 degrees. It was after midnight and Lloyd, who was supposed to be at a work function, was uncontactable. Intermittently, between bathing the baby with cold flannels, Sophie had tried his mobile number with increasing panic and desperation, until three in the morning when he finally came home.

His excuse was that the venue for the cocktail party was in a cellar and the reception on his phone had failed. But why hadn't he picked up her messages in the cab? Wasn't cocktail hour over by 9 p.m. at the latest? Sophie knew he had turned his phone off. It wasn't until a few months later that she asked herself why he would have done that. It wasn't as though Lloyd could have done anything to help Joanna, but Sophie would have found his presence a comfort. Joanna's temperature subsided, and experience later dictated that the temperature had been the result of teething, no harm done. Except that it was another tiny incident where Sophie realized she could manage on her own and another tiny resentment that she stored against Lloyd. Resentments that, when finally totaled up, meant Sophie wanted to live on her own.

Sophie wished she'd stop rehashing their past. It never did any good. No matter how many times Lloyd reluctantly apologized for one or other of the crimes he'd committed, he couldn't repair the damage he'd done.

"For your information, I talked to Greta earlier on this evening," said Lloyd, although he knew his ex-wife was barely interested in facts. She was ensconced in her version of things. A world that he believed had little basis in reality. She could be so exasperating. So argumentative. So willful. Spirited. Fun. Lloyd managed to shift from furious to curious in a matter of seconds.

He knew it was the drink, but at that moment he didn't want Greta. At that moment he wanted Sophie, and his daughter, and his old life back. He wanted that more than anything in the world. If they were a family again, he wouldn't be lonely. He wouldn't be alone in a crowd anymore. He wanted his old life. The life where he believed in happily ever after. The one where he was respected and envied.

His rambling desires were interrupted by a heavy sigh from Sophie.

"Can I go now? Some of us have to be up early in the morning, and not to dash down a ski run, cutting the first snow, but to feed Cheerios to an unwilling two-year-old."

Damn, Sophie mentally kicked herself. There, she'd done it again. The reprimand was loud and clear—Sophie's life was lonely and damaged because of Lloyd's selfish actions. The truth was Sophie was doing OK now, better than OK. She had long since left behind her the endless nights of reprisals, revenge plots and recriminations. She was sometimes genuinely happy. It wasn't always easy. Juggling a career and a small child on her own was complicated, but her daughter was such a source of undisputed, exquisite joy that the complications were nothing more than inconvenient. Her work was also a great source of pride and, not to put too fine a point on it, income.

For the first time in a long time, Sophie felt in control of her life and destiny, and she liked that feeling. So why was it that she found her treacherous tongue could not resist waging a pointless battle with her ex-husband? It was clear that the war had already been fought, the casualties counted and the dead buried. Why couldn't her treacherous tongue follow the instructions of her infinitely more sensible brain and behave with composure and serenity? Sophie wondered if she was over Lloyd. The loneliness had gone away, but her anger reared its ugly head at so many unexpected turns. She was angry with him when other women—her friends, for example—announced their second pregnancy or when she bumped into him and Greta in the high street, strolling along hand in hand, and smiling as though they hadn't wreaked as much damage as an earthquake measuring 7 on the Richter scale. She was angry when he announced he was taking a week's skiing holiday.

"What was your New Year's wish?" asked Lloyd.

Right at that moment, Sophie wished she had the courage simply to hang up on him, but she didn't. Even now she was pathetically grateful for his attention. Habit, she supposed. Because she had been deprived of it for the past couple of years, she naturally hankered after it, like an ex-smoker gladly inhaling secondary smoke in a bar.

"You don't have New Year's wishes. You're confusing it with birthdays. You have New Year's resolutions," she pointed out tetchily.

Lloyd didn't bother to ask her what her New Year's resolution was. He assumed he knew. It was likely to be to drink more water and lose ten pounds in weight. Those had been Sophie's New Year's resolutions for all the years they'd known each other. Besides which, he suddenly found that he had an agenda, one which had been developed with the speed and intensity exclusive to a drunk. He planned to stick, unwaveringly, to the agenda. It was the only way to secure success.

"My resolution is to grow my business by another thirty percent and to franchise the Highgate branch," said Sophie, even though he hadn't asked. Lloyd barely registered what she had said, so intent was he to push ahead.

"Well, my New Year's wish is that you were here, with the old gang."

He let his voice drop slightly, and Sophie knew that his eyes would be misting over. The two things, the drop in tone and the misty eyes, always came hand in hand. It wasn't exactly insincere, but it was a practiced technique. His huge, melting, puppy-dog eyes had weakened her resolve on many, many occasions in the past. But they were less effective over a telephone line.

"I wouldn't be enjoying myself if I were there," said Sophie truthfully.

"Wouldn't you? Wouldn't you, really?" Incredulity was always amplified after a beer or two too many.

"Mia would be making my life hell because I like makeup and I didn't go to an ancient university. Mistakenly, she seems to link the two facts. She'd be making snide comments about my 'party project' and ignoring the fact that I was nominated as Business Woman of the Year by *Red* magazine. Rich would be veering between correcting my grammar and accent, and trying to seduce me."

Lloyd lost his footing and slipped. He only managed to stay upright because he fell against the wall. He was glad that Sophie couldn't see just how drunk he was. "Oh, no, no, no, no. Rich wouldn't do that."

"Rich always did that. As did Jason. And Kate and Ted are OK, but I've been extremely disappointed with Kate of late. We were good friends, or so I thought. I've seen her once since you and I split up. I think that was due to curiosity—she wanted to hear me dish the dirt. Maybe I should have obliged. At least I'd have been more interesting, then maybe she would have called a second time. I don't think it's very decent of her to ditch me and Joanna quite as unceremoniously as she has. Even lepers get visitors, and leprosy is medically proven to be infectious. As far as I know, divorce isn't."

Sophie took a deep breath. She'd been meaning to say that for a while.

"Rich wouldn't be trying to provoke you. He's engaged now. You'd really like his fiancée, Tash." Lloyd giggled, as though indulging a small child. "I think she's running into the same problems with Mia as you did."

"Poor girl."

"Why do you say that? I'm sure they'll be very happy," argued Lloyd.

Sophie tutted, but realized she didn't know enough about the situation to comment. These weren't her people anymore. These weren't her problems.

"Soph, I thought you might pop on a plane and come to join us." Lloyd's voice was urgent and drunken. If he could get Sophie out to Avoriaz, away from all the distraction of her work, then maybe he would have a chance at convincing her just how sorry he was. He knew he'd been foolish, made a terrible mess, but the game was over now. He wanted to put things back to normal. "I bet you could get a flight or, if not, there's a train from Waterloo. It comes all the way into Cluses." He wondered if he sounded desperate.

He absolutely hated rejection.

And so he added, "The wedding is on Friday. You're a pal of Rich's, too."

Put this way, he hoped his proposal sounded friendly rather than romantic. A rejection of his friendship was easier to bear.

Sophie was almost amused at Lloyd's stupidity. She knew that he wanted her, very, very much. But she also knew that he wouldn't want her in the morning when he sobered up. If he remembered this conversation at all, he'd be mortified. He'd had plenty of opportunities to make it work between them. Opportunities he had shrugged away, with a casualness that was insulting. He was always prone to nostalgia, and that was all this was. Where should she start with pointing out just how silly a plan that would be?

"What would I do with Joanna? The wedding party is a child-free zone, isn't it? And what about Greta? I can't imagine she'd be too happy to hear I joined the little ski trip. And what about my work? You have no grasp on reality, Lloyd. Besides, I'd be damned if I'd just melt back into that scene at the first offer after months of being out in the cold. I'm surprised you have. Go sleep off the beer, and lay off the spirits."

Stung, Lloyd yelled, "You can't tell me what to do anymore, Sophie."

"I won't even try if you stop calling me. Good night."

For the second time in less than fifteen minutes, Lloyd found himself listening to the empty tone of a dead line. He didn't know what to do, so he decided to ignore Sophie's advice to go to sleep and to stop drinking. His only regret was that she couldn't see him march straight back into the club.

# 21

## *Not so Polite Small Talk*

Mia left her dance partner on the floor and went to stand with Rich, Tash, Kate, Ted and Lloyd.

"He looks really keen," commented Lloyd, pointing to the French guy that Mia had left languishing.

She shrugged and didn't even treat the guy to a smile. She'd spotted Scaley and Jayne emerging. They'd obviously found a private bit of the bar to chat and God knows what else. Damn. She was going to have to get a move on. Mia took a deep breath and once again tried to quash the rising panic she felt. She told herself that it was not impossible that Scaley Jase would have more than one flirtation on this holiday. In fact, it was probable.

"So what happened with the Frog Prince?" asked Jason, nodding toward the bloke Mia had left stranded. "He's a good-looking guy."

"Dull," said Mia, by way of explanation.

"Well, you didn't give him much of a chance to shine. He can hardly impress you with his conversation on the dance floor. He was a good mover—surely that ought to have got him through to the second round, even by your strict criteria. You never know, Mia, you might even have had some fun." Mia shot Jason a withering look. He ignored it and carried on. "Your problem is that you are already rehearsing your exit before you've even got their mobile number. What are you so scared of?"

"Inadequacy."

"Yours?"

Mia looked scornful. "Theirs."

It was true. No man had ever been good enough for her. Bright enough, sensitive enough, funny enough, passionate enough, rich enough, single enough. They might have had one or two of these qualities, but never the full house. No one except maybe Scaley. He was the last person on earth she would admit that to. She turned away from him and picked up a conversation with Kate.

Lloyd had bought a bottle of beer and paid with the last of his loose change. He'd hoped it would help him forget about the two abruptly ended calls, but he'd drained it and the calls were still the only thing on his mind, although he was halfheartedly joining in with a conversation about French cheeses. Lloyd was desperately trying to appear sober and therefore coming across as very drunk. "It is my round," he articulated carefully. "Can I interest anyone in a nightcap?"

"Yeah, I'll have one more drink," said Tash, as she'd finally come up for air after kissing Rich for what seemed to the others forever and seemed to her not long enough. "But better make it water. I want to be in a half-decent state tomorrow."

"I'll have malt," said Jayne, "Glenmorangie Black, darling. No ice, no water, as it comes."

"Hey, that's Rich's favorite nightcap," said Tash.

"I'll bring whisky for everyone, and I'll make mine a double," said Lloyd. It was only when he'd ordered a bottle of malt and eight glasses that he remembered that he'd run out of ready cash and needed to change more sterling into euros. He tried to pay with Visa, but the busy bartender was unimpressed and uncooperative. Kate kindly led him back to his seat and instructed Ted to take care of the bill.

"I think you've had enough," said Kate to Lloyd. "You are going to feel lousy in the morning."

STILL THINKING *of* YOU                    113

He slouched next to her and rested his head on her shoulder. The intimacy didn't seem inappropriate, more motherly than flirty. Kate's role in the gang had always been that of mother hen. If they'd been alone, he would have told her about the disastrous phone calls. He was unsure which one would have the most disastrous consequences. He hadn't called Greta back, which he'd meant to, and he'd asked Sophie to come back, which he didn't mean to. Fuck. Kate stroked his hair, and he allowed himself to feel temporarily soothed. He'd stay drunk and avoid the repercussions, that was the answer.

"This reminds me of old days in the college bar," said Lloyd, sentimentally. "Do you remember when Jason ran the bar and we'd have those lock-ins?" The university crowd nodded and smiled. "I think that was the last time I felt this cocooned," added Lloyd.

"No, it's just that that was the last time you felt this drunk," laughed Jason.

Ted came back from the bar with the whisky and water. Everyone accepted a glass, despite worries about early starts on the slopes tomorrow.

"I didn't really expect to be invited here," said Lloyd suddenly. The stark truth was spluttered, despite his desire to be affable.

"Lloyd, buddy, you are one of my oldest and best friends. I couldn't get married without you being here," said Rich.

"But you could go and play footers every week and not ask me along," said Lloyd sulkily. The combination of the term "footers" and the sulky tones made Lloyd appear about age eight. Luckily he was too drunk to be self-conscious. Besides, he had a point. Or, rather, he had made Sophie's point. Rich had been avoiding him. Rich had, and so had Jason, and Mia, and Ted and Kate, and the whole bloody lot of them.

"What are you talking about? You're welcome to come along to soccer anytime," lied Rich, embarrassed.

"Since Sophie and I split up, I can count on one hand the number of times I've seen you." Unfortunately, Lloyd had the grim determination of a drunk. He wasn't going to let his point go. He was oblivious to the discomfort he was causing the others.

"Rubbish," replied Rich, without turning to face Lloyd. "It's nothing to do with your split. If we've seen less of each other of late, it's because we're all busy. My biggest crime has been falling in love with Tash. She's all-consuming. But look at her, can you blame me?" Rich smiled proudly, oblivious to how insensitive his comment was. "The timing is coincidence."

"You are all the same. No one wants to see me or meet Greta." Lloyd pointed an accusatory finger around the table. Unfortunately, he used the same hand as he held his whisky in, and it slopped onto his jeans. It wasn't very dignified.

"Why didn't you bring Greta along? Doesn't she ski?" asked Jase innocently.

"Yes, she does, actually," admitted Lloyd. "I didn't bring her along because I didn't think she was welcome," he blurted.

"It's not that we have anything against you or Greta," said Kate untruthfully. In fact, she was wary of Greta. As a rule she didn't like women who went out with married men. Ted was a married man. She generally preferred to mix with married women. "Ted and I haven't seen you as much because we thought it was awkward. In truth, we liked Sophie." She jutted out her chin in defiance.

"Yes, I liked Sophie, too," added Jason, jumping on the bandwagon that looked vaguely like the moral high ground. It was true that he'd always thought she had great tits and nice cheekbones.

A general buzz went around the crowd. Everyone agreed that they did like Sophie. Mia forgot that she had thought she was rather common. She'd worn her ambition on her sleeve. She was an archetypal working-class, comprehensive-educated girl, with a chip on her shoulder the size of a Henry Moore sculpture. She'd been so desperate to prove herself. Which, Mia supposed, she had, when she made her business a success and received that award from whichever magazine she received it from. (Mia couldn't quite remember, despite Sophie going on about nothing but for several weeks.) She'd been nauseating when she'd gone to that ceremony at the Ritz, just because it was on some crappy satellite TV channel. She had no idea how to be gracious. Her sort never did. But Mia did like her now. Now that she'd seen her crumble into tiny, spiky shards of glass. The chip crumbling along with the rest of her.

"Why isn't Sophie here, then?" asked Lloyd reasonably. His grin was ridiculously wide and slack. He thought he was being extremely clever and that he'd just tripped them up in a complex interrogation.

"Because we were being tactful toward you, mate," explained Rich carefully.

"Right," said Lloyd, allowing his disbelief to show. The loud music blasted around Lloyd's head, drowning out common sense. He couldn't really understand why he was saying these things. He'd wanted to be agreeable, yet this was social suicide. He laughed into his whisky, drained it, then poured another. Rich noticed that his whisky glass was empty, too. He refilled it.

"Sorry, mate, that we didn't specifically invite Greta. Maybe we should have been more welcoming. We should have had you over for dinner by now. As soon as we get back we'll arrange it. But I think I did feel funny about having Greta over for dinner, so soon after Sophie."

"So you are saying you stopped seeing me in deference to Sophie?" challenged Lloyd.

"I don't know, maybe. Yes." Rich felt quite proud of himself for computing and confessing something so emotionally complex. Lloyd chose to throw cold water.

"If only that were true. If only you were making a moral judgment on my behavior. But you are not. The reason you don't see either me or Sophie is not because I behaved badly, or even because she's boring and always crying into her Chardonnay nowadays. It's because we don't fit any longer." Lloyd shouted this, and was drawing attention from other clubbers and drinkers. It was lucky he was British and the French expected little better of English tourists. "We're not throwing barbecues in the summer or dinner parties at any time. We don't make polite conversation. We're not perfect, successful or even happy. We hurt, and we bleed our hurt all over the place."

Lloyd waved his hand about, to demonstrate the point that he metaphorically bled profusely, and sent glasses crashing and smashing to the floor.

"We're not reliable dinner guests. She dates younger men, and that's embarrassing for you. We don't fit anymore; we can't get into your exclusive club. We don't fit, so we don't count."

Lloyd threw himself back into his seat and, for an awful moment, it looked as though he were going to cry. Everyone wished he would shut up, including himself.

"Now, come on. Let me get this straight. *You* are giving *us* a hard time about not inviting Sophie. Not being *nice* to Sophie. That takes the cake. You treated her like shit, mate. You dumped her. You were together for six years, married for three of those. Then you grew bored and you gave her and your kid the old heave-ho." Rich thought it was time to point out the obvious.

"I didn't give my daughter the heave-ho," shouted Lloyd.

"You did. You could have worked harder at it for her sake," argued Rich. He was really irritated that Lloyd was ruining his night like this.

"We are really sensible about time access to Joanna. I see her every Sunday."

"She's a baby, not a time-share in the Costa del Sol," snapped Kate.

"He needs some air," said Tash. "He's drunk a lot." She stood up, grabbed their coats and kindly led Lloyd outside before he

STILL THINKING *of* YOU117

could expose himself further. She felt uncomfortable because she had a feeling that his drunken ramblings were the worst kind—it was correct. As Tash led him away, Lloyd could hear the recriminations he'd left in his wake.

"What Lloyd did was wrong. He left a wife and child," said Kate.

"Well, strictly speaking, Sophie threw Checkers out. He didn't have any choice in the matter," pointed out Mia.

"She was right to throw him out. He had an affair," added Rich.

"I admit it was daft of him. He hurt himself but—" Ted interjected.

"He hurt her, not himself. People should say what they mean, or else what is the point?" bit out Kate.

"It is quite possible that there isn't one," shouted Lloyd over his shoulder, as Tash continued to shepherd him away. She was trying her best to get him to stay upright so that he didn't upset any more drinks or people. "And would you all stop talking about me as though I'm not here," slurred Lloyd, clearly disgruntled.

"Oh yes, sorry, mate. Habit," apologized Jason.

# 22

## *It's Cold Outside*

Tash and Lloyd stood outside the bar and didn't know what to say to one another. The freezing air was so cold it scratched at Tash's eyeballs and bit her cheeks, but, on the plus side, it seemed to help sober up Lloyd. They both wondered what to do next, and they both wondered if Lloyd was going to throw up. It was snowing heavily, shrouding everything in a thick white mist. Tiny silver fairy lights twinkled magically on roofs and fences, illuminating the wood with a warm amber glow.

"I'm sorry about that." Lloyd pointed toward the bar.

Tash shrugged. "No problem."

"I've drunk too much."

"I should say." Tash smiled. "It's nothing. God, we've all been lashed, then lashed out, said things we didn't mean."

"I did mean it, though," said Lloyd defiantly.

"Right." Tash moved her weight from her left foot to her right and concentrated on making patterns in the snow.

"Well, I think I did. I don't know. I'm not sure about—" Lloyd searched for the word.

"Anything?" filled in Tash.

Lloyd nodded. "I guess. Still, I am sorry. It's not the kind of stuff you want to listen to six days before your wedding, though, is it?"

Tash checked her watch. "It's technically only five days to my wedding."

"The countdown begins." He smiled and tried to look bright and sober; he felt he owed this nice woman that much.

Tash grinned back. "Should we walk back to the hotel? It's only five minutes, but we can get a horse and sleigh if you don't think you can—"

"No, I'll manage. The walk will do me good." Lloyd smiled.

Tash looked at him properly for the first time. As she'd only just met him and it had been such a busy day, she hadn't really had a chance to take him in. Rich hadn't been particularly forthcoming in his description of Lloyd. He'd simply revealed that he was initially focused and recently divorced. It didn't give her much to go on. Tash had got the impression that Lloyd was so much more ordinary than all of Rich's other mates. That sounded rude. She didn't mean to be rude.

She'd expected someone so typically run-of-the-mill that he had become a caricature in her head. Lloyd was a man who had been jealous of his wife's success and the time she spent on their baby, and therefore had an affair with a younger, blonder, less demanding woman, to secure a bit of attention. In the flesh, however, Lloyd was much more complicated than the caricature that Tash had allowed to settle in her mind. He was bleeding, just as he'd said. His face was tense with regret and pain. His eyes were wary, almost hunted. This man was clearly confused and at a complete loss as to how he ended up exactly where he was. Tash didn't know enough about his marital experience to know if he was a complete loser or not. All she knew was that this man needed friends. Tash found herself wishing Rich had been a better friend to Lloyd. Which surprised her—she always thought of Rich as an excellent buddy.

They walked to the hotel in silence, then Tash walked Lloyd to his room as she feared that he'd have a relapse and wouldn't be able to put his key in the lock.

"Thanks for the escort," said Lloyd when they reached the door to his room.

"No problem." Tash turned to leave, then stopped. She turned back to him, the tired, drunken man struggling with the mechanics of a basic door lock. "Look, I don't know how to say this without sounding corny, but, if you need someone to talk to, if you need a friend, then I'm happy to be it."

"Thank you," said Lloyd, "I'll bear it in mind."

Rich got back to their room only minutes after Tash. She had taken her boots off and was in the bathroom removing her makeup.

Rich crept up behind her and put his hands on her shoulders. He started to nibble her ear.

"It's been a long day."

"Hasn't it," she agreed.

"I'm sorry about Lloyd. What an idiot. He really spoiled a very good evening," said Rich, as he broke away from Tash and sat on the bed to pull his sneakers off. He was feeling more than peeved. He hated people who couldn't hold their drink. He didn't need this. Jayne being here, crashing the party, was bad enough. He didn't want to listen to Lloyd's self-indulgent, drunken rants. Didn't Lloyd know this was supposed to be a celebration? It was this miserable self-pity that had made Rich steer away from him over the past year. People falling in love didn't usually like to look at the carnage of a divorce.

"Don't worry. He apologized, too," said Tash.

Rich wasn't listening. He really had to talk to Tash about Jayne. He'd meant to earlier this evening, but then they'd gotten cheeky instead, and afterward it just hadn't seemed like the right moment. He could have said something tonight, he supposed. It wasn't as though Jayne's name didn't come up in conversation—the opposite was true. Tash had almost continually sung her praises. She'd gone on and on about how sweet Jayne was, how attractive and what fun. Clearly Tash had made Jayne her new best friend, but that had somehow made it harder for him to say anything, not easier.

Clearly now wasn't the moment. Not now that Lloyd had dampened the festivities. Rich wondered if it would be best to keep quiet altogether. If the matter ever came to light, he could always say that he had not considered it significant enough to mention.

"Actually, I feel a bit sorry for him. He seems lonely," said Tash, interrupting Rich's thoughts.

"He brought it on himself," muttered Rich. He didn't have any sympathy to share. Rich had quickly stripped himself naked and hopped into bed.

"Yeah, well, everyone makes mistakes," said Tash, as she started to pull off her multiple layers of clothes. "Not that I'm condoning his behavior. Be clear, I love you too much to be able to forgive you if you were ever unfaithful. I'd chop your balls off. Surely that is threat enough to keep you on the straight and narrow." Tash was now naked, and she climbed into bed next to Rich. "And if I ever had a dalliance, I give you full permission to break the heels off all my shoes." She smiled with the confidence of a woman about to marry the man she loves; she couldn't really imagine the situation they were joking about. More seriously, she added, "It's not infectious, you know."

"What isn't?"

"Divorce, unhappiness. You can't catch it from him."

"I hope not," he mumbled, as he stretched to turn out the bedside light.

# SUNDAY

# 23

## *Slippery Slope*

The conditions were perfect for skiing and boarding. The cobalt blue sky was split with white-hot sun rays. The spectacular mountains were covered with deep, fresh snow. The forecasts had proved on the nail; there had been a huge dump of snow last night. There were long, wide ski runs overflowing with fresh powder, and risky narrow tracks winding between fir trees that were weighed down with white blankets. Tash was feeling excited; Kate was feeling nervous; Jayne was feeling confident; Mia and the boys were feeling competitive.

"Are you going to throw some tricks?"

"What are the parks like here?"

"There are hips, quarters, tables, gaps, spines. You name it."

"Guaranteed thrills."

"Maybe we should hire one of those crews that video you in action, then we can have serious debriefs at the end of the day. It's the only real way to improve technique."

"You haven't got wrist protectors on."

"I never fall, mate."

"I'll do a couple of black runs just to get the lay of the land, and then I think I'll get over to Switzerland for some hot chocolate."

And so on. You could almost taste the testosterone.

Snow sports require a lot of preparation. Dressing in the morning is like preparing for battle. The boarder girls wore knee, wrist and bum protection, even though they bemoaned the fact that the question "Does my bum look big in this?" had never been so redundant. Thermals, Salapex or trousers, jackets, snoods, gloves, boots and goggles were essential wear. It took an age to get everyone dressed and out on the slopes, only to find that they'd forgotten the piste map, then water bottles, and then the walkie-talkies, so Lloyd, Rich and Jason took it in turns to run back to the hotel to retrieve the forgotten items. Despite a very early breakfast, it was past eleven o'clock before they reached the top of the slopes.

"At least we didn't have to queue for a shuttle every morning like we did in Chamonix," said Mia.

"Was that where we had to reserve the cable car?" asked Jason.

"Yes, dull bloody wait. But it was worth it. Wonderful snow, the best. It was as though we were the only people on the mountain." Mia smiled at the memory.

"It felt as though we were the only people on the planet," laughed Jason.

"It felt as though we were ruling the fucking planet," added Lloyd.

Lloyd was trying to be particularly lively and pleasant. He'd dashed about at breakfast, refilling everyone's coffee cup, securing extra croissants. He'd helped to tighten everyone's boots and adjust goggles. He was trying to compensate for his drunken outburst last night. No one referred to his ranting, and he was grateful. He wasn't absolutely sure exactly what he'd said last night, but he rather feared he'd been a bit of a bore. Bloody Sophie, she'd put the idea in his head that the gang had been neglectful of him, and then he'd gone and spewed her idea all over their party. It wasn't good form. He felt embarrassed, and was grateful for the gang's tactful silence on the matter. He wished Tash wouldn't keep giving him those obvious looks of concern. She was a lovely girl, he wouldn't want you to get him wrong, but what's said on tour stays on tour.

He was drunk; he didn't mean that stuff. Well, he did. A little bit. He meant some of it. Last night he'd meant all of it. But that was the drink talking. Wasn't it?

Lloyd shook his head. It was impossible to think straight with a hangover. He needed to get skiing. That would clear the cobwebs. He wondered just how cross Greta really was. He had no idea. And Sophie? God, he couldn't even think about Sophie. He'd made such an ass of himself. What had he been thinking of, asking Sophie to come here? A recipe for disaster. Not what he wanted. Not really.

Lloyd, Kate and Ted had decided to stick to skiing. Jason was a great skier, but he wanted to learn to board—and Mia realized that this was largely to impress Jayne. So she, who was also a long-term skier, said that she wanted to learn to board, too—largely to keep up with Jason. Jayne, Rich and Tash didn't even consider skiing, preferring instead the adventure and challenge of boarding.

At the top of the run, Mia watched with envy as Jayne effortlessly stepped onto her board, fastened her bindings in one swift movement and set off down the slope.

"She's a natural," laughed Lloyd. The entire group kept their eyes on the slight girl as she gracefully carved her way through the fresh snow.

"No, she's a master," marveled Rich. "Look at her technique. It's on the nail."

"She's always been a great sportswoman," commented Ted.

"I'm going to catch her up," said Tash. Pulling her goggles down over her eyes, she set off down the slope. All eyes were on her now. While she was a devoted and competent boarder, it was obvious to everyone that Tash's enthusiasm and speed supplemented a lack of technique and control. Rich was surprised; he'd always considered Tash an extremely good boarder. She was gutsy and tireless.

But he had to admit she looked clumsy in comparison to Jayne. He shook his head. It was a harmless comparison, one he'd made subconsciously, but he didn't like it.

Ted, Kate and Lloyd set off down the slope, too. They skied past, through and next to one another with a quiet, steady confidence that was a result of their learning and skiing together for years. Mia watched them go, a little bit of her wishing that she hadn't taken up Rich's offer to teach her to board. She hated learning anything new. Learning something, by definition, meant that you weren't very good at it.

"OK, you guys," said Rich, as he turned to Jason and Mia, and gave them a loose grin. "It's pretty simple, really. It's all a matter of confidence and balance. I'm expecting great things from both of you."

"Be careful, Rich: Mia's in a mood. The guy in the rental shop called her goofy. She nearly took a swipe at him," blurted Jason.

"Well, how was I supposed to know that he meant I lead with my right foot rather than orthodontically challenged? I'm a rookie, you know." Mia threw in the hip expression for novice, in an attempt to cover her mistake. How she loathed being anything less than impressively informed on all subjects. "Look, let's stop jabbering and get down to it. The sooner I get the hang of this, the better. There's some major off-piste to shred."

"Yeah, like, radical," sniggered Jason, who always knew when Mia was faking. "What happened? Did you swallow a boarder slang dictionary, Mia?"

Mia glared at Jason and continued, "I understand now. The plastic hoops on my boots face left on the board. If I were regular they'd face the other way, but what difference does it make anyway?"

"You're right, Mia. It's all irrelevant. You are probably going to come down on your butt no matter what," laughed Jason. Rich laughed, too, but Mia just scowled and vowed that she'd make Jason eat his words.

All she ate was snow. It was impossible.

Mia couldn't stand. She was fittish and firmish, with strongish stomach muscles, but she couldn't even stand up on her board. The only blessing was that she didn't get high enough to fall down; she simply slipped and slid, her feet constantly moving away from her despite being attached by a complicated series of muscles, ligaments and bones. Her calves stung with lactic acid buildup. She should have trained more. Jason was at least upright. He was practicing something called his "heel edges." God, she felt such a fool. This was hardly going to help her seduction of Scaley. He'd think she was a loser.

After half an hour of trial and error, Mia mastered standing up and balancing on the heel edge of her board. She grabbed on to Rich as though he were a life raft, and in many ways he was. He patiently encouraged, directed and cajoled in exactly the correct proportions to elicit the best performance he could from Mia. She inched down the mountain—stop-start, stop-start—just as Rich had instructed her to, so that she gained control of the board. As soon as her confidence increased, she waved at Jason, who was a few meters in front of her. He grinned, and shouted something, but she didn't hear what it was as she fell backward.

Shit, that hurt.

Mia, as a competent skier, had forgotten just how painful falling was. The shock pains screeched up through her bum, her coccyx and back. She felt the agony tingle, far away from the impact, in her earlobes and her toes. As she'd fallen she'd bit her tongue, quite badly, it appeared, as she could taste blood. Mia squeezed her eyes shut so the tears couldn't eke out.

"Are you OK?" yelled Jason, his teasing submerged by genuine concern. Suddenly he was at her side, rubbing her back. She waved him away with a dismissive flick of the hand, forced her very best wide grin, flashed it, and burst out laughing.

"God, am I a klutz?" she laughed.

The boys joined in with her laughter, relieved.

Mia knew that her strongest card, her deepest tie, with Jason was being one of the boys. One of the boys would not cry when they'd fallen on the slopes, however much their back hurt.

"Quite a spectacular fall, wouldn't you agree? But then, I've never been one for half measures." She grinned.

"That's my girl," said Jason, and then turned his attention back to practicing balancing on his toe edge.

Mia smiled to herself. Jason's comment was progress. Like her boarding, it needed lots of work, but it was progress.

# 24

## *Ladies at Lunch*

The girls had agreed to meet at 2 p.m. for a pizza. At the time of agreeing, Mia had thought that she probably wouldn't bother showing up. She'd imagined that by then she'd be boarding down the slopes, with Action Man and Scaley, and would not want to break off to eat. However, she had been clock-watching for an hour and a half, and was very grateful for the excuse to leave the boys to their lesson. Every bone was battered and every muscle was screaming in protest. It was actually quite hard to fall forward—gravity nearly always dragged rookie boarders onto their bums—but Mia somehow managed both. She even fell from the chairlift, one foot tethered to her board, like a ball and chain, the other flaying wildly. She was sore.

"How did you find the snow this morning?" asked Tash.

"Good," said Kate.

"Excellent," said Jayne.

"Hard," said Mia.

This just about wrapped up the ski stories. Unlike the guys, the girls did not feel compelled to relive every second on the slopes, exaggerating every trick, making every near miss that bit more heroic or scary.

It had been Jayne's idea for the girls to meet for lunch; she'd said it was a sort of hen party lunch. Mia had thought that the idea was ridiculous. Jayne was more obsessed by this wedding than Barbie Babe was. Last night she'd turned every drink into a toast to the bride and groom; every conversation somehow found its way back to the subject of the nuptials. This morning Mia had commented that the breakfast was good and Jayne had replied, "Can you imagine how fantastic *the* wedding breakfast will be?" Mia suspected that Jayne was trying to worm her way into Tash and Rich's affections because she had burst in on the party. Frankly, it made tedious conversation. Mia did not need reminders of just how loved up the whole planet was, particularly as she was a notable exception.

They found a cute pizzeria and chose to sit outside on the street, which was covered with a wooden layer of red-cedar shingle tiles which had not been seen for a while as they had become enveloped by the snow. The girls removed gloves and scarves, slackened boots and unzipped jackets. They turned their faces to the sun, which splattered light onto their sunglasses, the polished table and the drinking glasses. Sun-kissed and exhausted, the girls idly watched children being pulled along in sleighs and skiers skiing right up to shop and restaurant doorways. Hungrily they read the menu.

"I think I'll order some garlic bread and a pizza. I'm always starving after skiing," said Kate. "I can never bear getting back onto skis again with a full stomach, so I might as well have a glass of wine."

"Good idea. I'll have vodka," said Mia.

"I thought you were detoxing," said Kate.

Bugger, thought Mia, she had said that yesterday, hadn't she? And she hadn't known whether to be pleased or aggrieved that no one questioned her about this move. It was useful that she hadn't been cross-examined as to exactly which detox diet let you eat what you like (in enormous quantities) but not drink any alcohol, yet it was insulting that the gang clearly thought she needed to detox. Were they saying she was fat?

"One won't hurt," she insisted.

"Oh, go on, then, I'll have a glass of red," added Tash.

"Not for me, even though this is a hen party, I'm determined to get back on the slopes this afternoon," said Jayne.

Kate automatically placed her hand on her stomach as though Jayne's self-control were a direct criticism of her lack of it. Kate's Salapex was feeling a bit tight across the stomach and thighs, even though she only bought it last season. She wanted to believe that it was her bulky underwear, but she knew that was not the case. She thought she might have a snoop around the shops that afternoon and perhaps buy a new, slightly more generous one. She knew she was eating too much at the moment, but she couldn't seem to stop herself. It was impossible to think of salads in the winter. Never mind, well-tailored clothes hid a multitude of sins.

"Isn't this place darling? Sort of a cross between *White Christmas* and *It's a Wonderful Life*," gushed Jayne, who, Kate noted, was failing to show any of the symptoms of being the desperate, ditched soul she'd convinced Ted she was. Kate sighed. To her, snow more often than not meant lost gloves and runny noses. At least by leaving the children at home she didn't have to worry about them catching colds or chilblains. Not that she'd know a chilblain if she saw one, it was just something her mum used to worry about on her behalf, and now Kate worried about them on behalf of her own children.

Kate thought about the conversation she'd had with the children on the mobile that morning. Fleur had sent a picture text, one of them all eating breakfast. Kate had just about been able to make out the box of Sugar Puffs on the table. There was no sign of the homemade muesli she'd left behind, but then she'd had three pastries for her breakfast and that probably wasn't a good idea either. Kate let her gaze drift toward the kids' ski school, which dominated the center of the resort. Even acknowledging the chilblain factor, she wished her children were here with her. They'd be no trouble. They would be in ski school all morning, and she would have entertained them all afternoon. To be honest, she'd have much preferred to spend her time with them than on the slopes. She sighed, accepting it wasn't to be, and tried to avoid staring at the carousel that merrily twirled around next to the ski school.

Mia followed Kate's gaze and thought, Weren't they just too cute? Those children with their chubby, determined faces and awkward, uncoordinated moves. Adorable. One day she would bring her child to ski school.

"Look at that mother," said Mia, pointing to a vexed-looking mum who was yelling at her son for throwing down his sticks in a temper tantrum. "What is she teaching him by yelling at him? She's just making him cry louder. She's unfit."

"It's not always easy to keep calm," pointed out Kate.

Mia was incensed. She wanted to pick up the sticks and beat the bad-tempered mother with them, although she conceded that wouldn't be the best example to set the small boy either. Mia swore to herself that she'd never be unnecessarily harsh with her child. She'd be unwearied, serene and wise, 24/7. Although not a pushover.

"Doesn't she know how lucky she is, just to be a mum? Couldn't she be just a little more empathetic, a little more patient?"

"Probably not," said Kate. She was aware that the fantasy of the perfect mother was one only childless women could harbor. "Are you feeling broody?"

"I certainly am not. Can't bear the idea. Horrible noisy things, children. Ruin your figure. It's not like I have anyone to have a baby with, is it? Never have the chance to go to the loo on my own again. No thank you," snapped Mia.

The words were out before she even considered telling the truth. Kate thought it was sad that Mia had no idea how much children brought to your life. Mia thought it was sad that she couldn't tell even her best friend how much she wanted a child brought into her life. But she couldn't afford to reveal her plan yet. It would ruin everything.

"Imagine little Richards running around," said Jayne. "They'd be too darling."

Jayne smiled at Tash, but Mia noticed that the smile didn't reach her eyes. What was Jayne playing at? She certainly wasn't playing it straight. That was for sure.

"Give us a moment," laughed Tash. "We're not even married yet." Mia was just thinking that she'd escaped lightly and no one was going to talk about the bloody wedding.

"No. You're not," said Jayne, and then to Mia's surprise and momentary relief she changed the subject. "Are you going to book lessons at the school?"

Mia glared her response and tried to weigh up whether Jayne was being rude. Was she saying that Mia needed lessons? She did, of course, but she wasn't sure if she wanted anyone else saying so.

Jayne didn't wait for a response. "I think I might check in for lessons just because Pierre, the instructor, is so ruggedly handsome. I would so love to fall into those arms."

"I saw him. You're right, he's to die for," added Kate.

Mia was torn. She wanted to encourage Jayne in that direction— any direction away from Jase actually. After all, a fling with a ski instructor was almost mandatory for women such as Jayne, a perk of finishing school, but she found herself snapping, "I'd hate that. There's nothing worse than being taught something by a man who is infinitely better than you, other than being taught something by a man who is infinitely better than you *and* good-looking."

The girls giggled, and started to guess the girth of Pierre's forearms. They hotly debated the subject for a long ten minutes.

"So you've skied often?" Kate asked Tash.

"Boarded," Tash corrected, not for the first time. "Oh, yes, I got into it when I was about twenty."

"Where have you been?"

"All over. Courchevel, Pas de la Casa and Les Arcs in France. Limone in Italy. Narvik in Norway and Sugar Bowl, California."

"She'd never been to Avoriaz, though. Had you, Barbie Babe?" interrupted Mia.

Tash didn't respond to the interruption. "Not like this, of course. Never in a hotel. More often than not I've stayed in a huge self-catering apartment block with a big gang of mates, acquaintances and relative strangers. About ten in beds and another half-dozen overload floor-scammers, who paid their way with beer. Lots of smelly bodies, and steamy wet clothes, fights over the shower and stealing food from the fridge. That has been my usual boarding holiday."

"You paint such an irresistible picture," said Mia.

"I've always had a lot of fun," insisted Tash.

"Did you enjoy Pas de la Casa? I've heard it is pure holiday camp, designed for the world's welfare cheats."

"It is noisy and rowdy. It's lively. Good fun. You should go one day."

Mia glared. People were always implying that she could do with
a dose of fun, as though it could be administered in the same fashion as cod liver oil.


The girls chatted about the hotel, specifically the rooms and the
treatments they fancied at the spa. They discussed the pizza top-
pings and gently argued about the number of calories in a hot
chocolate. Tash noticed that Mia seemed fractionally less competitive when the boys weren't around. She didn't seem compelled
to talk about the latest Pulitzer Prize novel she'd just read or art
exhibition that she planned to visit. The conversation was not so
liberally scattered with phrases such as "sourly forceful" or "thoughtfully compelling," as though she were a walking art compendium,
and Tash was grateful. They drifted into the occasional lull as they
watched other groups of friends and families order pizza and drink
beer.

  Tash thought what a wonderful moment this was. She loved
her limbs feeling tight and exhausted after a workout on the slopes.
She felt high on fresh air, and there was no better sensation than
the sun shining on closed eyelids. She felt relaxed and happy. This
was a good moment. She wallowed in it, then blurted, "Don't you
think it's funny that I am a Richardson, Natasha Richardson, and
I'm marrying a Richard. Sort of exchanging one Richard for another? It's that kind of thing that makes me believe in fate."

  Kate and Jayne nodded and smiled genially.

  "You are not serious, Barbie Babe?" snapped Mia, who clearly
hadn't grasped the concept of politely-going-along-with-the-bride-
because-after-all-she-is-the-bride in the same way as the other guests
had. "So you are marrying Action Man because his name coin-
cides with your surname?"

  "No, she's marrying Rich because he's hot in the sack," interjected Jayne.

"Barbie Babe, what did you do? Look up the birth registry for, say, 1969 to 1973? In which region?"

"I didn't say that, exactly." Tash suddenly felt like an idiot. The relaxed atmosphere instantly vanished. She wanted to beat herself with a huge stick and wear sackcloth and ashes for the rest of her days as a punishment. Why did she say such stupid things? It wasn't because of a coincidence to do with names that she believed in fate. It was for a number of reasons to do with how her life had panned out so far, reasons that suddenly had become elusive and ephemeral, and she couldn't explain to Mia. Mia who was supposed to be her friend, but seemed distant and discouraging. She couldn't explain here at this lunch, which was supposed to be a hen party lunch, but now seemed about as much fun as a condemned man's final meal.

"Hey, Barbie Babe, did you limit it to the UK, or did you include Europe, just to see how many boys were named Richard in that period? Did you then drop them all an email until you got lucky with our Richard? Inspired." Mia was laughing. Kate, who didn't think Mia was being funny, and Jayne, who did, both joined in to varying degrees. "I might do the same search with Philip, as my surname is Philips. I hadn't thought of it before."

Tash knew that she should probably count to ten. She should remember that Mia was one of Rich's best friends, that she was here as a guest to celebrate her wedding. That's what she should do. Fuck it. Mia was a bitch, and Tash had had enough.

"Really, how odd, when you seem to have done everything else, including Internet dating, small ads in *Time Out* and sleeping with every guy you meet, including the groom and best man," snapped Tash.

God, that was satisfying.

"How do you know that?" Mia demanded.

"Well, obviously, Rich told me," replied Tash. She felt a smidgen shamefaced. After all, it was never nice to know that people had been talking about you. "Don't think we were gossiping, we were just . . . chatting." At least she'd managed to keep quiet about Ted, but that was more out of respect for Kate than respect for Mia.

"You've slept with Rich?" asked Jayne.

"Yes," muttered Mia.

"And you knew?" Jayne asked Tash. Tash nodded. "And you still let her come here?"

Kate looked around for the waiter. She hoped that by the time she ordered another bottle of wine the conversation would be forgotten.

"We don't keep secrets from one another. I fiercely believe in honesty. I don't much care what Rich has got up to in his past. He's a good-looking, clever, funny guy. It would have been odd if he hadn't slept around a bit. But I do believe that we have to be honest with one another about our past sexual conquests because past sexual conquests say a lot about a person, don't they?"

Mia shrugged. Tash thought that it had probably been such a long time since Mia had had an intimate conversation with a lover that she probably couldn't relate to Tash's theory or practice. Mia and her lovers swapped saliva, not stories.

"Our entire relationship is based on trust. No secrets, no lies, just one hundred percent respect and honesty. Aren't all relationships?"

"So you know everything there is to know about Rich's past, then?" asked Jayne.

"Yeah, pretty much. I could just about name every one of Rich's significant exes and detail the circumstances of the most interesting seductions. Well, at least as clearly as Rich can. He's sometimes a bit vague about names or the order of his flings. Spread himself a little too thinly at times." Tash grinned. "Don't worry. I'm fine with it," she added, turning back to Mia. "Well, it was all such a long time ago and it was just—"

"—a fuck," stated Mia.

"Yes, that's what Rich said." Tash closed the conversation with a guilty sense of triumph.


# 25

## *Ninety-five Percent Honesty*


"Hi." Jayne beamed at Rich and waved excitedly.

"Hello," he replied, nodding in her direction, but not breaking away from the queue for the ski lift.

"Are you trying to get in one more run before the lifts close?" she asked.

Rich nodded again, then started to fiddle with his goggles.

"All the other girls gave up at lunch time. I've been boarding on my own since then. Do you mind if I join you? I was just deciding whether to go back to the hotel or try for one more run."

This wasn't actually true. Jayne had been waiting by this lift for over an hour hoping to track down Rich. She'd heard him plan his routes this morning and knew he was the type of man who stuck to his plan. She'd figured that she would see him, eventually, at La Frontalière, the black run at Avoriaz, if she was patient enough.

Jayne was very patient.

Rich didn't reply, but he moved his board an inch or so to the left, to acknowledge that he had to accommodate Jayne and allow her to join the queue. Jayne turned to the grumbling people she was pushing in front of and made their holiday by flashing one of her gorgeous smiles. The smile silenced the objections. Rich saw the guys behind him melt and couldn't help but grin to himself. He had to admit she was a stunner. Any red-blooded male would get an erection within ten meters of her, let alone if she pressed her dainty derriere into their crotch as she edged into the queue.

The lifts were getting busy as everyone tried to squeeze in a last run before the light was completely lost, so Jayne and Rich found themselves sharing the chairlift with someone else. The French guy was in his sixties and clearly a seasoned skier—he didn't feel the need to make polite Franglais chitchat as the lift rose. Jayne and Rich were left to themselves.

"Isn't it darling?" sighed Jayne, waving her arm at the landscape, indicating, Rich supposed, that she was talking about the view. Rich scowled. Nobody said "Isn't it darling?" anymore, not unless they were the princess in a Disney animated movie. Jayne was no princess.

"The snow has lain so thickly that the mountains look as though they are wearing tablecloths and the trees look as though they are dressed in paper doilies, a veritable tea party. Don't you think so?" Jayne turned to Rich, whom she wrongly assumed thought she was charming.

"I don't know what paper doilies are," said Rich, turning his head to tighten the strap on his helmet.

"Darling, you *do* know. Snowflake-shaped bits of paper. Grand-mas put them on plates of scones." He looked at her blankly, so she gave up and simply muttered, "It really is beautiful." They stayed silent for some seconds before Jayne asked, "So, how have you been?"

"Good," replied Rich.

"You look good." She smiled encouragingly. "But then you always did."

"Thanks," replied Rich. Good manners and poor judgment forced him to add, "You look good, too."

"Thank you," said Jayne, and then grinned, clearly delighted with the compliment, although she had heard several more verbose ones in just one afternoon as she'd hung around the lifts. Those gushing compliments meant nothing: Rich's reluctant one meant everything. Jayne knew she looked fantastic. She'd mastered the mix-and-match earthy color scheme favored by boarders and was wearing blues and beiges. She'd instinctively known to avoid the top-to-toe pink-patterned numbers that ski bunnies chose, although she'd happily worn those in seasons of old. She preferred the snowboard outfit. That and because Rich boarded were her two reasons for choosing the sport.

"I've missed you," she said, getting straight to the point. Rich moved a fraction away from her, although the tiny lift seat allowed little room for maneuvering. He stared straight ahead, refusing to meet Jayne's eye. Jayne knew instantly that she'd overstepped the mark. She'd tried to move him on before he was ready for it, so she added, "Natasha seems lovely."

"She is," confirmed Rich cautiously.

"You've done very well for yourself there."

"Haven't I."

"Who'd have thought it? Rich the old rogue settling down."

Rich was determined not to be drawn, and so they fell silent again as the lift reached the pinnacle of the slope. They both expertly hopped off the chair and scooted to a safe distance away from the rotating seat. They fastened on their boards, and Jayne turned to Rich.

"And isn't Tash cool, the way she's so friendly toward me. Despite our past and everything?"

Rich froze. Jayne's radiant smile did nothing to melt him. In fact, it was her wide grin that sent shivers up and down his spine. After a long pause, he admitted, "She doesn't know about you."

"Doesn't know about me?" Jayne appeared shocked, but it was, of course, pretense. Before she'd wangled an invite onto this trip she'd been pretty sure that Tash wouldn't know about her. After all, none of Rich's friends knew about their relationship. Jayne

would have been more worried if Tash *had* known about her and
Rich; it would have shown that Tash's trust in Rich was justified.
That would have been the death knell for Jayne. But Tash's lunchtime conversation about Rich's sexual partners had confirmed
that, despite Tash's belief in Rich, he was not being 100 percent
honest with her. Tash knew about Mia, but not about Jayne. Jayne
was delighted.

"No. She doesn't know about you," sighed Rich. He'd feared
this conversation from the moment Kate had cadged an invite for
Jayne.

"You mean us," said Jayne pointedly.

"There's no reason why she should," insisted Rich. He was trying to sound calm and controlled, when in actual fact he was extremely nervous. He refused to look at Jayne. "We were over an
age ago."

"Hardly, darling. I was still sucking your cock this time last
year."

Rich breathed in quickly; the cold air whipped the back of his
throat and silenced him. He'd always found that extraordinarily
sexy—the way Jayne seemed so entirely proper, with her ancient
lineage and smart received pronunciation, and then the next moment she could be so filthy. Her statement was as coarse as it was
candid.

"It's interesting that Tash insists that the two of you have no secrets *at all*. She says that your entire relationship is based around
respect and honesty. 'Aren't all relationships?' " Jayne was quoting
Tash directly, and she was pretty sure that Rich would know that.
She wanted to see him sweat. "Odd, then, that she thinks she can
name every one of your significant exes—"

Rich tried to interrupt; he wanted to argue that Jayne wasn't
significant. He'd found a loophole.

Jayne didn't allow him his moment, but carried on, "—*and*
detail the circumstances of the most interesting seductions. I

think you have to agree, I come under the category of the latter, if not the former."

The loophole was closed.

"What's your game?" he asked.

"Game?" Jayne looked out at the beautiful vista and shrugged. Rich grabbed Jayne by the arm and tried to get her to look at him.

"Don't play the innocent with me." He'd tied her up in ropes once. They'd had anal sex. There was no point in her feigning innocence now. "Why are you here?"

"Didn't my darling brother explain everything to you? Some bastard dumped me and I'm heartbroken. I'm here to recuperate."

Jayne finally turned her beautiful brown eyes on Rich. He stared into them and tried to read her expression. It was hopeless. Jayne had perfected the art of deceiving him. In all the time she'd known him, she'd been very careful that whenever she looked at him she did not allow the love she felt to radiate out of her eyes. And now, she had no intention of showing him her desperation.

"What's that got to do with me? *I* didn't dump you," insisted Rich.

"You fucking liar," she snapped. "You were in my life for over ten years, then nothing. I call that dumping."

"But we haven't seen each other for months."

"It seems like yesterday to me. Time hasn't moved."

Rich felt a slow panic rise up his body. "I'm with Tash," he insisted anxiously.

"For now," replied Jayne.

"For ever," said Rich, but he wasn't sure whether Jayne heard because his words were swallowed as she pushed her lips onto his. He was too surprised to know how to react and remained stone still for a fraction longer than he would have done if his wits hadn't deserted him. Remembering himself, he broke the kiss and pushed Jayne away. He stared at her angrily and then, somewhat pathetically, wiped his mouth as though she'd sullied him. Jayne appeared unperturbed by his rebuff. She winked, then sped off down the mountainside, leaving Rich afraid and confused. He shook his head in an attempt to clear it, as he knew that a fair share of his confusion stemmed from the fact that as she sped away his final thought was, "Great ass."

# 26

## *Barflies*

It was a good bar to have chosen, Kate thought. For one, she wasn't the only woman sitting alone. There were two others. One was protected by a magazine which Kate assumed was the French equivalent of *Hello!* while a weighty novel shielded the other. There was also a family of three. A mother and father and a boy aged roughly eleven, not older. He smiled too much to have hit his teens yet. Kate immediately scrabbled for her mobile phone. She called Ted's mother and was assured that all the children were fit and well. She talked to everyone, even Aurora, who chatted contentedly and incomprehensibly down the phone. After saying goodbye half a dozen times, Kate finally hung up.

There were two men sitting at the bar. One had his back to her, but she had a good view of the other, who was the epitome of Frenchness. Dark floppy hair, elegant limbs and movement, and well-cut jeans, a sweatshirt and loafers. Neither of them noticed Kate. She was relieved.

The bar was perfect in many other ways, too. The person serving behind it was female, the floors were clean and the music was 1980s. They played people such as Paul Young and Annie Lennox, tunes Kate recognized and even knew the words to. Important, they played tunes that *had* words. She ordered herself a hot chocolate and found a warm corner to enjoy its powdery creaminess. This was the only time on a skiing holiday that Kate felt completely peaceful.

She didn't like snow.

Kate was not sure hell was hot at all. She imagined it would be icy cold. She'd skied every year since she was an undergraduate, so she was competent at the sport. But she simply didn't get it. What was all the fuss about? You went up a mountain, then you came down again. Sometimes you fell, sometimes you didn't. Either way the whole process had to be repeated. To what end? Kate didn't get the thrill that everyone talked about; it was as elusive as multiple orgasms. Besides, physically Kate was no longer ideal for this sport. She was fifty pounds heavier than when she'd first hauled herself up a mountain, when she was eighteen. She'd felt every ounce of those fifty pounds this morning. Kate had been grateful for the three years when she had been pregnant and was able to sit by the fire, with hot chocolates and a legitimate excuse.

Kate sighed and ordered a second hot chocolate. Her already weak willpower definitely suffered in the cold. She was ravenous again, even though she'd had that huge pizza at lunchtime. She looked longingly at the menu. They'd be having dinner in a couple of hours; surely she could wait until then. It would be a four-course dinner. But, on the other hand, if she had a crêpe now it would take the edge off her appetite and she could eat a dainty portion more akin to Tash's and Jayne's. Kate ordered a banana, chocolate, nut and cream crêpe.

This morning someone had suggested that they might go bowling or to the cinema tonight. Kate hoped that they'd choose the cinema over bowling, and a romance or a comedy over an art film. But she knew that if there was a consensus in favor of something arty and bleak, she wouldn't voice her objections. Kate was not a stranger to silently participating in things that she didn't really enjoy. For example, she found herself on the motorway traveling to Devon every weekend throughout the summer, and had done for five years now. Kate loved Devon, but the Lewis-Ponsonbys went there for sailing, and Kate hated sailing. She wasn't a very good swimmer and more than a little bit nervous of boats. She'd never said so. She would seem such a disappointment. They'd spent a fortune on buying the boat, employing a crew, hiring a summer house, getting lessons for the children. It would be madness to admit that she didn't enjoy the sport. Besides which, they'd made some great friends at the sailing club. Well, some fun acquaintances at least.

She felt the same about classical music and opera. At least once a month, Ted would blow more than £500 on tickets for Glyndebourne or Kenwood, or a box at Covent Garden. She did like the champagne during the interval, and it was nice taking her friends along, but frankly she was much more of a musical type of girl at heart. She had *Phantom of the Opera, Cats, Chicago* and *Les Misérables* on DVD. She watched them by herself when Aurora was taking a nap and there was no one else in the house. She had *Jesus Christ Superstar* on CD in the car, and she knew every word. She'd play it as she went to pick up the children from ballet, or school, or horse riding. Once the children were in the car, the preferred form of entertainment was Harry Potter on tape, and she enjoyed that, too. It just wasn't very vogue to admit to a passion for musicals, was it? People had passion for opera and mere affection for Julie Andrews belting out "My Favorite Things" in *The Sound of Music*.

Kate wondered if Natasha might like musicals or whether she was too trendy. She had a hope that at least Natasha wouldn't mind that Kate liked them. As much as Kate adored Mia, she would never dare admit her love for all things Andrew Lloyd Webber to her. She could imagine the tongue lashing. Kate sighed and returned to her hot chocolate, comforting herself with the thought that either bowling or the cinema was preferable to a club.


Jayne stomped into the bar. It was convenient to pretend that she was trying to knock snow off her boots, when in fact she was simply furious. She failed to notice the rustic charm of the bar, and her first thought was, God, what crap tunes they're playing. Fucking Meat Loaf, going on about wanting some woman and needing her, but not going the whole hog and loving her. Two out of three was lousy in Jayne's opinion. What a pointless, senseless—and, worst of all, poignant—lyric. It could be her personal theme tune. Where were the Coldplay tracks? And Air and Zero 7?

Jayne marched up to the bar—a woman serving, typical, not even a tasty barman to flirt with—and ordered a glass of red wine. The bartender's eyes involuntarily and reproachfully flicked toward the clock on the wall. It was 5:30 p.m. Jayne glowered. She knew that the bartender would assume that she, like many British tourists, was planning on drinking constantly from now until the early hours of tomorrow morning. Jayne picked up her glass, threw down a couple of euros and turned to scope the bar, as was her habit. She was looking for someone to flirt with. Someone who would reaffirm her attractiveness and buy her drinks. Someone who wouldn't wipe away her kisses. The two guys sitting at the bar had smiled at her the instant she'd walked into the bar. Dream on, guys. Not up to scratch.

Bugger, that was Kate. Jayne did not fancy making polite conversation with her dull-as-ditchwater sister-in-law. In fact, she'd rather self-administer a large suppository. Had Kate spotted Jayne? It appeared not. Kate was drowning in hot chocolate. Jayne acted quickly and settled into another dark corner, one that was out of Kate's view.

He had snubbed her! Wiped her kiss away. Denied her, even! Jayne hadn't even made it into his stories. Why not? Why *not*? Rich had told Tash about Mia, and Mia had fat thighs. Why didn't he talk about Jayne? Was she so insignificant? They'd once had sex in the loo of a bar. She thought that alone should have guaranteed her a degree of notoriety. Fucking bastard.

Why was he wasting his time with Natasha?

It was *such* a waste. Such a terrible, *awful* mistake. She couldn't let it happen. Every single bone in her body screamed in revolt at the idea. Every blood vessel was engorged with horror and anger. So many tragedies happened in this world. You had only to switch on the news to see disaster and cruel mishap. Just the other day she'd read this awful story in the *Metro* about some guy making a spur-of-the-moment decision to hire a private plane to get him up to Scotland for an important business meeting. The newspaper reported that he'd never expressed an interest in small planes to any of his friends. Then the plane he hired fell out of the sky. Killing him and the pilot. A needless disaster, resulting from a hurried, ill-considered decision. Jayne would not let Rich plummet to his death by choosing the wrong mode of transport. She would stop this disaster. There were things that were supposed to happen and things that weren't, and this wasn't. He belonged with her.

Jayne had spent an hour in her room examining the contents of a metal box, slightly bigger than a shoe box. She kept it locked, and wore the key on a silver chain around her neck.

Many girls and women kept similar memento boxes. There might even be boys who did the same thing, but it seemed unlikely. These boxes housed tickets from particular cinema visits, where their date had been especially solicitous, invites to weddings, old diaries, even the occasional pressed flowers. It wasn't just the Victorians that had a penchant for the sentimental. Jayne's box housed fourteen old diaries, dating back from her sixteenth birthday until last year. The diaries were all different, reflecting the tastes of a gauche teenage girl who had grown into a sophisticated woman; pink plastic covers were swapped for deep-brown buckskin. There were a handful of photos and numerous tube tickets, some as old as ten years. Jayne picked them up and carefully counted them. There were sixty-six—she knew that before she counted them. There were a couple of beer mats, three champagne corks and a dog-eared copy of *The Catcher in the Rye*. There was a torn envelope, addressed to her, and on the back, in a different handwriting, someone had written "Later X." There was another scrap of paper on which the word *plumber* and a telephone number were written. There was a small cardboard box inside which lay what looked suspiciously like toenail cuttings, curled and yellow, and two or three pubic hairs, curled and brown.

She took this box with her wherever she went. Even on holidays, despite the fact that it took up so much space in her suitcase and seriously affected what else she could pack. If Jayne's flat were ever to go up in flames, and she were only able to save one thing, she'd let her hamster burn and save the box.

Looking through her treasure box always cheered her up. Here was evidence of their relationship. The diaries detailed how Rich had taken Jayne's virginity on her sixteenth birthday and, while they hadn't actually met for the next five years, hardly a day went by when his name didn't appear in the diaries. None of the boys in her sixth form or at college could even come close. They were silly, inexperienced and, the biggest sin of all—as far as the teenage Jayne had been concerned—spotty. Most of them had those awful yellow spots that oozed or spurted gooey pus. Jayne couldn't imagine giving herself to those bags of hormones. Rich was, by contrast, beautiful. He was tall and lean and rugged. The handful of photos proved that. He looked surprised in all the shots. He didn't really like having his photo taken, and he'd always mess about covering his face with his hands or a magazine. As though she were a tabloid photographer and had caught him, a reluctant star. The only photo he looked peaceful in was the one that she had taken of him sleeping.

It was Rich who had inspired Jayne to become a management consultant. Not that he actually recommended the career path to her, but he was very helpful when she left the university and expressed an interest in becoming a consultant. He'd met her for coffee and laughed about the lousy hours and the lovely pay packages. It had been the obvious move for Jayne to apply to Peterson Windlooper because Rich seemed so inspired working there.

Their relationship had begun in earnest pretty soon after that, as soon as Jayne moved to London from college. The sixty-six tube tickets were gathered over the next nine years, two tickets for every time Jayne made the journey to and from Rich's flat in Islington.

Jayne had examined the scraps of paper that Rich had written on, the note he'd left for her, "Later X," and the telephone number of the plumber that she'd stolen from his flat. She'd fingered the book that he'd recommended that she read, and the corks saved from the bottles of champagne that she'd bought and they'd enjoyed together.

A fourteen-year relationship.

Clearly he'd confessed to dozens of scenarios to Tash, but not hers. Jayne couldn't understand it. Was he so ashamed of her?

Jayne reflected on this for a moment. Maybe there was another reason that Rich had never mentioned her to Tash, nothing to do with shame, indifference or neglect. Maybe he was protecting the sanctity of their relationship.

Jayne instantly felt cheered. Yes, that seemed possible.

That seemed probable.

The relationship between Rich and Jayne was so precious to him that he'd refused to spill out the details to Tash just for her titillation. It was perfectly possible that Rich was being a gentleman. Because he cared.

He cared for her.

Jayne thought she might order some champagne right now. She went to the bar and bought a bottle, ignoring the odd look that the bargirl insisted on bestowing.

He hadn't pulled away from her kiss straightaway, had he?

In fact, it sort of felt as though he'd kissed her back, or at least wanted to. Jayne took a sip of champagne, then another. It was obvious. Rich had found himself drawn into this marriage thing, but he wasn't serious about it. Not really.

Jayne took a massive gulp of champagne and half emptied her glass. The crazy bubbles danced on her tongue, demanding she lose her senses, which, after all, she was already keen to fling away.

If he was serious about marrying Tash, he would never have agreed to Jayne coming along on holiday. Clearly he wanted Tash to find out about them and to call off the wedding, so that he and Jayne could get back together.

Of course. It was crystal. Jayne took another massive swig, and this time she hardly noticed the sharp, almost bitter taste as she began to float, happily intoxicated. Jayne had always found that champagne took away the world's problems; luckily her lifestyle—scattered with expense accounts and devoted suitors— was such that she could drink lots of it without either appearing like a lush or breaking the bank.

And he hadn't yet called off the wedding himself because . . . ?

Because he was too kindhearted. Yes, that was it! He didn't want to hurt Tash. And, fair enough, Tash was a sufficiently nice girl. Jayne could admit this much now she was cocooned in the happiness that is champagne. Not a very special girl. Not good enough for Rich. But he was so kind that he didn't like to hurt anyone.

Jayne had already forgotten how Rich had hurt her for many, many years by denying and ignoring her, by breaking dates and failing to call. The tears that had threatened to overwhelm her as she walked into the bar receded. How could he not want her? Every man she'd ever met wanted her, and she wasn't even half decent to most of those. She was very sweet to Rich. Besides, she was clever and pretty, she supported his football team, played the same sports as him, read the same books, laughed at his lousy jokes.

Jayne was blind with passion, and so had never seen the disinterest in Rich's face as he flipped her over in the sack, preferring to take her from behind rather than risk acknowledging any intensity of emotion—love or need—that her face may have inadvertently betrayed. Jayne was blind to his rejections. She had always excused the fact that he would never meet up with her until after the pubs closed. She had never noticed that he'd never once said anything that remotely hinted toward a commitment or a future. He'd never said anything that would indicate that they were in a *relationship.* She never acknowledged that they saw each other on average once every four months. The facts that he'd stopped sleeping with her once he met Tash and that he'd proposed to Tash, that he openly, frequently and happily declared his love for Tash—all seemed irrelevant to Jayne.

She wanted him so much. More than she'd ever wanted a puppy or a Raleigh bike. More than she'd ever wanted anything else in her life. And for longer than she'd ever wanted anything else.

Jayne always got what she wanted.

The university place she wanted. The exam results she wanted. The job she wanted. The figure she wanted. The pay raise she wanted. She even got the shoes she wanted that just matched so perfectly with her handbag bought for that very special occasion. Not getting what she wanted was not an option! Rich had made a terrible error of judgment, an error she could correct, which he *needed* her to correct. He needed her help. She was the girl for him, not Natasha. She would stop this wedding, she had to.

But how?

At that moment Jase walked into the bar. Like Jayne, he had immediately scoped the room to hunt out any potential pickup. After all, he was on holiday and scoring was de rigueur. He was delighted to spot Jayne huddled in the corner with no company other than a bottle of champagne. He grinned to himself—that girl had a serious sense of style.

"Mind if I join you?" he asked. He was already holding a champagne flute.

Jayne looked startled, but immediately recovered her aplomb and then looked delighted. "Of course not, it would be lovely."

"Are you celebrating?" asked Jase, nodding toward the champagne bottle.

"I am now." Jayne smiled, patting the space on the bench next to her. As she leaned over to fill Jason's glass, she took care to let her breast brush against his arm. She was cold and her nipples were standing at attention. Jayne noticed Jase blush and was pleased. There was no way *he'd* ever brush off her kisses.

# 27

## *Another Night in Paradise*

Wow, Mia, you look amazing," said Kate, looking up from her magazine.

Kate, Tash and Jayne were settled on the sofas in front of the open fire in the hotel foyer. The scene was cozy. Kate was reading a magazine and enjoying a G & T. Jayne was dozing, stretched out on one of the sofas. Her magazine lay discarded and open across her chest. An empty glass of what had been red wine sat on the table. After finishing the bottle of champagne with Jason she'd decided it was best to carry on drinking, rather than stop and risk the onset of a hangover. She was resting her head on Tash's lap. Tash did not seem freaked by this, although Mia would have been horrified if Jayne, or any woman for that matter, had curled up with her so intimately. Tash was also reading a magazine, and she held it high and to one side so as not to disturb the sleepy Jayne. Despite their über-trendy gear, they put Mia in mind of Roman empresses, lolling on perfumed beds waiting for the return of their conquering heroes.

Kate and Mia sat a little distance from Tash and Jayne, excusing themselves by explaining that they wanted to chat and did not want to disturb Jayne. Kate was worried that Mia wasn't happy about Jayne joining the party. She couldn't quite understand why it would upset Mia as much as it clearly did, but she was sorry to have caused her best friend any disquiet. She did her utmost to make amends through flattery.

"Yes, those jeans really suit you, and your skin looks radiant. It must be all the fresh air."

"Oh, thanks," said Mia. She had made an effort. She'd spent the afternoon in the hotel's spa. She'd had a manicure and pedicure, and spent an hour in the Jacuzzi. In her room she'd tried on several outfits, only to discover just how hard it was to look fabulously sexy and keep warm at the same time. She didn't quite know how Jayne and Tash pulled it off, but she'd rather rip out her own eyeballs than ask either of them for sartorial advice. After considerable effort and numerous combinations, Mia had settled on a pair of Earl jeans and a black polo-neck cashmere sweater. The jeans flattered her bottom and thighs, and the sweater clung to her full, round breasts. Unusual for Mia, she'd taken the time to apply full makeup, including a red slash of lipstick on her plump lips. The overall effect was good. Only she knew that she was wearing Marks & Spencer minimizing panties and a thermal vest. She wasn't too worried about her underwear, as she didn't really believe that they would make their debut tonight.

Her plan tonight was to keep in the running, not to get knocked out in the early heats, so to speak. And while she thought that the proposition of competing with Jayne for Scaley Jase's affections was a little demeaning, she comforted herself with the fact that she wasn't really competing for a man's affections or even his attention, just a sperm donation. She told herself that this was scientific, practical, nothing to do with emotions. Still, she was grateful for Kate's compliment. Although she was determined not to acknowledge the fact, she was as nervous as hell.

"Goodness, I feel so drab in comparison to you three," added Kate.

Mia felt the marvelous effect of the compliment vanish, believing that it wasn't so much rooted in a genuine respect for Mia's own carefully chosen ensemble as in Kate's deep-seated lack of confidence. Good manners now demanded that Mia reassure Kate. She ought to say that Kate's new haircut was flattering. Which, indeed, it was. Or she could say that her shoes were fantastic—it was rare to see Kate in heels. Mia stayed silent. And grumpy.

Kate wondered if Mia had noticed her new haircut—perhaps it wasn't radical enough. What a shame if it wasn't noticeable. It had cost nearly £400 for the cut and color, and Kate had had to wait several months on a list to get an appointment with the award-winning stylist who, rumor had it, also cut Madonna's hair. She fingered the ends around the nape of her neck and sighed. In truth, she'd suspected that the cut was a little ordinary, but felt that for all the hype around the stylist *and* all that cash she'd paid, she had to be mistaken.

"How are you getting on with the boarding?" asked Kate.

"I'm not," Mia whispered, turning away from Jayne and Tash. "I can't get the hang of it."

"Well, you have only been trying for half a day."

"There might only ever be half a day," said Mia grimly. She shifted on the chair. She never thought she'd see the time when she bemoaned a lack of padding on her bum. "Scaley Jase is being depressingly impressive. He mastered his toe and heel edge; he can already traverse at some speed. I'm sure by the end of the week he'll be speeding down black runs brilliantly," spat Mia without doing much to hide her envy or irritation.

"Oh, come on, Mia. You knew he'd be marvelous. He's a great sportsman and totally fearless, almost bordering on the insane. That's what you love about him."

"I don't love anything about him," hissed Mia, further infuriated by Kate's choice of words. "Why would I love his insanity? I'm a very measured person, extremely considered."

"Exactly," said Kate, with a sigh. She didn't bother to expand. Mia would understand her if she wanted to. She paused before tentatively adding, "I'm not sure if I'll ski tomorrow."

Suddenly, Tash piped up, "Do you fancy an alternative buzz?"

"Quite," said Kate, who wasn't actually sure what Tash had offered. Mia glared. She hoped that Tash hadn't heard the entire conversation. It was private.

"Boarding?" asked Tash.

"Not boarding," said Kate, with a definite tone that no one questioned. Tash thought for a second. "There's quad bike riding, snowmobiles and climbing. I could take a day off the slopes, too, and join you if you'd like some company."

"That's very kind of you, but I was more thinking a walk, perhaps with a guide." In fact, Kate was thinking of a walk as far as the next crêperie, but didn't want to say.

"Well, just let me know if you fancy some company," said Tash, turning back to her magazine and fiddling with Jayne's hair.

"It looks like you guys cleared out the magazine rack," said Mia, as she idly picked up a couple of the mags that the women were reading, then dropped them again. She couldn't help but wonder at their shiny insincerity. None of them related to her. Not the titles that were aimed at the bimbo, the chatterbox, the bride or even the thinking woman. She wasn't interested in interior design or gardening and, while she did enjoy cooking, she didn't need a magazine to tell her how to do it.

There had been a period in her life when she had subscribed to *FitLife*. It was at that time that she had employed a personal trainer. It had been a successful ruse and for a while Mia's thighs were brought under control, for a monthly cost that was greater than her mortgage payments. She tried to remember why she stopped seeing her trainer. She had the feeling that it was because she decided that she could do without him. The way, in the end, she always decided she could do without everyone. Mia was a fast learner and had soon learned his routine. Five laps around the common. One hundred sit-ups. Eighty press-ups. Sixty lunges on each leg. Forty bench presses—against a felled tree, for God's sake. Twenty squats, and then cool down. La, la, la. It soon became very predictable. As it happened, she couldn't do without him, or rather, didn't do it without him. She never ran around the common and couldn't remember the last time she attempted a lunge. Instead she resorted to wearing flared skirts that camouflaged her growing thighs. She canceled her subscription to *FitLife*.

Mia noticed that Jayne and Tash had each purchased a clutch of beauty and gossip magazines—how predictable—and Kate was looking at the posh parenting one called *Junior*.

"Why do you waste your time and money on magazines that think highbrow is a new way to wear your hair and the deep articles are about how to guarantee multiple orgasms?"

"Is there more to life?" commented Tash dryly. She glared at Mia. The gloves had come off in the pizzeria this afternoon and Tash felt liberated. Mia was an intellectual snob. She was cold and disapproving. Tash couldn't understand why Rich numbered her among his best friends and she knew she would never feel the same.

"We're just killing time waiting for the guys," said Kate apologetically and diplomatically. In truth, she loved a good magazine. They were a mix between a best friend, a mother, a counselor and a personal shopper. Kate looked for another topic of conversation, and chose badly. "Jayne looks better every year, doesn't she?" she whispered.

"Yes," admitted Mia. Jayne's chestnut hair tumbled across Tash's thighs, catching the light thrown from the open fire and shimmering. Her skin was peachy smooth, and Mia wondered what it felt like. Velvet, she supposed. No doubt Scaley would be in a position to tell her exactly what it felt like, very soon. She sighed, depressed.

Jayne was, without doubt, dazzling. Mia liked to think that, as a feminist, she always looked beyond the superficial. She hated the way women were continually judged on their looks. And yet she found that she judged that way all the time.

"It just goes to show what money can do. I bet she spends every Saturday in the beautician's," whispered Mia, which was in fact what she did herself. Kate didn't—her beautician came to the house. Neither girl confided this to the other.

Instead Kate commented, "Natasha is beautiful, too, don't you think?"

There was nothing more annoying than an ugly duckling turning into a swan except, mused Mia, a girl who was born swan, lived swan and died swan. Tash *was* lovely. And while Mia hadn't personally known her at primary school, she was prepared to put a bet on the fact that Tash had always been lovely. She was the type of girl who played Mary in the school nativity play. (Mia had always been given the more vocal but considerably less glamorous part of a shepherd, Kate had always been a sheep and Jayne had been a tree. Jayne still smarted from the humiliation of having to wear nothing other than brown tights and a green roll-neck sweater on stage.) Tash was the girl who the teacher trusted to take the class goldfish home during the summer holidays. She was the girl who fueled every boy's early teen dreams in her secondary school. Mia knew this without even having to talk to Barbie Babe.

"Hello, ladies, have you missed me?" Jase bounced into the foyer. It appeared everyone had. Jayne stretched and sat up, apologizing for catnapping in public; Kate and Tash beamed at Jase, simply pleased to see him, as he always helped the group to gel. Mia grinned in delight at the arrival of her sperm bank.

"I wonder where Ted is?" said Kate. "It's quarter to eight. He's going to be late."

"He'll be here in his own time," assured Jase.

Kate leaned close in to her two old friends and said, "Can I ask you something?" Her normally strong face was crumpled.

"Ask away." Jase grinned.

"Have you noticed anything different about Ted?"

Mia and Jase stared at Kate, then exchanged confused looks.

"Different, how?" asked Jase. "Has he had a haircut? New snow gear?"

"No, no, don't be silly," said Kate, not realizing that Jase was being perfectly serious. "I, he's, I . . ." Kate wasn't sure what she wanted to say. "Do you think he's behaving oddly? More distracted than normal? Less communicative?"

Kate felt that she was betraying her husband by floating these ideas to their friends, but she didn't mean any harm, quite the opposite. She just had to know if she had an overactive imagination or if anyone else had noticed that Ted wasn't quite himself. He was not so jovial of late. Not so confident and loud. Obviously she would not mention to their friends that his sex drive, usually re-spectable, had nosedived off the scale over the past few months. Dried up altogether, actually. She hadn't noticed at first. They'd been together for so long, and the children were such a drain on time and energy, that loving had long since been confined to a once-every-couple-of-weeks activity. But then a month went by. Then several. She wouldn't dream of telling Mia and Jason this. She couldn't stand those horrible American-style confessionals. She had her pride.

Nor did she mention that he'd missed the parents' evenings at both Fleur's and Elliot's schools, and he was normally so involved with the children. He said he'd clean forgotten, even though she'd reminded him on the relevant mornings. He was always forget-ting things nowadays. The other day he went to the office having forgotten his watch, and he'd twice forgotten to shave. Thank God for casual dress and designer stubble because otherwise he'd stick out like a sore thumb. Could he be ill? His uncle on his fa-ther's side had been diagnosed with Alzheimer's disease. It was a tragedy to watch, but he'd been so much older, in his seventies. Ted was a young man. Although he didn't always act it.

"Do you think he could be ill?" she blurted.

Jason and Mia silently stared their response. Eventually Jason said, "He seems chipper to me." He nudged Mia, who was inter-nally fuming that Kate really didn't have enough to worry about. If the children were here, she'd have been imagining all manner of chills and coughs and colds. As she didn't have them to fuss over, she was diverting her smothering attention toward Ted. Poor Ted.

"Tops," said Mia, with a yawn.

Kate nodded, pleased to have received reassurance, however unenthusiastic. "I wonder where he is?" she repeated.

"Action Man and Checkers have gone to the pool hall," said Mia. "Maybe he's joined them."

"We'll all be late for dinner," fretted Kate. "What's he thinking of, wasting his time in pool halls? I think I'll go and find him."

Mia and Jason rolled their eyes at one another as she bustled off. Jase was sitting close to Mia. He put his arm around her shoulder, and she reciprocated by patting his leg.

"Big Ted and Ms. Monopoly can be really irritating," she confided.

"They're your best friends," Jase reminded her.

"I suppose, but I feel like I'm on holiday with my parents. The way Ms. Monopoly checks up on him all the time. Where is he? Has he eaten a good breakfast? Is he going to be on time? And Big Ted's turned into an old man. Have you noticed the way he has to zip up his coat, put on his hat and gloves and scarf before he'll leave any building, even if he's only going to be outside for a hundred yards? He's not Scott of the bloody Antarctic."

"Ah, that's what you don't like. They remind you that you aren't twenty. Because they act their age, they remind you of yours. You resent it."

Mia glared at Jason, and wondered how it was that he knew her so well. Better than she knew herself at times.

Scaley's gaze fell in the direction of Tash and Jayne. All thoughts of Kate and Ted disappeared. Jayne had been very flirtatious this afternoon when they'd stumbled into one another in that bar, thought Jason, and she looked so sweet snuggling up with Tash. It was fantastic that they were becoming great friends. Jase allowed himself to feel a bit warm and fuzzy once more. Talking to Jayne in the bar had started him off again. *If* he were to play with the idea of, or at least consider the possibility of . . . well . . . maybe . . . looking to date steadily. Well, then Jayne would be a perfect candidate. *If* he permitted himself, he could easily imagine a scenario where he and Jayne and Rich and Tash went out for cozy four-some dates or had informal supper parties at his flat. Yeah, he could imagine dating Jayne, Jayne becoming his girlfriend.

He was almost positive that it wasn't just the drink making him think this way.

It wasn't just that Jayne was a fox—although, fuck, was she ever a fox. That ass, those tits, those lips. They could have a really good time together. But besides her being one sexy honey—who was clearly coming on to him—she was also a really great person. She'd been so interested in him. She insisted that they'd met two or three times in the past, over the years, at family things of Ted's, but Jase couldn't remember talking to her at the various weddings and christenings they'd both attended. He knew himself well enough to know that the reason he couldn't remember them talking was that he couldn't remember Jayne looking this good. If he had remembered her as such a honeypot, then he'd have definitely struck up a conversation.

This afternoon she had been so animated, so interested. She'd wanted to know all about how Jase and Rich had met and what stuff they'd got up to over the years. She was a great listener and seemed to find the Jase-and-Rich seduction stories of old just as hilarious as, well, as Jase did. It was also very sweet the way she asked him about how he thought he'd recognize the One when she came along. Clearly she was fishing for compliments. She might have shrouded the inquiry in a question about how did Rich recognize Tash as the One when Tash came along, but Jase wasn't stupid. He got the feeling that Jayne really just wanted to talk about him.

Get in there!

When Jason had packed for this holiday he had packed with his usual inimitable style and care. He'd popped six Boxfresh T-shirts into his Hermès travel bag. Alongside his numerous pairs of Diesel and Helmut Lang jeans (different cuts, different shades). He'd also packed three pair of sneakers—Diesel and Nike Air Max to hang in, and a pair of Adidas Micropacers to train in (they had that magical little computer chip that measured the distance covered—disappointingly, it was never the distance he hoped). He didn't pack any of his Armani suits or Patrick Cox loafers, nor his Prada shirts; this gig was casual. He'd known that there wouldn't even be any strip joints, so he had no need of brogues. He'd packed a pair of Johnny Mokes especially for the wedding ceremony. He was planning on wearing a Dolce & Gabbana shirt and Armand Basi trousers, made to measure, Conduit Street. While playing down his sartorial elegance—after all, he didn't want to upstage the groom, let alone the bride—his outfit was the right mix of criminally expensive and understated. At the time he'd thought that his attention and deliberation would go unnoticed by anyone important, by which he meant anyone seducible. It was unlikely that the package-holiday ski bunnies would care what he was dressed in. But Jayne would. Now he was glad that he hadn't let his standards slip.

A vision flashed into Jason's mind. It was of him and Rich standing at the top of an aisle. He'd had that vision a few times since he'd agreed to be Rich's best man, even though Rich and Tash hadn't opted for the traditional church affair. A bolt of fear and excitement shot through Jason's body. In this imagined scenario, he wasn't the best man . . . he was the groom.

Jesus.

He wasn't saying that he wanted to marry Jayne, for fuck's sake. It probably was the champagne allowing these fantasies to float into his mind. But were they totally ludicrous?

Yes. They were. Frankly, he'd settle for a fuck.

Mia followed Scaley Jase's gaze. Jason was probably going to have to excuse himself to go and jerk off. She had been struck by the beautiful picture Tash and Jayne made. There was no way Jase was oblivious to it. Mia knew him well enough to know that this was the stuff of his fantasies, a tall blonde and a curvy brunette languishing on the sofa, chatting, giggling, gossiping together. To be fair, the girls probably made up the stuff of most men's fantasies. The only other more beautiful twosome that sprang to mind was Kylie and Dannii.

Mia squeezed Jase's leg and winked at him, mouthing the word *hot* as she popped the olive from her drink into her mouth.

Jase laughed, and asked, "How is it that you always know what I'm thinking?"

"Because you're always thinking the same thing," Mia laughed back.

# 28

## *Minuscule Talk*

Tash didn't really enjoy dinner. She should have been having a good time. After all, she was staying in the most beautiful hotel she had ever visited, *and* she was eating the most delicious food, *and* she had spent the morning boarding and the afternoon lazing *and* it was only days until she married the man of her dreams. The problem was she couldn't help but think that it would have been nicer if they'd been alone in this beautiful hotel and they were having a candlelit meal *à deux* and that she'd spent the day boarding with Rich.

Tash had barely seen Rich all day, as he'd spent it teaching Jase and Mia. She didn't want to appear selfish—she knew that it was

STILL THINKING *of* YOU          165

lovely that all of Rich's friends had joined them to celebrate their wedding. It was, after all, an investment both in terms of their time and of their finances, but . . . well, she hadn't asked them, had she? And frankly, she wouldn't choose to share the planet with Mia, let alone an intimate boutique hotel. And yes, the food was delicious, but the menus were in French and it was far too posh an establishment for them to provide a translation, let alone large plastic menus with green-tinged photographs of the dishes. Tash was extraordinarily grateful that the menu was set—at least she didn't have to make a choice. She might not have known what she was about to eat, but she didn't have to admit as much to anyone.

Tash had come to the meal with good intentions. She felt a teeny-weeny bit guilty about the conversation at lunchtime, but only a teeny-weeny bit—Mia had provoked her. Tash would have been prepared to call a truce, but clearly Mia wanted blood.

"Do you understand the menu, Barbie Babe? You mentioned that foreign languages aren't your forte."

"I'm fine, thank you," Tash replied, but she couldn't summon a smile, not even a fake one.

"I could translate for you," offered Mia. Tash doubted she was trying to be helpful. Tash was saved from further embarrassment by the beep-beep of an incoming text message. "My God, fancy that. I've just got a message from Giles Hewitt-Simpson," said Mia.

There were smiles around the table and general murmurs about what a good chap Giles was, a great pal.

Here we go, thought Tash, social bingo.

"How is he? I haven't seen him since the cricket season finished," asked Ted.

"Bloody marvelous. Says he's got a promotion and is off state-side in February," screeched Mia.

Two fat ladies—eighty-eight.

"Talking about people going overseas, I got an email from Clara the other week. She's about to emigrate, too. Hong Kong. Coutt's couldn't manage without her," said Kate.

Legs eleven.

"Sadie and Charles are moving to a place in the country, had enough of the smoke," added Lloyd, determined not to be left out.

Open the door, forty-four.

"Samuel has finally proposed to that banker girl. We got an invitation to the wedding. Should be fantastic. Her father is a lord, you know."

Clickety clicks, sixty-six.

"Me, too."

A duck and a flea, twenty-three.

"Yes, I did as well. I'm planning on buying a new hat."

Bingo.

Tash had to remind herself that these were some of the best-educated people in London and that they held down some of the most stimulating jobs available. It was a marvel, then, that their conversation always seemed to focus on catching up on news of people who weren't even there. Tash wondered if the gang really cared for these people or whether it was a game of social one-upmanship. Either way, she couldn't join in. She didn't know Giles or Clara or Samuel or Sadie or any of the people attached to these glamorous names and lives. Tash felt lonely at the end of the table. It was bad luck that she was sat opposite dull Ted and next to dire Mia. Rich was at the other end of the table, in between Lloyd and Jase, and opposite Jayne. Tash would have done anything to swap places. She feared her silence was all the more notable because everyone else seemed to be having a fantastic time. Banter and laughter darted up and down the table faster than Rich got down mountains or Jase got up women.

"More wine, Barbie Babe? Your glass is empty." Was it? Tash was surprised. She must be knocking them back at some rate, rather more hurriedly than steadily, and certainly more hurriedly than advised. Well, it was something to do. "You're drinking white, aren't you? We need to order some more. Any preference?" asked Mia.

"You choose," replied Tash.

"You must have a preference. A sauvignon blanc, Sémillon, Savagnin, Sylvaner?"

Tash wondered if Mia had listed all the wines beginning with *S* just to confuse her. "I really don't mind."

"Perhaps you have a regional preference rather than a grape? Would it help if I told you which are *les bonnes années?*"

"Not really." Tash shrugged. She just wanted the bottle open and the wine in her glass. In fact, she wanted to fast-forward to the stage where she'd consumed enough not to care about Mia's snobbery.

"Mia has a master's in wine tasting," said Ted.

Tash laughed. "A few of my friends could claim the same."

"No, I'm serious," said Ted. "She has a genuine qualification."

"Oh, I meant my friends have a genuine problem," giggled Tash. Ted didn't get the joke. He blushed and said that was unfortunate.

Tash noted that Rich wasn't in his best form either. Despite being at the fun end of the table, he was very quiet. Tash thought that maybe he was missing her as much as she was missing him. She couldn't reach him physically, so she tried to catch his eye and create quiet moments of intimacy in between the chat and chaos. It was impossible. He stared resolutely at his plate. Had he caught the sun? He was very red. Or perhaps he was flushed with alcohol. God, she longed to kiss him. When Tash kissed Rich, she was sure that he was the perfect partner for her. She forgot that Mia left her feeling grubby and not quite up to scratch.

"How are you getting on with the boarding?" Jayne asked Mia. Tash wondered if Jayne was being mischievous. She hoped so. What a pal. Perhaps she'd heard Mia patronizing Tash and was making a point that everyone couldn't excel at everything. The warm affection Tash already felt for Jayne cranked up a notch or two. "Would you call yourself a freestyler or a linderet?" Jayne pursued. Tash wanted to giggle.

Mia scowled. "I haven't reached the stage of developing a style," she admitted.

"What does that mean, a freestyler or a linderet?" asked Kate, who was trying to take the spotlight off what was clearly, for Mia, a sore point.

Rich explained, "I'm a freestyler, which works well here as Avoriaz is full of natural hits and big air opportunities." Kate nodded politely, although she was none the wiser. "Jason is likely to become a linderet as soon as he develops a style of his own."

"They play a lot, in parks, doing clever tricks," said Mia, who, Tash noted, had at least mastered the lingo, if not the toe and heel edges. "Linderets spend their time showing off, mostly," she added, as though she were already someone's mother.

"Still, you have the best teacher I could imagine. I'm sure you'll be flying down the slopes soon and not just on your bum," said Jayne. Tash wanted to kiss her. "I've learned such a lot of new moves from Rich, and my general technique has improved no end under his tuition," she added, with a smile and a wink at Rich. Tash noticed that Rich looked uncomfortable. He wasn't good at receiving compliments. But wasn't Jayne a sweetie? She was trying so hard to be nice.

"When?" asked Mia.

"We spent some quality time together this afternoon."

"I wouldn't call it that," said Rich.

"I can't thank you enough. I'll never forget it." Jayne gazed at Rich.

Rich looked up from his *raiole de foie gras* and glared back at Jayne.

"Really, it was nothing," he said, stonily.

"It meant a lot to me," said Jayne with a smile.

Poor Rich, you'd think he'd never come across a friendly woman before. He didn't seem to know how to deal with Jayne. Men are so vain, thought Tash, with an indulgent smile. Patently he thought Jayne fancied him and found it embarrassing. Yet it was obvious to Tash that Jayne was simply being friendly. Jayne had just been ditched, her confidence was at an all-time low. Women often became overly eager to please and be found pleasing at such times. That neediness, plus alcohol, did run the risk that friendliness became borderline flirtiness, but Jayne meant no harm. Tash would explain all of this when she was next alone with Rich. She'd tell him to go easy on Jayne and not to be quite so cutting. If she were ever alone with Rich again, that is. She was beginning to wonder if their wedding night would turn into a gang bang.

When the meal was finally over and everyone had eaten and drunk more than a sensible amount, Jase suggested that they make a move and go to a club. Jayne seconded it, and Mia and Lloyd passed the motion. Ted and Kate excused themselves, saying they were in desperate need of an early night.

"Whey hey, why not take advantage of a childless room?" said Jason.

"For God's sake, Scaley, do not judge everyone by your own mucky standards. The most likely thing on their agenda is sleep," snapped Mia.

While they bickered, Tash grabbed Rich's hand and whispered in his ear, "Shall we slip away?"

"And do what exactly?" he asked, smiling. Clearly Rich was happy to be judged by Jase's mucky standards.

"Not that," Tash giggled, immediately picking up on his lascivious tones. "Well, at least, not right away. I thought we could hire a horse and sleigh, and see the resort at night."

Rich didn't hesitate. They made a run for it.

# 29

## *Sleigh Ride*

Isn't it beautiful," said Rich.

"Really breathtaking," Tash agreed.

Tash and Rich sat under blankets in the back of the horse-drawn sleigh and looked out over Avoriaz. Although it was the height of the season and the resort was packed, the driver of the sleigh had driven them to a distance where they could make believe that they were the sole inhabitants of the mountains. The driver may have been only a meter away, but he was practiced at becoming invisible. Lovers such as Tash and Rich could deceive themselves into believing that they were entirely alone and allow the vast space around them to somehow become astonishingly intimate.

The freshly fallen snow muffled the rapturous and drunken shouts from the bars and games halls. Footsteps were cushioned, doors didn't bang and music didn't blare. It was as though the angels had turned down the volume and, to compensate, other senses were accentuated. Everything looked bright, shiny and fresh. The stars were large and lavish in the black sky, their brilliance so true that the sky appeared illusory. Tash felt like Aladdin in the dazzling cave of jewels. The alpine cleanliness seemed to swill out all the smoke and smog of city life harbored in their bodies and minds.

"I love you, Tash."

"Why? Why do you love me right this second?"

It was a game they often played. They told each other they loved each other many, many times a day, and they often demanded or gave a reason. Sometimes the reasons were huge— "I love your soul" or "I love your spirit." Sometimes the reasons were minuscule.

"Tash, I love you because you get worked up over penalty shoot-outs."

"Rich, I love you because with your new haircut you remind me of Bodie, as in Bodie and Doyle, which in turn reminds me of my childhood Saturday pop nights, complete with tubes of Smarties and dandelion and burdock pop."

"You love me because of dandelion and burdock pop?"

"Yes."

"Fair enough."

"I love you because of the way you laugh."

"I love you because you introduced me to *The Simpsons*."

"I can't believe you'd never seen an episode before you met me. I love you because you're kind to my mum and dad."

"I love you because of the great things you can do with your tongue."

The challenge was to always give a different reason. And yet it was always the same one.

"Right now?" asked Rich.

"Yeah, why do you love me, right now? What made you say it at just that moment?" demanded Tash.

Because he felt bad that he'd let another woman kiss him was not an acceptable answer.

"I love you because you are sharing this stunning night with me. Because there are mountains to be boarded down, snow to roll in and stars to ogle. And I know none of it would mean as much if it wasn't you who was sitting next to me," said Rich, as this had been the other reason he'd said "I love you" at that moment. Rich grinned, mostly at the fact that he could say such stupidly romantic things and not be embarrassed. Well, not too embarrassed. He wouldn't like anyone to overhear him, but he didn't mind talking to Tash this way.

Tash moved a fraction closer to Rich, even though she was already squashed so close to him that her arm was numb. She wiggled her fingers to try to bring some feeling back into them. They both fell silent again and allowed the spell of one another's company to weave its magic.

When Rich was sitting with Tash, Jayne didn't intimidate him. Her silly half-threats on the slopes and her pathetic innuendos at dinner were forgotten.

"Do you regret not going for the full flouncy dress and a hundred guests?" asked Rich.

"Oh, yeah, clearly I'm totally disappointed that right now I'm not spell-checking a hundred order-of-service sheets and arguing with my mother about canapés."

"So, no regrets?"

"None, other than I wish more people could have joined us. I wish Emma hadn't broken her leg."

"Yes, poor thing. But I bet you're glad that the gang came along after all, aren't you? Their company adds to the celebration, don't you think?"

Rich wasn't even sure he believed this as he said it. Yes, it was fantastic that his gang was here. He'd had a brilliant day in the snow and, on the whole, he'd enjoyed the dinnertime *parler*, it was great fun catching up. But if they hadn't been here, then Jayne wouldn't be here either, and he wished more than anything that Jayne wasn't here. She'd tried to play footsie with him throughout the meal. How pathetic was that? She was behaving like a floozie in a B-grade movie. At one point she'd slipped her foot out of her shoe and put her toes in his crotch. He'd nearly bit the bowl off his soup spoon. It wasn't funny. He pushed her to the back of his mind and thought about his other mates.

"They are great, aren't they?"

Tash paused. She'd like to have been able to smile and reassure him with an "Absolutely" because that was clearly what Rich wanted and expected to hear, but she was conscious that it would be a lie. It would be the first lie she'd ever told Rich. She stayed silent, hoping that he wasn't really expecting an answer. For the first time she wondered if her absolute honesty policy was realistic. No secrets, no lies, just 100 percent respect and honesty. What about tiny, little, feeling-saving white lies?

"You *are* glad they are here, aren't you?" repeated Rich.

Tash kissed him and said, "I'm glad it's made you happy." She busied herself with hunting for the flask of hot chocolate that the sleigh driver had thoughtfully supplied. She poured two large mugs, and handed one to Rich. Rich sipped the sweet, warm liquid. Fleetingly, Tash regretted that he wasn't a woman. If he were a woman, such delicious hot chocolate would wipe away all other concerns.

"Don't you like my friends?" he pursued.

"You have a chocolate mustache." She moved to kiss it away, but Rich quickly rubbed the back of his hand over his mouth, depriving her of the pleasure.

"So why don't you like them?" Was she avoiding answering the question?

"I didn't say that." She didn't have to. He knew her well enough to know that she was always verbose in her praise. Her silence spoke volumes. Eventually Tash said, "I like Jason a lot. He's great fun. Shallow, but a laugh."

"He's not shallow. He'd fall on his sword for me."

"You don't get much call for that nowadays, though, do you?"

"You know what I mean."

Tash conceded with a shrug. "I'm sure he would. I meant with women. He's shallow with women. I have the impression he doesn't treat them particularly well."

Rich stopped himself from pointing out that few men did. Until Tash, he hadn't treated women particularly well. He knew, however, that he wouldn't score any brownie points by highlighting that fact. Before he'd met Tash, people—his friends and family, and others—used to describe his life as shallow, too; he liked to think of it as simple. He ate when he wanted, he slept when he wanted and with whom he wanted, he farted when he wanted. He told lies if he needed to and if he thought he could get away with it. He didn't tell lies if he had a chance of being caught out. He never overpromised, overcommitted or overexerted himself. He never promised women *anything,* not even breakfast. He was an extremely intelligent man who worked ruthlessly well in a ruthless world. He was happy with his uncomplicated life, where the only thing he ever felt was hot, cold or thirsty.

Tash. Tash changed everything. Suddenly he wanted that intimacy that everyone harped on about. Suddenly honesty and fidelity seemed like cool options. He didn't want to tell any lies, not even little white ones. But that meant he had to reevaluate his life because, frankly, it wouldn't pass the Daz whiter-than-white challenge. He found himself ditching other birds. Jayne had been one of a number. He found himself turning down flirtatious suggestions and proposals. He found himself dating Tash exclusively. It wasn't that Tash demanded this of him, she just deserved it.

Rich no longer thought that the perfect Saturday was a lazy morning asleep in bed, followed by an afternoon in front of the

TV watching soccer, and then going to pubs and clubs with his mates to seduce anonymous girlies who gave good head. He no longer lingered in the office after hours because work was no longer the most important thing in his world. He didn't look forward to international travel that took him to sleek boardrooms and exotic lap-dancing clubs. Rich soon found that the perfect Saturday was just hanging around with Tash. They went to the movies, ate out, ate in, and lazed in bed, and it made him so happy.

So happy.

All the stuff, all the stupid clichés, were true. Love did make you feel complete and important. It did drive meaning into a previously rather questionable existence. It did make you look at sticky kids and think (just for a fleeting second), "One day." It did make the birds suddenly appear. For fuck's sake.

Tash was so incredibly beautiful. Looking at her made many men's trousers twitch. It was only when Rich's heart began to tighten every time he laid eyes on her that he knew he was in trouble. She was thoughtful and thought-provoking. Sensual and sensible. Funny and so bloody serious.

"Ted is deep. He treats women well," Rich observed.

"Yes," agreed Tash. "He seems very sweet, and I'm glad you told me that he's phenomenally intelligent because otherwise I'd have just thought he was phenomenally dull."

"Tash!"

Tash giggled. "Ted and Kate are lovely people, I'm sure. We just haven't got that much in common. When I mentioned that my mum and dad had a Lowry on their dining-room wall, Ted assumed that I meant an original, not a print from Athena. The estate I came from was a sprawling housing estate; his estate has been in the family for generations. It just means we have different outlooks." She shrugged. She wanted to make her point, but she didn't want to argue. She hoped Rich didn't want to either. "I think Lloyd's very interesting. I'd like to get to know him better."

Lloyd? Spend more time with Lloyd? Why? He was drunken and morose, not at all good company. He could be, Rich knew that, but he wasn't at the moment. What was she thinking of? As though Tash were reading his mind, she added, "I know he's not too much fun at the moment, but—"

"Mia is hilarious, though, isn't she?" interrupted Rich.

"Hilarious," Tash deadpanned back.

"You don't like Mia?" asked Rich, amazed.

"No." She could not dress it up. She could not find a redeeming feature.

"You don't like Mia?" repeated Rich, stunned.

"What is there to like?"

Rich sighed, admitting that it was a mystery but not a calamity that Tash didn't see eye to eye with all his buddies. She would. She'd grow to like them. Especially Mia. He was sure that one day Tash and Mia would be great friends. They'd swap recipes . . . Well, maybe not recipes, Tash didn't like cooking. They'd swap gossip.

Rich held Tash's face in his hands and stared into her eyes. They were the same big blue smiling eyes that he had stared into for the best part of a year. There was no point in being upset that she hadn't become bosom buddies with his pals yet. As if reading his mind, she leaned in and kissed him. They kissed for ages, but they were wearing too many clothes to consider anything other than kissing, and the driver's presence was not entirely forgotten. They finally stopped kissing and allowed themselves to be swallowed up by the splendor of the vista once again.

"I feel like a teenager," whispered Rich. "I'd have loved to be your teenage boyfriend. I'd have loved to have spent hours in your bedroom, listening to Duran Duran and trying to persuade you to take your clothes off."

"You would have been sadly disappointed. I was very prudish," laughed Tash.

"You wouldn't have been if you'd met me," he assured her. "I'd have unlocked your chastity belt."

"Possibly, I feel like a teenager. When I'm with you my hormones go into battle with my common sense on a regular basis. That's why I've often been late for work recently." It was true that there wasn't really ever enough time for a quickie, but there was also never a possibility that Tash would turn down Rich.

"Tash, it doesn't matter, does it? Not really."

"What doesn't matter?"

"If you don't instantly adore my friends. It doesn't mean anything insurmountable, does it?" Rich was at once stating his belief and at the same time looking for confirmation. He felt nervous. It was Jayne, bloody Jayne. She was blurring his vision. Not allowing him to think clearly. Was it important? Tash grinned and hugged him.

"Not at all. I like you. Most of the time—except when you leave the loo seat up or put an empty milk carton back in the fridge," she joked. Clearly she was trying to keep the conversation light. "I like Jayne. I'm glad she joined us. I'm glad you spent the afternoon with her. Did you get the chance to get to know her a bit?"

"No. Not really. We just boarded. We didn't talk much. Do you think these seats are hard?" Rich shifted uncomfortably.

"You should try to get to know her. You two have loads in common. She's a Man City supporter, too."

"That's bloody ridiculous. She and Ted were born in Suffolk. I bet she's got City mixed up with United and is a faux soccer fan. She probably just fancies Beckham. I hate women who pretend to like soccer."

Tash laughed. "You might have been born in Manchester City, but you only lived there until you were three."

"It counts," said Rich huffily.

"She drinks Glenmorangie Black."

"Millions of people do."

"Her favorite city is New York, like ours."

"Everybody loves New York."

"She blades and boards, not to mention the fact that you work in the same building. Haven't you ever come across her?"

"Once or twice."

"And, this is the funniest coincidence, she likes to listen to Nina Simone when she's making love, too."

Rich froze. "How do you know that?" Female intimacy scared Rich. Girls swapped their life histories and secrets as easily as blokes shared soccer results.

"She told me when we were at the airport."

The airport. Christ, what else would Jayne reveal by the time the week was up?

"I think I might ask her to be a witness at the wedding. You know, sign the paperwork. She is a girl I can get on with."

The temperatures were subzero, it was possible to see your breath dance in front of your mouth when you spoke, but until Tash had said this Rich hadn't felt the cold. Now he was sure icicles were hanging from his nose.

She continued, "She's very kind and principled, and yet she has a wicked sense of humour. She seems really spirited, great fun."

Rich felt his intestines liquefy. How could Tash have got it so wrong? Kate was the kind, principled one. Mia was the fun, spirited one. Jayne was the good fuck, mind fuck. It was a horrible thought: Jayne witness at his wedding. What if she decided to interrupt the service? She could choose that moment to confess all her sins. More to the point, all his. Why hadn't he ever mentioned Jayne? Why hadn't he included her in his stories? It wasn't as though Tash were shockable. Far from it. Christ, she'd taught him a trick or two; he'd admit it. And Jayne didn't mean any more or less to him than the other women he'd slept with. Jayne didn't mean anything. She'd never meant anything. Why hadn't he mentioned her? Rich knew that he had to tell Tash about his past with Jayne before Jayne did. He could just drop it into conversation now.

Right now.

He could just casually say something like "No way, not since I've slept with her; that would be weird." And then Tash would say, "I didn't know you'd slept with Jayne." And he could say, "Didn't I mention it? Well, it was years ago, when she was still at school. I'm sure I mentioned it." He wouldn't have to tell her that they'd had casual sex secretly for nearly a decade. He would have defused Jayne's bomb. He'd be safe. They'd be safe.

He'd tell her.

Sure, she would be a bit huffy. She'd probably sulk for a bit. Maybe all night, but he'd talk her round. She'd always said that she didn't care what he'd got up to, or whom he'd got up, as long as he was honest about it. It wasn't as though he'd slept with Jayne since he'd met Tash. He'd only seen her once and that was to call it a day. The meeting had been entirely platonic, despite Jayne's pleas for it to be otherwise. He'd tried to do the right thing at the end.

But what if he confessed and Tash didn't get over it? What if she was really angry and she called the wedding off? What if she became unreasonably jealous of Jayne and was inconsolably angry at him for keeping a secret from her? He came back to the crucial point: What if she called the wedding off? He could not bear that.

He could not risk it. He couldn't face it. Tash had such an unwavering belief in him. She was always going on about how important honesty is. She dealt honestly with everyone she met, but she took the gamble that her straightforward approach would not always be met with the same respect. But from him she *demanded* honesty. And he wanted to give it to her; it just seemed impossible now. Tash trusted Jayne. They'd become friends and swapped intimacies. Tash would feel a fool if Rich gave her the whole lowdown. It was too late now.

Rich took a deep breath and tried to tell himself everything was OK. They were a party of eight. There were 153 kilometers of piste in Avoriaz alone. Not to mention the other Portes. He could avoid Jayne. Yes, that was best. He'd try to minimize all contact with her and, if he could, he'd steer Tash away from her, too.

Today was almost over, tomorrow was Monday. On Friday, they'd be married. He could avoid Jayne for five days.

He'd often heard women accuse men of being emotional cowards. He thought it was a shame that they were right about this, when they were so wrong about many other things.

"I'm getting cold. Let's get back to the hotel," said Rich, and he kissed Tash's nose.

He loved her cute nose. He'd started and ended his day loving her. That had to be enough, didn't it?

# 30

# *Not Tonight, Darling*

I called home," said Kate. She was sitting at the dressing table massaging moisturizer into her skin. She made exaggerated, upward, time- and gravity-defying strokes.

"Good," replied Ted. He was sitting on the side of the bed. He was trying to take his snow boots off. But his feet seemed a long way down, and he wasn't sure if he could bend that far. How much had he had to drink at dinner?

"The children are all fine."

"Good."

"Fleur has been practicing."

"Good."

"Mum had to take Tiger to the vet's."

"Good."

"Ted, are you listening to me?"

"Yes, yes, of course I am."

"Tiger got into a fight with another tomcat and needed to go to the vet's."

"Serious?"

"I don't think so. He needed antibiotics and has to be kept indoors. Poor Mum, having to keep three children and Tiger indoors."

"How much?"

"How much what?"

"How much was the vet's bill?"

"I have no idea. Mum did say. I can't remember. One hundred and eighty? Two hundred and eighty? I can't remember."

Ted sighed. Bloody cat. They should never have bought a pedigree. They were bad-tempered with an overinflated assessment of their own hardiness. Tiger was always getting into spats with tougher kitties. They should have gone to the RSPCA and picked something up there. And now another vet's bill.

Kate slipped into her pajamas and dashed to hide under the duvet. It was cold and, besides, she'd eaten four large meals today. She wasn't sure that she could convince herself that huge overhang was water retention. She sat up in bed and reached for her hand cream. She always applied hand cream last thing at night. She always meant to apply it every time she washed her hands, as the magazines advised, but, despite having hand cream in every bathroom and next to every sink in the house, she never got around to it. She massaged the cream with swift, efficient strokes, then picked up her novel. It was the latest hyped faux lit, she felt she had to.

Kate watched Ted undress. His movements contrasted with hers. Where she was efficient, breezy and purposeful, he was languid, lazy and lethargic. Kate scowled. Was it just that he'd wound down faster than she had? Was he already in the holiday mood, relaxed and ready to be recharged? Maybe. Kate wanted to think so. But there was something about Ted's movements that suggested depressed rather than de-stressed.

"Isn't it fantastic to see the old gang again?" Kate commented. "Nobody has changed, have they?"

"Don't you think so?"

"Not at all. I thought dinner was just like old times. Everyone was in top form. I love the constant banter, the chat. What would Jason call it? The vibe."

"Yes, everybody does seem very jolly," agreed Ted. He hadn't really been able to follow the banter at dinner. He was stumped. He couldn't think of any clever stories or witty comebacks. That had always really been Jason and Rich's field.

"Lloyd seemed to have cheered up," added Kate.

"Hmmm." Ted wasn't sure. Who knew what was going on in another man's mind? "Mia is a little caustic, don't you think?" Mia's tongue had managed to slash through even Ted's self-indulgent fog of worry.

"She always was a little sharp," said Kate.

"But she is more so now, don't you think?"

"She's more confident now. Dares to say what she thinks."

"You think it's that, do you?"

"Don't you?"

"I wondered if she was happy." Ted often wondered who was truly happy nowadays and who was simply good at putting on a show.

"Oh, I think she is," encouraged Kate. Kate liked people to be happy and rarely looked for anything else. "Tash and Rich are very much in love, aren't they?"

"I imagine they are." Ted smiled. It was impossible not to be warmed by Kate's enthusiasm.

"And Jayne is fitting in nicely."

"Yes, no sign of her broken heart," said Ted wryly.

"No," confirmed Kate.

"I think she took us for a ride."

"Yes," confirmed Kate, pleased that her husband had reached the same conclusion as she had without her having to point it out to him. "She adores you, Ted. She just wants to be part of her big brother's gang."

"Do you think so?" asked Ted, surprised.

"She's been the same ever since college," said Kate, yawning.

Ted had finally eased himself out of his day clothes. He left on his boxers and hunted for a T-shirt to sleep in. It was too cold to think of going without underwear. He climbed into bed, pecked his wife on the cheek and turned out his bedside light.

"Night, night," he muttered, rolling away from Kate.

Kate sighed. She lay in the darkness looking at the ceiling.

It had been fun at dinner. Yes, she missed the children, but she had to admit it was rather lovely having dinner and just following the genial chat, rather than always keeping one ear alerted for the baby monitor or a call from the babysitter to say one of them needed her—that was if she had dared to venture farther than her front door. It was wonderful to drink one too many with old friends and know that it didn't matter if you did have a hangover. And even if Ted was right about Mia and she was a little bit snappier than normal, she was probably premenstrual. Kate knew that Mia was a true friend. Tash and Rich were a pleasure to watch. Kate had never been able to imagine the woman Rich would end up with. He'd never restricted himself to a type. Tash did seem a little young. But youth was lovely. Jayne was behaving herself. Jason was hilarious, and it was pleasant to see Lloyd again. She really didn't know why she had left it so long. The times the gang had had together in the past were so important, but the memories could only survive if they were nurtured by regular reminiscing and, more important, if new experiences were added to the old. If she didn't have to ski, this would be the perfect holiday.

And if she could persuade her husband to make love to her.

What was wrong with him? When she'd suggested an early night, she did not mean to sleep. How could he think she did? Kate stared at the bulk under the duvet. She knew from her husband's breathing patterns that he wasn't really asleep, just pretending to be. Didn't he fancy her anymore? Were her spreading thighs and vast breasts pushing him away? That would be so unfair. Ted wasn't the man she married either. He was twice the man. And she meant that in a nice way. Yes, he was fatter, grayer and a little bit balding, but he was also the man who had held her hand and rubbed her back through three labors. He was the man who provided for her and their children. She loved him more now than on their wedding day. Didn't he feel the same?

Kate, emboldened by drink, felt under the bedcovers and moved her hand toward her husband's thigh. She rubbed it for a few moments, then slipped her hand further around toward his penis. Ten years of marriage had taught her that in situations such as these lighting candles and covering his body with a hundred tender butterfly kisses would not get the job done. He was a man. Besides, she'd tried that over a month ago to no avail. Nor had her cooking his favorite dish, buying sexy underwear or asking him into the shower with her lit his fire.

She gently caressed and stroked and tickled, waiting to feel him stiffen. He did not. She increased the vigor of her stroke, even though that was a trick normally reserved until he was erect. Nothing doing. Ted's chubby penis flopped around in her hand, defying thousands of years of genetic programming. Kate wasn't a quitter. She gently rolled Ted onto his back so that he lay looking at the ceiling, rather than facing the wall, with his back to her.

She kissed him, using tongues and everything. Ted had an open mouth and open eyes, but a closed heart.

"What's wrong, Ted?" murmured Kate. She wiggled southward, hoping her kisses could manage what her fingers couldn't. Ted pulled her back toward him. They stared at one another. Kate was confused, scared, hurt and humiliated. Ted was, too, but more so.

"Nothing," he muttered, aware that he was compounding her fears.

Nothing. Kate was amazed. It was unlikely that "nothing" could persuade any man to pass up the chance of a blow job.

"I'm just very tired."

Kate rested her head on his chest, and Ted wrapped his arm around her. Cuddling was nice. Despite the disappointment, she was asleep in seconds. Red wine did that to her.

"I love you, Kate," Ted whispered to his sleeping wife.

# MONDAY

# 31

## Not-So-Good Morning

Rich thought that Tash might be just about to wake up. He'd lain and gazed at her for over an hour now, just looking.

He managed not to touch her. Not to trace his finger across her unsurpassable collarbone. He'd managed not to tenderly kiss those full pink lips. But only just. It took every iota of his self-restraint. She wasn't an especially good "morning person," and she might just be a bit irritated at being woken up before seven-thirty on holiday. But, God, he wanted to kiss her. And make love to her. Even though they'd made love most of last night and into the early hours, he wasn't satiated. He couldn't imagine ever getting to the point when he felt he'd had enough loving with Tash. He willed her to wake up. If she woke up on her own accord and not because he'd woken her, he would have a better chance of having sex. He smiled with anticipation; she was usually as randy as he was in the morning.

And if they had sex, and it was really spectacular sex, then he might tell her about Jayne. He was vacillating wildly as to whether or not this was the best course of action. Last night, high up in the mountains, under the duvet of black sky and brilliant stars, he had decided it would be unwise to mention Jayne. Later, in the throes of orgasm, when he'd felt so close to Tash that he believed they were melting and meshing into one another, he'd thought it was the only way forward. But it hadn't been possible. Tash was almost blokelike in her inability to stay awake and chat after orgasm. She'd instantly rolled over and fallen asleep. Rich had comforted himself that cocooned in that sort of intimacy Jayne couldn't harm them.

"Come on, wakey, wakey."

There was a loud banging on their suite door and, even before Rich could compute that it was someone knocking, the door swung open and in walked Jayne.

"Warm *pain au chocolat* and a cooked breakfast, surely that can tempt you from even Tash's charms." Jayne stood in the doorway of Tash and Rich's bedroom. She could smell sex, warmth and affection lingering in the air. Jayne thought she might choke. She snapped on the harsh electric light in an effort to banish their coziness.

"Come on, you two are supposed to be the keen boarders. Don't you want to cut some fresh snow, make some clean tracks? The slopes here are groomed with the same care as is lavished on the greens of expensive golf clubs."

Tash, rudely awoken, sat upright in bed, seemingly unaware that she was flashing her naked breasts at Jayne. Jayne tried not to look, but couldn't help but notice that her nipples were pink. Pink! Rich had always said he preferred brown nipples. How could this relationship last if her nipples weren't even the right color?

"Did we order room service?" Rich asked, as he stubbornly buried his head beneath the bedcovers. His tone was indisputably grumpy. He'd been hoping for a blow job, not bacon and eggs. Besides, Jayne's presence in their suite ruined both plan A and plan B. He could hardly build the intimacy necessary for a confession, and it was hardly what anyone would call keeping a distance from her either.

"No, but I wanted to treat you."

Jayne put the tray on their bed, revealing a tempting stack of pastries, yogurt, fresh fruit and juice, and two steaming cooked breakfasts. The tray was decorated with confetti and a single red rose.

"Wow, thanks, Jayne. That's really, really thoughtful, isn't it, babe?" Tash nipped her fiancé under the covers. "You are spoiling us," she said as she immediately picked up a fork and dived into the tray of goodies.

"How did you get a key to our room?" asked Rich, glaring at Jayne, as he reluctantly surfaced from under the covers.

"I asked at reception. Told them my plan to surprise you and treat you to a romantic breakfast *à deux,* and they were very accommodating. Breakfast was hectic yesterday, wasn't it? I thought you'd appreciate a bit more privacy. After all, this is your wedding trip." Jayne smiled at Rich. She looked a picture of fresh-faced innocence. In that instance, Rich despised her.

"Look, Richie, the bacon is crispy. Just how you like it," said Tash.

"Do you mind going so I can go to the loo?" said Rich.

"I'll turn my back," giggled Jayne, "although I'm sure you haven't anything to show me that I haven't seen before."

Rich froze and waited for Tash's response. But Jayne hadn't lobbed a hand grenade, only he knew she meant he *literally* didn't have anything to show her that she hadn't seen before. Rich sighed, got out of bed and wandered into the bathroom. When he came back, with a towel wrapped around his waist, Jayne was tucking into the breakfast along with Tash. The romantic breakfast *à deux* had clearly turned into *pour trois.* The girls were giggling. Tash's laugh was low and controlled. Jayne's was higher and slightly manic. Would she keep quiet or would she spill the beans? What was she playing at? Jayne looked at him and winked conspiratorially.

"Oh," she cried with disappointment, "you've found a towel. I wanted to check out your wedding tackle, see if you were up to scratch for the lovely Tash."

Tash grinned and assured, "No worries there, girlfriend."

Rich turned red, but not with embarrassment. He was angry and frustrated. He quickly snatched up his clothes from around the bedroom floor and fled to the bathroom to get dressed. The girls returned to their giggling and whispering. Rich didn't dare think what they were talking about. Jayne's actions had now made it impossible to confess. Clearly Jayne was enjoying this farce. She had always liked living on the edge. Indeed, the exciting, wild aspect of her nature had been the very thing that had made her so attractive to him in the early days. Now he was terrified of her. She could ruin everything.

"Babe?" Tash tapped on the bathroom door. Rich eased it open a fraction and pulled her inside. He could see Jayne sitting on the bed. She was casually flicking through his paper stack on the bedside table, and then she opened his bedside drawer and began to flip through the contents, her long, red fingernails touching his wallet, his tickets, his phone and his condoms. Why was she doing that? Had she no sense of what was acceptable and what was intrusive?

"Er, excuse me," he called from the bathroom.

"Darling, I'm horribly nosey. Apologies." Jayne smiled, then picked up the copy of *GQ* that was lying on the floor.

"Can't you get rid of her?" he hissed at Tash.

"Relax, babe. It's cool. Wasn't the breakfast a sweet idea?"

"I haven't touched it."

"Oh."

"I'm not hungry. Look, can't you just get her out of here? We need some privacy."

"OK. Jayne and I are going to board together today."

"Don't you want to board with me?"

"Babe, I'd love to, but I thought you'd agreed to teach Jase and Mia again today."

Fuck, he had.

"It's no problem. I think I might get the lowdown on that prick who ditched her back in London. I think she needs someone to talk to."

"Does she?" Rich looked at his feet. He was expecting to see the blood that had drained from his body in a puddle around his toes.

"Can you imagine anyone letting a treasure like Jayne slip through their fingers?" asked Tash.

Rich couldn't think of a reply.

# 32

## *Jason's New Love Interest*

Jason was making great progress with his boarding lessons. Rich was a considerate and dedicated teacher, and Jase was a natural sportsman. He was fearless, tireless and, if the occasion necessitated it, mindless, too. He did not become frustrated with repeatedly practicing the same moves over and over again in an effort to perfect a new skill, and his perseverance, a trait often lacking in daring sportsmen, paid off.

Mia had dutifully joined Jason for another snowboarding lesson from Rich; however, after falling over for what felt like the hundredth time that morning, she decided to return her board to the rental shop and get back onto her skis. She could not imagine that she would impress, let alone seduce, Jase if she slowed his progress and wept in pain.

She made light of her failure by mocking those who were successful at what she couldn't master.

"I've decided I don't want to join the baggy-trousered, peroxide-haired boarder girls, with their slouchy walks and their impossibly cool demeanors. They are so fake," she insisted.

"You don't have to be blonde to board," pointed out Jason.

"But I have a feeling it helps," added Mia dryly.

"Those girls know how to have fun at least," sighed Jason.

Mia pretended not to hear him and went to find Ted and Kate.

Rich was pleased to find himself alone with Jase. Jason was invariably sunny, and today he was positively bouncing. Rich hoped that some of his carefree attitude would rub off on him.

"Yessssss. I'm fucking brilliant, if I say so myself," yelled Jason, as he had successfully negotiated an entire blue run on his board, only falling once.

"Mate, you are too modest," laughed Rich.

"I am an Olympian hero," shouted Jase, holding his arms aloft like a weight lifter.

Rich smiled to himself. Jason was short, he had stumpy legs, he didn't look like a hero, and yet Rich noticed that women couldn't keep their eyes off him. Maybe, like Rich, they were attracted to Jason all the more because his confidence was as misplaced as it was abundant.

"Seriously, though, you have every right to be proud of yourself. I've never seen anyone take to boarding as quickly as you have."

"Yeah, well, I'm truly motivated." said Jason.

"Oh, yeah?"

"Yeah, I have honey girls to impress. And I think it's working."

Rich looked around him, to see if Jason meant anyone in particular. He had noticed a couple of Italian girls who had been flashing smiles and fluttering eyelashes when they shared the chairlift. They were beauties and, of course, promised hot Mediterranean passion. Rich had had the best everything-other-than-sex in his life with Italian girls. They were the consummate teases. In fact, it was his opinion that only Italian women knew how to strip so as to be sluttish and quintessentially unobtainable at the same time. He smiled fondly at the memory of his various Italian girl-friends, and then his grin broadened as he registered that, while he was buoyed up by the recollection, he wasn't in the slightest bit interested in these girls' flirtatious come-ons. Not now he had Tash. He was happy to retire from the game and enjoy living the chase vicariously through Jase.

"You mean the Italian girls?" he asked.

"Oh, no, I'm thinking of something much closer to home." Jason raised his eyebrows, and nodded to the left of Rich. Rich turned around.

Jayne.

Jayne was standing only meters away. She smiled broadly and headed toward them. Both Jason and Rich felt giddy, although neither of them suspected the other.

"Hi, guys. You looked fantastic out there, Jase. I've been watching you." Jayne scooted up to Jason and leaned in to place a full, lingering kiss on his mouth. Rich was pretty sure that she didn't use her tongue.

Pretty sure.

But she definitely meant to be more than friendly.

Jason grinned. "You think so?"

"You're a natural. I love sporty men." Her big smile dissolved into a pout, and then—and Rich could hardly believe that she really did this—she started to chew on her little fingernail as she cocked her head to one side. She ran her wet finger over her lower lip, leaving some saliva glistening. Rich sighed impatiently. She might as well have carried a sign saying "I give good head"—which, by the way, was true.

Her tactics were transparent. She was trying to make him jealous. How pathetically juvenile. It wouldn't work. The only loser here was poor Jase. He clearly had the hots for Jayne, and she was leading him to believe that the feeling was mutual.

"Is it OK if I join you?"

"Yes," said Jason at the exact moment that Rich spat out an emphatic "No."

"I thought you were boarding with Tash."

"I lost her."

Rich didn't know whether to be relieved or terrified. "We were just going to practice some more turns," said Rich. "You'd be bored."

Jayne didn't acknowledge Rich, but simply repeated her question to Jason, who of course agreed instantly. She grabbed his hand, and they made their way to the chairlift.

Rich climbed on the chair behind theirs and was forced to watch Jayne's show of affection as she flirted, caressed and whispered into Jason's ear for the entire ride. At the top of the run, Jayne took charge of Jason's tuition, leaving Rich feeling redundant. He toyed with the idea of boarding away and going to find some of the others, or just going to one of the parks and doing his own thing, but he didn't want to leave Jason alone with Jayne.

He was being irrational. Jason could more than look after himself where women were concerned and, even if Jayne were only paying attention to Jase in a misguided effort to irritate Rich, the chances were Jason wouldn't care. Like most men, Jason rarely questioned women's motivations for not wanting to sleep with him, and he *never* questioned their motivation when they did want to. All the signs were that Jayne did want to.

Still, Rich felt uneasy. They stayed together for a couple of runs, slowly making their way down and then back up the slopes. Jason's already good technique improved further under Jayne's tuition, and he wanted to try a longer run.

"As much as I'd love to stay and watch, I have got to get back. We girlies are meeting for lunch, then I'm going to the hotel spa. I have an appointment with a mud bath."

"Oh, lucky mud," said Jase, as he and Rich watched Jayne's lithe body float across the snow. "Great ass," he added. Rich shrugged, and refused to agree.

"I can't believe Jayne invited herself along," Rich muttered, ostensibly to himself, but in reality he wanted Jason to hear. He felt that they needed to talk. That was another thing Tash had done to him. Suddenly he was feeling things so deeply that he had overwhelming urges to bloody share them. He was British, for God's sake, and male. He didn't know how to deal with these impulses to communicate.

"Why, mate? What's the matter with Jayne joining the party?" asked Jason.

"Well, you know. Numbers and stuff. This isn't just a holiday, it's our wedding," Rich tried to sound indignant rather than terrified. "We wanted to keep it small, just very close friends. Christ, if my mother finds out that my friend's sister came along because of some spat with her boyfriend, after I've insisted that I'm keeping it to essential witnesses, she'll never forgive me." Rich was stalling.

"I'm not complaining," replied Jason. "She's über-fit. As far as I'm concerned, she evens the numbers up. Before she arrived I didn't have a chance of a lay, which I think you'll agree is a tradition for the best man. Nay, a duty. No disrespect, but I can't do Tash."

"No, you can't," bit Rich dryly.

"Kate is, well . . ."

"Fat."

"I was going to say married."

"Maybe, but you meant fat."

"Yeah, I did. And Mia and I have done it every which way. There's no challenge in a repeat performance. Jayne is a very welcome addition."

"She's Ted's sister," objected Rich, aware that he was being a hypocrite.

"Yes, true. But that doesn't have to be a big deal. I figure it will be worth the faux pas because she'll go like a train." Jason smiled to himself and contemplated with relish the moment that he'd get to find out for certain. "Anyway, she's clearly panting for me. It would be rude not to."

"I have her down as a prick tease. I don't think she'll follow through. You could spend your entire holiday trying to get one in the back of the net and never do it," argued Rich.

"No, she's there for the taking."

"What makes you so sure?"

"Let's just say that we got very close last night."

"How close?" asked Rich. He wished he knew why he wanted to know. His question was complexly motivated. He was curious, that much was certain—he was always curious about Jase's conquests, as Jase had always been about his. They always swapped details. Well, nearly always. Of course, Jayne was a notable exception. He was also nervous. Nervous because he didn't want Jase and Jayne to become close. That was nearly as bad as Jayne and Tash becoming close. Closeness inevitably led to confidences and, clearly, that would lead to trouble. Finally, he wanted to protect Jason. He didn't want Jayne to use Jason to get at him, and he was fairly certain that was what she was doing.

"Are you jealous, mate?" laughed Jason. His question wasn't entirely serious, nor was it entirely a joke either.

Was he?

"Funny. Why should I be jealous? I have Tash."

"Fair point. Tash is a gem. But Jayne, there's something irresistibly filthy about her, isn't there? Don't tell me you wouldn't be interested if you weren't with Tash."

"She's not my type," said Rich firmly.

"You have a pulse, don't you? Of course she's your type. Anyway, she put the blow in blow job for me last night and I tell you, mate, I was the best man." Jason winked, and set off down the mountain at a surprising speed, leaving Rich to take in the significance of his words.

# 33

## *Black Run Monday*

Ted and Lloyd had grabbed a light bite and quickly got back to the slopes. They'd lost sight of Rich and Jase that morning and, while the girls were meeting for lunch again, it was clear they didn't want the boys to join in. "Go away. We don't want you to join our lunch," had in fact been Jayne's exact words. Of course, she'd delivered them with that bewitching smile of hers, demonstrating she was only playing. The guys weren't offended. They thought it pretty slack to call it a day at 2 p.m. when there was still good light until at least four.

The guys took a lift to the highest point in Avoriaz, Les Hauts Forts, which was 2,466 meters closer to the clouds than the hotel. Their main motivation for selecting this difficult run was so they could mention it at dinner that evening; however, their initial competitiveness was blown away on first sight of the spectacular view and was replaced by something approaching awe.

"It's beautiful, isn't it? When I'm somewhere like this I can understand why Kate believes in God," mused Ted.

"Don't you?" asked Lloyd. "I assumed you did."

"Don't know," replied Ted thoughtfully. "I suppose. But not actively, if you know what I mean? Not actively until I'm somewhere like here."

Lloyd followed Ted's gaze and understood him. They sat in silence for some moments, drinking in the pink, blue and golden skies.

"Look, Lloyd, old chap, I'm glad that we've got this chance to . . . I wanted to say . . ." Ted didn't know how to say what he wanted to say. "About the other night, Saturday."

"Oh, let's not go there. I'd drunk a brewery," said Lloyd.

He was embarrassed that Ted had brought up the subject of his drunkenness. Since his outburst, he'd tried very hard to be the perfect guest. Last night he and Mia had enjoyed a few quiet drinks, then turned in before midnight. He had been careful to confine his conversation to subjects such as his work and the effects of GM crops on the environment. He did not mention his divorce, the lack of dinner-party invitations or Saturday night's outburst. He hoped, although didn't really believe, that everyone had forgotten it.

Still, if anyone was going to mention it, it was better that it was Ted. Ted and Lloyd had once been close friends. They'd both married and had children, which set them apart from Jason and Rich. That said, Lloyd was divorced now, which set him apart from everyone.

"I just wanted to say that I'm sorry we haven't seen much of one another recently," said Ted. "But it's not what you think. I'm not avoiding you. There's been a lot going on in my life, too, which, er, made it more difficult than usual to see friends."

"Oh." Lloyd waited to see if Ted was going to say anything else.

It wasn't their style to probe. They'd both been trained at public school and would rather eat their own innards than probe uninvited into their friends' personal lives. Ted would offer as much information as he deemed necessary. Lloyd would accept any detail he was given without asking further questions.

For a moment Ted thought he might want to say more to Lloyd. He really wanted to talk to someone, explain it to someone and get some advice. What a mess he was in. What a mess he'd got himself in. The stress of this enormous secret was taking its toll. He was comfort eating and therefore piling on the pounds. Everyone assumed that his recent weight increase was due to the numerous client dinners that he attended. If only. His body had never been very athletic, but this year Ted hadn't needed padding to bulk out the Father Christmas costume which he wore for the children's party. He should probably go to the gym. But even as the thought flitted into his mind he dismissed it. He knew he wouldn't. He used to say he didn't have the time, that worrying about getting fat was women's work. Now he had time, but he still didn't go.

He had no energy. No drive.

And yet he was hardly sleeping. He knew that he looked closer to a guy in his late forties than mid-thirties.

Even here in beautiful Avoriaz Ted couldn't relax. He had spent most of last night watching the digital numbers on the clock radio add up to 6:15 a.m. He'd lain rigid, pretending to be asleep, desperate not to wake Kate. Eventually, when time had crawled to 6:15 a.m., he couldn't stay still any longer and had decided to swing his legs out of bed and get up. It was a relief to stretch after spending another night feigning sleep. He'd slept for an hour, tops. He could have got up almost as soon as he'd gone to bed. Ted wondered whether if he did that often enough, and quickly enough, he could turn back time. Because Ted, who had always been a big believer in progress, would very much like to turn back time.

Of course, he knew it was impossible. The space–time continuum was nothing more than a little boy's fantasy. And a little man's fantasy.

He'd tried not to wake Kate. She was used to getting up early, as the kids demanded her attention from about 6:30 a.m. every day, but she might as well get the extra snooze time while she could. They were on holiday, after all. Besides, he didn't really want a postmortem of last night. He doubted Kate would push the issue of him turning down sex. It wasn't her style. They'd been together long enough to know that sex drives come and go, and that they don't always flow in sync with one another, tragically. Kate hadn't wanted sex for months in a row in the past; admittedly, it was usually toward the end of her pregnancies. But, still, he didn't want to risk having the conversation. It wasn't dignified.

Despite his care, Kate had sensed that Ted was awake, and she'd rolled over toward his side of the bed. She didn't open her eyes, but lifted her head off the pillow and smiled in his direction, the way she did every day. Ted loved that and smiled back, even though she was still too bleary-eyed to notice. Ted thought his wife was beautiful. He knew she worried about her weight, and it was true that her waistline was thickening and her boobs were sort of melting toward the floor, but Ted didn't care about that. That morning he'd watched her sprawled sleepily across the bed. Her skin warm, voluptuous and inviting, her brow a little furrowed, her stomach exposed, wearing her Caesarean scars like war medals, and for a moment he'd had difficulty continuing just to breathe in and out. His heart contracted with love, leaving him, even after all these years, breathless.

How could he have done such a terrible thing to her? To the woman he loved so much?

"What's the rush?" she'd asked sleepily. "No need to get up early this morning."

Ted hadn't bothered to reply. Instead he'd stepped out of his boxers and headed into the bathroom. He'd held his penis in one hand and used the other to scratch his head, his stomach and then his ass. He'd watched himself in the mirror as he did so. Maybe he would get a hint from his reflection as to what this was all about. His hair was thinning and actually turning gray. He patted and pulled at the skin on his face. It didn't help much—he looked tired. He turned sideways to check out his profile. He had at least two chins. Bugger, his urine had splashed on the floor. Kate wouldn't like that.

Ted liked the shower on full force and the temperature up high. He liked the feeling of the water drilling down onto his back. A good, hot, strong shower was the best way to start the day. He tried not to think about the time when he'd thought sex was the best way to start the day, but Ted honestly couldn't remember when he last had sex in the morning. When they were trying to conceive Aurora? Maybe, or maybe before then? He'd considered jerking himself off, but couldn't summon the energy for that either.

Ted washed with designer liquid soaps which Kate had packed, even though the hotel provided perfectly good toiletries. Kate would never use hotel toiletries. When he once asked her why she replied, "Because *nobody* does!" as though he were stupid for not knowing that particular piece of universal bathroom etiquette. Kate insisted that they spend a lot of money on "treating our senses," as she called it. She said Ted worked damn hard and needed to be pampered.

Fuck.

The designer liquid soap, to wash away his sweat, cost twenty-two quid a bottle. It did smell good, and it was thick and creamy—although Ted always liked the smell of Imperial Leather well enough, it reminded him of his father. His shampoo cost £17.50. His toothpaste cost £8 a tube. His aftershave, over fifty quid.

Fuck.

Ted got out of the shower. He left large footprints on the marble floor. He barely noticed that the tiles were underheated because Ted and Kate had the same at home. Underfloor heating cost a small fortune, but Kate didn't like radiators. She'd read

somewhere that they ruined chi. So, last year they removed all
twenty Bisque radiators which they'd had installed throughout the
house in 2001, installing underfloor heating instead.

Fuck.

Ted had stared at his heavy footprints and found them a comfort. Sometimes, recently, he worried that he'd disappeared. He'd
towel-dried himself with the Egyptian cotton bath sheet, which
took a long time because he was a very hairy man. As a teenager,
he had grown pubic hair and chest and leg hair long before anyone else. He'd been very proud of his hirsute state and enjoyed
walking naked around the locker rooms. He loved being so manly
when the majority of the others were clearly still boys, with high
balls and bare chests. He hated to admit it now, but he used to
whip the hairless boys with wet towels. Not that Ted was a particular bully, far from it; it was simply the done thing at his school.
No one complained.

Now Ted had hairy arms, back and shoulders. He even had
hairs sprouting from his nose, ears and on the backs of his hands.
He had grown into Mia's nickname. He'd become a large, rotund
teddy bear. Ted read a disproportionately large amount of articles
about how women find excessive hair growth a turnoff. He'd worry
about that, except Kate had never complained.

Kate didn't complain about things like that. About how he
looked, or even the things he said. She was very easygoing on
him. She swore it was because she loved him and thought he was
perfect. But Ted didn't need to look at his reflection in the mirror
this morning to know that he wasn't perfect. How could she love
him? Really love him? She might love the Ted Lewis-Ponsonby
package—in other words, the huge three-story mansion in Holland Park and the converted farmhouse in Bordeaux, the Jaguar,
the Range Rover, the private schools, private health care, the full-
time housekeeper, the designer wardrobe and the half a dozen
holidays a year. The chubby thighs, the paunchy belly, the thin-

ning hair and the slimming conversation were accepted as part of that package.

They would not stand alone.

Ted was thinking all of this as he sat with Lloyd on the mountainside. He did not turn to face Lloyd. He did not want to catch his eye. He needn't have worried. Lloyd was well aware that this was a very personal conversation, and therefore he had no intention of looking directly at Ted either. Guys only met one another's eyes when they were on safe ground, such as when they were discussing bottled beer preferences or horsepower.

"Things OK?" asked Lloyd.

He racked his brains as to what might possibly not be OK in Ted and Kate's world. He was clueless. Ted's parents were both healthy and lived very comfortably in their old pile in Suffolk. He knew that Kate's mother was well because last night she was saying that they had just bought her a house in the Cotswolds, for her to retire to. As far as he knew, the kids were doing fine at school. What could be wrong? Could Ted be ill? Lloyd stole a glance.

Christ, it was possible. He looked crap. Fat and sallow-skinned. Lloyd felt concern rising through his body, his heartbeat quickening. He'd been so engrossed in his own problems that he hadn't noticed.

"Are you ill?" he demanded.

"No, not ill," sighed Ted. Lloyd raced through other possible explanations. Something was very clearly amiss. What could it be? And then suddenly he knew. Of course. It appalled him, possibly more than the idea of Ted being ill. Of course, that's why Ted had chosen to confide in *Lloyd*. That was the thing everyone confided in Lloyd, and he was sick of it.

Ted was playing around.

God, it disgusted him that so many people thought that just because he'd once been indiscreet they could unburden their sordid tales to him. He didn't want to know if Ted was having an affair. He couldn't have cared less. It wasn't romantic, or amazing, or clever, or even different. And he should know. Lloyd turned to Ted to say as much, but something stopped him. Ted's eyes were fractured with worry, not bright with passion. His body was bloated with indifference, not taut with illicit pleasure. His face was a maze of anxious wrinkles. He did not look like a man in the middle of a fevered, dangerous liaison.

"What's the matter, buddy?"

And Ted wanted to tell him, as he'd wanted to tell Kate for several months now. The problem was that he couldn't find the words. He wanted to unburden himself. Just by blurting out his secret he would feel better, surely. Perhaps if he confided in Lloyd, Lloyd could be the one to talk to Kate. Maybe it would be better if this kind of thing came from a third person. But maybe not.

He'd let Kate down. Brutally. Dismally. Completely. He could not imagine a way in which he could put things right. He'd lain awake night after night coming up with plan after impossible plan to try to fix things. They were fantasies, not solutions. The very least he owed her was a bit of directness. Ted had to talk to Kate before he talked to anyone else.

"Nothing's the matter. I'm cool." Ted forced his mouth into, if not a smile, then at least a line. "In fact, I'm not just cool, I'm cold," he joked weakly. "Let's get going again." And before Lloyd could quiz him further, Ted was up and away down the slope.

Lloyd sighed, relieved. Thank God everything was OK with Ted and Kate. Their OK-ness was a given. An absolute. A necessity. Hearing that they were in the slightest bit shaky was tantamount to declaring a disbelief in sunny childhoods or happy endings. And Lloyd more than anyone needed to believe in happy endings.

Lloyd launched himself down the slope after Ted. He swept to the left and to the right, and then left again. He was pleased with his speed and technique. That was the amazing thing about snow. Every year he forgot just how fabulous it felt to be up on the slopes until he was there, and it made him feel fantastic. So bloody strong and in control. This was a tricky run, and only the extremely competent skiers even attempted it, so it was genuinely peaceful. It was possible to get to quite a speed and just enjoy the velocity without worrying about bumping into gaggles of boisterous novices from the ski schools.

Lloyd smiled to himself. Of course the gang wanted him to be here, why else would Rich have asked him? My God, he was beginning to be as paranoid as Sophie. Well, he felt welcome; he was relaxed. These were his people. This holiday was going to be the perfect antidote to the heavy days he'd endured of late.

Lloyd spotted Ted just ahead of him. A slither of competitive spirit glided up his spine. Ted didn't look as confident on his skis as Lloyd did, even though Ted had skied since he was a child. This black run was clearly too much of a challenge, as Ted was beginning to wobble. He was a bit close to the edge there. Was he going to recover it? Lloyd's delight at being the better skier instantly turned to fear that his friend was in real trouble.

Lloyd started to speed up and head toward Ted—although, through experience, he knew that he couldn't really do anything to help. In a split second Ted managed to pull himself away from the crevasse, but he'd taken the turn too suddenly. He panicked and fell head over heels. Ted landed with a violent thud. Even from a few hundred yards away Lloyd could see it wasn't good. Ted's ankle was twisted underneath him. The ski on that foot was still attached. Although his poles were splayed at a distance, and the other ski had flown over the edge. It was unlikely that they'd be able to rescue it, but more worryingly it showed Lloyd just how close a call the fall had been. Lloyd skied to a halt next to Ted.

"Ted, buddy, are you all right? Shit, that looked nasty."

Ted nodded, but said nothing. Lloyd looked around for help. A couple of other skiers were heading toward them, to see if they could assist.

"Didn't you see how close you were?" he asked. His tone was that of an angry parent reprimanding a child for wandering away from the cart in the supermarket, a collision of emotion, relief and fear. Ted remained silent and wouldn't look at Lloyd. Instead he sat up in the snow and slowly inched his leg from out beneath him. Lloyd decided that the best course of action was to recover the lost poles. Having done so, he returned to Ted and the small crowd of two or three skiers who were standing around being, in varying degrees, useful. One of them had a walkie-talkie and was radioing for help.

"Where does it hurt?" asked Lloyd. It was an automatic question—clearly the twisted ankle was causing Ted's face to curl in pain. "Can you move it?"

Ted moved his leg, then rotated his foot.

And then he let out a wail. It wasn't a wail of pain, more of despair. Lloyd was shocked and didn't know what to say.

"Come on, old chap, buck up. We'll get you down from here." He bent down to pat his friend on the back. He was embarrassed for him. There were strangers standing close by, and Ted was wailing like a baby.

"It's shock," explained Lloyd to the others.

One woman was wearing a rucksack; she opened it and produced a big bar of chocolate. She broke off a slab and offered it to Ted. He didn't even acknowledge her or her chocolate.

"It's OK, Ted. It's not broken." But Lloyd's words of consolation couldn't help. Ted began to sob. They were deep sobs that shook his massive six-foot-two frame and made him suddenly appear like a child. Tears, actual tears, began to pour down his face. Lloyd was stunned. He'd never seen Ted cry. None of the guys cried. Well, except for Jase when he went through that stage of doing drugs as a sort of hobby. He'd insisted that it was part of his job description. He'd had a few particularly hairy trips and come down crying. But that was chemical, not emotional.

"Mate, get a grip. It's not broken, you're just shocked."

"No, I'm not," insisted Ted. "I'm ruined. I'm fucking ruined." And then he fell back into the snow and lay staring at the blue sky while he howled like an animal.

# 34

## *Kicking Back*

Tash eased her feet out of her boots and wiggled her toes. She edged down her waterproof trousers and protective padding. The relief was enormous—she felt like a butterfly emerging from a cocoon. However cozy it was in that cocoon, nothing felt better than a good stretch. She reached for the ceiling, then bent at the waist and allowed her upper body to flop forward. She could comfortably place her hands flat on the floor, while keeping her legs straight. She practiced yoga at least four times a week, which left her supple and flexible. It was a hobby Rich encouraged. Tash stretched for about ten minutes, finishing with a stretch into the minibar to retrieve a packet of peanut M&Ms before she collapsed onto the huge bed, still dressed in thermal long johns, vest and socks.

Tash smiled to herself. Life was good. She'd had a fantastic morning in the snow with Jayne. They'd had a real giggle. Jayne was so sweet and interested. They hadn't got round to talking about Jayne's ex because all Jayne did was direct the conversation back to Tash the entire time. That was a sign of good breeding, genuine manners. Jayne seemed to be fascinated by everything Tash had to say. She wanted to know what schools Tash went to, where she bought her clothes, which gym she was a member at—everything including her favorite sandwich filling. And they'd covered some miles, until Tash had lost Jayne. Jayne was so much faster, they'd somehow lost sight of one another. Tash was exhausted.

The hotel changed the sheets every day, and yet as she lay on the bed a memory of Rich's lovemaking, the night before, seeped into Tash's mind.

Since meeting one another, Tash and Rich had made love in every imaginable way. Sometimes slowly, carefully, respectfully and sometimes hurriedly, frantically, filthily. They were daring, imaginative and experienced lovers, so they had naturally swung from one position to another, one location to the next. They prided themselves on ticking off "firsts"—their first time in the open air, the first time in a train—and they christened every room in both their flats, utilizing every surface that was sturdy enough to take their weight. They would fall onto a chair, the bed, the stairs, up against a wall, and vigorously kiss one another over and over again. Naturally interweaving their limbs so that it became difficult to know where each body started and finished. Their hands, tongues and lips would race to rediscover every part of one another's bodies.

Naturally, he knew the curve of her breast and the fit between her thighs as well as she knew his penis, balls and buttocks, but they also knew every other inch of one another's bodies. Many times he'd traced the fine blue veins that ran down the backs of her knees. He'd sucked each of her toes. He'd kissed, lapped and caressed every vertebra on her spine, the mole on her rib cage and the cuticles of her fingernails. And she had explored the mounds, the ridges, the sinew and tissue that curved to form his thighs, the crook of his elbow, the bridge of his nose, the knuckles on his hands. They knew the smooth bits, the soft bits, the hard bits, the tender bits of each other's bodies.

And yet last night had been different again. Quite a different sort of first.

Last night Rich had made love to Tash with a new intensity. He was always a considerate and accomplished lover. One who gave her great pleasure, somehow managing to combine familiarity and joyful surprises, shocking eroticism with a sense of well-being and peace. But last night as he entered her, he took her head in both his hands and stared at her. His look was strong, vibrant and purposeful. His lovemaking confirmed that he loved her and acknowledged that she loved him back. His raw, searching gaze was trying to communicate something more, trying to ask for something more. He knew her, and he was begging her to know him. To know him and to love him still.

Wordlessly, Tash had reacted to his needs. She tightened the muscles in her thighs and groin and held on to him. He moved leisurely and deftly, then more rapidly and vigorously. Nothing mattered except the two of them, at that moment, on that bed. She came. He came. They waited and repeated everything all over again. After the second time, the recovery took longer, but despite his exhaustion and her rawness he climbed back on top of her and started over. They bounced through their orgasms, falling, springing and shuddering.

"I want to stay here forever," he told her, "just here." A drop of his sweat fell from his nose and splashed onto her face. She blinked to stop it going in her eye. "I want to be joined to you. To be inseparable."

"We are inseparable," she assured him, and Tash trembled with joy at having found something so perfect.

What were the odds? Logistically everything was set against finding such perfection. The world was awash with hazards and miscommunications, pressures and lost opportunities that conspired to take you away from such happiness. But in that moment Tash enjoyed a bit of heaven on earth, and she had no reason to believe that it would be anything other than endless.

There was a knock at the door, which startled Tash from her luxuriant memories.

"It's me, Jayne."

Tash ran to the door and flung it open. "Hi, I lost you."

"Yes, but I found Jason."

"Was he with Rich?"

"Yes. Rich was there, too, being all macho and gorgeous. Darling, he is a beauty." Tash grinned. She knew that Jayne was the type of girl to scatter compliments liberally, but it was always good to hear nice things being said of Rich. "I'm not disturbing you, am I?"

"Not at all. I was lying here thinking life is pretty damn perfect and that can't be improved upon except by a bit of company."

"You are so lucky." Jayne forced out a small smile as she entered the room. Tash mentally kicked herself. It wasn't exactly tactful to gloat about just how perfect your life was to someone who had just split up from their boyfriend. "Listen, darling, I've booked us both into the spa. I'm going to have one of those mud wraps that promise to make me disappear."

"There's not a spare ounce of flesh on you," Tash pointed out, as Jayne knew she would. No matter how often it was said, she always liked to hear it again.

"Thanks. And I've booked you a massage. Then we are both having manicures and, if there's time, pedicures."

"My God, that's amazing. I was planning on getting all this stuff done, but I hadn't got round to booking anything. I was sort of imagining I'd get a last-minute appointment on Thursday."

"You can't leave anything to chance in these matters," scolded Jayne. "It's too important. What if there aren't any appointments on Thursday? That would be so tragic."

Tash was sure she'd have managed, even if there hadn't been any prewedding pampering. She couldn't imagine Rich calling the whole thing off because her bikini line wasn't neat, but like any woman she was thrilled by the prospect of spending a couple of hours in the beautician's. "I'll have to give you some cash. I couldn't possibly let you pay," said Tash, as she darted around the room looking for her swimming costume and bathrobe.

"Oh, don't worry. I put it all on Ted's room account. Big bruv is so stacked that he can treat us. Think of it as a wedding prezzie."

"No, I couldn't," said Tash, embarrassed. "Ted and Kate have already been crazily generous. They've offered to buy all the drinks at the reception, and Kate has ordered vintage champagne. Plus they spent nearly six hundred quid on bedding for our flat. Can you imagine six hundred quid on sheets and stuff? I can't thank them enough as it is."

Tash was ready; she picked up her key and followed Jayne out the door, making a mental note to herself to charge the cost of the treatments to her room bill.

# 35

# *Hot Water*

Jayne watched Tash dip her toe into the hot tub. They'd been asked to relax there until the beauticians were ready to begin the treatments. Tash's limbs were long, lithe and lily white. Her toe broke the surface of the water and sent ripples to the edge of

the tub. For some reason, the unwelcome image of Rich's cock
sinking into Tash clambered into Jayne's head. She fought it off.
The droplets of water glistened on Tash's shoulder, and Jayne
wondered if Tash perspired a lot when she had sex with Rich. Tash
had pinned her hair in a chaotic updo, but one or two rebellious
strands were insisting on tumbling down about her face. The
strands of hair looked like fingers, and Jayne thought of Rich tenderly cupping Tash's chin as he leaned in to kiss her lips.

"Fuck!" Jayne's expletive echoed around the watery chamber,
bouncing on the pool surface and off the tiny mosaic tiles, breaking the peace of the spa.

"What is it?" asked Tash.

"Oh, nothing. I just stubbed my toe," lied Jayne.

Jayne could see why Rich might fall in love with Tash and so
hated her. Her collarbone was sublime, her tits were tiny but pert
and her legs looked strong and muscular. Jayne loathed her.

"So, tell me how you met Rich?" asked Jayne, picking up on
where she'd left the conversation that morning.

"Usual thing, a party. A friend of mine from work was hosting
a 'spring into spring party,' and Rich came along with my friend's
brother."

"Was that last spring?"

"Yes."

"Oh, you haven't known each other very long, then, not even
a year." Jayne thought it was unlikely that she was the first person
to point this out to Tash, but she was determined to try to sow seeds
of doubt wherever she could. She figured that if she threw them
liberally enough, eventually one or two would take root.

"Seems like I've always known him," mused Tash.

Both girls fell silent, and the only noise was the hum of the
Jacuzzi and a drip, drip, drip somewhere distant. Tash found the
drip, drip, drip mesmeric and felt the tissue in her body slowly relax. Jayne thought the drip, drip, drip was deeply irritating, and

with each drop her shoulders tightened and she dug her nails deeper into her palm.

"They ought to get a plumber to fix that," she complained.

"Fix what?" asked Tash, proving to Jayne that she didn't have very high standards of what was acceptable in a five-star spa.

"You're so brave. Aren't you even a little bit worried that it's all so whirlwind? Do you think you've known each other long enough?" asked Jayne, forcing herself to forget the dripping.

"What is long enough? How can you measure feeling by clocks?"

"That's very romantic. I must be a bit of a coward. I'd only feel confident if I'd known someone a good few years before I made the most enormous commitment."

"How long have you known Jason?" asked Tash, with a huge grin.

"What?"

"You don't have to be shy with me. He hasn't made a secret of the fact that he is mad keen for you, and when Rich and I came back from our sleigh ride last night I saw the two of you slip into Jason's room, so I can only assume that the interest isn't all one way." Tash grinned, enjoying gently teasing Jayne.

"We didn't have sex," declared Jayne. Tash raised her eyebrows sceptically. "I don't sleep with men unless I'm in love with them. We just fooled around," insisted Jayne.

Tash had come across women like this before, but they were usually much younger than Jayne. They insisted that sex was only sex if there was penetration, and they were prepared to do everything in the sack other than that final deed, in order to convince themselves that they were somehow more reserved than was truly the case. Tash thought it was a misplaced prudery that allowed women to swallow cum, but still say that they hadn't had sex. Not least because they were often denying themselves their own orgasm. She decided not to say as much to Jayne. Jayne looked vexed enough as it was. Pointing out the folly of giving pleasure while receiving none was unlikely to put a smile on her face.

What was she upset about? Was she embarrassed? She had no need to be. Jayne and Jason were single, consenting and well past their twenty-first birthdays.

It struck Tash that Jayne was a peculiar cocktail of sophistication and immaturity. On the one hand, she appeared to be so sorted, the epitome of erudition and the ultimate girl-around-town. On the other, she was like a little girl, diving into her mother's wardrobe to dress up and play a part for which she wasn't ready. She might live in a flat in Chelsea and drive around in a soft-top BMW Z4 series, but both the flat and the car were paid for by her parents. Her friends were her brother's friends. And Tash could now see, as she was so up close and personal in the hot tub, that Jayne's boobs and nose belonged to a surgeon, probably one on Harley Street. It seemed that Jayne didn't have anything she could faithfully call her own. Jayne reminded Tash of a beautiful, handblown champagne flute, vulnerable and brittle. Tash was beginning to sense that Jayne wasn't as happy as she ought to be, or as she pretended to be. She supposed it was the recent breakup of her relationship. That's why Tash had been so pleased to see that Jason and Jayne were starting something up. If nothing else, Jason would provide a good distraction.

"He really likes you," Tash assured Jayne.

"Do you think so?" Jayne scooped up the water from the tub and let it trickle through her hands onto her face. She couldn't have cared less if Jason liked her or not. In fact, she was peeved that Tash had spotted her entering his room. She didn't want anyone other than Rich linking her to Jase, least of all Tash.

"Do you like him?" probed Tash.

"I was drunk, it was just a bit of fun," replied Jayne dismissively. She didn't want to waste time talking about Jason. "Tell me, how did you know when you met Rich that he was the One?"

Tash thought this inquiry canceled out the declaration that Jase was "just a bit of fun." She remembered asking engaged and married women the same thing, "But how do you *know?*" Tash had hoped to identify the secret formula before she met the One so that he didn't take her by surprise or, worse still, she didn't miss him in a crowd of also-rans. She'd always found the reply to her question horribly vague—"You just do." It was extremely infuriating. Therefore she was determined not to churn out the same cliché for Jayne.

"He makes my life seem more significant. Everything we do together, even the stupid, ordinary stuff, such as picking out microwave meals in the supermarket, is more fun when we do it together. He leaves me feeling gleaming, you know? Excited, sparkly. From our very first kiss, my existence took on a greater import. Clarity. I hadn't even realized it was fuzzy until I met him."

"You sound really lusted up," said Jayne. In fact, Tash had described falling in love with a pithy directness that Jayne resented and recognized.

"And the more time we spent together, the more I came to realize how compatible we are. We have the same values and priorities. Rich understands my belief that honesty is the foundation to, well, everything. Relationships, our sense of self, our sense of history and even our hope in the future. I mean, when all is said and done, our lives are just a series of stories that we tell, aren't they? That's why it's so important to tell those stories as faithfully as possible, because without that desire for sincerity we don't exist. I'd tried to explain this to men before and they never got it or, if they did, they weren't prepared to live by it. One hundred percent honesty isn't an easy thing to try to achieve. But Rich gets it. He gets me. And he wants the same level of integrity."

Jayne could tell her now. She could simply burst this stupid girl's bubble by telling her that he hadn't been 100 percent honest with her. That he had an enormous secret which he was trying to keep from her and planned always to keep from her. So, far from this marriage being built on principles of trust, fidelity and honesty, it was already swamped in deceit.

But Jayne knew that speaking out now was a risk. If she told Tash about her affair with Rich, Tash might not believe it; they had only known each other five minutes. She might suspect her motives, as well she ought.

Or, even if she did believe Jayne, she might find it in her heart to forgive Rich. If Tash were desperate and determined to marry Rich—which Jayne assumed must be the case, and she could relate to that—then she would sweep his indiscretion under the carpet. Lots of women did the same.

That wouldn't do.

The betrayal had to be absolute and present rather than historical. Plus she needed it to be revealed to Tash by someone other than herself. Tash's humiliation had to be complete.

"How do you get along with Rich's friends?" asked Jayne.

Tash hesitated. Her honest response, "Varies," was clearly not appropriate when Jayne had known them all for a long time; she was related to some, and sucking the penis of another. Was she a particular friend of Mia's? Where did Jayne's loyalties lie?

"Mia can be a bitch, can't she?" declared Jayne, clearing up the issue of loyalty.

"I haven't really got to know everyone properly yet," Tash said cautiously. She never liked this kind of conversation. She really had listened to the advice her mother had drilled into her as a child: "If you haven't anything nice to say, keep your mouth shut."

"I always believed Kate married Ted for our money," stated Jayne.

"Are you serious?"

"Yes, my mother thinks the same."

"They seem very happy," said Tash, stunned at Jayne's revelation.

"He's henpecked. He can't form an opinion on his own any-more. She has him tied so tightly. You must have thought the same thing." Tash wondered if she should allow herself a small nod. "And they are all terribly cliquey. They don't really take to strangers joining their gang, do they?" added Jayne.

"I do sometimes feel a bit of an outsider," Tash admitted. "I don't always know who they are talking about and, of course, they have so many shared memories that I can never be part of."

"And doesn't Mia like bringing up their past."

Tash nodded. "But I think things will get easier the longer we know each other."

"Don't bet on it," Jayne said grimly. She sighed, then added, "Poor Sophie."

"Sophie?"

"Lloyd's ex-wife. It's so sad. Lloyd and Sophie were so in love in the early days, but it's my belief that in the end she simply got sick of being lonely in company. That's why their marriage didn't make it."

"What do you mean by her being lonely in company?" asked Tash.

"You know what I mean," said Jayne, looking directly at Tash, meeting her eyes for the first time since they'd slipped into the tub. "I never understood what Mia had against Sophie. I guess she felt that Sophie wasn't a 'fit.' It's not as though Mia wanted Lloyd for herself. There was never a physical attraction there, not like with—" Jayne broke off and put her hand to her mouth. "Sorry, I've been indiscreet."

"What?"

"Well, Rich and Mia, they must have been attracted to one an-other once, mustn't they? He told you they used to be lovers."

"Not lovers, it was just a fling. A long time ago."

"I'm not saying Rich still feels that pull." Jayne paused and allowed her words to sink in. "It's just people rarely take an unmotivated dislike to someone, and I couldn't imagine anyone taking a dislike to you. Not under normal circumstances."

"So you think Mia dislikes me?"

"I'd be lying if I didn't admit to picking up on quite a bit of tension between the two of you. I haven't offended you, have I?"

"No, not at all. I agree that Mia has said some surprisingly cutting things. But I'd held on to a vague hope that it was nothing personal and that she just had some issues of her own, you know? I accept we don't have much in common, but no one wants to think they are actively disliked, do they? And Rich insisted that there was nothing really malicious about her. I'd begun to think I was exaggerating the situation in my mind. Rich kind of implied that was the case."

"He would say that, wouldn't he?" said Jayne, delighted that she'd tapped into one of Tash's concerns.

"What do you mean?"

"Their loyalty to one another runs very deep. Very deep indeed. Besides, if we are right in thinking that Mia does still hold a torch for him, he's bound to have noticed. He couldn't not have. She's always hanging around him, following him to the pool hall, insisting he teach her how to board."

"Do you think so?" Tash was surprised. Rich had never suggested that there might be a sexual tension.

"Yes, and he couldn't help but be flattered. Mia is very attractive. I'm not saying he'd act on it, not in a million years. He's just flattered." Jayne reached out and squeezed Tash's shoulder. "But there's nothing to worry about. You trust him, don't you?"

"Absolutely," agreed Tash.

"There, then." Jayne smiled, and then glanced at her fingertips. "I look like a prune. I'm going to hunt out the beautician and insist on my mud wrap now. Catch you later."

She pulled herself out of the hot tub and walked toward the treatment rooms, leaving Tash to nurture the seeds she'd sown. Jayne doubted that it would be difficult to grow some shoots of discontent. After all, she'd poured on enough manure.

# 36

## *Après-Ski*

Mia, Jason, Lloyd, Jayne, Rich and Tash sat around the dinner table. They'd all already sunk a couple of cocktails while waiting for Ted and Kate to join them. They all appeared to be in an indecorously boisterous party mood, and some genuinely were so.

"Wow, another delicious menu, and I'm starving," declared Jayne. "Can we just order, and Ted and Kate can order when and if they join us? All this lazing about in the spa has given me such an appetite."

For once Jayne was telling the truth, she was famished. Scheming had worked up an intense hunger. She considered her chat with Tash a huge success. It had taken less than thirty minutes to imply that Tash barely knew Rich, that the gang was intractable and unwelcoming, and she'd also managed to insinuate that Mia probably had the hots for Rich. Moreover, she'd implied that he knew that was the case, but hadn't thought to mention it to Tash, which rather pissed on Tash's honesty parade. Tash would have to be made of steel not to be moved to concern about one of those issues. Jayne felt she'd earned herself a huge steak and a large glass of red. She poured for everyone.

Tash was not made of steel, she was made of sterner stuff. Optimism, trust and hopefulness. While the conversation in the hot tub had unsettled her temporarily, the very soothing sixty-minute massage which followed had allowed her to calmly put things back into proportion. She did not believe that Mia felt anything other than friendship for Rich. And while that friendship was at times a little territorial, it wasn't sinister. She did not believe that Rich would keep silent if he thought Mia had designs on him. He didn't keep secrets from her. Nor did she expect people to understand the intensity of her feelings for Rich and was used to shrugging off the raised eyebrows at the speed at which they had decided they were made for one another. She didn't care. They'd known each other for nine months, which seemed an eminently sensible length of time to her. It wasn't as though they were getting married after a three-day acquaintance.

Rich was feeling sick. All the optimism, trust and hopefulness that he'd carried with him since he'd met Tash had somehow morphed into fearful desperation. Christ, what was he going to do? Everything was fine when they were on their own, but he could hardly keep Tash holed up in their suite, could he? No, he couldn't. He'd thought about it, quite seriously, and really couldn't see how the option could be made viable.

What the hell was Jayne playing at? Could she be serious about Jase? Maybe. And was that a good thing? Maybe. Or a bad thing? Maybe. Rich simply didn't know anymore. He did know that it was not a good idea for his fiancée and his secret fuck buddy to share a hot tub all afternoon—not even in his wildest fantasies was this acceptable. He wished that Jayne wouldn't wink at him like that. Nor should she address all her comments to him. He could not believe that when the conversation had turned to breast implants she'd confessed to her falsies and asked if he wanted to touch them! Like he hadn't already, dozens of times. He knew those tits pre- and postop—was that the point she was trying to drive home?

"Go on, darling, squeeze. It may be your last chance to get your hands on a pair of falsies," she giggled. "Even if I hadn't been in the tub with Tash today, I'd know that she was one hundred percent natural. No offense, Tash."

"None taken," said Tash, who liked her tiny titties. Tash refilled everyone's glass. Jason in particular looked thirsty—his tongue was hanging out.

Bitch. Dangerous bitch. Surely, everyone else had noticed those long, lingering looks that she threw him from under her eyelashes. And Tash bloody did touch them, didn't she!

She'd actually cupped his fuck buddy's tits. Not in a sexy way. Women could do that, couldn't they? Touch and look at each other's bits in a nonerotic, purely scientific manner. They had communal showers in the gym and didn't get aroused by one another. Jesus, he was getting aroused. Even through his excruciating fear he could feel his cock shudder. This was proof positive, as if he needed it, that he had no control over his own tool.

"They feel great," Tash had enthused. Typically complimentary.

Jesus, this was blowing his mind. Please God, don't let it blow his cover. Luckily everyone had had loads to drink and just seemed to think that the whole thing was hilarious. He didn't. He wished Jayne would spontaneously combust, leaving nothing but those stupid sacks of silicon.

"How's Ted?" the gang chorused in unison as Kate joined the table. Rich never thought he'd see the day when he was glad that the conversation moved away from breasts.

"Well, the doctor says he's fine. His ankle isn't even sprained," said Kate. She slipped into a chair next to Lloyd and immediately gulped back the wine he'd poured her. She picked up a roll and slathered butter on it. She finished off the roll in two bites, then picked up a second. Only when she'd consumed that did she continue.

"But I think he's in shock. He's very quiet." Kate turned to Lloyd with a look of concern on her face. "What happened out there, Lloyd?"

Lloyd coughed, and repeated the story of Ted's fall yet again. This time, as with all the other times he'd repeated the story, he omitted the bit about Ted howling and insisting that he was "ruined."

"You didn't have a falling-out, did you?" asked Kate. This was the question she asked Fleur and Elliot if either of them was behaving peculiarly.

"No!" Lloyd was offended that, whenever anything went wrong, people assumed that he was the root of the problem.

"Well, whatever," sighed Kate. The mystery was clearly beyond her. "Ted doesn't want to come down to eat, and he said he's resting up tonight. I ordered him some room service, but he hasn't touched it."

"I tell you what, I'll go and see if he wants some company," offered Lloyd.

"Would you?" Kate looked relieved. She didn't want to admit as much, but she had the distinct feeling that her fussing was doing more to irritate rather than comfort Ted. He'd been really cross with her for ordering room service, insisting that he wasn't hungry and that it was a waste. And it *was* a good idea for the doctor to come back tomorrow, just to be on the safe side. Why had Ted protested quite so vehemently? He was clearly very embarrassed about having to be rescued from the mountainside. It was his pride that was hurt, nothing more.

"What should the rest of us do tonight?" asked Jase. It wasn't that he was being insensitive toward Ted—he did feel bad for Big Ted—it was just that this was a holiday, and more than that, it was a celebration of his best mate's impending wedding. And still more than that, he had to make the most of the presence of the very lovely Jayne. He could not believe his eyes. He'd just watched Tash cup Jayne's tits. Through clothes, admittedly, but still . . . If that wasn't a come-on, he didn't know what was. Jayne had deliberately offered Rich the opportunity to cop a feel precisely because he was part of a couple and therefore unavailable. Women always paid attention to your best mate and/or the unavailable guy when they were flirting with you. He knew that he was really the one she was interested in because she made such a thing about blanking him. The blow job had been sensational last night, but he couldn't wait to get her clothes off.

"I'm keen for more of the same. A bar and then a club," he added. It couldn't do any harm to get her drunk and keep her dancing. He loved to see her gyrate. All those curvy, fleshy bits, wobbling just the correct amount. It was a treat.

"I liked the idea you had yesterday, the idea of going to the cinema, Scaley," said Mia.

In fact, it had been Mia's idea to go to the cinema, and she was the only one seconding it now. She wanted to keep Jason off the alcohol as much as she could. She'd peed on the stick before supper and this was it. Her window of opportunity was just opening. She had approximately four days. She needed to get on with the job and, while it was unlikely that Scaley Jase was about to jump her bones (Mia wasn't blind—he clearly was in the midst of his infatuation with Jayne), she still wanted to keep the alcohol level down as much as she could in the next day or so. Jase's infatuations rarely lasted longer than that.

Mia was kicking herself for not joining in on the conversation about cleavages. She had a great cleavage, easily as good as Jayne's

surgically enhanced one and way better than Barbie Babe's barely
there one. But she had remained silent. It shouldn't have been difficult to flirt with Scaley, to draw attention to her assets, and yet
she'd remained mute. Hell. Mia knew that it was time to start
making her intentions to seduce Scaley a little more obvious, his
infatuation with Jayne notwithstanding. He was not the type of
man who appreciated subtlety. If they went to the cinema, she
could whisper flirty innuendos to him in French, if the film afforded the opportunity. She was surprised to find that, now that it
had come to the crunch, she was finding it difficult making the
transition back from thinking of Jase as a friend to potential bed
partner or, more accurately, getting him to think of her in that
way. She'd watched him over the past forty-eight hours—he flirted
with everyone.

Everyone, that was, except her.

He flirted with Jayne—yes, that was understandable. And he
flirted with the air stewardess, the receptionist, the waitresses and
bar staff. He even flirted a tiny bit with Tash and Kate, for God's
sake. But he did not flirt with Mia. He talked to Mia. They had a
laugh together, but his hugs were matey, not sexy, and his compliments were reluctant compliments such as a brother delivered to
a sister. Mia knew her own worth. She was aware that a lot of men
found her attractive, and she knew that she used to drive Jase wild—
first with desire, then later with frustration. Maybe that was the
problem. But somehow she was finding it difficult actually word-
ing her proposal. Not that she'd been planning on telling him that
she needed his sperm. She'd thought that through and feared he'd
see the responsibility as crippling, even if she assured him she
didn't want or need anything other than the biological bit. Her
plan was to proposition him indecently, so to speak. All she
needed was uncomplicated sex. Surely that was Jase's life goal and
as such shouldn't be a difficult thing to discuss with him.

But it was.

Mia was finding it impossible to be suggestive or lewd, or even intriguing with Jason. She desperately hoped that the cover of darkness would help her become more eloquent and witty. Or, at the very least, it would afford her opportunity to bang her knee against his.

Jase was flattered that Mia had said she liked an idea of his. She wasn't big on compliments of any sort. And while he couldn't actually remember suggesting going to see a film, it wasn't a bad idea. He could ensure that he was snuggled in the seat next to Jayne's. He'd enjoy stealing glances at her in the dark, and there would still be time for a boogie at a club afterward.

Kate said that the cinema was a lovely idea. She'd have preferred to spend the evening curled up with Ted, but then Lloyd had just said he'd sit with him, and the cinema was better than going to a noisy bar. The bars were packed with people who all seemed decades younger than Kate. People who seemed to like music ricocheting through their lithe bodies. People who wore cropped tops and skirts that were just tiny slashes of material held together with a string of sequins. Their slim, pinched waists, flat stomachs and happy, optimistic laughs were similar to those badges the children got on their birthday cards, stating "I am three." Their line-free faces and copious, unrepentant drinking of shots said, "I am twenty-three." When Kate reached for her drink, she felt her upper arm wobble heavily—she only ever wore long-sleeved tops, even in the summer. She wasn't sure she'd ever been twenty-three.

"Do you understand French?" Tash asked Jayne. She feared she knew the answer. Jayne smiled and nodded.

"I get by, darling. I've got an A at A level, but I'm not fluent like Mia."

"Right," murmured Tash, the hope of her having a nonbilingual ally dashed. Tash's low grade in French loomed larger than ever. She could see it hovering above her head, and only just resisted the temptation to punch it.

Rich put his arm around Tash, "A movie sounds good, hey?"

"Not really," admitted Tash, "I don't understand French films when there *are* English subtitles. I won't have a chance without them. I think I'll give it a miss and get an early night. I might run though some of the wedding plans with the maître d'."

"Do you want me to stay with you?" offered Rich.

He hoped Tash would say yes. He didn't want to spend time with Jayne without Tash, even if there were other people around. It made him nervous. On the other hand, he didn't want to refuse to go to the movies because he didn't want to appear unsociable. After all, these were his mates, and they were all here at his invitation, for his wedding, and he couldn't exactly slope off without a good excuse. If Tash said she wanted him to meet with the maître d', though—that would count as a good excuse.

Tash didn't much feel like having an evening in on her own in the bedroom, however lovely their suite was. She already knew that it would not be a good idea meeting the maître d' as she was half drunk—she wouldn't remember anything they agreed about the wedding arrangements. She desperately wanted Rich to ditch the idea of the movies and take her upstairs to, well, take her again. But on the other hand, these were his pals, and she didn't want to be a millstone around his neck. She'd look so pathetically needy if she stopped him from going out and having a laugh.

Tash grinned widely and falsely, "God, no. I wouldn't dream of it. You go out with the gang," she said. It didn't count as a lie. She was being selfless.

"Really, you don't mind?" Rich smiled back with lots of faked enthusiasm.

"And if you want to go on to a club or something you should," added Tash, just to prove how un-needy she was. Rich hoped that no one had heard her offer, especially not Jayne.

"Great," lied Rich.

"Great," repeated Tash.

"Great," said Jayne, smiling, having heard every word. Her smile was genuine. Rich stood up and walked toward the door. He wasn't one for being overly dramatic, but he did feel like a condemned man walking toward the gallows. He stopped, turned and blew Tash a kiss. She smiled and pretended to catch the invisible token.

# 37

# *Ted's Story*

Lloyd knocked on Ted's door; there was no response. Lloyd didn't believe Ted was sleeping—he could hear the faint drone of the TV. It sounded like a cheesy game show, so he knocked again and called, "It's me, Lloyd." More silence, and then a sigh, and some bustling as Ted made his way to the door. He opened it, but didn't greet his friend. He simply turned and went back to bed, throwing the duvet over his head. Lloyd entered the suite and closed the door behind him.

"Nice room, mate. This is really something."

Lloyd let out a low whistle and although he knew he was there to have a "big talk" with Ted, and he knew that it was seriously uncool to be so clearly impressed with anything, he couldn't help himself. Besides, he never had to be cool around Ted. Ted didn't mind if Lloyd was just himself. Lloyd opened the cupboards and passed comment on the amount of space and the rare-but-sensible large number of coat hangers. He nosed around the bathroom, then opened the minibar.

"Do you want one, buddy?" Lloyd could just make out that the movement under the duvet was Ted shaking his head. Lloyd helped himself to a beer anyway. He didn't need to ask—Ted was always very generous and probably wouldn't even notice another beer on his minibar bill. Lloyd sat on one of the comfortable armchairs and addressed the mound of duvet. "God, this is like old times, isn't it?" Although, in fact, it wasn't much.

Lloyd and Ted had shared rooms as undergraduates, and neither of them could count the number of times they'd spent an evening together, sharing some beers, watching the TV, kicking back, chewing the fat.

They'd been great days.

The double-occupancy rooms at the university were coveted. Providing you got on with your roommate (which most undergraduates did, as they didn't often have the confidence to form dislikes), you had so much more space and hence the double rooms were usually the party rooms. Lloyd and Ted had more than got along; they genuinely liked one another's company. Lloyd had been immediately attracted to Ted's double-barrel name and entry in Debrett's, and after that he had formed a genuine respect and affection for Ted because Ted was generous, gentle, brilliant and, most amazingly of all, humble. Ted had thought Lloyd was a "great chap," full of principles and political theories which, although often naïve, were honestly and sincerely felt. Ted liked Lloyd's energy. His passion. He often referred to him as the "Red Radical."

"Yes, 1989 to 1992, they were good years," said Ted, who had finally emerged from under the duvet.

"The best," added Lloyd.

"Some of the best," qualified Ted. "I mean, you've had better since, haven't you? Meeting Sophie and having Joanna. I know the marriage hasn't worked out, but—"

"Oh, yes. Yes, of course," said Lloyd quickly. He knew how sad those people were who thought their university years were the best years of their lives. He didn't want to sound like one of those boring losers.

But it was hard not to think back fondly.

Lloyd, Rich, Jase and Ted's time at college had been a hedonistic whirl of parties, popularity, sex and success. The good times sure did roll, and roll and roll. Since then, well, yes, there had been good times. Better times, more real times, but not good *years*. That was the coolest thing about university days: there were so many of them. There were numerous lazy mornings in bed (or, occasionally, in a lecture hall). Followed by endless sleepy afternoons in front of the fire (sometimes books open, other times just with the fridge open). And then there were the countless nights at raves, in pubs or simply in young, uncomplicated women's beds. There had been so much time to look forward to. Now Lloyd often felt that time was running out, or at least the good times were running out.

Lloyd remembered feeling fire in his belly. He'd known that everything out there was his for the taking. They'd all believed that. And they'd been right. They all left with good degrees, high hopes and numerous notches on the bedpost. The world was their oyster. Throughout their twenties, the guys had hurtled their way up their respective career ladders. And while Rich and Jase had bought fast cars and apartments that were too big for single guys— and so they filled them with one-night stands and expensive audio equipment—Ted and Lloyd had happily become smug marrieds with kids. Those were the designated roles. Rich and Jase were playboys, and Lloyd and Ted were happily married.

But Lloyd wasn't married anymore and looking at Ted, who was at this second a mound of flesh shielded by duvet, there was little to suggest that he was in the least bit happy.

"We used to set the world alight with our ideas, right?" said Lloyd, partly as a reminder to Ted, partly because he was looking for confirmation that the boys he remembered had existed. "We were always laughing and joking."

"Arguing," added Ted, but as he said it he grinned at Lloyd.

"Well, yes, there was healthy debate," admitted Lloyd. "But imagine how I felt knowing I was sharing my wash basket with a bloke that killed foxes for a giggle."

Ted laughed. He couldn't imagine getting on a horse to chase across the countryside now—far too energetic. "Do you still campaign against fox hunting?"

"Of course I do," said Lloyd. "It's still an issue. Don't you watch the news?"

"It must be a good feeling knowing you are really making a difference," said Ted.

"I guess," said Lloyd with a grin. He'd been out of the way of feeling good about himself. The divorce had left him feeling like a failure. Lloyd didn't like failure, and he tolerated failure in himself least of all. At the first sign of trouble between himself and Sophie, Lloyd had panicked. He had frozen. He'd found it impossible to discuss their issues, hoping that if he ignored them they would go away. Of course they didn't. The cracks in their relationship widened to huge, sore gashes—a chasm that he'd filled with another woman. Ashamed of his reaction, Lloyd had lashed out and then withdrawn. Shame and loathing didn't allow for introspection. Lloyd had rolled himself into a solid, impenetrable ball.

Big Ted's compliment acted like a blanket settling around the solid, impenetrable ball. Their old friendship was somehow proof that Lloyd wasn't a failure. For a moment Lloyd felt how he hoped he'd feel on this holiday with his friends—wanted, not wanting. Lloyd watched the snow falling outside the window and allowed a little bit of self-satisfaction to seep into his consciousness. It was a good thing that he still campaigned against fox hunting. How many student saboteurs still gave a damn?

"What happened out there, buddy?" asked Lloyd, aware that he could no longer avoid the issue about which he'd come to see Ted. Surprised to find he didn't even want to.

"I took a fall."

"I know that."

"No big deal. I just wasn't concentrating properly."

Lloyd wondered if he could push on. Since Ted's fall, he'd been going over and over the circumstances of the tumble, and he'd been left with this awful thought. A thought so unpleasant he didn't know how to articulate it. He didn't know if he even should.

"Today, it was, you know, it was an accident, wasn't it?" Lloyd sat nervously peeling the label off his beer bottle. Clearly he was anxious and uncomfortable. Ted laughed dryly.

"You think I was planning on hurling myself off the crevasse, don't you?"

Lloyd blushed. Said aloud, the thought that had half formed in his mind and had haunted him all afternoon seemed ridiculous.

"Buddy, you've been acting so weird. And when you did fall, that wailing—" Lloyd left the sentence hanging.

"I'm not that barmy," Ted reassured. Poor Lloyd felt silly, but he also felt relieved. "In my family, the women are the ones with the history of being total and utter loons," added Ted.

"Jayne appears eminently sensible," insisted Lloyd, offended on her behalf by her brother's comment.

Ted raised an eyebrow. "You only think that because you fancy her."

"I do not," insisted Lloyd.

"Why? What's wrong with you?" asked Ted. Lloyd grinned and said nothing, admitting his mild infatuation through his silence. "Everyone fancies her," mused Ted, "and it's not doing her any favors."

Lloyd saw that he could now spend the evening chatting about Jayne, and Greta, and Sophie, too, if he wanted. What was it that Lloyd had longed for in the past year? What was he too proud to ask for and the others too shy to offer? He'd wanted someone to talk to, someone to give him some perspective and, if it wasn't too much trouble, some advice, too. Maybe that was why Lloyd looked back so fondly on his university years. The place was awash with advice givers. Role models, mentors, counselors and good, old-fashioned, chatty mates were around every corner. Here, at last, was his chance to get some advice, comfort and guidance. He could avoid the issue that had brought him to Ted's room and indulge in a chat about the things and people that were important in his life.

Lloyd looked up at Ted, who lay like a bloated and beached whale on his bed. He hadn't shaved since he'd arrived on holiday, but he didn't look relaxed, he looked unkempt. Despite the sun on the slopes today, Ted looked gray. It was clear that Ted needed a sounding board, but it was also clear that he probably didn't know how to ask for one either. At college they taught you how to debate, discuss and rationalize. They taught you how to pass exams and the port. They didn't teach you how to ask for help.

Lloyd stepped up to the mike.

"Look, I'm not here to talk about your sister, as delectable as she is," insisted Lloyd. "I want to know what's going on with you. What did you mean when you said you were ruined?"

Ted let out a long sigh. He looked exactly like a balloon several days after a party. Tired, dejected, useless. "Exactly that. I lost my job five months ago."

"What?" Lloyd was stunned. "Why haven't you said anything?"

Ted shrugged. He couldn't think of an answer. Why hadn't he said anything?

"Well, how are you managing? I mean, how did Kate take it? She still seems her old self." Lloyd wanted to be positive and upbeat. "It's obviously not getting you both down. You're pulling together. That's a good thing."

"Kate doesn't know," said Ted, deadpan.

"Doesn't know?" Lloyd was momentarily stumped. "How's that working? I guess there was a big payoff, right? And you're living off that, right? Are you waiting to get something new before you tell her, to save her the worry?"

"There was no payoff." The same blunt, resigned tone.

Lloyd didn't get it. "But if you are made redundant in the City there's always a payoff. I'm always reading about blokes who get a cool million, and then walk straight into another job." Lloyd jealously hated this type of bloke, but at that moment he desperately wanted his best friend to be one of them.

"I wasn't made redundant. I was sacked," said Ted simply. He sounded dulled, damaged.

"Sacked?" Lloyd was astonished and at a total loss for words. He wasn't exactly *au fait* with what merchant bankers did on a day-to-day basis, but he'd always had the impression that, whatever they did, Ted did it well. He was extremely bright, diligent and likeable. Why would anyone think to sack him? Ted answered the unasked question.

"Insider dealing."

"What?" Lloyd jumped to his feet. He simply could not take it in. He did not believe it. Could not, would not believe it of Ted. Not even if it was Ted telling him so. "But you didn't, did you?" Lloyd assumed his question was rhetorical. Ted was the very epitome of English gentlemanliness. He was fair, loyal and honest. He was not a cheat. Not an insider dealer. There had to be a mistake. "It's clearly a case of wrongful dismissal, isn't it?"

"No. Yes. A bit," said Ted, not clarifying the situation much. "Well, technically no, it is not a case of wrongful dismissal. I didn't mean to, but I broke the rules."

"How? Why?"

Ted sighed. After five months of horrible secrecy, he was amazed at how simply the words were pouring out now. "I was in Suffolk visiting my parents one weekend. Do you remember Miss Hollingson? Their lady 'that does.' She'd been with them forever. She's next to hopeless as a cleaner now—in fact always has been—

but she's part of the furniture. She'd finally decided that it was her time to retire, what with my parents spending most of their time abroad. She didn't like knocking about the old pile alone. My parents would never have asked her to leave, unless it was in a box. I think they were surprised and more than a little bit sad when she said that she wanted to move to her brother's, to be near his children and grandchildren."

"You've lost me," said Lloyd.

"The odd thing was I could have given her cash, a lot of cash, and I'd have happily done so. She taught me how to tie my shoelaces and recite the alphabet. You know?"

Lloyd didn't know. Ted was describing a different world. A world with live-in housekeepers was one which he could only imagine, but he nodded to encourage Ted.

"She wouldn't take my cash. Too proud. We were chatting about her family, and I passed comment on how excited she must be about going to live near them, and she said something a little odd, something that suggested that wasn't the case. She wasn't excited and nor were they. Worse still, she knew they weren't. They couldn't afford her was her view. Although, realistically, they probably just didn't want her. A great-auntie turning up on your doorstep with her duster and profligate advice on child care, well, it's not ideal, is it? She wanted to take a nest egg with her. A sweetener, if you like. Can you believe it, after all those years of working for my parents for a very fair wage, and yet she didn't have a pension? Hardly any savings to speak of? I was astounded. Nearly everything she'd ever earned she'd passed on. She'd lived comfortably and had no idea that it would end. It didn't even have to. My parents think of her as family. They didn't want her to leave."

A flash of frustration and regret passed across Ted's face. He was trying to sound reasonable, but in truth this terrible difficulty he found himself center of was all so unnecessary, and if there was one thing Ted loathed it was unnecessary hardship. Hardship was difficult to bear. Unnecessary hardship was insulting.

"Yes?" Lloyd gently prompted.

"So I gave her a tip. I knew of this smallish IT company that was going to float. You know, when I did it, I didn't think it was going to mean much. It was like passing on a good horse bet. I thought she'd make a couple of grand. Just enough for her to hold her head up high when she arrived at her family's door. I could have written her a check." Ted shook his head. "She made over two hundred thousand in a week. I thought she was going to buy fifty-odd shares. She hardly had any money to invest. But she passed on the tip to her bloody brother and his greedy family. Between them they made a tidy sum. Even then it wouldn't have mattered, except that she rang her local newspaper and told them what a lovely boy I was, to help her out in this way. Of course, she had no understanding of the consequences of her actions, but she mentioned my name and my company's name. One of the national papers picked up the story and ran a column. Just a space filler, really. Didn't name me, but they did mention my company again, and the name Miss Hollingson. They made more of it than there was. Tried to paint me as a modern-day Robin Hood. Sounds heroic, except Robin Hood is best known for robbing the rich and my job is . . . was . . . to make the rich richer. My old bosses are very hot on following their own PR. They employ people to track exactly what is written about them across the globe, so they soon spotted the story. It wasn't difficult to trace Miss Hollingson back to me. They were looking for people to let go. They needed to cut their workforce by twenty-two percent. I handed them an excuse and allowed them to avoid the cool million payoff. Which, you so rightly point out, is often necessary. My desk was cleared within twenty minutes, and I was escorted off the premises by an armed guard."

"Armed guard?"

"Stupidly over the top—they like the theater," Ted sighed.

Lloyd could only imagine the humiliation. He battled to be positive. He couldn't believe this could happen. Such bad luck. Such poor judgment. Such a mistake. These things didn't happen to people like Lloyd and his friends.

Except, of course, when Lloyd had slipped into Greta's bed and thought that he was "showing Sophie." Such poor judgment. Such a mistake. Lloyd felt sweat on his upper lip. Did this mean no one was immune?

"But surely you can appeal? There must be ways to clear your name. If you tell them about Miss Hutchinson."

"Miss Hollingson," Ted corrected, gently. "No. I did pass on secret information. Why? I can't remember. I think I was showing off. Can you imagine? How pathetic. A man my age and size showing off to the elderly housekeeper who thinks I walk on water regardless, and then, bang, I have no job and no references, so no chance of getting another job."

"And you've kept this all from Kate?"

"It hasn't been easy, but at first I thought I'd get another job. If the market weren't so dead I'm sure I could have talked away the indiscretion, and the thirteen years of good service would go some way toward making me employable, but the markets are flat. Even those who can wash their underwear in public can't find work."

"So what have you done all day, every day? How have you managed to convince Kate that you are at work? What have you done for money?"

"I had some family money. I cashed in my trust fund, and we had some savings. But it's all gone now. I've discovered that we live dramatically beyond our means. I've become the cliché. I am the man who picks up my laptop and coat, ostensibly setting off for work, but who goes to the park instead."

"Every day?"

"Well, at first I made calls, tried to pick up some old contacts, but no one wants to know you as you slide down the pole. I feed ducks; I sometimes visit museums if it's wet."

Lloyd felt sick. He could only imagine his friend's despair and loneliness, the disgrace and dishonor. He had no concept of the fear.

"You have to tell her."

"I do."

"How bad is it?"

"Couldn't be worse. We'll lose the house and our cars. Our shares are worth a fraction of what I bought them for. The children will have to come out of their schools . . ." Ted couldn't bring himself to continue.

"But you can sell the house in Bordeaux."

"I already have. The money from that paid the mortgage on our Holland Park pile for the past few months."

"But you've just bought your mother-in-law a place in the Cotswolds." Lloyd didn't understand.

"I didn't know how to get out of the promise without admitting to my situation. So I took another loan out to put down the deposit. I can't pay the mortgage on it or the loan payments. I'll have to hand back the keys. I've lost thousands on solicitor's fees, pushing through a purchase."

"Shit."

"I couldn't have put it better myself."

"The housekeeper, Miss Hollingson, she could give you some of that money she made."

Ted looked at Lloyd with genuine sadness. He didn't need to say anything. He would not ask Miss Hollingson for money; he had too much pride for that. Besides, she might not want to give it to him. She might have already given it to her family. If he asked and she turned him down, well, Ted would never recover from that cruelty. Such simple solutions and happy endings were confined to the pages of books.

"Why haven't you told Kate?" asked Lloyd, with bewilderment.

"She'll leave me," said Ted calmly. "Lloyd, Ms. Monopoly will not live a life as ordinary as the one I am now equipped to provide."

Lloyd didn't know what else to say. He didn't even have the spirit to fling out a few consoling platitudes. He thought it was pointless to suggest that everything would be all right or that Ted was mistaken and Kate would "stand by her man." Like Ted, he doubted that would be the case.

Ted continued, "I don't want to be divorced. I don't want to lose her, or the kids. I don't want to be—"

"Me."

"No offense."

"None taken," said Lloyd. He didn't want to be he either.

"Old chap, you should understand more than anyone."

Yes, he did understand. Lloyd lived in his own hell, made worse because he'd chosen it. At least Sophie could assure herself it wasn't her fault. She hadn't chosen to be divorced—although technically she had. She'd sued *him* for divorce, but, when he pointed this out to her, she simply said he'd left her no choice. She insisted that he'd chosen their paths when he stopped loving her. She had successfully disassociated herself from all responsibility. He'd tried to tell himself that it wasn't entirely his fault. Sophie wasn't one for forgiving and forgetting. She attached herself to grudges and grievances like a leech on bad blood; rehashing and revisiting, remembering and reviving the hurtful anger each time. So he had no choice either. But then he was the one who had put them on a path where there were no opportunities for U-turns. He sighed. Sophie's words, "You chose this," tossed at him with indecent regularity, had hit their target, wounding him.

It *was* his fault.

As this mess was Ted's fault.

The guys sat in silence for another two hours. The light faded around them, but neither of them moved to turn on more lamps.

The glow from the TV illuminated the room with a bluish hue. The drone of the French quiz shows and the occasional *pshuush* of a bottle top being eased off a beer bottle were the only sounds in the room. Lloyd wished he could be more useful. He felt his silence exposed his impotence. Ted thought his silence was sensitive and had never admired his friend more. Eventually Lloyd stood up. "I'd better get going. Kate will be back soon. Are you going to talk to her?"

Ted shrugged. He certainly felt braver and better for telling his story for the first time, but he wasn't sure if he was ready to confront Kate.

"Well, look, be careful. You know, look after yourself, buddy." Lloyd wondered if he should offer to lend Ted some money, but he had the sense to realize anything he could spare would be a Band-Aid trying to patch a severed limb. Instead he stuttered, "I'm here, right. If you . . . need . . . well . . . anything . . ." He felt very Californian.

"Don't worry, old chap. I'm not going to fling myself off a mountain. It wouldn't do any good. My life insurance wouldn't cover the debt I'm in." Lloyd grinned, pleased that Ted was trying to make a joke, however weak. At least he was trying to fit the affable, easygoing persona that he'd worn so comfortably throughout his life. "But seriously, Lloyd, thanks for the concern."

Lloyd closed the door behind him.

# 38

## *Showtime*

The cinema was surprisingly busy, despite the heavy-duty arty film that was showing.

"Even on holiday the French need to feed their intellect is apparent," commented Mia. She loved the French. They were so learned, and elegant, and imbued with a haughty, unapologetic sophistication that Mia yearned to ape. "It goes to show you can never underestimate the French love of culture," she added.

Or torture, thought Kate. It didn't surprise her that they had invented the guillotine.

Despite the popularity of the sepia-toned film—mostly about suicide and urban cruelty, as Kate had expected—the gang of friends managed to secure a line of seats. Kate sat next to Mia, who had wangled a seat next to Scaley. Jason hadn't needed to do much to ensure that he was sitting next to Jayne. He was flattered to see that she made quite a fuss to squeeze in between him and Rich, although she hadn't responded that well when he'd tried to put his arm around her shoulders as they'd walked here tonight. She had sort of shrugged him off. Still, it wasn't as though they were an actual couple. He could understand her not wanting to appear too "together" in front of all of the others. But then she had kissed him on the slopes in front of Rich today, so the message was a bit mixed.

Jase didn't care enough to think about that more. He was happy that they were sharing a Diet Coke and that she kept flashing her fantastic smile and cleavage. He was a betting man, and he thought that the odds were on that she'd sleep with him tonight. There was a slim chance that she'd be the type of girl to keep him waiting until the end of the week, but he didn't think so. Jason didn't come across teases too frequently in the world in which he lived.

Jayne wiggled in her seat, crossing and uncrossing her legs. The process somehow involved her toe sliding all the way up Rich's calves. He glared at her, and she responded with a wink.

Rich fidgeted in his seat, too. He stretched his long legs out into the aisle and away from Jayne. Then he folded his arms protectively around himself so that she couldn't accidentally weave her fingers around his—well, he wouldn't put it past her. How obvious did she want to be? Someone was going to think something was going on if she didn't stop pestering him. In addition to the frankly shocking show with the fakies, at dinner she'd laughed at all his pathetic jokes and—no false modesty—he knew he wasn't being particularly funny. Still, Jayne had laughed loudly and was behaving as though she thought he was more hilarious than Johnny Vegas and Ricky Gervais rolled into one. And she laid her hand on his arm whenever she was talking to him. He supposed it could just be interpreted as a friendly gesture, but it was very friendly and none of the others knew they were particular friends.

Not that he was saying they were particular friends, but, you know.

It was confusing.

It was a good thing that Tash was such a friendly, tactile and trusting person herself; she didn't think Jayne's behavior was odd. The others might begin to, though. Mia, for example. She had a nose for this kind of thing. He couldn't risk anyone associating the two of them beyond the acknowledged acquaintance. He didn't like finding himself sitting next to Jayne. He'd be more comfortable if he was sitting with Kate at the other end of the row. Or, better yet, if he was with Tash. A fleeting stab of anger hit

Rich. Tash should be here. Going to bed was selfish and unsociable. She should be here, protecting him. Rich was immediately embarrassed by his own thoughts. Tash wasn't selfish. She was probably exhausted and she had every right to say no to the film. Besides, he didn't need protecting. That was a ridiculous thought. Protecting from what? Little Jayne.

"Popcorn?" Jayne offered the carton to Rich.

He opened his mouth to decline politely. He didn't want anything from her, not even her bloody popcorn. But as he went to say so, Jayne quickly dropped a piece into his mouth. She let her beautifully manicured finger gently drag on his lip, just for a nanosecond. Miffed and stunned, he turned his head back toward the film, carefully chewing the popcorn with his mouth firmly shut.

He couldn't follow the film. To be totally frank, he held the same opinion as Tash about French films. He found them self-consciously clever, a bit too pleased with themselves. And what had they to be pleased about? The plots were all the same—very beautiful and intense youths doing unspeakable things to themselves, drugs, prostitution etc. All in the name of art. And he couldn't keep track of who was whom because everyone looked the same—in other words, not much like real people. Not even the good-looking real people he knew. He hadn't liked *Betty Blue,* not even when it reached cult status when he was studying. Not that he'd ever admitted as much. He, like every other undergraduate, had raved that the film was profound and moving beyond belief. But it had just been depressing. He didn't mind having a poster on his wall, though. The actress Béatrice Dalle was hot.

Jase was whispering something to Jayne, again. She smiled at whatever he said, again. He wished they'd shut up. They'd been whispering to one another throughout the film and it was bad manners, even if it was a bad film. Rich hissed a shush which just caused Jayne to giggle.

"No need to be jealous, babe," Jayne whispered in Rich's ear. He could feel her breath on the back of his neck, and it made his hair stand on end. Her lips almost brushed his earlobes.

"I'm not jealous," he snapped. Jayne smiled, believing she knew better. "I just can't follow the film if you are chatting. My French isn't good enough."

"You are so sweet," simpered Jayne, and she landed a light peck on his cheek.

Rich was incensed beyond words. He checked along the line of his friends' faces, to see if any of them had caught Jayne's kiss. It didn't look as though they had; their eyes were glued to the screen, brows furrowed in concentration as they attempted to deconstruct the bizarre plot. Rich stood up and marched into the foyer. Like a shadow, Jayne followed him.

# 39

## *A Big Joke*

Rich punched open the auditorium door. The plastic made a loud thwacking sound as it bounced back into place. Rich found that satisfying, but couldn't deny that he had an urge to thwack something else.

He was shaking. Was it fear? Anger? Shit, was it lust? *Was* he jealous of Jayne and Jase? Surely not. Had Jayne's not-so-subtle table show turned him on? Impossible. How was she managing to aggravate him so? There was a water fountain in the foyer. He walked directly to it and ran his face under the flow.

The water had the desired effect. Rich's smudgy head cleared.

It was not lust. He did not desire Jayne. On paper she was knockout; in reality, she was flipping him out. She could ruin everything. He had given her the power to ruin his life. He was afraid and then angry, and then afraid again. He felt a long fingernail trace the vertebra of his spine as he bent over the water faucet. Shit, she'd followed him out of the auditorium. He straightened, scowled and set off along the corridor toward the loos.

"We need to talk, babe," said Jayne, as she made short, determined steps to follow him.

"Oh, no, we don't," he replied. "We have nothing to say to one another."

"Why are you being like this?" she asked.

"Me? *Me?*" Rich turned to face Jayne, but pointed at himself. "Me being like this?" he asked, amazed. "I'm not being like anything. It's you who is being out of order." She laid her hand on his arm again, and he pulled away as though she'd scalded him

"Don't touch me," he bit out. "OK, this isn't funny now. These innuendos and the following me about, it's just not funny. You've had your giggle, now stop it," spat Rich.

"I can't lose you again," replied Jayne.

Rich thought he must be speaking a foreign tongue. Why couldn't he get through to this girl? She couldn't lose him again because she'd never found him. He'd never been hers to lose. He paused and studied her. She was at least a foot shorter than him. She was entirely pick-up-and-play, and he used to love that. He'd enjoyed flipping her every which way in the sack. Now he wished she was bigger. He felt ignoble that his adversary was so dinky. But at the same time he feared that her power was enormous.

She gazed up at him, and he had to admit she was cute. Or at least she would be if she weren't wearing that ridiculous expression. Her look put him in mind of his older sister gazing adoringly at the Donny Osmond posters Blu-Tacked to her bedroom wall. His sister had been about ten years old when she last wore that expression, and he'd thought it was soppy back then. Jayne could not be serious.

Suddenly Rich saw a ray of light.

This was a joke. The whole thing. Jase was probably in on it. He was probably trying to get his own back because somehow he'd found out about Rich having sex with Jayne on the sly, and his nose was out of joint because Rich had kept a secret from him. That's why he'd gone on about fancying Jayne when they were on the slopes today. Jase was probably hoping to force a confession from Rich. Bloody hell. Rich started to giggle. The relief was enormous. The bastard. Jase was a bastard, a funny bastard admittedly, but a bastard nonetheless. But thank God that this was a joke. A containable joke. Tash wasn't going to find out that he'd lied to her. He was safe. This was all a gag. Because this Donny Osmond groupie approach just couldn't be serious.

"What's this about, Jayne? Is this a joke?" Rich was tittering like John Travolta in those early scenes of *Grease* when he doesn't want to look uncool in front of the T-Birds. "You and Jase, you are having a laugh, aren't you? This is—" Rich didn't finish his sentence. If they were having a laugh, then Jayne was taking her role to the extreme.

"Don't be silly, Richie, babe. I want you. I want you more than any man alive, and I've only ever wanted you. This isn't a joke. Why would I joke about something as serious as us?"

"There isn't an 'us.' There's never been an 'us.'" Rich was aware that he was almost shouting, and so wrenched his voice back under control by the end of the sentence. The final "us" was issued like a hiss.

"Oh, Richie, babe, don't say such things." Jayne leaned toward him and hugged him. She nuzzled her face into his jacket and, if he wasn't mistaken, she was sniffing him.

Rich saw his hope that Jase and Jayne were having a laugh at his expense vanish in an instant. Sadly, his first theory, that she was a raving nutcase, was more likely to be true. Rich couldn't move. He wanted to push her away, but didn't know how to. He took a deep breath and tried to stay calm. What had she just said, she wanted him? Rich's mind searched frantically for another way of not facing up to the situation.

That was it, she wanted him. Her pride had been dented. He *had* been a little unceremonious in his exit, he supposed. Clearly she wanted to get him to the point where he admitted he still fancied her and then she'd back off. She'd have clawed back a little self-respect. She didn't *really* want him. She just wanted him to want her. It wasn't exactly mature, but that was women for you, all mind games, never played anything straight. She'd never wanted him in all those years when they were . . . well, not together. Because they weren't ever together. But, in all those years when they . . . had sex. She'd never once hinted that she'd like to take the sex further than that. He'd just say some nice things to her and then she'd back off.

"Look, Jayne, you are a very attractive girl."

Jayne broke away from the embrace, and laughed, "I know that."

She tossed her hair and sort of stuck out her tits, in one practiced move. Clearly she thought she was being irresistible. She put Rich in mind of a very expensive hooker he'd once hired for Jason's thirtieth birthday present. Rich shook his head and grinned. She was an odd one. Lacking in confidence one minute, brimming with it the next.

"You are a stunner, and a very clever lady, too."

Rich wanted to sound sincere, or at least smooth. He was aware, however, that he sounded like his father or even his grandfather—patronizing and dated. His throat was squeezed with stress. He didn't know how to adjust the tone of his voice and couldn't think of anything convincing, let alone truthful, to say.

"You could do loads better than me," he said, although he was aware that in reality no one ever minded shooting out of their league. "Why are you wasting your time with me? What you should be doing is concentrating your energies on working things out with that boyfriend of yours."

"What boyfriend?" asked Jayne, her dreamy look momentarily interrupted by a bemused one.

"The boy—" Rich corrected himself, "the man that you split up with just before you came here. The one that upset you so much that Kate and Ted were worried about you."

Jayne started to laugh, "Babe, I thought I'd explained when we were on the slopes yesterday. That is *you*. I was talking about *you*."

She was staring at Rich as though she were his mother and he was four years old. His crime? Something small and boyish, like eating a snail or refusing to say thank you for the gift of a sweet. Her expression was supposed to look stern, but the effect was blurred by the wide, indulgent smile.

"I know we've broken up before, but we'd always made up pretty quickly. This time you hurt me, babe."

"Is that how you see it, breaking up and making up?"

"Yes, of course."

"But we were never a couple. And will you stop calling me 'babe.'" Tash called Rich "babe." Jayne called everyone "darling." What was she playing at?

Jayne exaggerated her indulgent-mother-of-four-year-old-troublemaker look, and Rich thought he might laugh. This was comical, or it would be if it were happening to anyone else.

"Don't say such silly things. Not to me. Admittedly we weren't conventional, but we were a couple. You even met my mum and dad," said Jayne.

"You didn't introduce me. It wasn't as though you took me home for tea. I met your mum and dad at Kate and Ted's wedding. Ted is your brother and that means you happen to have parents in common," insisted Rich. Jayne tutted as though he were splitting hairs over an insignificant detail. "You are scaring me, Jayne. Look, don't take this the wrong way, but I think you need help."

"I love you."

Rich started to laugh. "Yeah, right."

He looked at Jayne again, and she hadn't moved a muscle. She was still staring at him with those dopy, droopy eyes and that lost-puppy look. He couldn't remember her eyes during sex, but he was pretty sure she'd never worn that expression. She'd been feisty. She'd been fun.

That was all she'd been.

But now. God.

"You can't love me."

But even as he said it Rich was already terrified that Jayne did think she was in love with him, which was much, much worse than her teasing him or playing with him. Women in love did peculiar things. Tash, for example, had agreed to marry him after knowing him for only a couple of months. Although he was delighted that she had, he did think it was a bit extreme. Scorned women in love were even worse; they were scarily extreme. They scratched cars with keys, cut holes in suits, sowed cress into your carpet. Women were bitter, vengeful and excessive. You read about it all the time in *GQ* and *Loaded.*

Rich was standing with his back to the cinema auditorium so he didn't see the door swing open and Mia emerging from the darkness, looking for the loo. Jayne did. It was fate. This was her moment. She lurched upward and passionately kissed Rich. Although she was much smaller than he was, she stole the advantage by taking him by surprise. She pushed him until he was backed against the wall and had nowhere to go. Jayne ran her hands up and down his shoulders, arms and hips. She grabbed at his buttocks. She'd closed her eyes, but opened them again, just long enough to ensure that Mia had clocked them. Mia had. She was far too cool to stand openmouthed and gape—instead she walked passed them, coughing loudly, then slipped into the loos.

The whole episode took a moment in real time. It played out as a year of agony in Rich's head and unlimited ecstasy in Jayne's.

Her lips were familiar, insomuch as they were no different from hundreds of others he had kissed. He had opened his mouth, just a fraction, as an automatic response and not because he was attracted to her. He wasn't even thinking about the kiss in terms of it being a kiss. He couldn't have been because, in the same second that he noticed she was kissing him, he'd noticed that the wallpaper was frayed at the edges of the skirting board and you wouldn't notice that if you were really kissing, would you? Jayne's neat little tongue had found the gap between his teeth and darted forward to massage the inside of his mouth. It wasn't awful, Rich thought. The tongue wasn't, the wallpaper was. Of course it wasn't awful. Kissing her had always been sexy. But it wasn't right. No, this wasn't right.

And then he saw Mia where the wallpaper had been, out of the corner of his eye. What would she think? Well, it was fucking obvious what she would think.

Oh, no. No. No. Shit.

Rich pushed Jayne off him. She gave up her grasp at the exact same moment, so his shove sent her lurching against the wall on the opposite side of the corridor. "I like it when you play rough," she said with a grin.

"You are fucking insane. Now get in there and explain to Mia what's going on," he yelled, pointing toward the girls' loos.

"What should I say, exactly? Would you like me to tell her that we've been lovers for years?"

*"No!"* Rich stared at Jayne in disbelief until she turned fuzzy at the edges.

"Babe, don't cry. We've got each other, whatever happens," she cooed.

She leaned forward and started to caress his head. Her long, cool fingers traced out the lines on his forehead. She kissed his jaw, tiny, little nibbling kisses. Rich was crying. Fuck, he couldn't remember when he'd last cried. But she made him so angry. Why did she insist on distorting things? Twisting things? Making more of it than there ever was? Why would she want to ruin his marriage? Surely she didn't really believe that, if she ruined his relationship with Tash, he'd turn to her and say, "Oh, well, never mind. You're free, aren't you? Would *you* like to marry me instead?" How fucking mad was this girl? She was a fuck buddy. Someone he had recreational sex with. That was all. And yet looking at her now— as she caressed him, rested her head on his chest and hugged him, looked back up into his eyes and smiled at him—you would be forgiven for believing that they were passionate lovers in the midst of a soul-searching argument.

Which is exactly what Mia did think.

"Excuse me," she said pointedly, as she reemerged from the loo.

Rich tried to break from Jayne's grasp. Jayne clung more tightly. "This isn't what it looks like," said Rich quickly. "Honestly, Mi, you have to believe me."

"None of my business, Action Man," she said. She threw out an efficient smile, one which wasn't meant to warm anyone.

"Tell her, Jayne. Tell her," insisted Rich. Jayne refused to say anything. Instead she looked at the floor, knowing Mia wouldn't be able to bring herself to think anything but the worst. Mia cheerfully raised her eyebrows as she grinned at Rich and said, "Leopards can't change their spots." She shook her head from side to side in mock despair, and returned to the film.

Rich watched Mia walk away and wondered if he could persuade her to keep quiet. He doubted it. On recent evidence it appeared that he wasn't very good at persuading women to do the things he wanted them to do. He used to have a knack for it, but looking at Jayne now, smiling at him like a mad Cheshire cat, he realized he'd lost that power somewhere along the way.

He was done for. Where had he gone wrong? He turned back to Jayne.

"I didn't take anything you weren't keen to give away. I never encouraged you to think we were anything other than . . ." Rich searched around for the correct word. ". . . anything at all," he finished.

"We were lovers."

"We had sex." Rich didn't even want to say they'd fucked. Saying they'd fucked sounded more involved than he wanted to admit to.

"It was more than that. We were more than that."

"No, we weren't."

"We were and by denying me you are admitting as much."

"What?" Rich was completely bemused. He leaned against the wall, took a deep breath, dropped his head into his hands, then thought it looked defeatist and so altered the gesture mid-maneuver to look as though he were simply running his fingers through his hair.

"You didn't tell Natasha about me. That proves I was significant."

"No, the opposite."

"This wedding isn't going to happen."

"You're crazy."

"Who is the crazy one, Rich? You or me? I fell in love with a man I had sex with for a decade. You denied I ever existed. Who is the most insane?"

# 40

## *Lost the Plot*

D espite Mia's love of French art house movies, she found it absolutely impossible to concentrate on the rest of the film. She would never know what became of any of the beautiful, nervy, floppy-haired characters. Not that it mattered, as she was jubilant. This result was better than she could have imagined. It took every ounce of restraint that she had not to lean over and whisper to Scaley Jase that he was wasting his time flirting with Jayne and he might as well father her child immediately. She knew she had to exercise *some* self-control.

Who would have thought it? Rich and Jayne? Mia was surprised. She didn't much rate Tash, but she'd thought Rich had. They'd appeared to be madly in love and they were days away from their wedding, for God's sake. What was Rich doing with his tongue down Jayne's throat? It didn't look like a first kiss. They definitely had history. Otherwise they'd both have laughed the incident off, dismissed it as a silly, drunken mistake. Still, whatever this meant for Tash and Rich, Mia hardly cared. The important thing was that, by default, Scaley Jase was once again available.

Neither Jayne nor Rich came back into the theater; Mia assumed they'd gone to find somewhere quiet to finish the business they'd started. Jason repeatedly looked back toward the door leading to the foyer, until Mia whispered to him that Jayne had grown bored with the film and gone on to a bar. They were to meet her there. This lie at least ensured Jason wouldn't call it a night straight after the film finished.

"Where are Rich and Jayne?" asked Kate as soon as the credits began to roll. She wanted to start up a conversation immediately because she didn't want to be drawn into a critical appraisal of the film. She had nothing to say about it because she never used expletives.

"Jayne's waiting for us at Bar de la Galerie, and I think Rich has decided to have an early night." Mia knew half of this was likely to be true.

"Very sensible," said Kate, yawning. "I'm going to hit the hay, too. I wonder if Ted will still be awake." Kate kissed the other two and said her good nights, congratulating herself that for two out of three nights she had avoided the bar. Jason and Mia zipped up their jackets and headed for Bar de la Galerie.

Jason pulled open the huge bar door and a cloud of noise, smoke and good-time vibe almost knocked them over. He grinned at Mia, and stepped forward confidently. Jason liked to be inside noisy, funky bars where conversation was often replaced by meaningful, loaded looks, slow drags on cigarettes and long slurps of cold beer. He considered himself a simple man.

Mia followed Scaley. She felt the beat of the current track bounce through her boots and rebound up her body. She swore her lungs, kidneys and heart were all internally dancing; only her rib cage stopped them escaping altogether. She was almost surprised to recognize the feelings of excitement and anticipation that came with having a good time. She'd forgotten how much fun could be had at a noisy, funky bar. It wasn't her recent scene. You were much more likely to find Mia enjoying a private supper or visiting an art gallery with a girlfriend. Kate said it was defeatist and repeatedly argued that Mia would never meet anyone like that.

Which was bloody rude.

Mia did not need to take romantic advice from Ms. Monopoly, thank you very much. Just because Ms. Monopoly was happily ensconced in la-la land, with the lovely, cuddly (and wealthy) Big Ted and their three perfect children. Just because Ms. Monopoly had everything Mia wanted, and more, was no reason for Mia suddenly to take advice from her on her love life. Everyone knew Ms. Monopoly was naïve beyond belief. She'd just got lucky with Big Ted. They'd both moved quickly before they, or anyone else, knew any better, and happily it had turned out OK. It was a bit of luck—it did not make Kate the grand master of all matters amorous.

Besides, in the not-so-distant past, Mia had visited more bars than Kate could begin to conceive. The bars she used to frequent in London were smarter than this one, the music was more obscure, the cocktail lists were longer, yet she never seemed to have much of a giggle no matter how many squashy leather chairs there were to lose yourself in, and no matter how many enormous vases of lilies were placed on the shiny mahogany coffee tables. Although, she did find those rain-forest-sized flower displays useful to hide behind if she didn't like the look of her date. Because, yes, she'd had blind dates.

After she'd dated every single male of her acquaintance and of her friends' acquaintance, after she'd followed up on every chance encounter and said yes to those guys who were nice enough but in fact not enough, after all of that—when she still hadn't found anyone who made her sides split with laughter, her panties leap with expectancy *and* her heart pound with the unknown (or, indeed, even one of the three)—she'd tried Internet dating, blind dates and, as Tash had accurately pointed out, even an ad in *Time Out*.

It wasn't that she couldn't find dates without resorting to these means, more that she couldn't meet anyone who "got" her, and she reasoned that she was looking in the wrong places. At least with an Internet profile she had the chance of meeting someone who knew their Claude Monet from their Édouard Manet. But they all looked like her uncles. Or someone else's uncle. Or maybe they looked OK and they knew their wines, but they didn't laugh much. Or they laughed too much, too loudly, too desperately. Or . . . well, whatever. There was always a reason that they weren't right, whether she met them in bars, at clubs or online.

So what did Ms. Monopoly know?

No matter now.

She had her plan.

It was a shame she couldn't have met someone like Scaley. In her extensive search she had never found that type of a man who knew when to say "Sorry," "Excuse me" and "Pardon." They always got that wrong. She had never met a man who was so entirely Colin Firth in front of the parents and Colin Farrell in bed. Scaley was. She liked the fact that even in bars without floral arrangements, but with damp walls instead, she still felt excited, alive, if she was with him. He was a man who took her seriously, but not too much so. Not as seriously as she took herself. He was a man who knew more than she did about Impressionist painters. He was the man who had made her feel genuinely relaxed this holiday, more so than yoga classes, aromatherapy massages or even a stiff gin and tonic.

A man who was currently craning his neck to look for another woman.

Mia pulled herself up short. She wasn't even drinking, why on earth was she indulging in this line of thought? Why was she viewing Scaley through rose-tinted glasses? It had to be her hormones. Definitely something to do with the time of the month. She remembered that time she flirted outrageously with the butcher on the deli counter in the Harvey Nichols store because he had strong hands. She temporarily forgot that, while in possession of ten big, manly digits, that was probably the amount of brain cells he had, too. He was totally unsuitable. And yet she had fancied him madly for five days and fantasized about the way he confidently picked up raw cuts of pork. She was mesmerized as he slapped the pieces on the scales and cheekily informed her that it was "a little bit over, but every girl likes a bit extra." She'd never eaten so much meat in her life as she did that week. She had been quite ill with indigestion. But then her obsession abruptly stopped as suddenly as it had started, coinciding exactly with her cycle. It was Mother Nature's way of trying to push her along, tell her to get out there and reproduce.

Scaley was just as unsuitable as the fat-fingered butcher, or the toy-boy banker-wankers, or the countless other five-day infatuations Mia had enjoyed. He was deeply unsuitable. He was a desperate, womanizing commitment phobe. He was old ground. She never traveled backward. They had nothing in common. He was exactly like the butcher.

Only brighter.

Stop it! Mia yelled at herself, almost frightening herself, she was formidable. OK, so she was on a high—the plan was back on track. But that was no excuse to get confused. Scaley Jase *was* exactly like the butcher only brighter, which made him the ideal sperm bank and nothing more.

"I wonder where Jayne's got to?"

Jase didn't want to appear keen in front of Mia, but on the other hand all he could think about was whether Jayne would show up and he'd get to see her tiny, lithe body writhing on the dance floor. Better yet that he might get to writhe with her both on the floor and in bed.

Mia sighed, and pulled her face into an expression that was supposed to convey sympathy. It was tricky when she wanted to give the air a euphoric punch of victory.

"You quite fancy Jayne, don't you?" she asked Jason. She had to yell very loudly to be heard above the music.

"No more than any other man," he lied. Not wanting to confess to fancying a woman who was possibly a no-show, despite the fact he'd been all but undressing her in public for the past forty-eight hours.

"Jayne, she's a regular package holiday, isn't she?" said Mia.

"What do you mean?" Until Mia had made that comment, she had managed to secure only about 10 percent of Jason's attention. She was sharing it with his attempt to catch the bartender's eye (and it did annoy her that even though he had a beer in his hand he was already trying to order his next one), his particular search for Jayne and a more general exploration of the dance floor as he eyed up any remotely attractive girl. It was habit. Mia's intriguing opener had guaranteed 100 percent of his interest, as she had known it would. She'd thrown him the line; he'd bitten. Now all she had to do was reel him in very, very carefully.

"Well, you get all the thrills and fun of a cheap, convenient deal. The only problem is you are off enjoying the holiday and the baggage arrives late. Late enough to ruin the whole shebang." Mia used the loud music as an excuse to lean in very close to Scaley Jase. Her breath was warm on his neck and her breast nudged his elbow.

"What are you talking about? Stop talking in clever metaphors. Just say what you want to say." Sometimes Mia's contrived cleverness really got on Jase's nerves, usually when he didn't know what she was being contriving and clever about.

"I don't know if I should say anything," said Mia cautiously. She knew that she had to appear reluctant. Elation was not a suitable response to uncovering a friend's infidelity.

"What baggage?"

"Look, I wouldn't have said anything if I'd thought you were interested in Jayne for yourself, but as you're not . . ." Mia paused for effect. She deserved an Oscar or at least a Grammy. "Well, I do need a bit of advice, and I have to tell someone." More warm breath, more breast brushing up against elbow.

"Tell someone what?"

"You probably know anyway, being so close to Rich and everything. I'm sure he's already confided in you, so I'm not gossiping." Mia's whisper was deep and husky, she sounded as though she smoked twenty a day—which indeed she had until she'd decided she wanted to conceive.

"What?" Jase almost shouted with barely contained excitement.

"About Rich and Jayne."

"Sorry?" Jason, usually the epitome of cool, spluttered into his beer and pulled away from Mia.

"I'd thought something was going on. They seemed to know each other beyond casual acquaintances, and they are always touching each other."

The penny dropped, nearly knocking Jason out cold. "They're having an affair, right?" He wanted to be wrong.

"Right," confirmed Mia.

Jason took another swig of his beer and concentrated on not moving his face so much as a fraction. First, he needed to decide which expression to settle into. What was appropriate? Raised eyebrows to show shock? Open mouth to show horror? Or a lewd wink that suggested his best friend playing away on his prenuptial holiday was entirely acceptable? Jase remembered that he was with Mia and so decided he didn't need to act. His face twisted with hurt.

"He's never said anything to me."

And oddly that was why Jason was feeling hurt. Not the fact that his latest would-be conquest had been conquered by someone else. All thoughts of Jayne's fantastic blow job and the promise of as yet undiscovered delights in the sack vanished. The fantasy of Jayne making a great steady girlfriend disappeared instantly, even faster than its admittedly rapid appearance. After all, there were always other fish in the sea. But the fact that Rich had kept something so mammoth a secret from him—that betrayal stung.

"I saw them kissing in the foyer of the cinema this evening."

Jason tried to compute this information.

"That's not necessarily an affair. Neither of them has confided in you, have they?"

"Neither of them bothered to deny it," said Mia. "They do work together, so it's possible. They've spent a lot of time together this hol. They clearly get along. Thinking about it, Jayne suits Rich better than Tash does."

Mia needed Jason to believe that Rich and Jayne were something of an item. If they were simply having a meaningless fling (his last and her rebound), then Jason would not move on from wanting Jayne. In fact, he would probably see her willingness to be a slut as a definite turn-on. Mia knew that neither Jase nor Rich was squeamish about sloppy seconds and had a number of past conquests in common. Herself included.

"Poor Tash," muttered Jase.

This startled Mia. She was so wrapped up in her own scheme that she had failed to consider how the consequences of this liaison would affect anyone but her.

"Suppose," she admitted grumpily. Mia rarely spared sympathy for women who had been cheated on. There were too many of them; it would be an endless and exhausting mission. Jase finally managed to catch the bartender's attention. He ordered two double whiskies. He pushed one toward Mia and downed the other himself. He immediately repeated the order.

"What are you going to do?" he asked Mia.

"Do?" She was confused.

"Are you going to tell Tash?"

"Hell, no."

"Don't you think you should?"

"It's not my business."

"Well, it sort of is, now that you know."

"You know, too. What are you going to do?" asked Mia, lobbying the ball of moral responsibility firmly back over the net toward Jason.

"Right now, I'm going to get very drunk and then . . ." Scaley Jase paused and looked around the dance floor. His eyes rested on a girl of about twenty years old who was wildly circling around her friend as though her friend was a pole in a Spearmint Rhino lap-dancing bar. Clearly very drunk already, she was strutting her not particularly funky stuff in a clumsy but amusing way. She wore a short denim skirt and a white boob tube. She was amply endowed and so she repeatedly had to hike it up because her enthusiastic dance movements were in danger of leaving her exposed. She wore too much make-up, even by Jase's standards.

"And, then, I am going to sleep with her, if she wants to," said Jason.

# TUESDAY

# 41

## The Morning After

Jason woke up next to the busty bottle blonde. He gently shook her awake and asked if she wanted him to order her a room service breakfast, before she left. They both knew that he was extending a courtesy by offering breakfast, but also making it clear that was all he was offering. The bottle blonde was young and resilient. She didn't want breakfast, but she did ask if she could take the toiletries from the bathroom before she headed back to the apartment that she was sharing with five other, similarly uncomplicated girls.

"Sure, and, look, maybe we can hook up again. Maybe tonight?" offered Jason. He didn't intend doing so, but, on the other hand, he didn't intend not to do so.

"Maybe." The girl shrugged.

Jason had been good at the oral stuff. She *had* enjoyed sex with him. She'd noticed before that tequila slammers made her particularly horny. But in the daylight, and now she was sober, he looked very old. He had wrinkles around his eyes that last night looked distinguished, but this morning they were just sad. And he had gray pubes—it was horrifying. She wasn't sure she'd want her friends seeing her with him again. Besides, she didn't really believe that stuff he'd spouted last night about him owning a penthouse pad in Soho and a Porsche Boxster. This meant that he was a prick for making it up.

"I'm going to bloody freeze getting back to my apartment," she moaned, as she wriggled into her minuscule skirt and boob tube. Jase gave her a Ralph Lauren sweater and the money to call a horse and sleigh. He knew he'd never see his sweater again, but he wanted to feel like a gentleman.

He gave the girl a perfunctory kiss on the cheek and, as the door closed behind her, he wandered into the bathroom and turned on the shower. He felt like crap, and it wasn't the one-night stand. He was male and incapable of understanding why anyone would feel anything other than marvelous about achieving a one-night stand. It wasn't even his hangover.

It was Rich.


Last night, after the farce in the cinema, Rich had rushed out of the foyer and fled to the hotel. He hadn't looked back. He didn't know where Jayne had gone, whether she'd returned to watch the rest of the film or not, and he didn't care. For all he cared she could have flung herself off the side of a mountain. In fact, that was the only favor she could do him.

Rich hadn't given any thought to what the others would think if he disappeared. He just wanted to be with Tash and only Tash. He had decided that he would tell her.

He'd tell her everything.

He'd tell her that he hadn't included Jayne in his accounts of his exploits. And he was sorry about that. That he'd had sex with her on and off for an age. And that he wasn't exactly proud of that. And he'd tell her that Jayne was trying to . . . what? Seduce him? And that he didn't want that. It sounded ludicrous. Why would any man be affronted by Jayne trying to seduce them? It sounded like a lie, a cover-up. What if Tash didn't believe him?

When he'd got back to their room Tash was already asleep. She'd fallen to sleep still grasping her novel, and she was sort of smiling. She looked so peaceful and relaxed.

Rich felt lonely.

For the first time since he had met Tash, Rich felt that they were operating in entirely different worlds. When they'd arrived at Avoriaz, they were so in sync with one another. Their lives were moving along in harmony, but now Tash slept soundly and he was full of despair. He resented her ignorance, and yet he had no one to blame for the new status quo except himself.

And, bloody Jayne.

He convinced himself that if Tash had been awake he would have followed his plan and told her all about Jayne, but he decided not to wake her to do so. If he did, he'd be lending the incident yet more import than it deserved. It would be better if he told her in the morning. Things were always better in the morning.

While Tash's sleep had been deep, Rich's had been fitful. He'd been plagued with nightmares of being gobbled up by a giant caterpillar. In his dream he'd called to Tash to rescue him, but she'd ignored him. It didn't take Freud to interpret that one.

Despite his fitful sleep, when he woke up Rich did feel a little better than he had the night before. The sun was shining into their room and, as he looked out of the window on to the slopes, the view calmed and soothed. Like yesterday, the slopes were beautifully groomed and as new. He wished that everything could be wiped clean so simply.

Rich decided to dress in silence and get onto the slopes before Tash woke. It wasn't that he was avoiding her—it was just that boarding would clear his mind. He was sure that out there, on the immaculate slopes, he'd find the correct words to explain his situation to Tash. Words that would at once absolve him and help to maintain her confidence and love. He couldn't find those words in their hot bed.

Rich was delighted to find Scaley Jase in the hotel foyer. It was almost as though Jason could sense when his friend needed him most. Rich shook his hand and leaned in to hug him in a way he was pretty confident was pretty manly. Rich always felt easier with male–male physical contact in Europe. After all, Italian and Greek men held hands and it didn't mean they were gay. Rich didn't go as far as holding Jason's hand, but he patted Jase on the back as though they hadn't seen one another for weeks.

Jase thought Rich was behaving like a man who'd just scored. He wondered if it was with Jayne or Tash.

"I was waiting for you," explained Jase. "I've already planned a route." Jase pulled out a map and started to discuss the business of the day. "Let's ride the Avoriaz to Les Crosets route, to start with. Get over to number forty-nine lift, do the Du Tour run down to Proclou. Then, if I'm not dead, which I might be because that is a bloody hard run, pick up Seraussaix to Quemont, or Du Baron-down to Tetras. Whichever. Then you can come down Super Morzine, but I'm going to take the lift as it's another tough run and, while I am fucking top on my board, I have only been on it for a few days. The estimated time is just thirty minutes, so we'll probably take anything between fifteen minutes and four hours, depending on the level of injury sustained." Jason folded away the map. "Then we'll go to a park."

Inwardly, Rich sighed with relief. He was so grateful that he was a boy and could avoid any emotional issue, if he played fast and hard enough.

# 42

## *Rich and Jayne's Story*

W ho are you looking for?" asked Jason.
        Rich had performed reasonably well on the slopes and
the park all morning, having fallen only twice, but clearly he wasn't
giving the boarding his full attention. He wasn't being daring, he
wasn't allowing himself to become absorbed. Instead he nervously
and repeatedly checked over his shoulder. He was expecting that
at any minute Jayne would pop out from behind an evergreen and
shout, "Surprise!" Clearly he wasn't being rational. They hadn't told
anyone where they were. Avoriaz was enormous. She'd have a difficult job in tracking them down.

Still, he couldn't relax.

"Let's get a hot chocolate," replied Rich, avoiding the question. He checked his watch. "It's nearly one o'clock, I'm starving.
I think I'll get a crêpe, too."

Jason and Rich found an eatery on the edge of the piste and
boarded to the door. They clicked out of their bindings and firmly
wedged their boards in half a meter of snow. They ordered a stack
of crêpes and some hot chocolate.

Jason, normally so effervescent, the reigning master of amusing small talk, had decided to remain stonily silent that morning.
His silence was partly to afford opportunity to Rich, if Rich did
decide he wanted to confide in him (and this was Jase's hope), and
partly because he was sulking that Rich hadn't confided as yet.
The technique worked.

"I find myself in a bit of a difficult situation," said Rich as he handed Jason a mug of hot chocolate.

They made their way outside toward a wooden picnic bench and sat down to munch on their crêpes.

"Oh?" grunted Jason, not turning to look at his friend, who was staring out to the horizon anyway.

"It's, er . . . Jayne. You know you were on about her the other day and you, er . . . you were wondering whether she goes like a train . . . well, she does."

Despite the seriousness of his situation, Rich couldn't stop the flashback forcing its way into his mind. Jayne was pure fire in the sack, and years of taking pride in such lays was a tough habit to break, he grinned to himself. Jase turned to him just in time to catch the grin subside, and irritation shot through his body like electricity.

"Why didn't you tell me?"

"I'm telling you now."

"Why didn't you tell me before?"

Rich didn't want to admit the truth, which was that he hadn't needed to tell Jason before, but now he'd discovered that Jayne was a psycho and Mia had caught them kissing, and there was a need. Even in his self-obsessed and distracted state he could tell that Jason was clearly affronted by the lack of confidence. God, if he felt slighted, Rich could only imagine the hurt Tash would register.

He searched for another explanation. "It was awkward. What, with her being Ted's sister."

"We're all adults," argued Jason.

Rich sighed and decided, due to lack of choices, to be honest. He thought back to when he first slept with Jayne and unearthed the reason he'd remained shtoom about his conquest ever since. "We weren't then, or, rather, only just."

"I'm not following."

"It was a long time ago. It was legal and everything," Rich rushed to justify. "Just," he added. "I was a sort of birthday present." Jason looked confused. Rich struggled to make himself clear, but shame tore at his vocal cords and reasoning. "Do you remember she came up to the college for her sixteenth birthday, which coincided with our first year Summer Ball?"

"I remember the ball. I can't say I remember Jayne being there."

"No reason you should. Everyone was smashed."

"So you slipped her the sausage. Hid the long yard?" Jason was trying to pull this confession into familiar territory. The pair was used to describing their sexual exploits in ludicrously crude terms.

Rich refused to meet him on common ground; he was too uncomfortable. "I've always felt bad about it."

"Why? She's fit. Nothing to be ashamed of."

Rich sighed. She hadn't been back then. She'd been a plain-looking schoolgirl, not the sexy siren she was now. Suddenly it was clear to him. Rich knew why he had been unable to tell Tash about Jayne—he was ashamed. Not of the way she looked—back in those days any hole was a goal. But she was a schoolgirl. Just sixteen that day, and he had been nineteen. A man. Something in the back of his mind, then and ever since, told him that Jayne had not been quite ready. Not as robust and sophisticated as she liked to pretend. He'd pretended to believe her faux sophistication because it had suited him.

He rubbed his hands together to try to create some heat. "Look, I was drunk. Everyone was. She was." It had been his justification then, and he held on to it now.

"She did want it, didn't she?" asked Jason carefully.

"God, yes, begging for it. Of course," Rich was offended. "What do you take me for?"

"Well, then, no big deal," said Jase, relieved. "Everyone has to have a first time, mate. Sixteen is legal, as you said. You did her a favor. At least you knew what you were doing. Better than a fumble with some spotty virgin."

It was true that by nineteen years old Rich wasn't exactly the splendid sexual specialist that he was now, but he had had several notches on his bedpost which made him the envy of his peers.

"Is that why you didn't want her here? Because of some ancient history?"

Rich played with a promotional leaflet that was propped between the cinnamon shaker and the sugar bowl; it advertised heliboarding and nighttime skiing. Rich fancied both of these activities, so the leaflet offered a legitimate distraction. He steadfastly refused to meet Jason's eye. But they knew each other too well.

"That wasn't the only time, was it?" demanded Jason.

"No."

"You did her again." Rich nodded, reluctantly. "When?"

"She moved to London when she was twenty-one. She looked me up. She used the excuse that she was going into management consultancy, like me. And so we met up for a couple of drinks so that I could give her some career pointers."

"And that wasn't the only point you gave her," snickered Jason. He always found it mildly erotic to think about his friends' conquests; he never analyzed this.

"We ended up in bed and then, er, well, have ended up there, on and off, ever since. It's just a casual thing."

"*A casual thing?* A casual thing that's lasted a decade?" Jason stamped the snow from his boots. Rich couldn't work out if the gesture was one of pride in his mate's antics or fury. It was neither. Jason was stamping his feet because he was cold.

"Yeah, well, almost a decade," admitted Rich.

"Shit."

"Exactly."

"Are you still . . . ?"

"No, no." Rich was quick to reassure. "I called it off when I met Tash. Once I met her I didn't want anyone else."

Jason wasn't going to let him off the hook that easily. "So what was last night? One for old time's sake?"

"Oh. Mia told you?"

"Yes."

"Well, I called it off, but Jayne doesn't seem to accept that it's over."

"Christ. She's sore?"

"Very. It's not as though it was a relationship or anything. It was just sex. Strictly after hours."

Jason took a deep breath, and all this information, in. He was glad that Mia had misread the situation and that Rich wasn't in the midst of a passionate affair with Jayne just days before he married Tash.

Jase liked Tash.

But then, Jase liked *liked* Jayne.

He felt slightly sickened. How could Rich treat Jayne so casually, so disrespectfully? Jayne was lovely, intelligent and funny. She was also that scary thing that all men should avoid in casual sex, she was deep. Deep was one step away from mad. Mad was miles away from discreet.

And then there was Jason's main concern. "Mate, how could you?"

"What?"

"Have sex with someone for over a decade and not even mention it to me. I thought we told each other everything."

"Sorry. Yeah. Like I said, it was complicated. A tricky situation."

The truth was wild horses wouldn't have dragged a confession out of Rich if Jayne hadn't turned up at his wedding party. His feelings for her were an ugly mix of lust and shame and guilt and fear. Not something he was prepared to share over a bottle of designer beer and a game of soccer on TV.

"You are so fucking lucky, mate," said Jason.

Rich felt about as lucky as the guy who had won a couple of tickets to see the World Cup final but didn't have a passport.

"You've lost me," he sighed.

"Well, Tash has to be the coolest babe on the planet to be dealing with all this, to have allowed Jayne here in the first place. You've really picked someone special there, mate. You lucky bastard."

Jase didn't think Rich deserved to be this lucky. He didn't deserve ten years of secret, no-strings-attached sex with sexy Jayne, let alone deserve to have found such an understanding *and* foxy life partner in Tash. Rich was a bastard with women. But, then again, Jason was a bastard with women, too, and also one of the great undeserving. Rich's story gave him hope.

"She doesn't know," sighed Rich.

Jason was aghast. "But I thought you two didn't keep secrets from one another. The pair of you are always going on about how honesty makes your relationship. I thought you told each other everything." Maybe not the making out last night, Jason mentally conceded, but the history, surely.

"Everything but this. Mate, I didn't even tell you this, how could I tell Tash?"

While Jason found this reassuringly flattering, he also saw his friend's dilemma. How could Rich treat Tash so dishonestly, so disrespectfully? Tash was lovely, intelligent and funny.

"Do you think Mia will say anything to Tash?" asked Rich.

"I doubt it. They're hardly bosom buddies."

"Don't you think so? I hoped they'd get on."

"Well, they don't," Jase stated. He was amazed that Rich could have missed this. Clearly he was self-delusional. "And you want to thank your lucky stars that Mia doesn't consider herself Tash's friend and doesn't think she owes her any girlie loyalty or honesty."

"You don't think she'd say anything out of spite, though, do you?" Rich panicked.

"No. Mia's too rational for that."

The guys fell silent. They were both thinking that the same reassurance could not be given about Jayne. Jason wanted to bolster his friend, but wasn't sure if he could.

"I thought she was OK with the arrangement and cool when I called it off. But, looking back, I wonder if it is coincidence that out of all the management consultancies in London she just so happened to end up working in mine. And just before we came away I got a memo introducing a new member of staff into my division. Guess who?"

"Jayne."

"Correct. Give the man a cuddly toy. Then she wangles an invite to my bloody wedding. I bought all that crap about her needing to be here as she was getting over an ex because—"

"You wanted to."

"Exactly. And then every time I turn round, on the slopes, in the hotel, she's there."

"Right." Jason nodded.

"Dropping hints, being indiscreet. She's showing signs of being a . . ." Rich didn't want to finish the sentence.

"Bunny boiler," confirmed Jason.

"Exactly. And finally, last night, she tells me she loves me."

"Oh, mate."

"Exactly." Rich realized that he was repeating the decisive and certain word precisely because he did not feel either decisive or certain of anything. "What should I do?"

Tension and panic had drained the blood from Rich's face so that if it wasn't for his ultrahip black Salomon jacket and trousers he would be entirely camouflaged against the snow. His tan sat uncomfortably on his face, red blotches against a pale canvas, reminding Jason of a kid's coloring book where splashes of color are clumsily applied.

"Did you ever give her anything?"

Rich looked at Jason, unable to hide his disgust. "You mean like herpes?"

"No. Mate, I know you well enough to know that you may not be too fussy about where you tuck it, but you are always careful to dress for the occasion. I meant like tokens. Letters, cards, anything at all that would incriminate you?"

"No. No, nothing at all. I keep telling you it wasn't like that."

"Then you're OK." Jason smiled, pleased to be on sure ground again, pleased to be able to offer his mate a solution. "If she says anything to Tash, it's her word against yours. Bluff it out. Say she's lying. Say she's demented."

"I couldn't do that."

"Why not?"

"Well, she isn't lying. And, more important, I don't want to lie to Tash."

Jason didn't want to be unnecessarily cruel, but he believed the situation demanded a certain measure of realism. "You mean you don't want to lie to her again."

# 43

## *Alone Together*

Tash had woken up with a nagging hangover, made worse by disappointment when she discovered that Rich had left early to go boarding. He hadn't left her a note to say when he'd be back or where he'd be, in case she wanted to meet up with him. She'd thought that she had plans of her own, but it was beginning to look as though they might not come off. Tash had stood in the foyer of the hotel, waiting for Jayne, for half an hour now, and there was no sign of her. Last night they'd agreed to meet at 9:15 a.m. to go snowboarding together, but Tash wondered if Jayne had forgotten altogether or simply slept in. She was just about to go and look for her when she spotted Lloyd coming out of the lifts.

"Hi!" Lloyd was thrilled to see Tash. "Would you like to join us? Kate, Ted and I are going to La Chapelle d'Abondance."

Lloyd was desperate for Tash to take him up on the offer. He knew that Ted was depressed and Kate was deceived, and as a consequence Lloyd was disheartened. Kate seemed to be aware of her husband's profound sadness, but could not understand how a fall on the slopes had brought about such an air of melancholy. She repeatedly asked Ted, and then Lloyd, for a further explanation neither could nor would provide. Ted had agreed to ski, but only because he thought that they could ski at a distance from one another, using the open space to hide in. Lloyd couldn't imagine the morning being that much fun. Perhaps if Tash joined them the mood would be less edgy.

Ted's confession weighed heavily on Lloyd's mind. He'd had no idea. Of course he hadn't. He hadn't seen Ted for months, not properly, not to talk to. And, besides, he'd been absorbed in his own problems. Lloyd felt a little ashamed. He'd called Greta late last night, hoping that she would offer some comfort or cheer. She did accept his apology for his call on Saturday, but she'd still been a little monosyllabic when it came to dishing out the sympathy toward Ted.

"I think he should talk to his wife. He's not being fair."

"Do you think I should talk to Kate?"

"Don't be foolish, Lloyd. It is none of your business," Greta had replied in her brutal, Austrian, plain-talking way. She had then turned the conversation to one about her setting up the video the previous night, but it recording the wrong channel. Greta blamed the video recorder for being too complex. Lloyd admired her confidence. He knew that in the same situation he would have blamed himself for being too simple. He couldn't really expect her to sympathize with the dilemmas of his friends, not when she hadn't even met them and they'd shown no interest in meeting her. At least she hadn't blown a fuse that it had taken him forty-eight hours to call her back. Sophie would have gone wild about something like that. Life was easier with Greta. He smiled at the thought.

Lloyd grinned hopefully at Tash. He could certainly do with some light relief, and he wondered if Tash was prepared to be just that.

"You'd be doing me a big favor. Things are a little tense between Ted and Kate."

"Oh, why is that?"

Lloyd stumbled. "Ted has been a bit belligerent since his fall." Lloyd blushed as he realized that he'd used the words "Ted" and "has been" in the same sentence. However innocently meant, it was too close for comfort. "I think he's a bit fragile."

Lloyd felt mean portraying Ted as the archetypal man who couldn't handle or admit to pain, but in many ways that was exactly what Ted was.

Tash liked Lloyd because of his drunken but excruciatingly honest outburst the other night and did want to get to know him better; however, she didn't fancy spending the morning with Ted or Kate. The thought of stammering her way through conversations about the headline news in *Les Echos* chilled her to the bone. No, of course she hadn't read the papers. She never read newspapers except on Sunday, and even then she mostly read the color supplements, and besides that, she was on holiday. And to top it all off, the newspapers were in French! Nor was she up to having to dredge up an opinion on League tables for preschools in central London. Her tongue and head were too swollen with alcohol and her stomach was having its own private rave.

"I'd love to, Lloyd, but I'm supposed to be meeting Jayne. If she ever turns up."

"Where's Rich?"

"Not sure. He might be boarding with Jason. He left before I woke up this morning."

"Well, I do know Jason had a very early start, too," Lloyd said.

"Really?" Tash could sniff gossip.

"He took a lady friend, and I use the term 'lady' very loosely, back to his room last night. Jase has the room next to mine. Honestly, I'm thinking of suing him for noise pollution."

Tash giggled. "You're just jealous."

"No, I'm not. Really. I don't want a string of minuscule chances at love. However busty and blonde and young that chance might be. I'm too old for those dance-floor encounters."

"You're the same age as Jase."

"Only in reality, and Jase doesn't live in reality," Lloyd said, and shrugged.

Tash wondered if Jayne had somehow got wind of the fact that Jase had been entertaining. Maybe she was upset.

"I'd better go and look for Jayne."

"Will Mia be joining you two?"

Tash shook her head. What did Lloyd take her for, a masochist?

"In that case, if you see her, tell her to call me on my mobile after her lesson with Pierre, and I'll come to meet her."

"She's having a lesson with Pierre?" Tash couldn't help but smile to herself. Mia had been so dismissive of the idea.

"Yes, but it's a secret. She wants to pretend she's a natural, so don't mention that I let it slip. She chose Pierre because, apparently,

he has very large forearms and that makes him a great boarder."
Lloyd winked and headed off toward the reception.


Tash knocked on Jayne's door twice before Jayne answered it.
Jayne opened the door just an inch or two. When she saw Tash
her beam disappeared and disappointment flickered across her
face. Tash realized that Jayne had obviously been expecting Jason.
Poor girl.

"Hi! I wondered if you were still on for boarding," said Tash.

Jayne stared at her, confused. She shook her head.

It had never occurred to Jayne that she could lose him.

She wanted to believe resolutely that now she had told Rich
exactly how she felt—no more games, no more playing it cool—
it was only a matter of time before he called off the pathetic and
stupid wedding to the pathetic and stupid Natasha, and flung himself into her open arms. She'd hoped it was him knocking at her
door. But he patently hadn't talked to Tash yet and, in light of last
night's conversation, even Jayne's extreme confidence in the power
of her love was trembling a little. It took every ounce of Jayne's
steely self-control to steer her mind away from the specific comments Rich had made. He couldn't have meant that they "weren't
anything at all," and when he called her "crazy" he must have
meant in an attractive, kooky sort of way, mustn't he? She would
not think about it. He did not mean to be offensive. He was taken
aback, that was all. Once he had time to think about her declaration, he'd find the courage to end the farce with Tash and be with
her. She knew he would. He had to.

Because if he didn't, she would.

He had said he thought she needed help. He'd told her not to
take his comment the wrong way, but what was the right way?
Fury bubbled up inside Jayne's stomach. She felt it clash and meld
with disappointment, humiliation and frustration. She feared that

despair might snuff out her hope that they could get it together, her belief that they should get it together.

Jayne had spent most of the night and all morning poring over her treasure box. The contents of which were at this moment spread across her bedroom floor. She momentarily considered asking Tash into her room. She could show her Rich's notes and recommended reading. She could show her the champagne corks and the tube tickets. That would wipe the smirk off Tash's frankly stupid face. Jayne dismissed the idea. The box of treasures, although priceless to her, wouldn't be of much value in terms of evidence of her and Rich's affair. Tash could explain them away if she wanted to. Jayne needed a more foolproof reveal. Jayne's face was twisted with concentration, and she hadn't slept well the night before. She looked terrible. Tash jumped to her own conclusion.

"You heard about Jason, then?" guessed Tash.

"What?" snapped Jayne. She was finding it hard to stay convivial with this wretched girl.

"He had someone in his room last night," Tash muttered, sympathetically.

"*Quel surprise,*" commented Jayne dryly.

Tash squeezed Jayne's arm. "Sorry. You seem upset."

"Not about him."

"So do you fancy some snow?" offered Tash. She did not believe Jayne's denial, but was prepared to pretend she did to protect Jayne's dignity.

Jayne weighed the situation. She could stay in her room all day, claiming that she was too tired to board. At least that way Rich would be able to find her if—no, when—he came to tell her he'd chosen her. On the other hand, it never did any harm to spend time with Tash. Tash was preposterously trusting and transparent, and was keen to share as though she were a native Californian. Jayne gained great insight into her and Rich's relationship as a result. She found out where they bought their groceries, where they drank coffee and which position was their sexual preference. Information was power.

"I don't want to board, I'm too hungover," said Jayne.

"Well, there are millions of other things to do. We could go scuba diving under ice," suggested Tash, who had entirely bought into Jayne's phony give-it-a-go persona.

Jayne looked horrified.

"Maybe not with hangovers," conceded the genuinely active Tash. "How about bowling or ice skating?" Jayne shook her head. "Take a walk. Or shop."

"Let's shop. I'll dress quickly and see you downstairs in ten." Jayne's face transformed from sulky to radiant in a flash. Tash sighed with relief and agreed. She wandered back downstairs to wait, unsure whether she'd imagined Jayne's initially chilly mood.

# 44

# *Retail Therapy*

Tash and Jayne drifted around the tiny clothes boutiques and souvenir shops. Although there were only a limited number of retail outlets, the girls still managed to find opportunities to flex their plastic—it was almost a matter of principle. Tash picked out a pair of pink, furry Quiksilver snow boots, which were as impractical as they were fun. Jayne bought the same pair in blue. Tash also bought a new pair of yellow, heart-shaped sunglasses and a tacky plastic snow shaker that dispersed shiny scarlet hearts, rather than snow, around a bemused-looking St. Bernard dog. Jayne bought two Roxy sweatshirts and the same snow shaker. They didn't have a second pair of the glasses, not even in another color. Jayne made a mental note to buy them once she was back in London. The retail therapy did as it was required to do and cheered both girls. Tash knew Rich would adore her purchases, and she couldn't wait to show him. Jayne had exactly the same thought.

It didn't take long to exhaust the small supply of shops, so the girls soon found themselves tucking into crêpes and a carafe of wine.

Tash could see that Jayne was much more relaxed and therefore felt brave enough to ask, "Are you disappointed that Jason took someone to his room last night?"

"That he screwed some easy woman?" asked Jayne, riding roughshod over Tash's tactful question. "Not in the slightest. I expected as much. Men are faithless bastards."

"Not all men," said Tash. She was thinking of Rich.

"All men," said Jayne, who was also thinking of Rich. "Is Mia boarding with Rich this morning?"

"No, I think she's having a professional lesson, but it's supposed to be a secret."

Tash didn't think it was an important enough secret to earn her respect or silence. She liked Jayne and didn't like Mia, so she also thought it was OK that they swapped smirks.

"Oh, I thought she'd be with Rich again," said Jayne.

"Well, she might be, I suppose. I'm not sure where he is. He left before I woke up."

"But he left a note, right?"

"Rich isn't good at that sort of thing. He doesn't think like that."

"Like what? Considerately?" asked Jayne. She pulled her face into an expression which approximated sympathy.

"He is considerate," Tash defended. "He just doesn't think about plans and arrangements."

"And consequences," added Jayne, raising her eyebrows. "Men. They're all the same."

Of course, she didn't believe this for a second. Rich was different from all men. Rich was her hero, her deity. She knew that when Rich was hers, in totality, once and for all, he would always leave notes detailing his plans. In fact, he probably wouldn't even have any plans that didn't include Jayne, so there would never be any need for notes, except love ones. It was just politic that Tash believe Rich was the same as other men. Jayne wanted Tash to be mistrusting of Rich. She wanted to fill her with hesitancy and doubt. Jayne needed to rupture Tash's peace of mind. She wanted Tash to interpret innocent situations incorrectly, to be consumed with jealousy and fury. Iago seemed a laudable role model. Jayne crossed her fingers because it really wasn't nice to say cruel things about Rich, and pushed on.

"It's no big deal. I had my own plans." Tash shrugged.

"Yes, but he didn't know that, did he? As far as he knows, you might be on your own today."

"He wouldn't have meant to leave me out. He's a live-for-the-minute type of guy. I love that about him." Tash beamed, not showing any sign of the Othello complex that Jayne was hoping to nurture. Jayne refilled Tash's glass.

"That devil-may-care attitude is always an attractive attribute in the beginning," agreed Jayne.

Tash stared at her crêpe. She was hoping that Rich's joie de vivre would always be attractive, full stop. Jayne could see that her approach was having all the effect of drilling a diamond with a toothpick. She tried another tack.

"Isn't it remarkable that Rich and Mia can be just friends? Considering that once upon a time he made love to her and all that involves—smelling her, tasting her, nibbling her nipples, kissing her thighs. Even now, she's always watching him, laughing with him, chatting with him. I don't think I could be friends with someone after I'd shared that intimacy." Tash took a huge bite of her chocolate crêpe. Suddenly she had an overwhelming urge for something sweet. "And, my God, you're amazing. If it were me, I'd be eaten up with jealousy thinking about that past closeness."

Tash shifted uncomfortably on her chair. "I don't let myself think about it," she said, truthfully.

"With my ex I was completely consumed by the green-eyed monster."

Tash was relieved that the focus of the conversation would now move away from her and Rich. She nodded for Jayne to go on.

"I hated the fact that there had ever been other women in his life. I wanted to be them all."

Jayne stared at her barely touched crêpe, unwilling to meet Tash's eyes in case she saw the tears of frustration and self-pity that were welling in her own.

"I hated them all. I wished none of them had existed, but, as they had, I had this weird, illogical fantasy. I wanted to be every girl he'd ever touched. The one who took his virginity, the college girls, the white ones, the black ones, the holiday flings, the air hostess, the ones he had loved, the stripper he slept with in Amsterdam for a bet. Even the ones he couldn't remember the names of."

"But that's impossible. What you wanted was impossible," said Tash gently.

"But it was how I felt," insisted Jayne.

Tash reached for the carafe of wine and was surprised to find it empty. How had they drunk it that quickly? She ordered another. Jayne could do with another drink. Hell, she could do with another drink.

"It's such a waste of emotional energy being jealous of someone's past. I don't want to be part of Rich's past—it's far more important being his future," said Tash. "And the fact is everyone has a past."

"My jealousy wasn't misguided, you know," spat Jayne angrily, incensed by Tash's clearly patronizing comment. "He was seeing some bimbo on the side, and eventually he—"

"Chose her?" asked Tash.

Jayne glared, "No, he didn't choose her. She forced him to leave me." Jayne's breathing was fast and shallow. Clearly she was still deeply moved by her ex. Tash reached out and patted her hand. Jayne snatched it away. "You have no idea," she snarled, then added, "Has Rich always been faithful to his girlfriends in the past?"

Tash was annoyed with herself for blushing. "Er, not absolutely."

"I think it's a yes-or-no issue. Not a gray area. Either he has been faithful or he hasn't," Jayne insisted.

"He hasn't been in the type of relationship where it was an issue. His affairs of the loins have always been casual," Tash explained.

"Always?"

"Well, he has had two or three girlfriends that have lasted six months or so."

"Was he faithful to them?"

Tash chose not to reply because she didn't like the answer. Instead she said, "Why do you ask?"

"Just because so few men are monogamists, and Rich doesn't appear to be that way inclined and I wondered how important fidelity was to the pair of you."

"Paramount," said Tash hotly. "The difference is Rich has never promised fidelity in the past, but now he wants to be exclusive. We both feel that, very strongly."

"And his past behavior doesn't worry you?"

"Rich may not have always behaved entirely honorably, but as I was the one who insisted that we talk about our old flames it would be crazy to distrust his future intentions because he was honest with me about his past actions. I insisted that we had no secrets at all. Our entire relationship is, and always will be, based on trust."

"Oh." Jayne nodded.

She wanted to laugh. She wanted to cry. This stupid girl had no idea. "I just wondered if you were going to go for one of these open marriages. I mean, you are so cool with the fact that he's had sex with Mia, and you have that one hundred percent honesty thing. I wondered if you were the sort of couple that didn't mind what you each did, as long as you swapped stories."

Tash felt grubby. She had always been so proud of her 100 percent respect and honesty policy. It was so simple, so full of morality and good intention. The way Jayne had interpreted it was grimy. Tash scrambled in her pockets for her purse. She pulled out a bunch of notes and threw them on the table.

"I think I need a nap. I've a headache. It must be the glare off the snow."

"Or the hangover coming for its second round of attack," said Jayne.

Tash nodded, and stood up. "That should cover my half."

"Oh, yes, more than," agreed Jayne, as she counted up Tash's money. "Go and have a nap before dinner. You do look pale. I'll settle up here." Jayne beamed.

Tash shook her head. It must be the hangover. She wasn't seeing things clearly. A second ago she thought she'd seen malice in Jayne's eyes, but that couldn't be right. Jayne was her friend. A friend who was clearly a little weary and battle scarred, but . . . Tash didn't try to complete the thought. Jayne's situation was nothing to do with her own happy one. She must not let the things sad and cynical Jayne said spoil anything at all. Tash stumbled back to the hotel and waited for Rich.

# 45

## *A Lot to Digest*

D inner on Tuesday night was devoid of buoyant moods, flirtatious chat, hilarious anecdotes or giggly overindulgence in
food and wine. Instead the atmosphere was drenched with deceit,
despair and despondency. It wasn't just that everyone was battling
with now almost permanent hangovers. The gang of old friends,
who had been sure they knew everything about one another and
who had prided themselves on their intimate history, were now
beginning to sense that there was a lot they didn't know about one
another. Furthermore, anything they had recently discovered was
shocking, scandalous and serious.

If there had been a competition to see who was the most miserable, it would have been a close-run thing with a photo finish.
Ted, Kate and Lloyd had skied all day, and yet had filled the hours
with superficial chitchat about weather conditions. Rich agonized
over his confession to Jason, and Jason agonized over the fact that
he'd been taken for a complete fool by Jayne—plainly she had
used him to try to make Rich jealous. And while Jayne knew that
she had upset Tash and disturbed her almost Zen-like calm and
confidence (she didn't believe that headache story, not for an instant), she still agonized over what Rich would do next. Why hadn't
he had the big talk with Tash yet? It was overdue.

Rich had returned to the hotel only twenty minutes before
dinner. He'd stayed out as late as he dared because he didn't want
to be alone with Tash. When he was, his conscience stung and

fought miserably with his sense of self-preservation. The battle left him feeling like the bastard he was.

"Where have you been?" Tash had asked the moment he walked in the door. The tone of the question was a curious mix between relief at Rich's return and anger and indignation that he had been away at all. She was sitting at the dressing-room table in her bra and knickers, applying her lipstick. Her hair was still wet and wrapped in a huge towel, which was twisted turbanlike up on top of her head. She wished he hadn't caught her in this half-dressed state—she looked comical and not at all glamorous. He thought she looked beautiful.

"I've had a great day on the slopes with Jase," Rich'd replied, kissing Tash briefly on the forehead. He'd wanted to kiss her lips. He longed to. He knew he'd feel safe there. But would she taste Jayne's kiss? Would she somehow know?

Of course not. He wasn't being logical. Her skin was almost translucent. He kissed her cheekbones, her nose. She closed her eyes, and he kissed her eyelids. He broke away. "Then we went to a bar."

"Which one?"

"The one next door."

Tash fumed, "You could have come to find me."

"Sorry, babe," called Rich. He was in the bathroom, towel-drying his hair, which was damp with snowfall. "Mia said you were ill, needed a nap. I didn't want to disturb you. I know you hate people fussing around you when you're feeling rough."

It was true that Tash didn't require much in terms of bedside manner when she was ill. She'd much rather hide under the duvet until the thing had subsided, then reemerge. But today she wasn't really ill, or at least not with anything infectious. She could have done with some company. But, then, Rich wasn't a mind reader.

"Mia was with you? I thought you said you boarded with Jase."

"I did. We bumped into Mia at about six-thirty. She'd been out with Jayne. It was Jayne who told her you were ill."

"Right," said Tash because she didn't know what else to say.

In fact, it wasn't right. Nothing seemed in the least bit right. She wasn't happy that Rich had left her alone all day. She wasn't ecstatic with the conversation she'd had with Jayne. It had stirred up an ugly cocktail of emotions—jealousy, fear and distrust, to name but a few. And while she knew she was being irrational, she was also unhappy that Jayne had spent the afternoon with Mia. It seemed like a betrayal. Of course, it wasn't. She was being silly. Jayne had every right to spend time with whomever she liked. And she hadn't ever said she didn't like Mia. Not in so many words. There was no real reason Jayne ought to dislike Mia. After all, it wasn't *her* boyfriend Mia was trying to seduce.

*Aaghhh.* It was all too much.

She didn't like the idea of Rich, Mia and Jase sitting around a bar, drinking and laughing without her. About her?

No, that was ridiculous.

Tash had wanted to tell Rich all of this. She'd wanted him to sit down with her and allow her to offload a number of preposterous ideas that Jayne had slipped into her mind. Ideas which Tash could not shove out again. She was sure he would stroke her back and play with her hair. Kiss her lips and tell her everything was OK. Instead Tash sighed, saying, "You'd better get changed quickly. We're booked for an eight o'clock dinner."

Only Mia was feeling sparky.

The fertility test had shown a bright green light today. She was slap bang in the middle of the most fruitful part of her cycle. That information, combined with the discovery of the relationship between Rich and Jayne—and Scaley Jase's predictable response to the news (random sex with a stranger)—meant that her plan was back

STILL THINKING *of* YOU 291

on track. Yes, it would have been ideal if Scaley had turned to her for consolation last night rather than that time-wasting tart, but it wasn't a major disappointment. Jayne had been genuine competition, but she couldn't believe that the touring loose women would be.

It was novel that when she arrived at dinner she found that she was the most high-spirited.

"My God, why the long faces?" she asked, as she slipped into the seat next to Jason. No one replied. "Glad to see you're feeling better, Big Ted," she said with a smile. Ted nodded politely. "Are you feeling rested, Barbie Babe? Jayne said you had a headache. Shame you missed out. We went boarding. Great fun, wasn't it, Jayne?" Jayne smiled and nodded. Mia's fun would have been increased tenfold if Jayne had taken the opportunity to discuss the "Rich foyer kiss," but both girls had discreetly avoided the subject. "Great snow, hey, you guys?" The question was thrown out to include Kate, Lloyd, Rich and Jason. More nods and more silence. "What is it? Have you all worked out that you've already broken your New Year's resolutions and it's still January?" joked Mia.

"I hate New Year's," said Kate, not answering the question.

"I thought you loved New Year's, Ms. Monopoly," said Mia in surprise. "You always throw the best parties."

"I love it," said Jayne with a fake smile.

Jayne knew that she had to rouse herself. This was a crucial time. She knew that her self-appointed role in life was to be extremely enthusiastic about everything from cute puppies, to dangerous black runs, to New Year's Eve. Men such as Rich didn't want moaning Minnies. In truth, Jayne wasn't fond of New Year's Eve celebrations. She had spent too many on the edges of Kate and Ted's parties, hoping that Rich would acknowledge her. He never had, and sometimes he'd even arrived at those parties with another woman. Some gawky, hopeless girl or other. On those occasions, Jayne always went home early and slept through the midnight hour. However, this was not the moment to share.

"It's all so pressurized. New Year's Eve is the time when everyone asks, 'What have you achieved this year? Have you scaled a mountain? Popped out a baby? Run the New York Marathon?' I hate it," said Kate. The group stared at her.

"That can't be a problem for you," said Jason. "You achieve so much every year. You do regularly pop out babies, or renovate new overseas homes, or buy new yachts. You always have good news. If accounting for your past year is a challenge, it's one that you more than rise to."

Kate felt ashamed. She shouldn't have said anything. She should have just continued to pretend to love New Year's. Just because these were her dearest friends, it didn't give her license to be so honest, not if her honest opinion had a dampening effect on the evening. What was she thinking of?

"I so missed your champagne bash this year. It has become the most important feature on my calendar."

"I'm sorry," apologized Kate, blushing at the compliment that her parties were a success and the guilt of not throwing one this year, when it was expected of her. "It will be back next year, bigger and better. We didn't bother this year because Ted was working on something massive in the office and we simply didn't have time for all the prep. Isn't that right, darling?"

Ted nodded, and turned pink to match his wife.

"What were you working on, Big Ted?" asked Mia, as she hungrily bit into a bread roll. She liked to show an interest in her friends' careers, particularly cerebral, thriving careers. She hadn't ever had the urge to find out exactly how Tash dressed windows.

"A merger," replied Ted.

"Oh, which one? Will I have read about it in the Financial pages?"

Ted buried his nose in the wine menu. "No, it's all very hush-hush."

"That's right, Mia. Ted wouldn't even tell me the details," said Kate with a smile.

She adored the fact that her husband worked on top-secret projects. It made him appear very 007, even though he worked in the City and not for Her Majesty's Service. In truth, Kate hadn't questioned Ted too closely on the exact nature of the work that would mean they couldn't throw their regular New Year's Eve party. She'd meant to show the proper interest, but Christmas was such a busy time. The children all needed costumes for their various pantomimes, and there were endless parties to drop them off at and collect them from. Not to mention the extra cooking and the shopping. She hadn't even said anything when in December it turned out that Ted managed to keep regular office hours and didn't have to work into the early hours of the morning as he'd feared. She was just grateful to have him around.

Kate had been delighted to have a legitimate excuse to avoid throwing the hundred-fifty-guest bash. She wouldn't say so. It seemed rude when the gang was among the hundred fifty guests she had to provide canapés and champagne for, but the parties were exhausting. There had been a time when she really enjoyed their New Year's Eve parties; back in the mid-1990s when the guest list was limited to a more modest forty or so friends. In those days she had managed to talk to everyone, ask if they'd had an enjoyable Christmas. Last year, she hadn't even recognized some of the guests.

"You should have hired Sophie's company," said Mia. "I've heard that her parties are a huge success. She did the Ephron-Eagleton wedding and the Beaumont-Parsons wedding, and I understand one of the Guinness cousins is thinking of using her for a wedding anniversary in the spring."

Mia had never acknowledged Sophie's career in the six years she had spent time with Sophie, but now Sophie was so eminently successful she wanted to make it clear that they were chums, still in touch, still on first-name terms. No matter if they weren't. No matter if it was the last name on earth Lloyd wanted to hear at dinner.

"I'm with Kate on this. For the past ten years, I've pretty much had the same resolution, which is to cut down drink," said Lloyd. "Sticking to my resolution makes January, an already dreary month, absolutely hellish."

Lloyd reached for the bottle of wine and refilled his glass. No one had seen any evidence of abstemious behavior. But, then, Lloyd had broken resolutions in common with the majority of the rest of the Western population.

"Guys, guys, it is not that bad. New Year's Eve is a great time to reminisce and also to look forward," said Mia forcefully. No response. She decided to ditch the small talk and change tack to a more tried and tested route. "My God, this is a wedding, not a wake. Get the champagne in, Big Ted, that's what we need."

"No, no, I'll get it," said Lloyd, jumping to his feet.

"Sit down, man," instructed Mia. "The waiter actually gets it. All you have to do is give a room number."

Lloyd dropped back into his chair feeling slightly foolish, but he felt better when he caught Ted's eye and saw that Ted was smiling at him. His gesture was appreciated.

"Do you know what these dinners put me in mind of?" asked Mia. Again no one responded, but she plowed on regardless and answered her own question. "Formal dinners in Hall back in our college days. God, they were fun, weren't they?" Tash rolled her eyes to the ceiling. "We all had to get dressed up. The food wasn't up to the des Dromonts standards, of course, but we were impressed at the time. It used to be such good sport watching the kids from the comprehensives worry about which fork to choose." Mia grinned so that no one took her bitchy comment seriously. Her ploy worked for everyone except Tash, the only one who had attended a comprehensive. Despite always knowing the "outside-to-in" rule, she took the comment to heart. "It's just the same, only with better hairstyles. Guess what I brought with me?" continued Mia.

No one guessed.

Mia bent down and pulled from her Louis Vuitton handbag a fat leather photo album.

"My album of all our best photos from college."

This wasn't a spontaneous move on Mia's part. Indeed, there was no such thing. Before the trip she had thought that it was a good idea to bring the photos of the old days when she and Jason were an item. It wouldn't harm to nudge his memory toward those heady, lusty days of their youth. Days when she wore grunge and he wore his jeans turned up at the ankle so that everyone could see his Doc Marten's.

She had sorted through dozens of packets of photos, carefully selecting the ones where she looked lovely. She'd brought photos of smiley, successful days; ones that showed the gang picnicking in the park, hosting big dinner parties with poor food and screw-top wine. The photos showed them emerging victorious from the playing fields or looking ludicrous as they dressed up for rag week, when the students raised money for charities. The photos showed the gang in clusters, in pairs and in their entirety. They were rarely alone. They stood, happy and confident, arms draped around one another's shoulders or lying on sofas or floors, relaxed and replete after eating and drinking too much, limbs and lives not so much tangled as comfortably intertwined. In Stalin-esque style Mia left behind the ones where either she or Scaley Jase had their arms around any other undergraduate.

Suddenly the miserable crowd was roused. No one could resist a peek at their younger selves, and both Tash and Jayne were keen to see photos of Rich.

"Tash, I bet you didn't know that Rich had a liking for women's clothes," laughed Lloyd, as he pointed to a photo of himself and Rich dressed as characters from *The Rocky Horror Picture Show.*

"I did, actually. I've told you, we don't have any secrets." She laughed at the boyish version of her fiancé dressed in drag.

"Oh, my God, what were we thinking of?" giggled Kate, as she stared at a photo of her and Mia with hairstyles that must have required at least a tin of hair spray each to maintain.

"We thought we were the height of style and sophistication, didn't we?" chuckled Mia. "I think you are on one or two of these, Jayne," she added. "Yes, that's you, in the background, isn't it?"

Mia pointed to a picture of the gang posing at their first-year summer ball. They were holding glasses of Pimm's and wide grins, and were all dressed up waiting for the revelry to commence. The boys didn't look too cringeworthy, as black tie doesn't date, but the girls looked outrageous in their pearls, big hair and silky dresses with enormous wide skirts, the type of dress that is now the staple of every charity shop window, but can't be found anywhere else. In the background of the shot Jayne loitered.

She was holding a glass of lemonade in one hand, despite both arms being folded across her chunky waist. She had her head tilted to one side, not in a flirtatious manner, as she might today, but because she was painfully shy. She was dressed like the older girls in a wide taffeta gown, only hers was stretched at the seams where she had squeezed herself into a size fourteen, refusing to entertain the idea of wearing a sixteen. You couldn't see the stressed seams in the photo, but Jayne knew they were there. For her they were always there. That had been the day she caught Rich's eye, or at least caught him at that stage where he was drunk enough to be irresponsible but not quite so drunk as to pass out. It had been enough for the gauche but ambitious teenager.

"Is it, really? I can't remember you ever looking like that," mused Kate, as she leaned closer to the album to get a better look at the dumpy Jayne. She couldn't believe that there was a time when she was better-looking and slimmer than her now very gorgeous sister-in-law.

"I'd never have recognized you," confirmed Tash. "How old were you then?"

"Sixteen." Jayne snatched the album away from Tash's gaze and quickly turned the page. "Here are the boys playing rugby," she said, trying to divert attention away from her less attractive, pubescent self. Jayne scowled at Mia. She didn't like seeing old pictures of herself and she definitely didn't want Rich seeing them.

"Sixteen. Ah, just a baby," laughed Jason, then he remembered his conversation with Rich on the slopes that morning. He mouthed "Sorry" at the scowling Rich, and tried to put his comment into context by adding, "While we were poncing around in our black-tie getups, you were probably still playing hopscotch, Tash."

Tash howled, pretending to be outraged. "I'm not that much younger. I'd have been thirteen. Believe me, hopscotch was well and truly behind me. But I admit I was probably still practicing on the recorder."

"That's a gorgeous one of you, Mia," said Kate, as she reached the final page.

It was a stunning shot. Mia had purposefully left the best until last. Jase picked up the album in order to take a closer look. She watched as he swallowed, his Adam's apple rising and falling as she knew it did when he was agitated.

"Yup, no denying it, you were fucking hot totty." He grinned, then added, "In your day."

Mia was elated. Scaley couldn't take his eyes off the shot, except to stare her down as he added the less sensitive part of his comment. She knew he was joking, that was his style. He never paid her a straight compliment. He always wrapped his praise in a punishing punch. She did the same to him. It was all a bit playground.

She watched as he pored over the photo of her studying in the library. He was transfixed, as she'd hoped he would be. She wondered if he was transported. Did he remember that he was the one who took that photo? Did he remember creeping up on her and tapping her on the shoulder? She'd looked up and blinked as he snapped the photo. The sunlight flooded through the window, enveloping her in a warm halo of light. She was writing a dissertation which was to form part of her final grade and had totally given up even halfhearted attempts at personal grooming. Her hair was pulled up in an untidy ponytail, her fingernails were badly bitten and she wasn't wearing any makeup. She was wearing one of Scaley's rugby shirts. But she was young and happy. She looked more beautiful than most brides do on their wedding day.

She wondered if he remembered that he'd insisted she leave her books, that he'd taken her back to his digs and that they'd made love all afternoon. That the lovemaking had been so stupendous, so energetic, so relaxed, then hard and fast, and then slow, that she had literally cried with delight and fear at such intimacy. A state she had never reached again. She hoped he remembered all that.

Although she didn't necessarily want him to remember that was the last time they'd made love.

The starters arrived and stole away everyone's attention from the photos. Mia's ploy had worked on many levels. Everyone seemed a little more chatty and relaxed as they started to dissect the delicious food and guess the ingredients and preparation techniques.


Ted allowed the prattle to go on without him. He picked up the fat leather album. It was Prada; it must have cost Mia a fortune. He never used to notice what things cost. He never cared. He would always have been able to tell you the share index of any of the FTSE (*Financial Times*/Stock Exchange) 100 on any day of the week, but he had no idea how much a loaf of bread cost or what the current retail recommended price was on a CD.

Ted reverently turned the pages of the album, deferentially drinking in the images, luxuriating in the memories. He paused at one of him with Rich, Lloyd and Jason. He had his arms flung around the shoulders of Lloyd and Rich; Jason was jumping up and down behind the three of them. Jason had probably set the timer on the camera, then dashed into view. Ted couldn't exactly remember. Not that the memory of the four of them wasn't important or special. It was just that they had a number of these carefree, careless moments. There were countless photos of the foursome grinning inanely at life and the lens.

Ted turned the page and paused at the photo where Mia and Kate had laughed over their hairstyles. He knew that Mia was considered the beauty of the pair and Kate thought of as the more dowdy one, and he admitted the hairdos did seem a little extraordinary now, but when he looked at the photo all he could see was Kate's beauty. Kate had such stunning eyes. Eyes with soul, which radiated kindness, warmth and intelligence. Eyes which made her far more beautiful than any treatment in a spa could make any woman. He knew that she didn't like her pale skin, which tended to burn rather than bronze, and he knew that she didn't appreciate her curvy, sensual plumpness, although she ought to. To him, Kate was the more stunning woman in the picture.

She was the most stunning woman he knew.

And while she looked amazing back then, it was his firm opinion that she had only become more delicious as time had passed. Was there a man alive who didn't believe his wife was divine during childbirth? Fat, yes. Sweaty, yes. Bloody, yes. But undoubtedly a goddess.

Ted stared at the slightly trimmer, slightly darker-haired version of himself and asked the young lad if he knew how it had all gone so badly wrong? Ted felt he'd let the young chap in the photo down, rather terribly. The young Ted had the respect of the lovely Kate. He'd earned it by being courteous, studious, funny and decent. The young Kate had stared at him with eyes which were kind, warm and intelligent, true, but she'd also looked at him and sensibly weighed up his prospects. Prospects that had been shimmering. The young Ted was stuffed full of promise, opportunity and good fortune. Big Ted barely recognized him.

Ted looked up and caught Kate's eye. She was watching him study the photos. She noticed that Ted was very pink and sweating. She watched as he pulled out his Paul Smith handkerchief and dabbed his forehead, chin and eyes. Ted thought Kate looked more cross than kind. Rather more irritated than warm, and certainly more confused than intelligent. He'd done that to her. It was his fault. How was he ever going to tell her? He knew he must. If it were possible, he would live with the charade forever—at least that way he'd keep his Kate. But it was not possible.

Although he'd switched his mobile off throughout the day, tonight he'd forced himself to listen to the increasingly irate messages left by his bank manager. While Kate had showered, he heard that the bank manager was demanding a meeting, no doubt to ask him to hand over the keys to their home. All cards had been withdrawn, both debit and credit. The situation was critical. He knew it would be a very short time before Kate's eyes shone with derision and scorn.

Oh, God, where had it all gone so badly wrong?

# 46

## *The Bar Scene*

Ted, why are you being so maudlin? Get the drinks in, bruv. You'll feel better," Jayne instructed.

Ted had been silent throughout dinner. He had pored over those stupid photos that everyone other than her seemed to derive

so much pleasure from, but he'd said very little. Jayne couldn't imagine that he was upset because the photos showed how much weight both he and Kate had put on. Neither of them looked well now compared to their more youthful image. Whereas, on the whole, time had been kind to everyone else. But Ted wasn't the sort to be bothered by such things. It was possible that he was still in pain from his ankle, although he said not, and he had been out on the slopes today. Jayne could only imagine something dull, domestic and probably very minor had gone wrong. Wasn't Fleur taking a flute or piano exam, or something or other? Perhaps she hadn't fared as well as Ted had hoped she would. Ted and Kate were horribly ambitious for their children. That was just the sort of crisis her big brother had to deal with.

Jayne didn't bother inquiring whether her guess was correct and whether a failed music exam, grade I, was the issue. She didn't know how she'd fake interest in Ted's response. Her brother was a lovely man, and normally she had a lot of time for him and his family, but, really, they didn't know when they were well off.

She had very pressing issues of her own. She was desperate for some more champagne. The single bottle at dinner hadn't gone far (how typical that Lloyd wouldn't stretch to a second one). Admittedly, the wine at dinner had been good. She'd drunk plenty, almost too much. She normally avoided red wine—it stained her teeth, besides which it brought her down. Red wine wasn't a party drink, and Jayne wanted to party. She oscillated between feeling nervy and excited, pessimistic and expectant. Why hadn't Rich said or done anything about finishing with Tash yet? And why was Tash giggling and kissing Rich, smooching up to him despite Jayne's conversations. On the other hand, Rich didn't look exactly comfortable. Maybe he was just waiting for his moment.

Jayne didn't know how to fill her evening. It wasn't possible to flirt with Jase anymore, and he'd made that patently clear. He'd been very monosyllabic with her all evening, almost rude. He'd spent his entire evening deep in conversation with Mia. Mia must have told him that she caught Rich and Jayne in a clinch. Or possibly Rich had come clean with Jason—they were, after all, best friends. Maybe Rich had admitted that he was in love with Jayne. Jase would have backed off immediately then. It was an encouraging thought. Jayne allowed the optimistic side of the scales to rise again. She felt like celebrating.

"Come on, Teddy, how about some champagne?" she asked.

"Why don't you get the drinks in? I've bought all the drinks since we got here, except for those at dinner tonight, which Lloyd kindly bought. It must be someone else's round. Yours, perhaps," spat back Ted.

The truth of Ted's statement did nothing to alleviate the embarrassment caused by him making it. There was a thoughtful pause while everyone considered whether they had ever heard him speak so aggressively.

No. No one had.

How odd.

Kate put her hand on Ted's arm and used her other hand to fish out their platinum Amex. She handed it to the barman and ordered three bottles of Veuve Clicquot. Her gesture was especially flamboyant, as she hoped to detract from Ted's rudeness.

"No." Ted snatched the card out of the bartender's hand.

"Ted, you are making a scene," hissed Kate.

"Believe me, I'm avoiding one," he slurred.

"Maybe we ought to have a kitty?" suggested Tash.

"What?" asked Mia. "I don't think that's appropriate, Barbie Babe." Tash couldn't see how it was as inappropriate as cadging drinks off Ted all holiday. She stared blankly at Mia. Mia elaborated, "It's not as though we can't afford to stand our own rounds, and I've always thought kitties were so lower middle class."

Tash glared and was about to point out that no one did stand their own drinks when Jason interrupted. "Ted is right, you are a bunch of bloody freeloaders," he laughed, in an attempt to break the tension. "I'm stacked, I'll pay."

Jason would ask for a receipt anyway. Q&A, the agency which paid him his enormous salary, would no doubt see the bar tab on his expense sheet next week.

The bartender took Jase's card and proceeded to open a bottle of champagne. He hadn't even poured the second glass before Ted had swallowed back the first.

"Steady, darling," said Kate.

Lloyd was extremely tense. He'd swear he heard the click as the pin was pulled from the grenade. "The snow was fantastic today. Best yet, I'd say," he offered.

The conversation quickly turned to who took the worst fall and made the best trick that day. With full glasses and the false confidence that they provide, Lloyd, Rich, Jason, Jayne and Tash began to relax into the evening. Mia was drinking water, but still felt buoyant, especially when Scaley Jase (who was drinking steadily and chatting merrily) waved her over to the dance floor. This was her moment.

Kate stayed with Ted and propped up the bar. She was becoming seriously concerned about his behavior. She wondered if the painkillers the doctors had prescribed after his fall were having an effect on his mood. Perhaps the pharmacy had given Ted the wrong medication. It seemed unlikely, but there had to be an explanation as to why Ted was being so grumpy. Ted was generally a gregarious drunk, but this holiday he had been self-pitying and aggressive by turn. It simply wasn't like him. He wasn't being her big, cuddly Ted.

"What's the matter, darling?" asked Kate.

She squeezed his arm and tried to catch his gaze. Ted glared at his empty champagne glass and would not look at his wife. Even the bubbles, normally a guaranteed thrill, a sure sign of good times, tasted flat and empty. Flat like his life, empty like his bank account. The analogy was a little pathetic, but Ted was too drunk

to care. He wondered how he could force the descriptors "pointless" and "ridiculous" onto champagne, too, because they fitted his
life. He gave up. He was too drunk to hold the train of thought
long enough to finesse the analogy. Besides, he'd never been very
good with words. He was good with numbers. Always had been.

And now, he was just a has-been.

"Aren't you enjoying yourself? Is it Jayne? Don't worry, she's
fine. She seems to be getting on very well with both Tash and Rich.
I honestly don't think anyone minds that we brought her along."
Ted didn't respond. He didn't seem to know Kate was there. She
tugged harder on his arm. "Ted, you are scaring me. What's up?
It's not the children, is it? They're OK, aren't they?" Ted nodded.
"Why were you mean about the champagne?"

"I wasn't mean. I'm just not the bank of fucking England,"
snapped Ted.

"Ted." Kate's remonstration was low-key. Although Jason,
Rich and Lloyd swore as naturally and frequently as they inhaled
and exhaled, her husband was usually a little more refined. Kate
didn't like cursing.

"Do you love me, Kate?" Ted turned to his wife, his eyes finally
meeting hers. Haunted, hunted eyes. Eyes that she didn't recognize.

"Of course I do." Kate shifted uncomfortably.

What an odd question. Wasn't it obvious? She looked over her
shoulder to see if any of the others were listening. She hated scenes.
No one was listening. Instead they were happily quaffing free
champagne and dancing. Mia and Jase were arguing over the words
of the latest Finlay Quaye track. They really seemed to find it impossible to agree on even the smallest thing, thought Kate. She
turned back to Ted. Kate had drunk two glasses of wine at dinner
and half a glass of champagne so far, a lot by her standard, and the
music was loud so she couldn't quite catch what Ted was saying.
He was very pink. He'd put on a few pounds over Christmas.

"—uined," he yelled.

"Sorry?" asked Kate, leaning her ear toward his mouth.

"Ruined. We're ruined," yelled Ted, finally desperate to be heard.

"What's ruined? Ted, stop being obscure. What do you mean?"

"I'm trying to be very clear." He glared at his wife and slowly, with the careful deliberation of a drunk wanting to appear sober, Ted said, "We have no money. We have nothing. Only debts. I've lost my job."

Some of his spittle hit Kate's cheek, then he turned and abruptly left the bar.

# 47

## *Alone at Last*

Where have Ted and Kate gone?" Tash asked Rich. They'd done with dancing for now and retired to a small table in the corner of the bar.

"I don't know. I think they are having some sort of domestic," replied Rich with a shrug.

He had enough to worry about without babysitting Ted and Kate; he always thought of them as pretty self-reliant. Where was Jayne, for instance? Not far away, he'd bet. He turned to look over his shoulder; Jayne was standing only yards away. She beamed and waved. Rich tried to ignore her. He'd played this all wrong. Well, obviously he had. But Rich meant that he'd played the salvage operation all wrong. He should have asked Jase to keep tabs on Jayne. If Jase had turned on his charm and really worked her,

Jayne might have forgotten about Rich. Rich sighed. He knew it was a pipe dream. Jayne was a determined woman, a determined scorned woman, the worst type of determined woman. She wasn't going to just change her mind. Besides, Jase wouldn't have anything to do with her now he was aware just how crazy she was. If only Rich had had half the sense.

"I thought you said that Ted and Kate never had domestics," challenged Tash.

Rich had said this. It had been one of the many virtues he had extolled about Kate and Ted's family life. Besides describing Kate as the "perfect mum," Rich had described the children as the most affable, polite and intelligent he had ever met. Obviously Rich assumed one led to the other, and Tash also hoped that affable, polite, intelligent children were guaranteed if you were a perfect mum. Because that would be fair, wouldn't it?

But what was a perfect mum?

"They have both been acting strangely all night," she commented, "but, then again, everyone has." Tash sighed, and took a slurp of beer.

"What do you mean by that?" Guilt made Rich's tone harsher than he planned it to be.

"Jayne has been a bit odd. I spent this morning with her, and—"

"What did you do that for?" he snapped.

"Lack of alternatives," said Tash dryly and pointedly. "She was, I don't know . . . sulky. I assume that is something to do with Jason, who's also been quieter than normal."

Plus Mia had been lovely. She'd been inclusive, funny and chatty, which was all very odd. Tash resisted saying as much.

"And I think that Ted and Kate are arguing, and whatever they are arguing about Lloyd is privy to, or perhaps even caused," speculated Tash. "He can't look Kate in the eye. I had a chat with him. Earlier he said things were a bit tense between Ted and Kate."

"I hadn't noticed," confessed Rich. In truth, he was too absorbed with secreting his own drama to have the time, energy or inclination to unearth anyone else's.

"I hope it's nothing serious."

Rich stared at Tash. Her brow was furrowed with concern. Her hair was tied back in a ponytail. It had been neat and tight at the beginning of the evening and she'd looked sophisticated and sexy. Now the clip had worked loose; bits of hair had escaped. Strands framed her face so that now she looked scruffy and sexy. Rich reached up to tuck a strand behind her ear. She blushed, and he smiled.

"I bet I look terrible, all sweaty and smudged eye makeup, right?" she asked.

"You're lovely," he replied.

And she was.

She was truly lovely to look at, but more than that she was a really lovely person. She was concerned that Kate and Ted were arguing; she'd watched them interacting with Lloyd to try to work out what was going on. She cared about people. She wanted to understand them and help them, and that was lovely.

Shit.

What if she turned the focus of her attention and intuitiveness toward the tension between him, Jayne and Jase? That wouldn't be lovely. That would be a fucking bloodbath. He pulled his hand away from her hair as though he were scorched.

"I don't think it's healthy to obsess and speculate about other people like that. You could be miles off the mark. It's dangerous."

"Dangerous?" asked Tash, somewhat taken aback by the sudden change in Rich's tone. She'd been enjoying the sensation of him stroking her face, fiddling with her hair. It had felt calming and intimate. "What's dangerous about saying I think they are arguing?"

"What did you mean when you said Lloyd was involved? Why are you connecting him to Kate and Ted? What are you suggesting?"

"Nothing. I'm not suggesting anything." Tash met Rich's irritated accusation with fiery indignation.

"Next, you'll be saying that just because Jayne and Jase are acting a bit weird, there is something going on there, and that it's my fault."

Fear and booze emboldened Rich and allowed him to drive closely to the truth. He was almost daring Tash to say yes, that was exactly what she thought. Then he could confess. And that would be a relief. That was what he wanted. Oh God, no, no. It was the last thing he wanted.

"Don't be silly." Tash grinned, and stretched across the table to take hold of Rich's hand. "There *is* something going on between Jase and Jayne, or at least there was. I'm not so sure now. But why would that be your fault?"

Tell her. Tell her, a voice in his head was almost hoarse with screaming. Still he ignored it.

"Jayne admitted to me that she and Jason fooled around a bit on Sunday night, but this morning Lloyd saw a young blonde number stagger from Jason's room, so the thing with Jayne is probably all over before it even began. Poor Jayne, she really doesn't need to be messed around at the moment. It's making her very cynical. God, Jason is a one, isn't he? Can't keep it in his trousers, can he?"

"I don't like you gossiping with Lloyd," snapped Rich. He drained his beer and signaled to the waiter to bring them two more.

"You're joking, right?"

"No, I'm not. People can get the wrong end of the stick about situations, and that leads to trouble."

"Maybe, but in this case the girl left Jason's room sticky and sordid at seven in the morning. I don't think there are two ways of interpreting that situation. Why are you being so huffy? I thought you'd be pleased that I'm building relationships with your friends. Swapping confidences."

"Swapping gossip, more like."

Rich had forgotten that only a matter of a few days before he had fantasized that Tash would swap gossip with Mia. Now he wanted everyone to be quiet. To stay still and say nothing. Until he was married, at least.

The bar was hot and heaving. The dance music blared so loudly that Tash could feel the base beat throb through her body and head, or maybe that was the alcohol. Alcohol always seemed like a good idea at the time and rarely was. Tash massaged her temples. What gossip? What was Rich so touchy about? She didn't want to allow Jayne's nonsense to drift into her head and affect her clear thinking, but . . . well, Jayne *had* known the gang longer than Tash had. Maybe there was something more to the Mia situation than Rich was letting on. Why else would he be so defensive about her getting close to his friends? Did they know something she didn't? Was there something between him and Mia? Tash sighed and rubbed her eyes. This train of thought was madness. She felt strung out.

Rich continued to lecture her. "I think it would be best if you didn't get too involved in people's affairs—I mean, business. From now on you should restrict your conversations to—"

"The weather? For fuck's sake, Richard, what are you thinking about?" Tash's finely stretched patience suddenly snapped. Rich wasn't thinking, he was panicking, but he couldn't explain why. "Get off your high horse, Richard. I'm doing my best here. I'm trying very hard to build new relationships with your friends, and I'm doing that for you."

"We're not talking about diplomatic efforts on the scale of negotiating the Belfast agreement here, are we?" asked Rich sarcastically. "Since when has making friends been such a hardship?"

Immediately he regretted his alcohol-induced anger and question. For a start he wasn't really angry with Tash; he was furious with Jayne. And besides, Tash would insist on answering his question *honestly* and actually he wasn't sure he wanted that.

True to form, she replied, "I don't know. Up until very recently, there was hardly a soul on the planet that I couldn't get on with. The security guard at my gym is a little overofficious, but generally, Richard, I expect to get on with other people."

"So you don't like my friends. It's not a big deal. I can see them on my own."

"I didn't say I don't like them," cried Tash defensively. "I do like them. I especially like Jayne. It's you who has the problem with Jayne. Jason is amusing, and Lloyd is a bit mixed up, but I think we're getting to know each other and he's an interesting guy. I haven't got a great deal in common with Ted and Kate, but I can see that they are decent people."

She took another slug of her beer, then scowled at the bottle. She should keep quiet. Perhaps the honesty policy should not come into play when they were both drunk and tired. As her mind decided to hold back, her mouth contradicted her and she blurted, "OK, OK, I don't like Mia."

"Why don't you like Mia?" Rich was stunned.

He must know. He must have heard the snide jibes and outright put-downs. Why couldn't Rich see any wrong in Mia? He was blind.

Love was blind.

No, it couldn't be that, could it? Jayne could not be right, there was nothing going on between Rich and Mia. But there once had been, hadn't there? That was a fact because Rich had told her as much. What was it that Jayne had said earlier? Something about Rich smelling Mia, touching Mia, nibbling her nipples, kissing her thighs. No, no, that was in the past. Not now.

"I think there are a number of unresolved issues that Mia is harboring."

"Unresolved issues? What are you talking about?"

"Is it possible that she has the hots for you?" Tash only just resisted asking him to answer honestly. It was unnecessary—they only ever answered one another honestly, right?

"That is the most ridiculous thing I have ever heard."

Tash was relieved that Rich's outrage was genuine. She exhaled deeply, somewhat calmed. "It was just that, earlier on, Jayne and I were talking about stuff."

"What stuff?"

"Monogamy, our deal to be completely honest with one another, ex-lovers, that sort of thing—"

"What? What the fuck were you talking about that sort of stuff with Jayne for?" Tash didn't know how to answer. Rich's outrage was definitely unwelcome this time.

"Just girl stuff," she stuttered.

"Well, don't. Don't talk to Jayne. She's a horrible, malicious scandalmonger. She's not to be trusted. Why can't you make Mia your friend?"

"You're telling me who I can and can't talk to?"

"Jayne is not a suitable friend."

"You sound like a Victorian husband," said Tash, aghast. "You are scaring me. Next you'll be saying I can't work when we have children, and you'll dish out housekeeping and tell me not to buy anything frivolous."

"Don't be stupid."

Her fears didn't feel stupid. They felt very, very real. The couple fell silent.

Rich was thinking about the fabulous summer that he and Tash had enjoyed. They'd played tennis together, rode their mountain bikes around Richmond Park. They'd been to countless bars and clubs. They'd shopped, slept, loved, laughed, played, cooked and eaten together. They had lots in common. Rich lost himself in a specific memory: he and Tash Rollerblading in Hyde Park last August.

They were both fairly accomplished, although personally he had thought he was marginally better until suddenly Tash started to do these clever little tricks. Nothing too adventurous at first, just tiny jumps and turns, but there had been a group of gay guys

picnicking nearby and she'd caught their attention. They'd enthusiastically whooped their encouragement with the joie de vivre that
the French are famous for but the gay community actually pos-
sesses. Tash had responded marvelously, her confidence growing
with their mounting praise until she attempted complicated twirls
and short sequences. Tricks she'd learned as a girl, when she used
to ice skate, she later explained to Rich. The picnickers became
quite raucous in expressing their appreciation. They cheered and
clapped with glee, which in turn attracted more onlookers. In the
end there was a crowd watching Tash perform, as though she were
some kind of professional.

Rich had felt so proud, so totally and utterly proud of his
beautiful Tash, who could do tricks on Rollerblades. It was possibly
the proudest moment of his life, way more exciting than passing
his degree or getting his first job. It amazed him to recognize that
this moment was more enchanting for him than losing his virginity or buying his first apartment. It was love. It delighted him that
the woman whom everyone was watching, the woman everyone
admired and adored, loved him. And suddenly everything had
seemed right with the world. He believed the world was a better
place because the crowd recognized the wonder of Tash. Complete
strangers could see how spectacular she was—and he didn't just
mean the simple act of being able to gracefully execute some clever
blading tricks. He believed that they were cheering the essence of
her, the total brilliance of the woman he was in love with.

Tash was still fuming that Rich had called her stupid. She
abruptly stood up. "I need some air."

With that, Tash turned on her heel and strode out of the bar.
Tash had probably only walked a few hundred yards back to the
hotel, and all Rich's best friends in the world were nearby in the
hotel or here in this bar with him.

Yet.

He felt very alone.

# 48

## *Cold Comfort*

Tash marched out of the bar into the night. The bar door closed behind her, sealing in the noise of blaring loudspeakers and a hundred voice boxes. She gratefully breathed in the cold air and calming silence.

"We meet again. We'll have to stop doing this or else people will talk."

Tash was startled and jumped. It took her a second to place the voice.

"Lloyd?"

"At your service, ma'am," he slurred. Lloyd tried to salute, but succeeded only in hitting himself in the eye with the beer bottle he was holding. The effect was comical, and Tash needed a laugh. She giggled.

"Ouch, that must have hurt."

"It would have except most of my body is numb with the cold and the other bits have been anesthetized by alcohol," replied Lloyd. He carefully enunciated every word; it was clear that he was trashed.

"You are drinking too much, Lloyd," said Tash, with her signature honesty. "You ought to cut down. You're not doing yourself any favors."

Lloyd shrugged, accepting her comment, but not intending to act on it. He was sitting on a wooden bench. He hadn't bothered to wipe the snow away before he sat down, but didn't seem to notice it was melting, creating a large sodden area on his jeans.

"What are you doing out here alone?" Tash asked.

"I saw Ted and Kate leave the bar, quite abruptly. I thought they might need me."

"In what way?"

"Oh, just to hail a sleigh because of Ted's injured ankle, that sort of thing," said Lloyd vaguely. "Jingle bells, jingle bells, jingle all the way," he sang, waving his beer bottle around as though he were conducting an orchestra. "Whoosh! I love the sleigh bells, don't you?"

"Yes. I thought Ted's ankle was OK now. He skied today, didn't he?"

"It's complicated," replied Lloyd. Tash couldn't understand how catching a sleigh for a ride of few hundred meters could be described as complicated. She was convinced that Lloyd was holding something back.

"Are they arguing?" she asked bluntly.

"Well, that's the odd thing," replied Lloyd. "I thought they were. They ought to be. But they weren't. I followed them out here, and I saw Kate take hold of Ted's hand. Like this." Lloyd grabbed hold of Tash's hand, very tightly. She flinched, and he noticed. "Sorry. Maybe not as tightly as that, but like—affectionate tight. I realized that they didn't need me at all. No, no, no, not at all. Which is good because, well, it is." He hesitated. "But I did like being needed, even for that short while."

Tash didn't think Lloyd was making much sense. Why "ought" Kate and Ted to be having a domestic? And, if they were, how on earth could Lloyd be of any help? She wasn't really interested enough to ask either of these things, and instead asked, "Are you going to go back into the bar?"

"I don't think so. I have all the company I need here." Lloyd waved his arm toward a shopping bag.

Tash could see that he'd visited the local mini-mart and bought a six-pack of beer and, quite endearingly, a kilo bar of Toblerone. She'd always assumed it was only women who comfort ate.

"Aren't you having a very nice time?" she asked as she lowered herself on to the bench next to him.

Good manners dictated that Lloyd would assure Tash he was having a wonderful time—after all, this was her wedding party. He paused for a second and stared into her large blue eyes. He knew she'd detect his bullshit if he tried it.

"Everyone is a couple," moaned Lloyd, with an accuracy that startled them both. "You and Rich are all loved up and into each other. Quite rightly, I mean it's days off your wedding." Tash didn't interrupt to say she'd just walked out on Rich. "Ted and Kate, of course, and Mia and Jason."

"Mia and Jason aren't a couple." This time Tash did interrupt.

"Oh, yes, they are; they always have been. Even though they aren't together in a romantic sense, they are always a team."

"I thought Jason fancied Jayne, and that blonde you told me about, and oh, well, any of a number."

"Oh, yes, he fancies those women, but Mia is the one he talks to."

"They are always bickering, always at each other's throats."

"I know. It's as though they are married already, isn't it?" said Lloyd with a grin.

"But Mia isn't interested in him, is she?"

"She is. Very much so, if this week is anything to go by. She's obsessed with him."

"With Jase?"

"Yes, Jase. She's always watching him, laughing with him, chatting with him."

This was all too much for Tash to take in. She'd had nearly the identical conversation with Jayne this morning, but about Mia and *Rich*. Could Lloyd be right and Jayne mistaken? Was Mia interested in Jase, not Rich? Maybe that's why she took boarding lessons and maybe that's why she was always hanging around the pool hall. Oh, God, she hoped so.

It wouldn't explain why Mia seemed to dislike Tash, though.

Tash tuned back to her conversation with Lloyd. "Well, look on the bright side, that leaves you Jayne to chat to, and Jayne is gorgeous."

Lloyd shook his head. Yes, Jayne was a beauty, and she was without doubt informed, clever and chatty, but he felt too old for late-night flirtations in loud bars. He regretted . . . what? He was too drunk to articulate exactly what he regretted. The regret fluttered around his head, like a flighty red admiral butterfly, always escaping his net. He certainly regretted being here alone. He should have insisted that Greta was invited along, too. Why hadn't he?

"No one seems to be having a very good night, do they?" admitted Tash. She didn't see any point in pretending it was otherwise. "A superstitious bride would be worried about that on the run-up to her wedding."

"Are you superstitious?" asked Lloyd.

"Not normally." Tash grinned at Lloyd.

"Sophie, my ex," added Lloyd, as though Tash would have forgotten who Sophie was, "she was very superstitious. She wouldn't walk under ladders, was forever throwing salt over her shoulder and on the first of the month she'd pinch and punch me." Lloyd took another swig of his beer.

"What?" asked Tash slightly bemused. She was pretty sure that Lloyd wasn't a victim of domestic violence. So what was he going on about?

"You know. 'Pinch, punch, first of the month.' We would race to say, 'White Rabbits,' on the first day of the month, then sort of playfully pinch and punch the one who'd forgotten to say it. All nonsense, of course. Couple stuff."

Lloyd took a drag on his cigarette. Tash didn't think this was the moment to point out that he didn't smoke. Lloyd looked wistful. Tash was cold and fed up. It had been a long day, and she wanted to go to bed and shut out all this confusion and mess. She needed to sleep on all the conversations she'd had today and try to draw some sense from them, but she'd honed in on Lloyd's need and couldn't ignore it.

"Tell me more about Sophie. What is she like?"

"A bit like you, actually, in the beginning," replied Lloyd truthfully. Immediately he started to apologize, "Sorry. That wasn't a come-on."

"I didn't take it as one."

"Thanks. It's just so many people seem to take everything I say in the wrong way at the moment." Lloyd paused. "Well, for a while now. I've come to the conclusion that Sophie was right about that, at least. I'm not a very good communicator. Com-mun-ee-kate-oor."

Lloyd repeated the word. He wished he'd been given a pound for every time someone had asked him to communicate better. It annoyed him intensely. It wasn't as though he were deliberately obscure. Perhaps the civil service wasn't the right field for him if he was such a dismal communicator.

Or perhaps it was.

Tash nodded toward the shopping bag of beer. "Do you mind if I join you?"

"Help yourself."

As Tash settled back onto the wooden bench, accepting the inevitability of a cold, wet bum, she asked, "So, go on, what is she like?"

Lloyd thought it was odd that Tash spoke of Sophie in the present tense. No one ever did that nowadays. They talked about her in the past tense, and often in whispers, as though she were dead. And in many ways she was dead, at least to him.

"Bubbly. Funny. Loud. Emotional." Lloyd listed his ex-wife's character traits as though he were reading a train timetable until he said, "Honest," when he became more intense. He grappled with the word. "Her honesty, her ability . . . no, her need to say what she feels is the thing that reminds me of you."

"Oh, I wondered if it was our unpopularity."

"You're not unpopular." Lloyd was genuinely surprised. The boys hadn't really discussed Tash much, beyond "Good legs" and "Good laugh," but that general consensus of approval was high acclaim in boy world.

"Not normally, no."

"All the guys think Rich has done far better than he deserves. He's a very lucky chap." Lloyd hoped he didn't sound as though he were flirting. He needn't have worried, he didn't sound as though he were flirting. Flirting had never been his line.

"I guess I've been hoping for too much."

"You have a problem with us, his old gang, don't you?"

"No. No, not at all." Lloyd raised one eyebrow and looked skeptical. "A little bit at first. I guess I felt left out," Tash admitted. "I pride myself on not being jealous of his past romances, conquests, liaisons, call them what you will. But I find myself simply jealous of his past friendships. I felt I had to catch up on years of history in just a couple of days. It's not possible."

"Sophie used to say similar things. She said that we were a very exclusive crew."

"She was right. I hadn't realized that I was about to enter some secret society with passwords and handshakes and everything."

"You're exaggerating."

"Am I?" Tash felt irritated that her new friend wasn't endorsing her point of view more wholeheartedly.

"I don't believe you haven't fallen under Jason's spell. He's a delight."

"I have," confessed Tash. "I think he's great, and I really like Jayne, but Rich doesn't."

"Doesn't he? Why not?" Lloyd was surprised. He'd seen Rich and Jayne together quite a lot. He'd thought they got along fine. Lloyd could not imagine a man alive that would not have a soft spot for Jayne. "Kate has a heart of gold," Lloyd pointed out. Tash nodded. "And if Ted is a bit distant at the moment it's because he has things on his mind. I know Mia can be sharp, but—"

"But what? What's her excuse for such constant rudeness? She has relentlessly worked to make me feel barred and unwelcome."

Lloyd shrugged and chose not to reply. Tash had thought Lloyd would understand how it felt not to be accepted as part of the select crew, as he had so clearly been excluded of late. Hadn't he noticed? They were both on the outside. It annoyed Tash that he was blinded by what she considered to be misplaced loyalty.

"So Mia is the problem."

"She seems to do her utmost to make me feel inadequate. I am so sick of listening to her historical anec-gloats! I feel I'm marrying into a mafia."

Lloyd chuckled. "That's exactly what Sophie used to say. She was always making jokes about finding a horse's head on her pillow." Tash didn't see the joke. "*We're* mates, though, aren't we?" asked Lloyd.

Tash looked at him and smiled. "Yes, we are," she confirmed. Tash patted Lloyd's leg, pecked him on the cheek and stood up. "I've said and drunk too much. I'm going to bed to sleep this off. Good night."

"Night." Tash strode through the snow. It crunched under her new pink fluffy boots. "Nice boots," called Lloyd.

"Thanks," yelled Tash back into the blackness; she was already fifty yards away. She ground her footprints into the snow. Bloody Rich hadn't even noticed them. Barbara Cartland pink, furry, knee-high boots, and he hadn't even noticed them. What was he thinking of? Tash wondered if she had the courage to ask. The pitch darkness helped. Lloyd wouldn't be able to see her humiliation.

"Lloyd?"

"Yes?"

"Do you think there is anything going on between Rich and Mia?"

"Hah. Good God, no."

Tash grinned, cheered by the emphatic answer, and went on her way.

Lloyd listened to the sound of her feet scrunching through the fresh snow. He listened until the scrunching died away, then he listened to the silence of the black night and the huge Alps. Lloyd couldn't decide if he was simply very, very drunk, but he felt strangely buoyed up, almost elated. This was twice on this trip when he'd set out to offload some of his problems and found himself in the position of confidant. It felt rather good. He felt important and needed.

Lloyd wondered if he should make his way back to the hotel, too. It wouldn't do to get so drunk that he passed out. He'd get hypothermia.

# 49

## *Kiki*

S he's cute, her. Look over there." Jason was pointing toward a mass of girls on the dance floor. They still had flawless skin and puppy fat, most of which was on show because they all wore very short skirts and tiny, strappy tops.

"Which one? They all look alike," Mia moaned. She was bored with indulging Scaley Jase in his game of pointing out "cheeky chicks." She actually wanted him to stop looking around the bar and look at the girl who was standing right next to him.

"That one there. The one with bra-strap-length hair."

Sometimes it wore a little bit thin, the constant sexual innuendos. Mia wasn't prudish, but there had been a couple of occasions when she'd thought it would have been more agreeable, more grown up, if Scaley Jase didn't insist on commenting on the tits or buttocks of every girl he came into contact with, every pop star snapped in magazines and even the cartoons pictured on the rude postcards.

"Can't you just say shoulder length like everyone else?" she grumbled.

"No, it's not as horny."

"And that's the be-all and end-all, is it, what's horny?"

"Well, it is important." Jase grinned. "I'm looking for some action between the sheets. Of course I'm looking for someone foxy to play with."

"What about what's real?" asked Mia, exasperated, but Jason wasn't listening to her as he was offering to buy someone a drink. The girl at the receiving end of his attention was unlikely to be older than twenty. She wore very heavy, dark eyeliner and layer upon layer of mascara. It was a wonder she could open her eyes with the weight.

"The nightlife here is entirely seaside resort," moaned Mia.

"I know. It's fantastic, isn't it?" Scaley grinned, missing her point.

"I preferred the bar we were in last night," she shouted above the noise. Jason shrugged and started to hum the chorus of "YMCA," which was currently playing. Mia marveled. Jason was normally so London. He usually spent his time in the most chic and groovy clubs in town. He had private membership to the clubs Home and Soho House (which Mia had always found confusing and which had led, on one occasion, to her waiting for him at Home when he was at the House—such poor planning to have the names of two of London's most coveted private members' clubs being so similar; she wondered whom she should write to to complain). How could he be happy knee-deep in cheese and tack? She had forgotten that last night she'd believed that it did not matter where you were, just who you were with. Her limited supply of patience was quickly being spent. She had seen Jayne off, she'd accepted the inevitability of Jason indulging in a quickie with the busty bottle blonde, but enough was enough. When was he going to notice her? What did she have to do? Strip naked and tattoo "Take me" across her boobs?

Jason paid for the drink, then started up a conversation. The girl was Dutch. Scaley Jase became visibly more excited when she revealed this. He clearly thought that because sex workers were legal in Holland every woman born there was more likely to be open to the weird and wonderful. After a few minutes of pleasantries, the girl picked up her drink and walked back to her gang of friends.

"Crashed and burned?" asked Mia, hardly able to keep the joy out of her voice.

"On the contrary." Jason smiled. He folded up a beer mat and slipped it into his jeans pocket. "She gave me her apartment details and told me I should swing by at about eleven for a few drinks with her and some of her friends."

"She did what?" asked Mia, amazed. "You'd only been talking to her for two minutes."

"That's my fatal charm," confirmed Jason.

"But you could have been anyone. You could be a rapist or a murderer. What was she doing giving you her details so quickly. She must be brainless."

"I expect she knows how to look after herself. Besides, I'm not a rapist or a murderer," pointed out Jase.

Mia huffed crossly. She felt old. But, then, even when she was young she couldn't remember being so idiotically trusting. Jason could see that Mia was upset and so tried to reassure her.

"I let her see my platinum card. It happens all the time."

"What?" He'd failed. Mia's disquiet turned to fury. "Are you saying that the girl is only interested in you because she knows you are rich?"

"Well, I like to think I'm great company, too, but as you pointed out she hardly had time to find that out. Mia, don't sweat it, she's a certain type of girl. She wants a good time, and she knows I can pay for it. It's all just a bit of fun. I tell you, that girl will be able to handle herself."

At that point their conversation was interrupted. A small, plump girl approached Jason. She wore her hair in a blunt, raven bob, except for her fringe, which was scarlet.

"I saw you flashing your money about, mate. You don't want to be wasting your time on those foreign birds, they never follow through. All Catholics are prick teases. Now, mine's a Malibu and Coke. The liquid variety, that is, unless you have something else to offer."

The girl winked and laughed. Her laugh was deep and gravelly. She was clearly confident that Jason would buy her a drink, which he did.

"Actually, she was Dutch and the Dutch aren't an especially Catholic nationality, even if your stereotype about Catholics were correct," said Mia snootily.

She really wished Jason wouldn't waste their time by messing around with this sort of girl. Mia had to admit she had a pretty face, big smile and large brown eyes, but she needed to cut back on the pies and, in any case, she was clearly very common.

"Whatever." The girl didn't feel it was necessary to talk to Mia. She looked like someone's mother, she was unlikely to have a platinum credit card and, even if she did, she would not buy the Malibu.

Mia stuck by Jason for another hour. She didn't join in their conversation, which was mostly about bands she hadn't heard of and TV programs she didn't watch. She loathed reality TV and prided herself on the fact that she hadn't ever watched a single episode of *Big Brother*. The girl's conversation was depressingly predictable, mostly about how she "got right fookin' smashed and vommed everywhere." Mia suggested they all dance because at least that way she wouldn't have to listen to the ridiculous chatter. Unfortunately, at the moment Mia made the suggestion, the tempo of the music changed to a slow, romantic number. Jason grabbed the hand of the Malibu-and-Coke girl and led her onto the tiny dance floor.

Mia was left alone propping up the bar. Her body ached from the boarding bruises, and her head ached with what felt like the onset of a hangover. She hadn't even been drinking. Slowly her optimism eked away. She had begun this evening so sure of her plan. She'd been convinced that the photos had done the trick. For a while Jason had looked at her in, well, a different way than normal. More intensely, more carefully. He'd talked to her all evening, and they hadn't stopped laughing. Even when they were arguing it had been fun. (He was wrong about the Finlay Quaye lyrics. He needed his hearing tested.)

Mia watched as Jason and the girl crawled all over one another. She had seen Scaley Jase dance with countless women. She had seem him emerge disheveled from women's bedrooms the morning after the night before. She had been privy to endless stories of his conquests; it wasn't as though his provocative dancing really marked anything different from everything she'd seen before.

And yet.

Yet.

She felt odd.

She felt sad. Weary and disappointed. Clearly if Scaley slept with this floozie tonight instead of her, her chances of conceiving were obliterated, but it was more than that. She was too good for this. She shouldn't be standing on the sidelines of a dance floor waiting for a drunken ex to notice her again. And Jason was too good for this. He shouldn't be dancing with a girl whose fingernails, eyelashes and boobs were fake.

Jason came back to the bar. "Do you remember where I left my jacket?" he asked. Mia pointed to the floor. Their jackets were rolled into tight balls and shoved under a bar stool.

"Are you leaving?" she asked.

Jason slid his arm into his jacket sleeve. "Oh, yeah, I think my luck's in."

"Of course it is, she was hardly going to present a challenge," snapped Mia. Jason didn't reply to that.

"Kiki has just gone to get her jacket. You can walk back to the hotel with us if you like, or are you planning on staying here for a bit longer?"

"Kiki?"

"It's not her real name."

"Thank heaven for that." Mia bent down to pick up her jacket. Not even her own name. How could he ever get close to someone if the people he cavorted with didn't even know who they were? Sunday had been Jayne. Monday, the busty blonde. Tuesday, Kiki. With every day and every lay, Mia saw her chances of conceiving recede.

She was going to have to revisit the idea of a sperm donor. Her plan was preposterous. Jason wasn't fit to be a father, even in the most perfunctory sense. He was still a child himself. She would accept the offer of an escort back to the hotel, order a hot chocolate and then read the next chapter of her novel. She would not demand, "Jason, how could you sleep with a woman like her?"

Whoops, it just sort of popped out.

"And how is she, *exactly,* in your opinion, Mia?" Jason asked with irritation. Even if Mia hadn't been expecting to pour scorn on the situation, Jason had been expecting her to do so. Sometimes he knew her better than she knew herself.

"Well, she can barely string a sentence together. The only view she expressed all evening was that Diet Coke makes Malibu taste 'fookin' 'orrid,' and her idea of a discussion on current affairs is saying that she likes Posh's hair extensions."

"I'm not looking for great debate." Jason smiled. Was Mia jealous?

"She's stupid. It's demeaning. The people you choose to have sex with say something about the type of person you are." Mia was surprised to find herself quoting Tash.

"She's not stupid, she's very street savvy. Besides," he added, with an annoyed shake of his head, "I just want a lay, and it may come as a surprise to you but stupid people, as you call them—poorly educated people, as I prefer to see them—have fantastic sex, too, you know. It's the great leveler. They possibly have even better sex than you do because, more often than not, they swallow."

"How do you know whether I swallow or not?"

"I remember."

Mia froze. In the thirteen years since they split up neither one of them had ever alluded to the fact that they once were boyfriend and girlfriend. The rest of the gang openly talked about what a great couple they'd been, but Scaley Jase and Mia had studiously avoided the subject. It had seemed to be the only route to take if they wanted to remain friends. And they did want to remain friends. Neither of them could imagine a world where they weren't in each other's lives.

"Oh, do what you like," said Mia. She grabbed her coat and stomped out of the bar, not waiting for the escort back to the hotel.

"I always do," Jason replied to the empty space she left behind her.

# 50

## *Kate's Response*

I love you," he said.

"I know you do," sighed Kate. She'd never doubted that.

Ted stared at the top of Kate's head because she refused to look up and meet his gaze.

"I'll go immediately. I'll get right out of your life. I understand I've made a terrible mess of things and you can't be expected to forgive me, or live with it. I'll go."

"Go where?" asked Kate.

Ted raked his hand through his hair, "Er, I haven't thought about that. My parents. Anywhere. Out of your sight."

"You stupid, stupid, selfish man," she yelled, her calm blown away.

"I know. I know. Really there's nothing you can say that I haven't said of myself, but say it anyway if it makes you feel better. It's your right."

Kate stared at her husband. There was snow in his hair, he'd catch a chill if he didn't towel-dry it. But what did she care? He'd told her they were ruined in a bar in Avoriaz, miles away from home. He told her they'd been broke for months, but he'd booked them into this plush suite in this luxury hotel anyway and, even though they'd walked out of the bar hand in hand, he was now telling her he was leaving her. What a stupid, idiotic, cruel gesture.

She stood up and got him a towel from the bathroom. She passed it to him, and he took it as though it were a live serpent. Ted struggled to interpret the gesture. Kate struggled to recognize her husband. The change was eerie. Ted was dressed in designer casual wear as usual. Ralph Lauren polo shirt and chinos, but the labels no longer shielded him. Her husband looked like a boy—the fat, bullied, unpopular boy who smelled stale and sat at the back of every classroom. How was it possible? Her cautious, steady Teddy, who always weighed up the pros and cons, why hadn't he seen the consequences of his actions? Hadn't he seen that giving Miss H a tip would be considered to be insider dealing?

"I don't want you to leave, you idiot. Didn't you just say you love me?"

"Yes."

"Well, prove it. Stay and sort this mess out with me."

Ted could not believe his luck. He had married the most fabulous woman in the entire world. And he hadn't even known it. Yes, he'd always loved her. God, he loved her so much. He'd always been amazed that Kate had accepted his proposal in the first place, which had been nothing more than a rashly hopeful pitch. He'd always believed her to be kind and clever, and then she'd turned out to be such a fantastic mother and she was lovely to his friends and parents. He's always been proud of her at his corporate events. She chatted easily to his boss and never got drunk, yet she had fun and didn't ever come across as dull or snooty, as some corporate wives could.

He'd always been her biggest fan.

But now this. This was amazing. This took his breath away. Nothing could have prepared him for this level of fabulousness.

Finally, it all came tumbling out. He told her everything. Stop-start, stop-start. It hadn't been easy. Telling your wife you were a bankrupt failure was not easy. He'd cried, again. It was becoming an embarrassing habit. He'd hardly dared look at her. He didn't want to see her disgust, or anger, or despair. But then she'd put her hands on his face and gently but firmly lifted his chin.

"Why didn't you tell me?" she asked.

"I couldn't. I didn't know how. I didn't want to disappoint you."

Then Kate cried, too. She'd failed her husband because he hadn't been able to talk to her. He didn't trust her enough. He hadn't been able to depend on her. Kate began to retrace their steps over the past five months. She imagined her husband pretending to go to work, preferring to sit on a park bench than talk to her, and she felt sick with self-loathing. What kind of woman did he take her for? He should have had more confidence in her and in himself. It was truly pitiful. She pieced together his lies and excuses. Temper tantrums and sulking that had seemed inexplicable were now too horribly understandable.

"This is why we didn't have a New Year's Eve party. Obviously you weren't working on a secret merger."

"It would have cost us thousands."

"So this is why you were angry about the cost of the doctor."

"Yes."

"And my ordering room service and à la carte."

"Yes."

"And, tonight, we can't even afford a couple of bottles of champagne?"

"Our card would have been rejected, probably cut up in front of everyone."

"My God. I'm sorry," said Kate, shocked.

"No, no, God. No, I'm the sorry one, Kate. My angel, Kate."

Kate blew her nose and said, "I thought you were sick. I thought there was someone else."

"Really? You thought that of me?" Ted didn't know whether to be amused, insulted or flattered that his wife assumed he could still attract someone else and that he would ever act upon it.

"Well, not seriously." She smiled.

He'd thought telling Kate would be his final undoing, the ultimate humiliation, but she stunned him. Throughout the night she asked all sorts of questions and gently probed to establish the severity of their situation. She suggested they consider suing for unfair dismissal, but he told her he had already talked to their lawyer and that they had no case. She did not allow the disappointment that she felt to flicker across her face. She suggested names of friends and acquaintances in the City—perhaps they could help to find him something new. He gently explained how he'd called all those people. If his calls had been returned at all, the news was never good. Often, his calls were ignored.

"It's a tough market at the moment. I'm sure people would like to help if they could," he said because he wanted to believe this was the case. Kate mentally crossed these names off her Christmas card list.

She insisted that they'd manage. That they'd make economies, that they'd take out loans, sell the house, do anything and *everything* to make it all OK. At first Ted pitied Kate. He vaguely remembered when he had been optimistic about their situation, when he'd believed there was a solution. Now he was numb with fear because there wasn't. However, as Kate continued to repeatedly reassure him throughout the night, he allowed some of her hopefulness to seep into his consciousness. Slowly he was drenched in her love and doused with her confidence. Perhaps, together, they *could* deal with this. Ted bathed in her sensible, composed attitude. It felt like peace.

They talked until the sun came up, then Kate insisted that they should try to sleep.

"Things always look better in the morning, and we can't do anything right now, anyway." She yawned. "I'll be happy to see the back of the boat. I never really took to sailing, and not having the party this New Year's Eve was actually a relief," muttered Kate, who was weary with weeping and thinking. "We don't have to go to the opera every month. We can watch *My Fair Lady* on DVD."

Ted looked doubtful, as any thirty-three-year-old man would.

"It's a wonderful film," insisted Kate. "I've always preferred musicals to opera. I must have seen it at least fifteen times. I used to watch it when I did the ironing. Not that I do the ironing anymore, not now that we have Mrs. Walker coming in every weekday." Kate paused. "We won't be having Mrs. Walker anymore, will we?"

"No," said Ted, "and don't try to tell me that you are looking forward to doing the ironing."

"No, you can do that," she'd said, and then she closed her eyes and fell asleep.

# WEDNESDAY

# 51

## *What Kate Did Next*

Ted felt three stones lighter.

He'd woken early and crept out of their room to go to the mini-mart to buy croissants and yogurt. He couldn't face meeting the others at breakfast, and room service was out of the question. Now that his credit had been severed, they'd be struggling to find a means to pay for the room without running the debt any higher. Even knowing this, Ted felt more relaxed, more confident and hopeful than he had in five months.

He dropped a plastic bag onto the bed, and Kate stirred.

"Why didn't you tell me before?" she asked again, before she even thought to say good morning, before her eyes were entirely open. She noticed that the yogurt and the croissants had been purchased at the mini-mart, and appreciated the small economy. She sat up in bed and accepted the plastic spoon Ted proffered.

"I was scared that you'd leave me."

"Why would I leave you?" she asked, as she peeled back the tinfoil lid. She was ravenous. Unfortunately, stress made her hungry. She wasn't one of those women who could comfort themselves that at least, during the bad times, they'd drop a dress size. Kate knew the opposite was likely to be true.

"I have so little to offer now. I've made a terrible mistake. I've ruined our lives."

"Everyone makes mistakes," said Kate matter-of-factly, as though she were excusing him of buying the wrong toothpaste brand.

"I have no salary. I've spent our savings."

She stopped spooning yogurt into her mouth and said carefully, "Ted, it's never been about the money."

Ted wondered how this could be. When he had sat lonely and directionless on benches in London parks, he'd found himself whiling away the hours by calculating how much his lifestyle cost. Lifestyle, rather than life, because as he sat on a park bench in the drizzle, with nothing but an enormous shameful secret to keep him company, it seemed that he had no life.

He wore shirts that cost a hundred fifty quid a throw and cashmere suits, made to measure, anything over a grand, swathed his body. His ties were Hermès and cost £150. If one included socks and underwear, it cost him nearly £1,500 just to get dressed in the morning. His watch, Dunhill, cost a couple of grand. His cufflinks averaged £300 a pair. His wallet another two. In his briefcase he carried a Nokia with built-in camera (Kate had one of her own) and a color iPAQ (Kate had one of those, too, so that they could synchronize their calendars). His laptop was a top-of-the-range Sony VAIO. He certainly didn't care about such things; he'd always thought he was dressing for Kate.

Since the first day of their married life, every morning as he left the house, Kate would kiss him good-bye and say, "Make a million, darling. We're depending on you."

By "we," she didn't just mean herself and the children. Some mornings he left the house as Sally, the florist, was arriving. She visited once every two weeks to tend to the houseplants and fresh-cut flowers (she didn't touch the garden, they had a horticulturalist to deal with that). Besides Sally and the horticulturalist, other staff that visited (more frequently than their families) included Mrs. Walker, the housekeeper; Jill (or was it Jackie?—he couldn't remember), the girl who did the jobs that Mrs. Walker felt were beneath her; the seamstress (who seemed to be forever at Kate's beck and call, letting this out, taking that up); the window cleaner; the man who cleaned their aquarium; the teenage boy who walked the guard dog; and Kate's masseur and beautician. Ted had always believed they were *all* depending on him. It was this huge responsibility that, in the old days, had spurred him on so that on occasion he did make a million. More recently, it was this awful overwhelming thought that caused him to sit on the park bench, carefully place his case down next to him, then hold his head in his hands as he despaired.

But now Kate was telling him that it had never been about the money.

"Really?" he asked. It seemed too good to be true.

"I love you," said Kate carefully. "I'm horrified that you thought I loved your bank balance more than you or, worse, instead of you." Kate paused. If she had been a more hysterical woman she would have felt insulted. As it was she simply felt sorry that poor Ted had got it so wrong.

"Money comes and goes, but it doesn't make any difference." Ted raised his eyebrows to express his disbelief. Kate wanted to be as clear and straightforward as possible. She reconsidered what she'd just said and added, "Well, it does, a bit. It makes our lives easier, but we had so much money it had started to turn full circle and make our lives harder."

Kate put her hand on top of Ted's and squeezed hard. It was vital that he believe her. They only had a chance if he listened to her very, very closely and accepted what she was saying. Their marriage would not work if he thought she resented him or pitied him. She wanted him to understand what she was trying to say and the tiniest part of her dared to hope that he agreed with her, too.

"I felt I was this Edwardian lady running a home with staff and charities and such like. There are expectations that come with money, such as which schools to send the children to and which shoes to buy and which hairdresser to visit."

"You did everything so beautifully, though, like a swan gliding."

"Swan's glide along the surface, but paddle like fury under the water."

"You loved all that, Kate," said Ted. He was staring intently at a picture on the wall just behind Kate's left ear. He couldn't say what it depicted, although he'd looked at nothing else for a good ten minutes.

"At first I loved it. I liked being a good Edwardian lady, but only in the same way as I like being good at anything I turn my hand to. Being the spender was my new job. But, recently, I've found it a little overwhelming. I don't need it, Ted. I need you. I need the father of my children."

"We're not even going to be comfortable. We're going to be uncomfortable." Ted wanted to be clear that Kate knew what she was getting into.

"For a while, but we'll find balance again. I can get a job. We can move out of London. We can go to that house we've just bought Mum in the Cotswolds and live there."

"Actually, we can't. We don't own it. We have to give the keys back. I can't afford the mortgage payments."

"Oh."

The severe reality of their situation was slowly boxing Kate in and pinning her down, but to her surprise she wasn't scared. Maybe she was. Maybe she was so terrified that she was in shock. Maybe, but she honestly didn't think so. At that moment she didn't care if she had to grow her own vegetables to eat. All she wanted was for them to be together.

"So what are we going to do?" asked Ted.

It was a ridiculous question. He knew there were no quick fixes, no easy answers. If there were, he'd have exploited those months ago. But Ted believed in Kate, and he thought that somehow things could be better now, now that he knew she was on his side.

"We should leave here. Go back and deal with things at home, draw up lists of our debts and assets. We need to establish exactly where we stand."

"I'll go and let Rich and Tash know, and you could start to pack," said Ted.

He slowly moved toward the door. Kate knew that he must be smarting with the humiliation of telling their friends about the change in their fortunes. She ran to him and wrapped her arms around his neck and kissed him on the lips. It was a closed-mouth kiss, as was their habit, but they pushed their lips into one another's for an age until her lips parted and his tongue probed. They kissed like lovers, and when they broke apart Kate reassured him once more.

"We'll be OK, you know. I believe in you, Ted."

Ted straightened his shoulders and left the room.

# 52

## *Big Breakfast*

Breakfasts were hearty in des Dromonts. The literature the hotel provided politely suggested that hearty breakfasts were necessary for an energetic day on the slopes, which was true. But a hearty breakfast was also essential for soaking up the enormous hangovers, of which there always seemed to be an abundance.

Tash shivered as she lifted the stainless-steel lid off the dish. The meats were practically still bleating, grunting and mooing, and the cheeses were so pungent her nose itched. She searched around for something a little more English. She gratefully grabbed a box of cereal, not caring if the milk tasted weird. She also piled her plate with pastries.

She really had drunk too much last night. Why else would she have become so disgruntled that Rich had called her stupid? Of course he didn't mean that he really thought she was stupid. And how had she got it into her head that there was something going on between him and Mia? She had no evidence. No reason to suspect him of anything untoward. And, if Mia did have the hots for him, it was hardly his fault. It was possible that he was oblivious. She was embarrassed that she'd stormed out of the bar like that. She wished she hadn't said so much to Lloyd. It was disloyal. Although chances were he wouldn't remember. He'd drunk more than she had. And even if he did remember, Tash was pretty sure she could trust him to be a confidant.

She'd hoped that Rich would follow her. How drama queen was that? She'd behaved like a petulant teenager walking out of a school-hall disco in a huff, expecting her puppy-dog boyfriend to hurry after her. Of course it wasn't like that at their ages. If you walked out on someone, they respected your right to do so. They believed that you could judge your own need to be alone, and they would not come chasing after you.

More is the pity.

Crap. She felt foolish.

Rich had stumbled into their room at about 3 a.m. She'd pretended to be asleep because she didn't want to—

What?

Argue with him?

Or talk to him?

That was so daft. They'd apologized to one another this morning. They both admitted that they didn't know where the row had come from. They'd both agreed that they'd probably had too much to drink and that they should probably have a night off the booze tonight. There hadn't been time to make love, which Tash would have found reassuring, as Rich spent ages in the bathroom. Probably very hungover, he'd let the shower run and run forever.

Tash had gone down to breakfast alone. She felt edgy. Of course, it was unrealistic, childish even, to expect to have a relationship where there were never any rows. Still, a little bit of her had daydreamed that, when she met her soul mate (and Rich was definitely that), she *would* have a relationship where there were no rows. Tash didn't believe that they had truly made up. She believed that they had settled into a wary, grudging truce. It was inadequate.

She needed more food. This hangover was ravenous. Tash eased the lid off another enormous stainless-steel cauldron, only to immediately drop it again in her hurry to block out the smell of scrambled egg. Instead she picked up a yogurt and a bunch of grapes.

By contrast, Jayne was gliding through her hangover. If all things were equal, she would have a fuzzy tongue and furry teeth, her breath would smell as bad as the boys' rooms. But her breath smelled of Listerine, not an old beer keg. Her eyelids did not need to be stapled to the back of her eye sockets to remain open, and she had full control over her hands and feet. Neither her coordination nor her circulation had been drowned or pickled. She felt fully awake and alive. She was always more sparkly, more sensational, in Rich's company, and this morning she felt particularly bright, exhilarated, vital. Victory was within her grasp. She could almost smell her success.

They had danced all night.

Jason and Kiki were there, too, but only in matter, not in spirit. In spirit, Jayne and Rich had danced alone. Initially they had both danced quite conservatively. Jayne, in particular, knew how important it was not to look as though you were having too much fun on the dance floor; it was hardly cool. Instead she swayed gently to all the tracks, irrespective of whether it was a pop ballad or a rough, modern, urban beat playing. She allowed her jutting hip to occasionally bang against Rich. In the beginning it was clear that Rich was uncomfortable. Jayne wondered if he was going to turn out to be a good dancer after all. In all their time together they hadn't been out to a club, so she didn't know for sure, but she'd always assumed that he would be good. What type of music did he like to dance to? She knew he liked Nina Simone playing when he was having sex, but she didn't know that he listened to Linkin Park when he was driving his car and that he always played House of Pain's "Jump Around" as his "get-them-on-the-floor" track at parties. Jayne had never been invited to one of Rich's many parties.

The more Rich drank, the more relaxed he became. Jayne noted—with an indulgent sigh—that he was in this way the epitome of an Englishman. By 2 a.m. neither of them was particularly worried about whether they looked cool or not, which was a good thing because they did not. Both had drunk more units than they could count. Quite a feat, as Jayne had a first-class degree in mathematics. The music playing was uninspirational Eurotrash, without distinguishable beat or lyric or melody. The only possible response was to manically thrash their bodies and flay their limbs as they bounced around the floor. The dance floor was heaving. It seemed to sway and sink with the weight of the boisterous partying crowds. Girls climbed on their boyfriends' shoulders and screamed with fake terror and true excitement as their boyfriends bowed and buckled beneath their weight. It seemed that nobody

STILL THINKING *of* YOU

could stay upright. Countless people bumped and banged and knocked into each other. Jayne didn't really like the sweaty bodies pushed up against hers—who was a fan of strangers' sweat? But she envied the beads of sweat that slid down Rich's torso.

He'd kissed her. Not her kissing him and him halfheartedly responding. Not an uncertain kiss or even a tentative kiss. He'd kissed her with passion, purpose and eagerness. He'd walked her back to her room and he'd lingered outside the door. She opened the door and flashed her eyes from him to her bed and back to him. He'd moaned quietly, then hooked her head in his hand and forcefully pulled her face to his. He kissed her again, with tongues. A sexy, demanding, curious kiss. A kiss about which there was no ambiguity, only longing.

"Are you coming in?" Her voice was husky with drink, cigarettes and shouting above the noise in the bar.

"I can't," said Rich, shaking his head. "Not this time." He stumbled back down the corridor toward his and Tash's room. He put his arm in the air and waved, without turning around. In that moment, Jayne was certain that she was established. She was utterly celebrated, the sweet bits and the bad-girl bits. She felt sexy, complete, victorious and vindicated. Her life of waiting and longing was about to become something more vital, something real.

She went into her room, closed the door and fell onto the bed without giving a thought to removing her clothes or makeup. Her body was incapable of performing anything so mundane.


Jason was finding breakfast a strain. Lloyd had barely said a word. It was unlike him not to be able to bounce back from a big session. It was worrying. Jason was aware that the entire gang thought he was the party fiend with alcoholic overtures. He was so firmly entrenched in this stereotype that they had failed to notice that he'd drunk slightly less than everyone, and significantly less than some, throughout this trip. But characteristics bequeathed by old buddies were harder to break than the bad habits themselves. The issue being no one had noticed just how much Lloyd drank these days. Lloyd was considered staid, almost boring, not a party animal and therefore unlikely to go wild.

"You OK, buddy?"

Lloyd nodded, but didn't look up from his plate or pause as he shoveled scrambled egg into his mouth.

Jason wasn't able to wrestle much conversation out of Tash either. She was clearly preoccupied, and so she should be. He wondered what she'd say if she knew all he knew, or if she thought—even for a moment—that after she'd stormed out of the bar last night Rich had consoled himself on the dance floor with Jayne.

Fuck, Jase hoped Rich had kept the consolation to the dance floor. He stole a look at Jayne. She was beaming. Her happiness radiated. It was almost blinding and, in the face of the multiple hangovers, Jason thought her blatant cheeriness a little insensitive. Had Rich done the dirty deed again? Surely not. Maybe?

Fuck, this was a mess.

And then, that thing with Kiki. Jason parked the thought. He could not deal with it now. He didn't have to. Jason chose to stick to safe small talk.

"Where are Ted and Kate?" he asked. "It's not like them to be late."

"Are they late? I hadn't noticed. Oh, yes, of course, there are croissants left for everyone else. I should have guessed," said Jayne. She giggled as she made her comment, sure that she'd secure a few cheap laughs with her cheeky remark.

No one replied. Ted and Kate did eat more than everyone else. Everyone had noticed, but no one would have passed comment. Yet, as they had noticed, it would be hypocritical to chastise Jayne about her less-than-polite observation. Jayne immediately sensed that she'd stepped over the mark. She was usually careful to suppress any leanings toward cattiness, presenting herself as entirely sweetness and light. She knew the importance of being a crowd-pleaser, so she added, "I love people with proper appetites. I can't stand pickers, can you?"

The table chorused their agreement, and they were left feeling mildly guilty that they'd interpreted Jayne's initial comment as anything less than charming.

"Have you heard?" Mia cried in a loud stage whisper from the entrance of the breakfast room.

She hurried to the table and slipped into the chair next to Jason. Her expression bounced between excited and shocked, a little like those drivers who rubberneck as they pass an accident on the motorway. She ordered coffee from the waitress, and shooed away the waiter who was trying to drop a napkin on her nap.

"I can manage," she snapped at him. Her impatience was out of character—usually she loved the excessive attention secured at a luxury establishment such as this, but today she was intent on gossiping. "Have you heard about Big Ted and Ms. Monopoly?" she asked again.

Jason, Tash and Jayne looked blank. Lloyd looked like he often did at his weekly status meetings with his boss, when he had some bad news to deliver and was hoping the spin wouldn't be too transparent. He looked wary.

"They are broke," said Mia triumphantly.

It wasn't that she was pleased that Kate and Ted were broke; if she'd paused to think about it she would have realized that the opposite was true. Kate and Ted's financial collapse was devastating. It was just that it was *such* a divine piece of gossip, and Mia loved bestowing choice scandal.

"Broke?" asked Jason, confused. "In what way? What do you mean?"

"Totally bankrupt." Saying the word made Mia think about it. She paused, then added, "Isn't it awful?"

"Are you sure?" asked Tash. It seemed impossible. Kate and Ted were rich. Was it possible to just stop being rich? Tash feared it probably was.

"Certain. I've just bumped into Action Man in the corridor. Big Ted had been to your room to tell you that they have to go home immediately and try to sort things out."

"I'm afraid it's true," added Lloyd. The group turned to him. They looked at him with surprise; it was so easy to forget he was there at all.

"You knew?" asked Mia. She was rather disgruntled that she wasn't the first with this gem, after all. Lloyd nodded, then told the full story of Ted's fall, literal and metaphorical. It was, in many ways, a relief to share the burden of the secret.

"How awful," said Tash. "Jayne, do you want me to come with you?"

"Where to?" asked a confused Jayne.

"Don't you want to go to your brother? You might be able to help."

"What help could I be?" Jayne asked. She was genuinely surprised that Tash thought she could be of any help at all. Jayne didn't do the tea-and-sympathy thing.

"Well . . ." Tash hesitated. To her, it was obvious. Jayne could offer some practical support. She could fly home with them and help with the children, so as to allow the couple as much time as they needed to talk, to act, to deal with this horrible situation. She could hand out tissues, make the odd meal. She could just be there, to smile when no one felt in the least like smiling.

Jayne looked embarrassed. No, she did not want to go to her brother. No, she definitely did not want to go home with Ted and Kate. No way. Not when Rich had just kissed her. If she went home now he might forget all about her. All her hard work would be undone. Cloying, needy Tash would trick him into going through with this ridiculous farce of a wedding. Going home now was a ludicrous, dangerous, ridiculous idea.

"I won't be any use to them. Kate and Ted are very independent. They look after me, not the other way around. I'm the baby sister, don't forget."

Jayne smiled quickly, then turned the smile into a pout. Lloyd and Jason dropped their heads and stared at their breakfasts. They knew Jayne was being selfish, but they also knew if they caught her bewitching glance they'd think what she was saying made perfect sense.

"Normally, they look after you but, in this case, surely . . ." Tash trailed off. There was something in Jayne's eyes, which she'd angrily flashed in Tash's direction, that told Tash it was a pointless argument. Jayne was not going to get involved.

"I think it's best if we leave them to it," added Mia. "They won't want to be crowded." Tash stared, openmouthed, at Kate's best friend.

"But think about the old saying, 'A friend in need is a friend indeed.'"

"We don't want to look like vultures," added Jason. "What can we say that would comfort?"

"You're a copywriter, surely you could find the right words," argued Tash.

"That's just a job," said Jase, with an apologetic shrug. He would genuinely have liked to be a comfort to Ted and Kate, but honestly couldn't see what he had to offer. Tash was stunned. For all the gang's constant talk about friendship, they didn't seem very friendly toward each other right now when the chips were down. Tash didn't think she knew Kate or Ted particularly well. She had found them reserved and at times remote, but she wouldn't wish this disaster on her worst enemies, not that she had any. She felt out of her depth. There was a need to say or do something, but what? Surely the gang knew.

"Do you think she'll leave him?" Mia asked Jason.

"It's a very difficult one for any couple to get through," he admitted. "Kate certainly isn't going to like giving up her lifestyle."

"I can't see her in rubber gloves," added Mia.

"What will Mummy and Daddy say?" asked Jayne.

"Will they be able to help out?" asked Mia.

Jayne looked embarrassed. "Unlikely. They are not as wealthy as one would imagine. That old ruin they insist on hanging on to bleeds us dry. Goodness, by default, I'll look like the perfect child following this scandal. All I've ever done to embarrass them is remain ringless on my thirtieth birthday. That's small fry compared to fraud."

"It is awful, though, isn't it?"

"Simply dreadful."

"Poor things."

Lloyd pushed back his chair and stood up. He carefully folded his napkin across his plate. "I'm not great with words. Even so, I think I'll try to find Ted, if you'll excuse me."

# 53

## *Put the Kettle on*

Tash listened at the door. She could hear movement, but not voices. She'd hoped to catch Kate on her own, so she knocked again. The movement immediately stopped, and there was silence. Tash waited, then decided to go. Maybe the others were right. They knew Kate best after all. It was obvious that she didn't want to see anyone and, even if she did, Tash was probably the last person she'd want to see. It had been a stupid plan. Tash didn't want to upset her further. She turned away from the room and set off back down the corridor.

"Yes?" Kate opened the door and called after Tash.

"Hi." Tash walked back to the door, but noticed that Kate didn't step aside and invite her in.

"We're just packing," said Kate. She was holding a laundry bag and clearly thought Tash would be looking for an explanation.

"I know," said Tash. "Ted talked to Rich and explained the situation." Tash fell silent. Her rehearsed speech had scampered to the darkest recesses of her mind, and suddenly she didn't know what to say. She didn't know what could be adequate. Certainly not "I'm very sorry to hear about your problems," which were the words that spilled out.

"Come in," said Kate, remembering her manners. "I can make you a cup of tea."

"No. I don't want to be any trouble."

"No trouble. It's complimentary, and I want to feel we got our money's worth from the room." Kate smiled, and Tash thought it was brave of her to make a joke about money, so she felt she had to agree.

The room was in chaos. There were clothes everywhere—in the wardrobe, on the backs of chairs and on the floor. Only some had made it into the suitcase that lay open on the enormous double bed. Tash edged the case to the side and sat down.

She took a deep breath and dived in. Still unsure of Kate's response, it felt right to her to make the offer.

"I came to say that we haven't opened the bed linen yet. Your wedding gift, I mean. And, well, you've been so generous throughout the trip; you've already given us gifts enough. I wondered if you'd mind if we returned it."

Tash blushed. She didn't know if her offer would be seen as rude or thoughtful. From what Lloyd had said, £600 was a drop in the ocean compared to the extent of the debts that Kate and

Ted were in, but, surely, every little helps. Besides, she just knew that she'd never have a good night's sleep on those blasted sheets.

"That's very kind of you," said Kate. Her smile was weak but genuine. "I'd appreciate that very much."

"Really?" Tash beamed, pleased to be of practical help.

"Yes. John Lewis has a generous returns policy. We can get the goods credited straight back to the card. It would be useful."

Kate had already decided to return the new china set that she'd impulse purchased before Christmas. It was an eighty-piece set, very pretty, silver leaves embossed around the edges. The set had cost over £1,000, and yet she hadn't even taken it out of the packaging yet.

"I *am* very sorry," said Tash again. "If there is anything we can do—"

"We'll ask," assured Kate.

Tash grinned. There was something confident in Kate's declaration that she would ask for help that cheered Tash. Kate's spirit was entirely British "make do and mend;" it was heartening. Tash had expected to find Kate prone, in bed, sobbing helplessly and indulgently, perhaps calling her husband stupid and unreliable. It would have been understandable—forgivable, even. But she wasn't. It was clear that Kate hadn't enjoyed a good night's sleep, and it was clear that she had spent much of the past night and morning crying, but she certainly didn't appear defeated or even angry.

"We're going to have to leave our home, which will be distressing for the children, but we're hoping to find somewhere cheap to rent until we sort out something permanent. I had hoped that we could keep them in their schools, at least until the year end, but I think we'll have to move out of London altogether. It's so frightfully expensive."

Kate was bent over the enormous suitcase. She repeatedly picked up garments of clothing, started to fold them, then discarded them again, only to pick up the same thing a second later.

Tash doubted that she'd ever finish packing at this rate. Carefully Tash reached out and picked up a sweater and started to fold it. It was Burberry cashmere. Tash knew clothes; this little number alone would have cost a fortune. Tash mentally shook her head. Poor Kate wouldn't be visiting Burberry's again in a hurry. Still, on the bright side, at least economies could be made; they could buy their sweaters from M&S from now on.

"Where will you move to?"

Kate's braveness wavered. She ceased her attempt to pack and straightened up. "I haven't a clue. One normally lives near one's work, but neither Ted nor I work. Now, about that tea." She put the kettle on and found a cup and saucer in the wardrobe. "I'm terribly sorry that we won't be able to stay for your wedding."

Tash had temporarily forgotten that they were in Avoriaz for her wedding. There was so much going on. She couldn't believe that Kate had the presence of mind to be polite enough to apologize for her nonattendance.

"I'm sure you understand." Tash nodded, but was speechless. "We simply have to stop hemorrhaging cash, immediately. Even saving a couple of nights' hotel bill will help. Besides, we need to get back to the children and start sorting this awful mess out."

"You really seem to be dealing with this so well," blurted Tash.

Kate shrugged. "What's the alternative? I won't achieve anything by crying, 'Woe is me.' I do wish Ted had told me earlier, but . . ." She hesitated.

Tash sympathized with Kate. She also believed that the saddest part of the whole situation was that Ted hadn't had the courage to be honest with Kate. Kate was so practical; perhaps she could have turned their fortunes around. She would have probably begged for his job back and, if that hadn't worked, she would have dealt with the bad PR, found a new spin and helped him to secure interviews at other companies. At the very least, she could have stopped him buying the house in the Cotswolds and running up the enormous debts of the past five months. Maybe she wouldn't have made any material difference, but maybe she would have. Now, they would never know, and they both had to live with that.

But, on the other hand, Tash also sympathized with Ted. Kate was formidable; he'd obviously been scared to confess to his wife. Kate must be saddened and chastened by that. Ted must be kicking himself now that his wife was being so eminently sensible and so entirely supportive. He'd be wishing that he'd unburdened himself earlier, before the situation had spiraled out of control.

"I love Ted," stated Kate, "and when we married we did say "'for better for worse, for richer for poorer' in our vows."

"Maybe, but nobody really expects the downside of the deal," commented Tash.

Kate laughed at the truth of this. "Maybe not, but we should." Kate handed Tash a cup of tea. "It's made with a bag, I'm afraid, and the milk is that awful UHT stuff. I'm sure it will be horrid."

Tash took the tea anyway. She realized that it had been made because women like Kate make tea in times of crisis and the right thing to do was to accept it.

*Women like Kate.* Tash mulled the phrase over in her mind. Did she really know what Kate was *like?* She had thought Kate was spoiled and cocooned. She had assumed she was girlie, overly pampered and would be useless in a crisis. But here she was being sensible, measured and loyal. Attributes Tash admired. Attributes Rich had said were there, and Tash hadn't been able to see. Tash had thought Jayne was the sympathetic one, but at breakfast she'd appeared more than a little selfish and irresponsible. Rich had been right.

How had she got Kate so wrong?

"Funny, this is the first time we've sat down together alone, isn't it?" commented Kate, as though she had somehow tapped into Tash's subconscious and was answering the question for her.

"I do hope we get more opportunity to get to know each other a little better. After the wedding and when we are a little clearer on where we stand."

"Yes," mumbled Tash. "I'd like that."

As predicted, the tea was awful, so Tash put down her cup and picked up another sweater that was lying on the floor. She folded it neatly and put it in the case. Kate went to the wardrobe and pulled out some of Ted's shirts and started to fold them. The women passed the next hour quietly packing. They didn't talk much. For all of Kate's extreme braveness, she was patently distracted, and Tash didn't think this was the right moment for a postmortem or deep discussion of any kind. The silence was comfortable, compatible, and they worked alongside one another with efficiency and no fuss. At midday, Ted came back to the room and reported, with some relief, that he'd managed to get their flight times changed at no extra cost. This wasn't surprising, as they had initially bought the most expensive but therefore most flexible tickets available.

"Right, well, I'll leave you two to get on your way," said Tash. She hugged Ted and Kate. She instinctively squeezed them tightly and planted a huge kiss on Kate's cheek. A left, right, left air kiss was out of the question.

"Thanks for your help with the packing," said Kate.

"We'll call you after the honeymoon," assured Tash.

"Yes, do. We'll want to see photos. I'm sure you'll find Mia a big help if you want any support with arrangements. She's good with detail," said Kate.

Tash looked at her feet. She didn't want to be rude to Kate, who had so many more important things on her mind than planning a wedding breakfast, but she couldn't imagine her and Mia having cozy little chats about seating plans. Kate clearly sensed Tash's reluctance and added, "Really, you would find her a big help, if you let her be."

Tash smiled; she didn't express her skepticism and set off back toward her room to try to find Rich. She wasn't exactly sure why, but she needed to hold him.

Tightly.

# 54

# *In the Deep Stuff*

"Scaley Jase, do you think we ought to have gone to the airport to see Ms. Monopoly and Big Ted off?" Mia asked.

After her initial reluctance to comfort her friend, which was little more than shyness in the face of adversity—something Mia would never admit—Mia had popped by Ms. Monopoly's room. But Barbie Babe was in there, being all tea and sympathy. Mia had thought this was an imposition. It wasn't as though Barbie Babe and Ms. Monopoly were particular friends. Mia believed that two is company and three is a crowd, and decided that she'd leave them to it. She told herself that her friendship with Kate was so long-standing that she could call later, to see how things were after they'd talked to the children. Mia didn't need to rush around and apply emergency aid. She convinced herself that this decision was nothing to do with the fact that Scaley Jase was heading off to the slopes and she was pushed for time if she wanted to join him.

"See them off at the airport? Hardly." He looked at her with incredulity. "It's not exactly a bon voyage moment, is it?"

"No, I suppose not."

Mia and Jason were sharing a chairlift heading up to the top of the fairly challenging Les Gets runs. Jason had wanted to see the Les Gets, Portes du Soleil, since he arrived, and asked Mia if she would join him. After hearing about Kate and Ted's bad luck they both had an unexplained need to be with each other, though neither was prepared to say as much. Jase suggested that they spend the day skiing together, alone.

"You're sure you are happy skiing rather than boarding?" he asked.

"I am so bruised that I resemble one of those inkblot tests that psychologists use to analyze their patients' moods," confessed Mia, laughing. "I don't think it's my sport."

"And if I saw you naked, what would your inkblot test of a body reveal?"

"Just that you were horny. Situation normal." Mia batted off the suggestive comment without noticing it. She took a deep breath and owned up, "I've been disappointed with my ability to snowboard. I was expecting to sweep up and whizz down. I'm used to my legs operating independently, but at least cooperating with one another. But when they are stuck together, like glue, and the board seems to have an entirely different agenda to mine, well, let's just say I didn't shine. I am happy to get back onto my skis."

Jason shook his head. "You are too harsh on yourself. You were making good progress on the board. You can't expect to go from rookie to expert in a couple of days," he said sympathetically.

"You did," argued Mia.

"Yes, but that's different. I am a superstar."

Mia laughed at his arrogance, partly because she agreed with him.

She hadn't exactly apologized for her behavior the previous evening, but Jason chose to interpret her good mood as a form of apology, and he accepted it with good grace. He was enjoying learning to board, but he put on skis today for Mia.

Jason hadn't exactly apologized for his behavior the previous evening, but Mia chose to interpret his offer to ski as a form of apology, and she accepted it with pleasantries and polish. She knew he put on skis today for her.

"Did you have a good night?"

Mia wished she hadn't asked the moment she heard her own sentence. Indeed, all morning she had been telling herself she wouldn't ask anything of the sort. She was no longer intent on getting Scaley's sperm, so what did she care what he got up to or whom he got up. So how had the question slipped out? It infuriated her that, while she could bend most other people's wills, she could not, it seemed, control her own. She asked the question without looking at Scaley Jase, keeping her eyes firmly fixed on the snow-dusted evergreen trees below her.

"Yes, thank you," said Jason, coolly.

He wasn't telling the truth. Yes, the pretty plump poppet had happily accompanied him back to his room and, yes, she had been very keen to strip off and slip between his sheets. Like the Jason of old, Kiki clearly thought that holiday screws were part and parcel of the vacation—a bonus, so to speak, like duty-free shopping. However, Jason was stunned to discover that he could not summon the necessary enthusiasm. His penis was more of a sponge finger than the magnificent pole he was used to waving.

Jason racked his mind for an explanation and excuse. Kiki obligingly licked and massaged; she even did a bit of DIY on herself, and watching a girl masturbate had never failed to get him in the mood in the past. Kiki was quite drunk and after putting, if not her heart and soul, then at least her lips, spit and elbow grease into the job in hand, she had become disinterested. She'd raided the minibar for as much chocolate as she could find, and then she'd fallen asleep.

It was humiliating. Being replaced by a large bar of Nestlé's Crunch was humiliating.

It wasn't even that he was more interested in the Dutch girl who had been an option. He wanted to believe that it was the drink, but he knew he hadn't drunk *that* much. The problem was every time he kissed Kiki's juicy, willing lips he thought of Mia's broad smile and deep-red lips. Mia's lips were full, like Kiki's, but somehow Mia's lips were more sophisticated, sexier and more splendid.

There had to be some fucking mistake.

Mia was a nag, a bitch, a whiner. She was not sexy, sophisticated and splendid. She had been. Yes, OK, he'd admit it. He had been the most envied undergraduate in all of the university because he was the only one who was ever able to describe himself as her boyfriend. Admittedly, seemingly scores of men could describe themselves as her lover, but only he knew how she liked her tea and toast.

But that was all a long time ago. That was before she finished with him. Oh, yes, Mia had finished the relationship. Switched it off. Snuffed it out.

The official line was that they mutually agreed that they were too young to settle down and that they both needed time to see what else was out there. Only Jason knew that what really happened was that, as soon as Mia started mooting ideas about it being "a big world" and needing "a bit of space," he had seen the writing on the wall. Instead of telling her that he didn't want to chase skirt and that he only wanted to see the world if she was by his side and seeing the same sights, Jason had rushed to disassociate himself from their relationship. He didn't tell her that he loved her and believed she was his One. On the contrary, he told her that he quite fancied the little blonde fresher girl that she was mentoring at the time, and he asked if she'd put a word in for him.

A man had his pride.

The path Jason had chosen was cool. He had a great life. He loved his job. He believed working in advertising was the ideal career opportunity for all Peter Pans—he was ridiculously well paid for not growing up. Unfettered by a wife or kids, with demands for country houses and fees for posh schools, he was free to squander his money on cars, a penthouse flat, champagne and the other things that attracted the constant stream of young, nubile and willing ladies—all of whom he considered to be little more than a perk of the job.

It wasn't as if he lay in bed thinking about Mia every night for the past thirteen years. He'd never done that.

Not until last night.

He didn't know what circuit in his brain had been tweaked to make him suddenly think of her in a different way. It could have been that he'd discovered Rich hadn't been honest with him about his relationship with Jayne in the first place. That had stung—he thought they told each other everything. He'd believed that Rich was the one person in the world he could rely on, but, no, he wasn't. Which meant Jason didn't have one person in the world he could rely on. Or it might have been because, despite the most extraordinary array of women that had trailed in and out of his bedroom since he and Mia split, their exoticism only seemed to expose how alike they all were to him.

The problem was that when Jason told Mia he remembered she didn't swallow, the intimacy of the moment sent a searing sensation up and down his body. A bolt of curiosity, sensuality and affection set him alight. It was quite unlike anything he had experienced in years, despite all the tiny, frilly Agent Provocateur panties he'd edged down silky thighs. He had suddenly, and with great clarity, remembered that she kept a box of tissues by her bed. He remembered how she turned her head. The way she discreetly emitted his sperm was somehow very endearing. Her particular brand of prudery ought, logically, to have been a turnoff, but it never had been. Love was odd like that.

At that moment Jason had known that all he wanted to do was kiss Mia. Kiss her so hard that she finally stopped moaning in a bad way and started to moan in a good way. Kiss her so hard that she started smiling again. Of course, Mia hadn't given him a chance to act on that crazy impulse. In a split second she'd picked up her jacket and stormed off in a huff.

As usual.

Why would he be thinking about her unwilling, unsmiling lips when he had Kiki's willing, smiling ones ready and waiting? He didn't know. Jason looked at Mia in case the answer to his question was written on her forehead. She grinned at him. A wide, genuine, warm smile. He tutted. Bloody hell. The last thing he needed right now was for her to start being amenable.

"So, you scored?" asked Mia.

She hated herself for needing to know this, but she did need to know, for reasons she wasn't prepared to analyze.

"I had a fantastic night, thank you," said Jason, without telling a direct lie.

Because he had had a fantastic night laughing and chatting with Mia. It had been pure comedy looking through those old photos that she'd brought along and a right giggle acting silly on the dance floor. A fantastic night—until Mia had got the huff.

They jumped off the chairlift with grace and ease, righted themselves, adjusted their goggles and turned to scope out the slopes. They had chosen a fairly inaccessible run, away from the vast majority of skiers. Most of the snow in their view was virgin.

"Wow, however often I see clean, uncut snow, it never ceases to take my breath away," said Mia.

Jason took a deep breath. "And nothing on earth smells as clear as mountain air. No wonder Unilever and Proctor and Gamble spend a not-so-small fortune on trying to recapture and re-create that smell in laundry detergent and disinfectants. God, even I would be moved to do some housework if they ever really successfully managed it."

"No, you wouldn't," laughed Mia.

"No, maybe not, but I'd definitely get a housekeeper."

They laughed, high on the view, the snow and each other's company.

"Are you happy, Scaley?" Mia blurted.

Jason blushed. He hated the way women asked questions about how he was feeling, particularly because these types of questions were always asked at inopportune moments.

Women often asked him how happy he was when he was at a movie. Wasn't that odd? He knew the subtext, of course. "Are you happy?" was girl-speak for "Do I make you happy and when are you going to propose?" Not that he thought that was Mia's subtext. No, this ice queen was not the type to look for love—when she opened her legs, she dispensed ice cubes. But other girls, ordinary girls, would ask him how he was feeling as he watched the latest romantic comedy from Richard Curtis. It was insane. No amount of cinematic confetti made him feel like proposing. Why would it? His answer would always be that he felt like buying a hot dog or some popcorn. If a woman were to ask how he was feeling as he watched a DVD of any of the *Star Wars* or *Lord of the Rings* movies, he would have been able to answer that he was ecstatic, really excited, but they never asked you how you were feeling then.

They would nearly always ask after sex—that was one of the all-time favorites. Well, the answer was obvious, wasn't it? Exhausted.

Jason didn't understand why women wanted to talk about their feelings all the time. What did it prove? What did achieve?

Jason shifted on his skis. He wasn't expecting the "feeling" question from Mia. Mia was normally too rational to feel much, and too selfish to care if other people were feeling anything at all. To be honest, he quite liked that about her. Jason didn't like Mia wandering into the feeling territory, it wouldn't do at all. He tried to think of an answer which was as bland and noncommittal as possible.

"Yeah, I'm happy, I'm cool. I'm having a fantastic time. I'm here with all my mates. I'm scoring with almost indecent regularity."

Mia interrupted him. "I was just thinking about Kate and Big Ted."

Chastised, Jason stuttered, "Of course, of course."

Of course Mia wasn't suddenly going to turn into one of those girls who went on about romantic stuff, emotions and feelings in an ungrounded, unfounded way. She'd asked him if he was happy because she was worried about her mates.

"Kate knew there was something wrong. Do you remember she asked us if we'd noticed anything different about Big Ted, and you know what? This makes me feel so ashamed—I hadn't. I don't notice Big Ted much at all. If pushed, I might have said he was a little more irritating than normal—"

"Yeah, you said that to me—"

"All right," Mia guiltily cut off Jason.

She would have preferred it if he didn't remember her foibles quite as well as he so clearly did. She'd prefer it if raking over her shortcomings was her sole territory and, even then, she wasn't one for feeling unnecessarily guilty about her actions.

"We're supposed to be best friends, and we didn't have a clue how much trouble he was in. He couldn't tell us. It scares me that we don't really know what's going on in one another's lives."

"Don't be too hard on yourself. His own wife didn't know what was amiss. Ted's a very clever man; he worked hard at deceiving us."

"And just maybe we wanted to be deceived."

"What?"

"Well, that thing Tash said this morning about a friend in need is a friend indeed."

"What are you trying to say, Mia?"

"Oh, nothing." Mia waved her hand dismissively. "I'm just saying, well, maybe we should all take a bit more care of one another. So that's why I asked you if you are happy. I mean, is this holiday turning out as you expected?"

"I didn't really have any particular expectations beyond having a few bottles, chatting with my mates, catching up."

"Seducing some easy lays," added Mia sarcastically—she just couldn't help herself.

"Exactly. Don't worry about me, honey. I'm delirious, always am. Now, shouldn't we just put all this worrying behind us and try to have a good day skiing? Let's make the most of this gorgeous snow."

Mia nodded. She didn't want to drop the conversation, but she knew he did. She wanted to ask Scaley if he ever got bored with waking up with another face without a name. She tried not to resent that he hadn't done the polite thing and asked her if she was happy, as she'd half hoped he would. It was perhaps better he hadn't asked.

She wouldn't have known what to say.

# 55

## *In the Library*

Tash found Lloyd in the hotel library, but Rich was nowhere to be seen.

"Have you seen Rich?"

"No, I'm afraid I haven't."

Tash sighed, frustrated. She wanted to find Rich, to kiss him. She wanted to reassure him that their silly spat the night before was pointless and groundless. She wanted to tell him she loved him, and that was all that mattered.

"Not skiing today?" she asked Lloyd, who was dressed in warm casuals, but not in a Salapex.

"Maybe later."

They both looked out the window. It was another beautiful day. They'd been so lucky with the weather. It had snowed just about every night, but been clear all day. The sky was cloudless. The mountains, slapped onto the backdrop of pure blue, looked magnificent, powerful and important. In comparison the library looked almost gloomy, whereas in fact it was an almost impossible mix of stylish and cozy.

"Are you thinking about Kate and Ted?" Tash asked.

"Yes."

"Poor things."

"Lucky bastards."

"What?" Tash didn't understand.

"Oh yes, the money thing, very disappointing. It's a mess, I agree, but I can't help thinking that they are lucky bastards."

"You mean because they are pulling together?"

"Quite."

Tash nodded. The same thought had crossed her mind that day. She had been amazed at Kate's capacity to forgive, almost instantly. Her love had immediately transformed Ted from a grieving, self-loathing wreck into a man with purpose, with hope. Ted was remarkable, too. This awful event had occurred because he was trying to do a good deed, but had he railed against the injustice of it all? No, he had not. His only concern was his family. His only care was how he'd let his wife down. He hadn't become in the least hung up with misplaced macho pride or stifled by a sense of life's unfairness. All they needed was one another. They completed each other. Made one another whole. It was exquisite.

"Their love for one another seemed to be fortified, not diminished, by the episode, wouldn't you agree?" asked Lloyd. Tash thought of Kate's calm courage and Ted's renewed hope, and nodded. "I know it's more drama than you'd ideally hope for on the run-up to your wedding, but they are a fine example for marriage, aren't they? They've made their mistakes, but they've forgiven one another. They've got through it. It makes you think, doesn't it?" Tash nodded again. Lloyd continued, "I envy you, too, you and Rich, at the beginning of your journey, starting out fresh, hopeful, optimistic, expectant. It's a lovely place to be."

It was obvious to Tash that Lloyd was not so much talking about what she had, more about what he had lost. She tried to rally.

"You're in the same position. You and Greta are just starting out."

Lloyd sighed, and shook his head a fraction. "It's a little different second time around. It's not the same. I wish it was. I have lost my belief in forever. I would do anything to find that again."

Tash's head ached with the intensity of his confession. She wanted to be with Rich. They needed to be on the mountains together. Where was he?

"I'd better go and find Rich," she said, as she eased herself out of her seat and away from Lloyd.

Lloyd barely noticed her leave as he muttered, "It makes you think."

# 56

## *Rich and the Barman*

Fuck, fuck, fuck. It couldn't be worse. It couldn't be more horrible. Or rather *he* couldn't be worse. *He* couldn't be more horrible. Rich was drenched in regret and self-loathing.

Had he been in the least bit sympathetic toward Ted? He wasn't sure. He'd tried to listen to what Ted had been saying, but it was hard to take in, and Rich had problems of his own. He hoped he'd said the right things. He thought Ted appreciated the hug and backslapping, and he did seem interested when Rich had suggested a career change. Rich couldn't believe that Ted *hadn't* considered management consultancy, for instance. A bit of fraud was a positive attribute in that field, given the right spin. Rich thought that maybe he had been of some practical help. He hoped so, but he wasn't certain. It was at moments like that when Rich wished he were a woman. He tried to imagine what Tash would say. Women generally, and Tash in particular, always knew how to comfort. What to say. What to do and how much touching was acceptable. Still, that was the only moment he'd ever swap places. The childbirth thing, the hostage-to-hormones bit and the lower salaries didn't attract in the slightest.

Ted would be all right. Surely.

This morning had been excruciating. Tash had woken up feeling fretful and frisky by turn. Normally he'd welcome the opportunity to exploit fully the frisky feeling, but today he'd leaped out of bed as though it were a pit of venomous spiders. He dashed into the bathroom and slammed the door behind him, but he couldn't bring himself to shave because he didn't want to look in the mirror. Rich had hung about in the shower until his skin resembled that white stuff girls ate. What was it? Cottage cheese. Eventually Tash had taken the hint and gone down to breakfast alone. He'd only emerged when he heard Ted hammering at the door. He'd rather never eat again than face breakfast with Tash (who knew nothing) and Jase (who knew something) and, oh, hell on earth, Jayne herself . . . who knew everything.

What in God's name had he been thinking of? The answer, of course, was not much. Jayne was there, Jayne was clearly willing and Jayne was hot. Tash—in that moment—was none of those things.

Jayne was there. That was the thing. She was there, grinding her tiny little body next to his and edging her ass into his crotch as she did a provocative rendition of Nelly's "It's Getting Hot in Herre." She was ready and present, and Tash was in bed in their hotel room, sulking.

Jayne was willing. He knew that. She always had been. In his experience, plain or fat girls were often way better at sex than stunners. They were grateful and wanted to pull back the disadvantage, so to speak. Good-looking girls always thought they were doing you a favor by simply lying back and thinking of England. Lots of good-looking girls didn't like to work up a sweat, as it ruined their hair and anything involving a bit of bending ran the risk of breaking a nail. Jayne was no longer plain Jane, she was a beauty now, but as she didn't believe it in her heart she still offered it up with enthusiasm. Even changing the spelling of her name from Jane to Jayne had done nothing to help, nothing at all, except infuriate her parents. It was almost too good to be true, a cutie with an ugly-girl mentality. He remembered that she slipped, flipped, slid around, under, over, in front and behind him. She was game for anything, any time and anywhere. It had always been easy.

Almost too much so.

But he couldn't wriggle out of it by saying Tash was unwilling or that she was the type of girl who lay back and thought of England. Under normal circumstances she was very keen and very accomplished. They'd had a great sex life back home and on this holiday, too. Some of their best. He wasn't saying that Tash was losing her edge or her eagerness. Tash was hot, scalding, but last night, for a brief and fatal moment in time, she'd grown distinctly tepid. Instead of whipping her tongue over his cock, she whipped him with her grievances over Mia. It was no fun.

And . . .

And Jayne was hot. She was indefinably dirty. There was something about her. Something base and animal and overpowering that compelled him to go back and back and back over the years. She roused him, almost goaded him into doing things that he knew would be better left undone.

Like the kiss.

It wasn't the same as the night in the cinema foyer. She hadn't kissed him and caught him unaware. *He'd* lurched at *her.* The responsibility, the initiative and the blame all rested squarely with him. He'd wanted to kiss her lips—hard. He'd wanted to bite them, to have them, to have her. He'd tasted blood and wanted more. She'd immediately put her hand on his crotch and, of course, he was erect. Of course, for fuck's sake, he was only flesh and blood. She'd grinned, that crazy, sexy, wild grin, and kissed him back. The kissing was vigorous, intense, almost frightening. Fucking horny. They fell against the corridor wall and she brought her leg up and around him, hooking him like a fish. His hands moved swiftly from cupping her face to cupping her tits, and then to her firm little ass. His fingers had stretched under her. At that point she'd broken away and panted an invite for him to join her in her room.

Her timing was out of kilter. It was just her poor timing that saved him. He hadn't drunk quite enough. He wasn't absolutely devoid of his senses. He wasn't entirely immersed in careless lust. One more drink, a few more moments grabbing her ass, and he'd have been hers.

He hated that.

He'd backed away from her and staggered along the corridor. He hadn't dared look back. She'd called his name, and he'd made a gesture which was supposed to indicate that she should shut up, go to bed, go away.

Ideally, disappear altogether.

What had he done? He had opened Pandora's box. Prior to that kiss, it had been just possible that he could have got away without this situation blowing up in his face. He could have faced Tash with his not-quite-white conscience and said, "OK, I hold my hands up, there's history." He could have, given the right opportunity, explained to her that that was all Jayne was, history. Only now she wasn't. Now she was very present.

He didn't want her. Not in the cold light of day. Not when sober. She was a mistake.

But was she an irreparable one?

Rich thought through his options. Option one, he could hunt out Tash and come clean. He could explain everything, lay it all out for her and throw himself at her feet, begging for mercy, understanding and forgiveness. The problem was that he couldn't visualize the scenario. When he tried to, he kept seeing visions of Tash kneeing him in the balls and bringing him down to her feet before he got a chance to willingly prostrate himself there.

Option two, he could track down Jayne and explain to her, firmly and fairly, that last night was a drunken mistake. He wouldn't have to tell her that he was beginning to think that every episode with her had been a mistake—he didn't need to be unnecessarily cruel. He could ask for her mercy, understanding and silence. He could brush the whole incident under the carpet. Again, it was hard to sincerely believe in this scenario. He was plagued with memories of Jayne's whispered innuendos and threats. Her perpetual insistence that she would not allow him to marry Tash.

As far as he could see it, his final option was to find a quiet bar and hide there until Friday. He wouldn't see or speak to anyone between now and then. Not even Tash. He'd just be unavailable. And he wouldn't enter into any discussion as to why he was unavailable, not with anybody. Then, on their wedding day, he'd dash up a slope with Tash and marry her quickly. Whatever happened after that, it was too late; she was stuck with him.

Scarily, option three seemed the most viable and appealing.

Rich pulled on his clothes, boots and jacket, and went in search of a bar that was open this early in the morning. He found one as far away from the hotel as he could manage, up a slope and just past the tourist office. It took an exceptional bar to make an impact early in the morning, and this was not an exceptional bar. The bar wasn't particularly trendy, or swish. It was full of chairs, with wooden legs that needed a varnish and plastic seats that were ripped but had been clumsily mended with Scotch tape. At night-time, the twinkling lights around the window and collection of snow globes above the optics may have appeared cute; in the harsh day-light they simply looked tired. Rich didn't care. As a hideout, it suited.

The guy staffing the joint was just taking the stools down off the bar top. They'd been put up there so that the floor could be washed. Rich arrived just as the cigarette butts from the night be-fore were being swept into a dustpan and the floor was being swilled with disinfectant in an effort to erase all traces of spilled beer and an unfortunate circle of vomit. Rich wished he could be swilled in disinfectant, too. The tall, lanky French guy seemed disinterested in Rich's early morning visit. He carried on with his cleaning. Not that he was fanatical about that either. His ap-proach was languid and did not seem to require him to take his cigarette out of his mouth, despite the fact that he scattered more ash as soon as the floor was clean. Rich watched for a while and wondered if the cigarette was actually a surgical addition.

"I'd like a coffee, please. Black and strong." He ordered in English, too fatigued to rustle up his charming French accent.

"Non, you non want coffee." The guy tutted and proceeded to pour a Bloody Mary. "The bollocks of a dog, as you English say," said the bartender as he banged the glass onto the bar.

"The hair of the dog," corrected Rich. He then tasted the Bloody Mary, which was very fine. "Or the dog's bollocks," he conceded.

The bartender shrugged, clearly not bothered whether his English idioms were correct or not. He was a good-looking guy and needed very few words to seduce the English women, who were pleasantly loose. Rich wondered if anything bothered this man. He doubted it. He couldn't imagine the elegant, slightly stooping French guy of indeterminate age ever becoming concerned about anything, let alone creating a god-awful mess. Rich wished they could swap places. Rich suddenly didn't want his big flat in Islington, his plasma TV or even his DVD collection, unsurpassable as it was. He would have traded it all in to be this careless French guy who came to Avoriaz for the season, had indiscriminate sex, then disappeared again, leaving neither regrets nor recriminations in his wake.

Rich sighed. It was not possible. Swapping his life with this stranger was an attractive fantasy, but he was wasting his time dreaming about the scenario. He should be concentrating on the issue at hand and trying to find a solution. That was Rich's forte, that's what he was paid a lot of money to do—"solution management." Besides, while he would happily walk away from all his worldly possessions—right now, if he had to, or if it would help—he could not walk away from Tash.

The thought surprised and horrified him in equal parts.

He did not want to lose her. He wanted to marry Tash, to have children with Tash, to grow old with Tash. It wasn't quite so horrific to contemplate saggy flesh, commodes and arthritic limbs if Tash were by his side. This was a remarkable admission, as Rich had been one of the few men of his acquaintance who had become seriously depressed about his mortality when he turned thirty. He had refused to throw a party or join the gang go-kart racing, as they'd arranged. Instead he had ignored the whole event and carried on as though it were any other day. Aging was his biggest fear. Or it had been.

Now his biggest fear was losing Tash.

And this thing that he'd had with Jayne, while lasting more than a decade, was nothing in comparison to all that he felt for Tash. And the incident last night was less than nothing. It was a drunken, meaningless, pointless kiss.

But it could be the most important kiss of his life if he couldn't find a way to contain the mistake.

Rich drained his Bloody Mary and, as if by magic, but in fact as a result of the experience of the bartender, a dark, molasseslike coffee appeared from nowhere. He sipped it gratefully and considered that Avoriaz village wasn't a big place to hide. He feared he could be found if anyone really wanted to find him. He was hoping, in vain, that no one would.

# 57

# *Rich and Jayne Share a Bloody Mary*

J ayne did want to find Rich.

"Babe, I've been looking everywhere for you." She beamed from the doorway. She rushed toward him, pulling off her beanie and letting her hair tumble free, creating the same sensation as a huge wave creates in a surfer's heart. Rich noticed the previously impassive bartender adjust his expression into one of admiration. Before Jayne had walked into the bar, the bartender had probably pitied Rich, if he thought anything about him at all. Now he admired Rich because this honey called him "babe."

Rich wanted to shrink.

"Is that a Virgin or a Bloody Mary?" she asked, sniffing his glass. "A Bloody, you bad boy. I'll have one, too." Jayne giggled, then sat down on the barstool next to Rich's. He felt overwhelmed by her presence. She shuffled closer and slipped her legs onto the rung on his stool, somehow intertwining her legs with his, as though she were a vine. Jayne ruffled his hair and gave him a peck on the lips.

"Don't take this the wrong way, babe, but you look terrible." Jayne enjoyed this gentle teasing. It was how boyfriends and girlfriends behaved with one another; they touched and teased with ease. She'd longed for this intimacy.

Rich climbed off his stool and moved it farther away from her, then climbed back on it again. He felt a little ridiculous doing so, particularly when he caught the bartender's eye, who, from the look on his face, clearly thought any sane man should be moving *toward* Jayne and not away from her. Rich was embarrassed to be fortifying the French stereotype of the English as repressed and cold, but he didn't feel he had a choice.

"Jayne, about last night."

"Wasn't it wonderful? I had the best time. You did, too, didn't you? Of course you did."

"Well, yes, it was a laugh, but—"

"I respect that you couldn't, you know . . ." Jayne leaned into Rich and whispered, ". . . fuck me, until after you finished everything with Tash. It is best to keep things clean."

"About that . . ." Rich had the words in his head, all he had to do was say them. That couldn't be too hard, could it? All he had to say was, "I'm not going to finish with Tash." But it was the way she said "fuck"—it threw him. Not that he wanted to, but somehow she pronounced it as though he wanted to. It was confusing.

"Have you told her? What did she say? I don't imagine she took it that well, poor girl." Jayne had absolutely no sympathy for Tash, not an iota, but she realized confessing as much would make her look callous.

"No. I haven't told her—"

"Well, you must get on with it. Now would be a good time. What with all this fuss about my brother and Kate, Tash will be able to lick her wounds relatively privately. Did you buy her a flexible plane ticket? Because she'll want to go home. But we should stay. We could take a sleigh ride tonight. I imagine that will be awfully romantic."

"It is," stuttered Rich.

He had to stop this. He felt as though he were on that carousel near the kids' ski school. He was on a beautiful, colorful but entirely false ride, and he was going around and around, but not getting anywhere. He felt dizzy. Stop the world, he wanted to get off. All he had to do was tell her, spell it out. Why couldn't he find the words?

In the past, situations such as this had always been much easier to handle. Women generally had more pride and intuition than Jayne had. Rich—like many, many men—would rather walk over hot coals and eat cold lard than actually finish with a girl. He employed a host of cowardly techniques to drop hints if his ardor was cooling. He'd fail to return calls, he'd turn up for dates late or leave early. He'd use the wrong name in bed. In his experience, women who sensed that Rich was about to give them the big heave-ho invariably scrambled to pip him to the post. If they really didn't take a hint, he could always just disappear. Not call at all. Not turn up at all. But there wasn't much chance of ignoring Jayne when they were holed up in the same hotel. For the first time in his life Rich wished he had a bit more experience at being mature about breakups. He wished he knew a sensitive and sincere, but, most important of all, *final* way of drawing the line with Jayne.

He wondered what Tash would do in a situation like this. It was a difficult leap of imagination. He couldn't envisage emotionally mature and perpetually honest Tash landing herself in a similar scenario. But if by some unlikely twist of events she had, Rich

knew that Tash would be handling things better than he currently
was. Not that he was handling anything at all. He was mute. Mute
seemed to be his latest physical manifestation of burying his head
in the sand. He wished he could ask Tash's advice. He needed her.

Jayne leaned across the distance he'd placed between them and
draped her arms around his neck. She gazed into his eyes, or, at
least, would have done so, if he hadn't been resolutely staring at
his boots.

"What do you want to do today? Should we board? Or would
you like to hole up here and just stay cozy?"

Rich knew that the most difficult moment of his adult life had
arrived. Far harder than proposing to Tash—that had been so natural, a snap. Far harder than pitching for hundreds of thousands
of pounds' worth of business and far harder than consoling Ted
this morning. But he had to reach out. And up. He had no choice.
He had to become the man that Tash thought he was. He had to
be honest. And, as he heard himself tell Jayne that he didn't love
her, never had, that he was sorry that he'd mistreated and misled
her—and he could now see he had done just that—as he heard
her scream that she would tell Tash everything, destroy their relationship, and even as he heard her sob that she'd see to it that he'd
never, ever be happy, he knew that he had done the right thing.

The bell on the bar door merrily tinkled, a taunting contrast,
as Jayne angrily slammed the door behind her. Rich watched as
she ran away, yelling obscenities and truths back at him. If Jayne
went directly to the hotel and Tash was there, he calculated, he
had about ten more minutes to live life as a man that was lucky
enough to marry Tash Richardson. It was cruel that, by finally being as honest as Tash wanted him to be, he had lost her. Because
he had surely lost her. Not even lost, but thrown her away. He'd
held in his hands this amazing, enchanting, fabulous woman, but
he hadn't taken care. Rich wanted to cry, but he didn't think he
deserved any pity. Not even self-pity.

# 58

## *Rich and Tash Share a Bloody Mary*

Jayne left the bar and turned right. There wasn't much to the right of the bar, a couple of souvenir shops and a pharmacist; it was the pharmacist that she was hunting. Her head pounded. The pain was excruciating.

Tash approached the bar from the left, missing Jayne by a matter of seconds. Rich was often luckier than he deserved to be. Tash spotted Rich sitting at the bar staring aimlessly out the window; she waved cheerfully. It was all he could do to wiggle his fingers in response. His arms felt like lead weights superglued to the bar top. Not here. Oh God, no, not a public showdown here in the bar, in front of the bartender who made good Bloody Marys. He'd watched Jayne turn right. What if she spotted them as she passed again? She was bound to look in at him. That was her style—a final, lingering look. And then she'd see him with Tash, and his life would be effectively over. Rich thought he might explode with tension.

"Babe, I've been searching high and low for you," Tash said from the doorway. She rushed toward him, tugging off the scarf which she had wrapped around her neck, chin and mouth to reveal a 100-watt smile of which Cameron Diaz wouldn't be ashamed. Rich felt his world grind to a halt. That smile, her smile, how would he manage without it? He'd become used to it. No, more than that, he'd become dependent on it. He needed it to get up in the morning—and he didn't just mean to get *it* up in the morning.

"Is that a Virgin or a Bloody Mary?" Tash asked, sniffing his glass. "A Bloody. Fantastic, I need one, too."

The irony wasn't lost on Rich, and it was positively enjoyed by the bartender, who carefully poured Tash a Bloody Mary and at the same time caught Rich's eye. Having jumped to a conclusion—the right one, as it happened—the bartender was clearly amused. Well, great that someone was having a laugh.

"It's on the house." He smiled. He figured that he was going to get a certain amount of entertainment in return for the drink.

"Oh, thanks," said Tash, beaming. "Why are you scowling, Rich?" she whispered, noticing that Rich was glaring at the barman.

"Nothing. Er, I was just worrying about Ted and Kate," he lied.

Tash's beam disappeared. "It's awful, isn't it? I feel terrible for them. I went to see Kate—"

"Did you?" That was so typical of Tash, rushing around trying to help. The only mention of Ted's misfortune that Jayne had made was in passing, on how the situation could be used to her advantage. Her own brother.

"Yes, Kate's amazing, Rich. You were right about her. She is a wonderful person. That's why I was keen to find you. I wanted to say I am so sorry if I wasn't as warm with your friends as you'd have liked. These things take time, don't they? But I should have thrown myself into it with more zeal." Tash looked at Rich with a face as open and honest as a child's. "I think I was a bit annoyed because your friends sort of hijacked the wedding trip, but I see now, it's like you always said, their company makes it a better wedding. More, I think I was a bit jealous because your friends were actually here and mine weren't. After all, whatever I think, or thought, about any of them, they all love you enough to want to celebrate with you. None of this is your fault, so it doesn't make sense that I took it out on you, but, then, emotions don't always make sense, do they?" She gushed on, "Kate is an astounding person. I felt humbled in the face of her calm and loyalty today. And the other thing I wanted to say was I am so sorry about . . . Rich, are you listening?"

"Duck."

"What?"

"Duck, it's Jayne." Rich pulled Tash off her stool and crouched on the floor. Tash complied, but started to giggle.

"What are you doing?" she asked, understandably confused.

"I don't want her to see us." That much, at least, was true.

"Why?"

Rich looked into Tash's large blue searching eyes. Eyes that trusted him, eyes that radiated love, amusement and, at this particular point in time, just a little bit of bewilderment. He could tell her now. Here, this moment. Why not? So they were crouched underneath a bar with the smell of pine disinfectant drifting up from the floorboards, just masking the smell of beer and wine; it was as fitting a place as anywhere else.

Rich put his hands on either side of Tash's head. He automatically rotated his thumbs to massage her temples. She naturally surrendered to his stroke, leaning her forehead into his so that they were touching.

"I love that," Tash said.

"What?"

"The way you massage my head."

"I wasn't aware that I was massaging your head."

"No, I know. You just touch me in the way I want to be touched. You just seem to know." She paused, and then they both spoke at once.

"Rich, I wanted to say—"

"Tash, there's something I need to talk to you about."

"You first," they chorused.

Tash took the initiative. "I just wanted to say I am so sorry for giving you such a hard time about Mia. I got it all muddled.

For a while there, I thought . . . Oh, well, it hardly matters what I thought, but I was wrong not to trust you and to trust your judgment."

Saying sorry was easy for Tash. She didn't really understand why people did make such hard work of it. Saying "I love you" was easy, as was asking for a pay raise, explaining to a shop assistant exactly why you were returning faulty goods and talking her way out of a parking fine. Tash could always find the right words. Communication was her forte.

"You were right about Kate's qualities, and that suggests that you probably know what you are talking about with Mia, too."

Oh, God, she hoped so. It would be perfect if they could all just get along. If they could love Rich, like each other, have a laugh. Life would be cool.

"I'm going to be different from now on in. I'm going to try to see things more from her point of view." Tash just wanted everything to be OK again, like it was when they were back home, curled up under the duvet or riding their bikes through Richmond Park or watching movies. They did so many nice things together. And it could be all OK again, she knew it could be. "And the other thing I wanted to say is that I am so sorry we rowed last night." Oh, God, she was, she was.

And he was, so, so sorry. Because look where the row had led. Rich also wanted everything to be OK again, but, with the benefit of an intimate acquaintance with all the facts about their situation, he wasn't as hopeful. How could it all be OK again?

"This awful business with Ted and Kate puts things back in proportion. I love you. You love me. That's all that matters. Agreed?"

"Agreed," said Rich, smiling. "I do love you, Tash." Rich leaned in and kissed her.

He held her tightly and kissed her hard. All ideas of confessing or explaining dripped away. She was right. All that mattered was that they loved one another. They could go back to being chilled and thrilled with one another the moment they were out of here, as soon as everything was back to normal. Jayne was not important. Only Jayne thought she was. They sat hunched under the bar and kissed until their jeans felt uncomfortably tight at the backs of their knees, until the bartender coughed and until Jayne was well out of sight.

"What were you going to say?" asked Tash, standing up and flexing her legs. "Before I made my big speech."

"Nothing, er, well, the same as you. I was going to say that I love you and you love me, and that's all that matters."

Rich paid the bill, but avoided the bartender's gaze. He no more wanted to face the bartender's knowing smirks than his own conscience.

# 59

## *Jase and Mia Have Dinner*

"You all alone, Checkers? Where is everyone?" Mia asked Lloyd.

It was 8:30 p.m. Mia and Jason had spent the best day in the snow yet. They had skied until 5 p.m. when the lifts closed and then they had, through a silent tactical agreement, headed straight to a bar for a little après-ski action. It didn't occur to either of them to go and get changed into dry clothes or to invite anyone else along. They were having such a marvelous time that they just wanted it to go on and on. Mia ordered a G & T.

"What about your detox?" Scaley Jase asked.

"What?" Mia had momentarily forgotten the excuse she'd
made up to explain her abstinence. "Oh, yes," she said, suddenly
remembering. "I'm giving up on that."

And she was. To hell with it. The fresh air had cleared her
head. She could see her plan for what it was—improbable at best,
farcical at worst.

It was very unlikely that Mia would ever get Scaley into bed.
In fact, it was inconceivable, thought Mia, laughing at her own
pun. In the queue of "women-likely-to-get-into-bed-with-Jason-
Clarke," she stood behind every other woman in the resort. Every
other woman seemed to be able to attract and secure Scaley's attention with ease. He simply didn't see Mia in that way. She'd
done her best to be witty, attractive and available for the entire
week, and yet Scaley insisted on sleeping with girls who were not
as witty and not as attractive (although she admitted Kiki probably had her beaten in the available stakes). Last night had been
soul destroying. She'd played all her best cards. While they had
had a fabulous day together, joking, playing, chatting and skiing,
it was clear that he saw her as a cross between his primary school
teacher and his big sister. It was undignified. Mia had had enough.

Besides, even if she were to get him into bed, she'd calculated
that her chances of conceiving were pretty slim. She was kidding
herself that one attempt would be enough. She was thirty-three,
for God's sake. She knew the scary statistics about fertility nose-
diving with every candle she blew out. Mother Nature was a tyrant.
It seemed to Mia that she'd spent all her twenties avoiding getting
pregnant—in those days it had seemed a genuine possibility at
every turn—and now the opposite was true.

But, then, maybe it wasn't Mother Nature who had flawed
planning.

Anyway, Mia reasoned, even if the first miracle did occur and
Scaley somehow suddenly saw her as a bedmate, instead of a big

mate, for approximately twenty minutes (that would do, wouldn't it?), *and* if, by some fluke, the second miracle occurred and somehow she got lucky after just one attempt, she figured she'd have a pretty determined fetus on her hands. Not the type of fetus to be in the least bit concerned about a couple of glasses of G & T.

"Make mine a double, Scaley."

They'd had a great day. They had swooped and swerved down mountains and through trees. They had glided and fallen with good humor and no style. They had chatted about, well, something, although neither could remember exactly what now. Both recalled that there hadn't been a single uncomfortable silence. They had felt a little naughty, absconding from the group and breaking away on their own, but they had both enjoyed breaking the rules —just a little bit.

They'd spent the day unthinkingly re-creating the intimacy and exclusivity that had always been so abundant in the past. They'd had fun. And neither of them had wanted the fun to stop. It was only the fact that they both felt duty bound to join the gang for dinner that brought them back to the hotel. They comforted themselves with the thought that the food was excellent. When they arrived back at des Dromonts, Lloyd was sitting alone in the bar, nursing a whisky.

"So, what's with the ghost town?" asked Jason.

"Dunno where Jayne is," Lloyd slurred, betraying that this wasn't his first whisky of the evening. "I haven't seen her all day. Tash and Rich went boarding together. Decided to go to Switzerland and had this madcap idea to stay in another hotel tonight. No idea why. This one is fantastic, and they'll still have to pay for it." Mia and Jason exchanged looks.

"Maybe they just wanted some time alone," said Jason.

"More likely that Rich is avoiding a certain someone," said Mia sotto voce. Jason nudged her, indicating it was wisest that she kept her thoughts to herself. He turned his attention back to Lloyd.

"I feel lousy, mate, really sorry. You should have come out with us, rather than stay here on your own all day," said Jase as he threw himself onto the comfy, cushioned seat next to Lloyd. He said this with the full knowledge that his generous invitation was impossible to exploit after the event.

"No matter, old man, gave me time to think." Lloyd forcefully prodded his skull with his forefinger.

"Oh, yeah, about what?"

Lloyd put his finger to his lips. "It's a secret, at the moment. But I'll let you in on it as soon as I can."

"Goodo." Jase smiled with total indifference. "Want another drink?"

He never had any curiosity to hear anything someone didn't want to tell him. Mia was the opposite and considered pushing Lloyd for more info. On the other hand, she really wanted to change out of her snow gear and put on something suitable for dinner. She excused herself and left Scaley and Lloyd to their drinks.

Mia bounced up the stairs to her room—well, metaphorically at least. Other than on the slopes, it was very difficult to move with real animation in ski boots. She dashed into her room and checked her reflection.

Yes! She'd thought so. She looked amazing. Obviously the fresh air agreed with her. It was only yesterday that she'd read in one of Tash's magazines that the air in the mountains was excellent for the skin, something to do with oxygen levels. She didn't like admitting that she'd read one of those terrible mags, let alone that she'd found an interesting article. It was just that she'd been hanging around the foyer waiting for the others and she'd seen it poking out from behind a cushion, carelessly abandoned she imagined, and, well, she'd just picked it up through idle curiosity. But then she'd found she couldn't put it down. She had to confess that the next half an hour had flown by and the articles weren't as imbecilic as she'd imagined. Two or three had actually been quite interesting and fairly well written. For example, the article about natural ways to make your skin glow had recommended a number of expensive creams, mountain air or falling in love as the best boosters. She hadn't had the opportunity to buy the creams yet, so it had to be the mountain air.

Mia quickly jumped in the shower and, although she was in a hurry, she hunted for her DKNY body wash. It smelled fantastic, and she always used it on special occasions. Not that having dinner with the gang was particularly unique, but today did feel like a distinctive and exciting occurrence. She dressed at great speed, not sure, or at least not prepared to recognize, what or whom she was hurrying for.

Scaley Jase.

His name popped into her head as she lathered her body with silky bubbles. Then again as she pulled up her cotton briefs, and again as she snapped on her bra. They'd had a fantastic day. Such fun from start to—

Mia didn't want it to finish.

That had to be the G & T's, didn't it? They'd gone straight to her head. She'd been off alcohol for a couple of weeks and suddenly she was Lady Lightweight. Well, Jase would be pleased, she was a cheap date. Not that she was his date. It was just a saying. If they did spend the evening together, as friends, he'd be pleased to see her so *relaxed* on a couple of G & T's. Maybe she shouldn't have had doubles, but she did feel deliciously light-headed.

Wasn't it just the way? Her whole purpose for being on this trip was to conceive a child with Scaley, but from the moment they'd met in Heathrow her plan had seemed doomed. Typical, then, that now she had accepted that it wasn't going to happen, all the problems that had stood in the way had suddenly disintegrated.

When Mia had been actively trying to seduce Scaley, she had struggled to secure time together alone. If they ever did have any time together alone, she was always struggling for conversation that was even remotely interesting, let alone sultry or flirty. But now that she had acknowledged that the idea was more of a pipe dream than a plan, she had suddenly become funny, dirty, happy and suggestive by turn. All week she had constantly analyzed Scaley's every move against criteria that she had drawn up to assess the suitability of his sperm and genes. Invariably he'd failed to meet her exacting standards. She hadn't liked the fact that he drank so much (that would damage his fertility and virility). She hadn't liked his legs, as she suddenly noticed that they were a little short in comparison to the rest of his body (would the baby inherit that?). She hadn't liked the company he kept—the girls were silly and cheap.

However, now that Mia had established that Scaley's service as unwitting sperm donor was no longer required, she suddenly saw things in a new light. Scaley wasn't really drinking that much at all. He'd only had one beer today, and his legs weren't especially short. In fact, he had a great swagger which some women might even find attractive. She still objected to the company he kept, although he hadn't been quite so obvious when leering at other women today. She'd only caught him checking out T & A on two occasions.

Mia rushed around her room. She didn't bother to consider which top would make her look most appealing—it no longer mattered, and her main concern was to return to Scaley as quickly as possible. Mia was slightly afraid that the magic spell which had made the day so relaxed and right might be broken if she stayed away too long. That could happen. In the past, Mia had been on dates which were going swimmingly when suddenly a dynamic was changed and the whole thing fell apart. It could even be a small dynamic such as moving venue or even table. Something intangible but important, and Mia didn't want that to happen tonight.

*Not* that Mia was on a date.

She was just saying it felt a bit datelike.

Mia realized that she was holding her breath.

When she returned to the foyer, Lloyd had disappeared. Apparently he'd palled up with a group of Belgian tourists at lunchtime and had arranged to meet them in the pool hall to shoot some balls.

"He's made friends?" Mia asked, without bothering to hide her surprise.

"He's a good and interesting bloke. You've just forgotten," laughed Jason. "So, it's just you and me for dinner tonight. Any objection?"

For once Mia couldn't find one.

The restaurant was busy, but not crowded. The entire clientele were guests at the hotel, so the atmosphere was friendly, almost intimate. When Mia and Jason walked in all the other guests looked up from their plates and nodded or called out greetings.

"You look lovely, tonight, my dear," said one elderly lady, who had on a regular basis chatted to the group about the day's snow and the seasoning on the salad and such. She dined with her husband, but he never said a word.

"Thank you," said Mia, beaming, a little taken aback by receiving a compliment from a stranger.

"You do," said Jason, which caused Mia to turn scarlet. Oddly, receiving a compliment from Scaley was worse. How come he told her she looked good tonight? Tonight when she wasn't trying, hadn't agonized over her outfit, hadn't poured herself into minimizing underwear. Tonight when it no longer mattered what he thought of her. Typical!

"You make a very handsome couple," said the old dear.

"Oh, we're not a couple," objected Mia, which seemed to cause the whole restaurant to titter.

"Why are they laughing?" asked Mia with a hiss, as she sat down to face Jason. He was grinning, too.

"I think it was the tone of your denial that amused them. I have to say I haven't heard you utter anything with such passionate conviction for years."

"Ha, ha," sniped Mia. "I just didn't want to give anyone the wrong idea." Jason chuckled, and accepted the menu from the waiter.

Mia relaxed, happy to find that she wasn't offended, or embarrassed, or irritated, or anything bad. The magic hadn't gone just because she'd had a shower and changed clothes. Mia sighed contentedly, selected a bottle of wine, then sat back in her chair, ready to enjoy a pleasant evening with her old friend.

They peppered the starter with conversation about work. Mia realized that, while she was always first to brag about how Scaley was "massive in advertising," she had no clue what he did on a day-to-day basis. Jason was flattered that Mia had asked and surprised that she genuinely listened to his answer, although if she was impressed she didn't say so. Being impressed wasn't her thing. Mia talked about her work, too.

"So what's next for you, Mia?"

"Well, the next step on the ladder to secure promotion would be for me to do another stint abroad. But I'm not sure I want to."

"Why not? I thought you'd enjoyed your time in Belgium."

"I did."

"And Hong Kong."

"Yes, it was fascinating."

"And you loved Peru."

Mia nodded. She'd spent seven years out of the past twelve abroad. She'd seen the world and been impressed and impressive while doing so.

"I'm so glad I had those opportunities and experiences, but I'm not sure I'm prepared to leave everything and everyone again."

The truth was she couldn't see how being a single mum would fit in with being a diplomat.

Jason sighed. He wasn't exactly sure why he was relieved to hear Mia would be hanging up her traveling boots, but he was. Despite email and the ease of travel, he'd missed having her close by.

Jason coughed to clear his throat, poured another glass of wine for them both and then said, "I meant to ask earlier, is the holiday meeting your expectations?"

Mia nearly choked on the Merlot.

Had she just heard that question correctly? Was Scaley Jase asking her something personal? Something serious?

Probably not. Probably just making small talk.

Should she tell him? Could she tell him that the sole reason she was on this holiday was to make honorable his wayward sperm and that by definition, as she hadn't done so, the holiday had not met her expectations? Mia giggled to herself; the whole idea was preposterous. Scaley, a father? Even in the most nominal, biological sense, no way. Her wineglass was empty again; she refilled it and took another glug. The entire thing was nonsense born out of desperation.

"What's the joke?" asked Jason.

"Oh, Scaley, if you knew what my expectations were for this holiday, you'd be laughing, too."

Jason grinned, wanting to be affable, keen to be in on the joke. "Well, tell me, then."

"I came here to seduce you," laughed Mia.

Jesus, how much had she had to drink? Jason stared, too stunned to respond. Mia barely noticed as she sped on, her words tumbling out onto the tablecloth between them.

"Are you surprised? Honestly, I thought it would be a snap. You being such a tart and me being, well, not unattractive. But I might as well have been invisible. Admittedly, I hadn't factored in Jayne's presence, and you always were a sucker for fresh blood." Mia smiled to indicate that there were no hard feelings. "So, I guess you could conclude that the holiday has failed to live up to my expectations as we haven't got grubby together."

Mia was choosing to be flip and funny. She was scared that if she hesitated, even for a second, her giggle would become less amused and more of a morbid cackle. Oh, God, she wanted a baby. She longed for a baby.

Not a woman who was normally keen on swapping confidences, Mia felt an overwhelming urge to disclose how much she wanted a child. She wondered if she should tell Scaley about her plan, now that he wasn't part of it. It would be a relief to talk about her secret longings. It was odd that none of her close friends had any idea what she wanted most in life was a new life. It had been impossible to tell Jase about the plan to have a child on her own when it was his child she wanted to bring up on her own, but now there was nothing standing in her way. She felt a tremendous compulsion to explain how desolate she felt, how purposeless. She was sure that a child would eradicate all feelings of loneliness. He or she would imbue her life with an indisputable sense of meaning. Would Scaley understand her longing? Maybe if she told him it was like longing for a Lamborghini Murciélago. The analogy seemed inadequate. Scaley was her best friend, but would he understand how wretched she felt? Could he comprehend just how reckless she had been tempted to be? Mia needed his empathy and compassion. If he laughed at her crazy plan to conceive a child with him, she would be crushed.

Best to keep quiet. Best to allow him to believe he was simply irresistible. Mia tried to stay upbeat.

"But you know what, Scaley? I don't really mind that we haven't got it on. It's probably a good thing. How could I have gone to bed with you? I have big boobs and big thighs, and you've been living in silicon city for over a decade."

"But you were my first love," stuttered Jason, finally finding words.

"Yes, and I was still defying gravity at the time. It's better to let the memory live. The contemporary reality would be a shock."

"My first *love*," repeated Jason, placing the emphasis on *love*. He took a deep breath and held Mia's gaze. He hoped she'd understand. He needed her to understand. All day he'd been wondering what would it be like to hold Mia close to him again. To smell her skin. To kiss her lips. To smell her sex. To kiss her tits. He'd been having these thoughts and simultaneously been dismissing them. Telling himself such fantasies were pure madness, a direct result of too much mountain air. He'd been telling himself that Mia would never, ever look at him in that way again. But to hear Mia say that she wanted to seduce him, too—well, it was amazing.

"My first love," he said again. He wanted to add "and only," but didn't have the courage. How much had she had to drink?

Mia rolled her eyes around her head and her wine around her glass.

"That hardly matters. It's the last lay that is the important one. No, it could never work, we've tried too much. Too much variety. There's been too much water under our respective bridges."

Jason was irritated that Mia dismissed the idea of them sleeping together as quickly as she'd brought it up. The woman could be so fickle!

"And, anyway, something else really positive has come out of my not being successful in my quest."

Jason really couldn't imagine a positive aspect to their not having renewed carnal knowledge.

"Something really amazing has happened anyway, don't you think so?" asked Mia. "I've had a great day today. I really feel I know you again. I feel so close to you, and there's no way that consequence would have come out of our having sex," she said with a wry smile. "I've missed our friendship, so in that sense the holiday has surpassed my expectations—" Mia would have carried on, but Jason leaned over the table and kissed her.

Tender, plump lips that she'd never forgotten.

The kiss was persistent, but slow. A confident kiss, full of assurance and intention.

Mia didn't exactly kiss him back, but she didn't exactly push him away either. For once in her life she surrendered to the moment. For a moment. Then she broke away and demanded, "What was that for?"

"I felt like it?"

"Why did you feel like it?"

Jason laughed. "I don't know. It just felt like the thing to do. You are right, we have had a lovely day. And you are right, you are not unattractive. In fact, for a moment there you were extremely attractive, and I just wanted to kiss you."

Mia thought about this. Was this what she wanted now? Now that she'd decided Scaley Jase wasn't the right man to father her child. Did she still want him?

"Stop thinking, Mia. Just allow your feelings to take control for once."

Mia thought about how she felt. It was a compromise.

The kiss had been good. No denying that. It was lovely, it was firm and gentle and sexy all at once. It was . . .

Jason leaned across the table and kissed her again. This time she kissed him back. The kiss made them feel strangely rooted and stirred up. Fervent and ardent kisses that were utterly familiar and fascinatingly unique. They kissed as though they had never kissed one another before, and yet they felt as though they had never touched any other lips except each other's.

"Let's leave dinner and go to bed," Jason whispered, when they finally pulled apart. "Let's make sure that this holiday meets your expectations and surpasses mine."

They scraped back their chairs and rushed out of the restaurant, not caring that they were leaving before the main course had even arrived.

# 60

## *Jase and Mia, Again*

They ran through the hotel lobby and up the stairs, not wasting any time waiting for the lift. All the words that they had bandied and brandished between them suddenly seemed redundant. Neither of them had any idea how to articulate the desire that now overpowered them. They did not care if it was longing that had lain dormant for thirteen years or if it was craving whipped up by a cocktail of alcohol, mountain air and expediency. They ran holding hands and hopes, toward Mia's room. As Mia scrambled about in her bag for the key, Jason threw her up against the wall in the hall. Without pausing to check for privacy, Jason started to kiss and bite Mia's lips.

Their lips meshed together, they both kept their eyes wide open, not prepared to miss a single second. His hands explored her body, running up and down her ass, waist and tits, inside and outside her clothes. When his fingertips brushed against the lace of her bra, he felt scalded. He knew what was in there. He knew the exact roundness and softness. He knew what they looked like, her breasts, at the moment that they escaped from her bra. They bounced a little. A perfect amount. Who would have thought after chasing endless new thrills that the old ones could be quite so dynamite?

It was difficult to focus on unlocking the door, but eventually they did so, and they fell into the room and straight onto the bed. Jason lifted Mia's sweatshirt above her head. She assisted him, maneuvering, wriggling, twisting and writhing to facilitate their mutual stripteases. He slipped off her T-shirt, and she pulled off his sweater; he struggled out of his jeans. He was a little broader than she remembered, and he had gentle curves of flesh around his waistline. Mia felt reassured. More, she felt turned on that his boyishness had developed into manliness, even if manliness inevitably meant stout bodies and the occasional gray chest hair.

He tugged her jeans off her legs, showering her body with kisses as he did so. He kissed her stomach. Yes, slightly rounder than thirteen years ago. He loved it; it was so womanly. He kissed her thighs. Were they more spread as she'd insisted? Probably. God, he loved them. They felt soft and yielding, every bit as delicious as they had felt the first time he'd tentatively fingered the lace on the leg of her panties. And the smell of her! It was the same. He doubted that she still used the same soap or laundry detergent, but it seemed familiar. Certainly the slightly musky, sexy smell was the same. Jason buried his face into her panties and breathed in deeply. Mia felt his warm breath shimmy up between her legs, swirl around her stomach and up into her chest. It was as though he were breathing life into her. She felt like a regular Sleeping Beauty, suddenly reawakened. None of the lovers that had found his way to the space between her legs had ever found his way to the spaces in her head and heart.

It took only a few short minutes until they were both naked. They had wasted a lot of time, and neither was inclined to waste any more. Jason lay on top of Mia and expertly slipped his cock inside her.

"You're sure?"

"God, yes," she said, nodding enthusiastically. "I want you."

"I want you, too, Mia."

She wanted him in every sense. She wanted to ride him, she wanted to talk to him, she wanted to taste him, to touch him and to have and hold him. God, she'd missed him. She hadn't realized how much until this second when his fat cock was plugging her, filling her with hope and happiness, and releasing her, too. Releasing her from the relentless search, the terrible loneliness. Sex had always been good between them. Honest and adventurous and open. At that exact moment, Mia realized that it had always been that way because they had always been honest, adventurous and open. More so than with any other living soul.

Imagine that. Oh, shit. She could carry on. She could let him have sex with her and maybe, just maybe, he would impregnate her. Then she'd never be lonely again. She'd have her baby. She would have his baby. She could pour all her dormant love onto the child. She could have a life that always felt as amazing as today had felt. She'd have a life full of fun and laughter and joy, pure simple joy, instead of a life full of wisecracks and angry emails about time sheets and holiday forms. Her life would have meaning.

But. But. How would he feel if he ever found out he was the father? He was bound to ask her if she got pregnant after this. If she told him the truth, would he feel responsible, trapped? But, if she didn't tell him, denied that the baby was his, then one day the baby might need a blood transplant or something. That always happened in soap operas. Then it would all come out. Then how would he feel? She hadn't thought this out. She'd thought of nothing else for months, and she was a rational and intelligent woman, but she hadn't really thought this out.

But the blood donor thing, that wouldn't happen in real life, would it? She wasn't thinking clearly. She wasn't thinking at all. She was feeling. Feeling very deeply. And keeping quiet didn't feel right.

"I want you and I want your baby," she blurted.

Jason laughed. "God, I love that about you, Mia. You're always having a laugh. Always there with the quick comebacks. God, I've missed you." He kissed her magenta nipples and gently continued to move inside her.

"I'm not joking. I want your baby." Mia paused, and pushed Jason away so that she could look into his eyes. "That's why I wanted to seduce you. I want to have a baby with you." Mia felt Jason's cock melt inside her. "No, no, don't panic," she pleaded.

What had she imagined? "I want your baby" had never been the type of bedroom talk that was likely to turn Jason on. She quickly clenched her pelvic muscles in an effort to entice him back into action.

"I wasn't expecting you to get involved or anything," she rushed to explain.

"What?" Jason pulled away, sat up and grabbed the duvet to cover his now 100 percent flaccid manhood.

Mia looked sulky. Crap, she shouldn't have let that slip out. Now everything was ruined.

"It's OK," she soothed. "Think of it as a donation. Charitable donation, if you like. I've looked into sperm banks, but I didn't trust the CVs, so I thought—"

Mia broke off. It was a difficult proposition to word with your panties flung onto the bedside table.

"As I say, I wasn't expecting any long-term commitment from you, not at all. Just a few minutes of your undivided time and—" Jason looked furious. "I should have said something earlier, not just sprung this on you. I really, really want a baby, and I can't do it on my own, can I? Well, I can. Most of it. All of it. Except the actual conception. It's just an idea."

Mia paused, dropping her gaze. Jason looked incensed beyond words. Mia played with the sheet, manically twisting it around her forefinger.

"To think I wanted to screw your brains out. It looks like someone else has beaten me to it."

"What?" demanded Mia, leaping off the bed and swiftly pulling on her abandoned sweatshirt to cover her exposed breasts.

"Have sex just to make a baby?" Jason spat out the idea as though it were poison.

"That's what sex is for," yelled Mia.

"What an outrageous, contemptible, infantile idea."

Mia was taken aback. "You're calling me infantile? It's you who's stuck in adolescence."

"You think so?"

"Yes."

Actually, only minutes ago Mia had stopped thinking that Scaley Jase was an irresponsible forever-juvenile. She'd started to think of him as a rather sophisticated lover and soul mate. But no, he was reverting to type. God, how stupid could she be? He blows on her panties and blows out her mind. After all these years, you'd think she'd know better.

"So, you think I'm permanently adolescent, but fit to be a father? Isn't your argument somewhat flawed?"

"Biologically fit to be a father. I told you I wouldn't want you to be really involved. I'd do it all on my own. I want a baby."

"Babies aren't like Gucci bags. You don't just fancy owning one and go and pick it up. They are not this season's must-have accessories," yelled Jason.

"I never said they were. Don't be insulting." Hot tears sprang into Mia's eyes.

The bastard. He had no idea. Gucci bags, indeed. She'd never coveted a single fashion accessory in her life. Didn't he know anything about her? He clearly wouldn't ever be able to understand her aching for a baby. He had no idea that she wandered around Mothercare on her Saturday mornings. Mothercare, not even Baby Gap. It wasn't as though she indulged by just looking at frivolous things such as cute Babygro sleepers and socks. She did serious research on the unglamorous stuff, too. She'd already picked out the exact pram she wanted (one with an attachable car seat) and the changing mat and the baby bath. And what she didn't know about breast pumps really wasn't worth knowing. This wasn't a passing phase.

"Babies are magical," shouted Jason.

"I know that," counterargued Mia. "That's why I didn't want to go to a sperm bank—"

"Any child I sire will be a sum of everything that's gone before me. Some Neanderthal had to rub a couple of sticks together before he could get his end away so that my ancestry could begin."

"What are you talking about?" demanded Mia, confused. "Your ancestry isn't particularly impressive. I didn't even consider your ancestry. You are entirely new money, but besides that I'm not asking for your money." Mia was baffled. Why couldn't he give her this one little thing? It was just sex. That's all he had to do. It wasn't so much to ask, was it? Jason had sex with all sorts. Only five minutes ago he'd wanted to have sex with her.

"You are insane."

Jason started to move around the room collecting his clothes. He pushed his foot into a sock and threaded his leg through his trousers in a couple of double-fast moves. "Have my bloody money. You are welcome to every last penny of it. You are welcome to everything I own. Well, except for my porn collection, perhaps. Some of the tapes I have are irreplaceable, and I can't imagine you having much use for them, anyway." Jason shook his head as if to clear it—he didn't want to be sidetracked. "But what you are asking for is far more precious. Far more valuable. You're asking for a bit of me. Possibly the best bit. My future."

"And is that so bad?" Mia yelled back because she wanted to match Jason, and he was shouting very loudly.

"Have you any idea what you are suggesting? What you'd be taking on?"

"There are plenty of single mums out there."

"Not many of them opt to be so. You are so arrogant, Mia. Even this you think you can do on your own better than with help." Jason stopped yelling and tried to breathe deeply. He needed her to understand, and he wasn't sure he was making a good job of explaining. He was dressed and had his hand on the doorknob. He wanted to get out of the bedroom, which was, in reality, comfortable and spacious, but in his mind was claustrophobic, threatening.

"Let's just play out this ludicrous scenario. Imagine if I did do, do—" For the first time in his life, Jason was without the ability to find a word to describe sex. He pointed at the bed. "Imagine if I do what you want me to do. What would you teach this baby that I surrender up into your hands? How to have a good time? How to enjoy life? How to love? I don't think so. All you are capable of teaching is how to be hard and calculating and mind-blowingly selfish."

"I know how to love, Jason. I know how to love," she yelled. But Jason didn't hear her, as he'd slammed the door behind him and stormed down the corridor.

Mia grabbed a pillow and folded her body into it. She was used to pillows providing nighttime company and all-time consolation. She fell asleep quietly sobbing.

# 61

## *Drunk and Sentimental*

I t's me."

Sophie yawned, and stretched to reach her bedside clock. She squinted at it. The big hand was pointing to the twelve and the little hand was pointing to the two. She shook her head. She really did have to get out more. All her conversations, even those she had in her head, were conducted as though she were having them with a two-year-old.

"Lloyd, what on earth are you doing ringing me at this time of night?"

"It's not so late for you as it is for me," Lloyd reasoned. "Besides, it's a special occasion."

"Is that why you are drunk?"

It worried Sophie that Lloyd drank so much, and it annoyed her that she still worried about him. She sighed, confused and exhausted at her own, sundry emotions. She knew she should just hang up. It was lucky that he hadn't woken Joanna, yet she found herself asking, "So what's the occasion?"

"Tonight, tonight is . . ." Lloyd paused. Sophie knew he was checking his watch, she knew him very well, sometimes, she thought, too well. "Or today, as it is in fact already tomorrow," Lloyd's explanation was drunken, but Sophie managed to just about follow it. "Today is the first day of the rest of my life!" said Lloyd grandly. Quite pleased with himself for making it to the end of his sentence.

Sophie remembered the first time that she heard that expression, "Today is the first day of the rest of my life." She, too, had been struck by its hopefulness and elation. She'd thought it was profound, but then she had been about fourteen. Now she was almost thirty-four, the saying sounded tired, even clichéd.

"Lloyd you're drunk and making a nuisance of yourself. I'm going back to sleep."

"Don't! Don't hang up," cried Lloyd.

God, the Belgians could drink. He could barely walk, but he'd left them at the pool table still challenging one another to another game and another beer. They'd been a fun group, though, very pleasant company. But for all their chatter, Lloyd had not been able to give the foundling friendship his full attention.

"Ted and Kate have already left. In fact, that was the main reason I called."

"What, the guests are thinning out and the numbers need a boost?" asked Sophie with disbelief and the fragile ego of a woman who has been rejected.

"No, no, nothing like that."

Lloyd gave a brief synopsis of the events relating to Kate and Ted. Sophie managed to understand despite the drunken tangents Lloyd veered off on, over and through.

"I'm very sorry for them," said Sophie with genuine sympathy. "I'll call Kate and see if there is anything I can do to help."

"Like what?" asked Lloyd.

Sophie seethed, resenting the implication that she could never be of any genuine use to anyone.

"Like offer her a job. She knows everything there is to know about party organizing, and she's incredibly well connected. Maybe she could manage the Highgate branch for me, rather than my selling it." Sophie was being rash and thinking aloud, but the idea wasn't absolutely out of the question, it wasn't ludicrous.

"Brilliant. My God, Sophie, that's a brilliant idea. I wish I'd thought of it."

"It's just a thought. I'll put it to her." Sophie wished she still didn't sparkle in light of his praise. The ex-couple fell silent.

"Look, Sophie, I need to talk to you."

"We've talked before. I'm all talked out."

Sophie was now sitting up in bed. Her eyes had become accustomed to the dark. She rested them on the familiar objects that filled her house and made it a home. Next to her bed were two photographs of Joanna and one of her parents. The frames were ornate and feminine. When Lloyd had left, the first room Sophie had redecorated was their bedroom. She'd thrown out the green duvet cover and the practical but rather ugly wicker laundry basket. She'd sold the pine chest of drawers and both wardrobes. Empty, the room revealed itself to be surprisingly large. She bought an antique sofa, bookcase and dressing table to fill it. The sofa was permanently covered with feather boas, silky shift petticoats and shoe boxes, the things she bought for their beauty and frivolity that never quite made it into her wardrobe. The dressing table was laden with tiny jeweled boxes and bottles. Strings of beads and fake pearls hung around the mirror. The bookcase swayed under the weight of embroidered cardigans and beaded pullovers. The carpets were plush, the lampshades Art Deco inspired. The room screamed "boudoir."

"Kate and Ted were inspirational. I think they are going to pull through it, I think they'll stay together," said Lloyd.

"I'm sure they will. They love each other very much," agreed Sophie.

Lloyd was surprised. None of the others had had the same confidence in Kate and Ted's relationship. How did Sophie know so much about love? "It made me think, Soph. Maybe we gave up too easily."

"You bastard." Sophie was grateful there was a channel separating them. Anything less and she'd have happily throttled him. She smoothed the patchwork duvet cover with the back of her hand—the sensation was somewhat calming.

"Would you have forgiven me if I'd got us into debt?"

"Yes, if you'd wanted my forgiveness."

"But you can't forgive my actual mistake?"

"You never wanted my forgiveness for your infidelity, which I assume is the mistake you are alluding to."

Sophie was Scottish and, although she'd lived in London for over a decade now, she would never get into those namby-pamby ways of calling a spade a digging device. To her it was a shovel. It would always be a shovel.

"And what if I said I wanted your forgiveness now?"

There was a moment of silence. Lloyd did not dare breathe, Sophie could not.

"I'd say you were drunk and sentimental, which is a lethal and insincere combination."

For a fraction of a second, Sophie wished she didn't know him so well. She wished that she could believe that he wanted her forgiveness. He certainly believed it, and he'd go on believing it at least until his hangover wore off.

"Maybe you just didn't love me enough," said Lloyd sulkily.

"I wish you'd died rather than left me, that's how much I love you," assured Sophie with a sigh.

"That is a terrible thing to say," said Lloyd, aghast.

"Is it? I think it's the biggest compliment I've ever paid you. If I hadn't loved you so much, I could have let you go more easily. As it is, I am stuck in a state of perpetual grief. Logically, true love would mean that I just wanted you to be happy somewhere, even if it wasn't with me. This isn't the case. I don't want you to be unhappy, but I just don't want you to be. There's no going back for us, Lloyd. We went too far."

And then she hung up.

It had taken over a year, but Sophie slept well that night. She slept sound in the knowledge that he hurt, too. Not in the way she did. He didn't ache that the world was so hellish and disappointing. It was unlikely that he doubted everything and everyone. He managed to hold together a relationship because he didn't recoil from intimacy, as though it were a stinging jellyfish. But he hurt, too. Maybe only when he was drunk and sentimental. Maybe only when he couldn't get hold of Greta. But somewhere it had finally registered in the deepest recesses of his brain that he'd lost out. Losing Sophie and Joanna was a loss. Thank God. She'd begun to think that she and her baby were a product of her imagination. She knew that after tonight's good night of rest she'd wake up feeling a whole lot better.

# THURSDAY

# 62

## *The Hideaway*

Tash rolled over. The duvet slipped slightly, allowing a rude draft to ripple up her bare legs, buttocks and back. She shuffled toward Rich and snuggled into his warm body. He was still asleep, which pleased and surprised Tash. She'd noticed that Rich hadn't slept too well since they'd come away. Despite des Dromonts' firm and comfortable mattresses, despite hours of exertion on the slopes each day and in bed most nights, he'd been waking up several times a night and always getting up before her in the morning. It was good to see him resting and peaceful.

Tash chewed on her thumbnail. She felt very guilty. It was obvious that her not seeing eye to eye with Mia had caused him a lot of distress. It must be that, as Rich was not the sort of man to get nervous or stressed over wedding preparations, and yet he had not been his relaxed self of late. Now she'd vowed to see the best in Mia, he seemed so much more chilled. Tash felt a weight of responsibility not exactly resting on her shoulders, more hovering above her head. She was responsible for Rich's happiness. Not all of it—obviously, he was a grown man and had to take responsibility for his own life—but suddenly she realized that she held an enormous power. The power to make Rich happy or unhappy. It seemed obvious, part of her brain had always known this, but suddenly she understood exactly what that meant. They were a team. Soon they would be married and they would always have to think of each other. Not just in the little things, such as what do you fancy for lunch? Or whether they should see a Merchant Ivory or a Tarantino at the cinema, but big things, too.

Tash could have made this holiday a better one for Rich. She could have spent more energy on getting to know Rich's friends. She should have trusted his judgment or at least respected his history. Rich had tried so hard to make this holiday fabulous for her, traveling club class, visiting a five-star hotel, taking her on sleigh rides, they'd almost swum in champagne. Tash felt ashamed.

Maybe Tash should ask Mia to do a reading or sign the register. Would she like that? wondered Tash, who momentarily felt like a six-year-old in a playground wanting to ask the most popular girl to be her best friend. Tash shifted uncomfortably. It felt a little forced, and friendships ought to be organic, not genetically modified. Still, she thought, it clearly meant a lot to Rich; it meant enough to afford him a good night's sleep.

Tash propped herself up on her elbow and looked around the B-and-B room. They had checked in late last night. They'd boarded over to Champéry, got pleasantly drunk in a small tavern and soon it was too late to find a way back to Avoriaz. She mentally hugged herself. What a magical day yesterday had been. She already knew it was one that she'd remember forever in Technicolor. The skies had been bluer than she'd ever seen before, the snow cleaner, the hot chocolates creamier. They'd pushed themselves physically, covering more ground than they had on any other day, and it was a fantastic feeling. Away from des Dromonts, Rich had transformed. He'd suddenly relaxed back into his articulate, loving, challenging, amusing self. And for her part, she'd cast off the role of nag or worrier, and reemerged as her happy-go-lucky, warm, humorous and doting self. When they'd checked in to the not-too-pretty B and B, they had not minded the ripped lino floor in the reception or even the smell of stale smoke that lingered in the bedroom. They'd slowly undressed, movements impaired by beer consumption and sore, overexercised limbs. They'd collapsed onto the bed and fallen into sound sleeps. No talk about weddings, or friendships, or feuds, or anything remotely "big." No talk at all, and it was lovely.

In the cold light of day, Tash could see that, to be totally frank, the B and B was not up to scratch and was pretty dismal in comparison to Hôtel des Dromonts. The mattress was too soft and covered in stains that Tash didn't even want to contemplate the origin of. She'd nipped to the loo (which was down the corridor and communal) as soon as she'd woken, and discovered not only was there only one bathroom to share among five rooms, but also the B and B didn't provide towels—she would have to dry herself with a sheet. Tash decided she'd skip a shower; she already knew it would be nearer to a trickle anyway. She'd enjoyed their getaway adventure. They had found privacy and intimacy, the perfect prewedding retreat, but Tash missed the power shower and sachets of bubble bath and body lotion. It surprised her how easy it was to get used to the good life. No wonder Mia was such a snob about accommodation and travel, after living in the lap of luxury for so long.

Tash kissed Rich's shoulder, and he trembled, almost imperceptibly. "Morning, gorgeous," he muttered.

Tash delved down under the duvet and felt for his erection, which she knew would be there. Not disappointed, she muttered, "Morning, glorious." It was their usual morning pattern, neglected of late. Rich rolled onto his back and lifted up his arm so that Tash could crawl under it and rest her head on his chest. She snuggled into his pit and marveled that love made even the slightly spicy smell of his sweat-soused skin attractive. They lay together, she lightly trailing her fingernail over his chest, he running the palm of his hand up and down her arm in an attempt to keep her warm. Tash felt so relaxed she almost dozed in their comfortable silence.

Rich was rigid with fear.

Oh, my God. Oh, my God. What now? What could he possibly do to avoid Tash meeting Jayne? They were OK here. Safe. Secure. But the moment they went back to Avoriaz she'd be there, waiting. Oh shit, what to do? What to do? He could tell Tash. Now, now when she had nowhere to run to, no way of hiding. She'd have to listen to his entire explanation. And it would be better coming from him. That way at least Jayne couldn't put her poisonous and inaccurate spin on things. He could start by telling Tash about the kiss. It was only a kiss, for fuck's sake. He didn't have to tell her about the tit feeling. Well, he probably would have to tell her because her first question was bound to be "Just a kiss? Are you sure?" By the very nature of confession he'd have to tell her that his hands had run up and down Jayne's firm, provocative little body. Would Tash think it was a greater or lesser crime if he told her that it wasn't the first time and in fact Jayne was an ex-lover? Would she think it was a big deal at all? Maybe not. Tash was cool with this stuff. She wasn't irrational or jealous of any of his exes, so why hadn't he told her about Jayne? He'd tell her now. This minute. Now.

"Let's get married here."

"Here?" asked Tash, looking around the grubby room with damp patches on the Artex ceiling and badly executed still-life prints on the wall.

"Not exactly here. But somewhere on the Champéry slope. Not in Avoriaz. You wanted a private wedding. Let's go back to plan A and have just that. We'll get married here, today. Just pull a couple of witnesses off the slopes."

Tash looked at Rich. Love him. He must have been lying quietly thinking the exact same thoughts as she had. He must have been considering how his actions impacted on her and how he was responsible for making her happy. He was making this gesture because he thought it was what she wanted. The idea was romantic. But it was also rash and wrong.

"We can't do that now, Rich. We've come too far. Mia, Lloyd, Jase and Jayne have all spent a fortune to be with us. They'd be so disappointed."

"They wouldn't be. They'd understand."

"No. It's really, really sweet of you to offer, and I know that you are offering to do this for me because you think it's what I want, but it isn't. Not anymore. I told you last night, your friends are my friends now. This is a fresh start. Besides, you'd regret it. In your heart of hearts, I know you want to get married standing up in front of your . . . our friends."

"I don't," insisted Rich. He wished he'd told her. Last night would have been perfect. Now would be OK. Why was he such a coward?

Tash squeezed him. "I don't think it would be possible, even if we wanted to. We have a registrar back in Avoriaz, and we have clearance from the tourist board. I don't think you can just change your mind on a whim. We've gone too far now. We have to see it through."

But that was his point! Would they get a chance to see it through? Not if Jayne had her way.

# 63

## Face the Music

They climbed back into their slightly damp snowboarding gear and took as direct a route as possible back to Avoriaz. Rich insisted that they go straight to their rooms to shower and change clothes. He had the vague hope that, if they followed this plan, Jayne would have gone out onto the slopes with the others. Maybe, he prayed, she'd have given up on the idea of splitting up Rich and Tash, and accepted that they were going to get married tomorrow. That's what most women would have done. Rational women. Rich shuddered, unsure whether he actually knew any rational women in real life. They mostly existed in his imagination.

Well, his room was as safe a place as any. And as dangerous.

"I don't think I'll go out on the slopes today. I want to call Ted and see how things are at home. It's better for him not to waste any more time. We need to draw up an instant plan of action. I wasn't totally with it yesterday. I'm not sure I was as responsive or helpful as I could have been," he added.

"It was such a shock," agreed Tash. She was sitting on a chair massaging her feet. They'd only been outside for a couple of hours, but her fingers and toes were so cold that they throbbed as they warmed up. It felt as though she'd sustained multiple bee stings. She wanted to believe that Rich could somehow magic from thin air a new career for Ted. She wanted everything to come good for Ted and Kate, and she enjoyed the glow she felt watching Rich behave with such purpose, care and confidence. He was 100 percent superhero as far as she was concerned.

"Now I've had time to sleep on it, I'm sure there are some guys I could call that would meet with Ted."

"It's a start." Tash nodded, smiling. "I'm sure Ted and Kate would be grateful for any leads you could scare up." It was so great that he'd put himself out like that. He was a good mate. He wasn't ducking out because Ted was in a mess. Tash smiled. Rich's simple, unselfish action showed her just what a magnanimous, thoughtful guy he really was.

At least in his room he could just refuse to answer the door. It would be ideal if he could persuade Tash to stay with him, so Jayne couldn't get to her either, thought Rich.

Rich knelt in front of Tash and took her small feet in his large hands. He carefully rubbed warmth into them.

"The problem is Ted is almost too honest for his own good. I'll have to brief him on what to say and what not to say. We're going to have to plan an exercise in damage control. I may have to be on the phone for a good couple of hours. Why don't you stay here and read a book? It won't be any fun if we are apart." He hoped he sounded casual and sincere rather than desperate and terrified.

"I'd love to, babe, but don't forget that we are meeting the chef and the maître d' at two o'clock. And we've got an appointment with the registrar before that."

Tash kissed Rich, but he barely responded. His mind was whirling, and he'd never been good at multitasking. He had to go out! How was he going to manage that? She'd be there lying in wait for him, ready to pounce, he knew it. He'd have to get hold of Jason and ask him to get Jayne out of the way, otherwise how was he going to be able to move freely around the village?

Tash left her clothes in a pile on the floor as usual and walked to the bathroom. She turned the shower on to full power and started to sing. Rich closed the bathroom door, making gestures that he couldn't be heard on the phone with background noise, and then called Jason's room. The phone rang once before it was snatched up.

"Jase, mate? You're not boarding?"

"No, didn't feel like it."

"Where are the others?"

"No idea."

"I need to know where Jayne is."

"I'd like to know where Mia is."

"Could they be together?"

"Anything's possible."

"Are you OK, buddy? You sound strange." Rich was surprised to find himself asking this question. He thought he was the only one with problems.

"Bit fucked up, to be frank. Mate, I'd appreciate it if we could have a beer. You wouldn't believe the shit Mia hit me with last night."

Rich checked his watch impatiently. He had to call Ted, he had to meet the chef and maître d' and, above all, he had to avoid Jayne. Now Jason wanted to meet for a beer.

"I wouldn't ask, only—"

"Yeah, buddy, cool. But I can't go out. I'll explain why when I see you. I'll come to your room."

Rich knew that Jason wouldn't ask unless it was important.

# 64

## *Jayne's Rampage*

Yesterday, Rich had said he loved Tash, and Jayne had believed him. She hadn't believed it was love when he stopped seeing her and every other woman when he'd met Tash. After all, she was used to long, barren periods when he'd had crushes on other women in the past. Sadly, theirs had never been the type of relationship where the regularity and frequency of the meetings could be counted on. She hadn't accepted his plea that he wanted to be exclusive with Tash; she'd thought Tash was putting pressure on him and that ultimately Rich would come back to her. He'd always tired of other women after indecently brief periods in the past. Jayne hadn't believed Rich loved Tash when he proposed marriage; she'd excused him, assuming he'd gotten caught up in the moment. She'd never expected him to actually go through with the wedding. Since they'd arrived in Avoriaz, he had on countless occasions insisted that he loved Tash, and still she hadn't believed him.

But she believed him yesterday morning.

Yesterday morning he knew that if he rejected Jayne, he'd lose Tash anyway. Jayne would see to it. But he'd still rejected Jayne. He loved Tash so much he'd rather be alone than with someone else. The pain. The humiliation.

It scorched her entire body. Flames of loneliness, disappointment and emptiness licked every inch of her skin. Jayne had never felt anything quite so searing. She wanted to run away and hide, but she couldn't hide from herself and it was her own mind that tortured her most.

How could he not want her? She had done everything she could to secure him. She had become everything she was to attract him. He was her motivation, her ambition, her reason for getting up in the morning. She felt bloody and bare. She grieved for him, or in fact the vision of him, with an unruly, brutal passion.

She had wasted so much time. Ever since she was sixteen, he had led her on. He'd used her. He'd taken the best years of her life. He'd had sex with her, over and over again, every which way, and now it turned out that that was all he'd had, sex. He'd never made love. She'd put his dick in her mouth, and it was just sex. He'd never seen that as a loving or doting act. She wished she'd fucking bit it off. He'd encouraged her to believe that they had some sort of relationship, that they had some sort of future. He might not actually have said anything for her to think that, but he'd never said anything that would stop her thinking that either. Or, maybe, if he had said something explicit about them being good fuck buddies, but him not being the sort to settle down, then she'd have assumed he was just playing hard to get.

Because he had kept coming back for more.

For a decade he'd come back and back and back. When he'd said he thought it was a good idea that she see other men, she'd never really believed him. After all, she said it was a good idea for him to see other women and she hadn't meant that for a second. It's just what people do, isn't it? They play it cool. They say the opposite to what they mean. It's part of the game.

The game was over. Even Jayne could see that. Rich was never going to be hers, but he was not going to be Tash's either. She would stop this wedding. Rich would not find his happily ever after with Tash. She would not allow it.

As well as the grief and the pain and the scorching sting of humiliation, Jayne felt a foul and an unutterable rage. Fuming, livid, mad. Vengeful. After Jayne had rushed back to the hotel and dictated a hurried note to the concierge, more or less demanding Tash's immediate attention, she ran to her room and slammed the door behind her. If only she could really lock the world out. She had been fired with rage, but the instant she was alone in her room the fury had been swallowed up by self-pity and a cold awakening.

Rich had never loved her. He had never said he loved her, and he had never done anything to give her the impression that he was in love with her. She pulled out her memento box and stared at the pathetic contents. Bits of scribbled handwriting, not even intended for her, photos of him as he slept because he would never willingly smile for her or even for her camera. Toenail clippings, secretly retrieved from the bin at night. It didn't amount to a relationship.

He hadn't even acknowledged her existence during his drunken, debauched chats with his best mates.

She flung the box at the bedroom wall. It made a satisfying crash, and the contents flew out. Tube tickets fluttered around the room like confetti. Jayne looked for something else to break. She swept the contents of the dressing table onto the floor. The expensive glass bottles, full of perfume and other lotions and potions, clattered and scattered to the floor. The ointments and gels oozed onto the carpet. She'd have to pay for the damage, but she didn't care. She'd flung open her wardrobe doors and clawed at the contents, ripping delicate, lacy tops and breaking the heels of her astonishingly expensive shoes. She wanted to destroy it all. None of it meant anything at all. Without him she did not have a life. She picked up the bridal magazines and her novel, and tore at the pages, scrunching the pages into balls and tossing them away. She smashed the bottles in the bathroom and her bedside table lamp. Her hurricane-like path of destruction only began to wane when her arms ached with pulling things apart and her fists bled with cuts and tears. Then she collapsed onto the bed and howled.

# 65

## *Jayne's Reveal*

Tash checked her watch again, then tapped it lightly because, for dubious, unscientific reasons, people did that to see if their watch was still working when time was dragging. Of course her watch was still working. It just seemed stuck as she'd stared at it so much in the past hour.

Where was Rich?

He'd explained that he had to go to Jason's room, said Jason was upset about something. What in this world would upset Jase, who was so laid-back he was horizontal? Then he had the calls to make on Ted's behalf, but he had promised he'd be in the foyer in time to go for the meeting with the registrar. But Rich was nowhere to be found, and Tash had to attend the appointment on her own.

She'd liked the registrar instantly. He was a jovial, rotund chap in his early fifties. He laughed a lot and oozed confidence and assurance. He told her that he was a demon on his skis and had patted his stomach and insisted that she should not be deceived by his girth; he'd confidently manage a ceremony on the slopes. He reassured her by telling her that marrying on the slopes was not unprecedented, but then, not a common occurrence. The right blend of individual but not barmy, attainable but not predictable. The registrar ran through the details and legalities. The wedding ceremony had to be performed in French and English, but as he was fluent in both a translator was not necessary. Tash was glad, as she didn't want the officials outnumbering the guests. The registrar gave her a brief list of things to double-check. Validity of lift passes, the hours the lifts opened, that they both had birth certificates or passports with them. Tash had already checked and double-checked everything on the list, and everything was in order. She left the registrar's office walking on air. It was lovely to know that her big day was in such remarkably capable and congenial hands.

Tash returned to the hotel and asked the concierge if there were any messages for her. There were five from Jayne, but none from Rich. Two of Jayne's notes had been left yesterday, and the three more demanding ones had been written this morning. Jayne's notes asked Tash to contact her "immediately." Jayne had given her room number and mobile number, even though Tash had these details, and even the hotel's phone number, which Tash thought was a bit odd. The notes were full of exclamation marks and underlinings and, while the intensity of the request did vary slightly, they all ran along similar lines.

*Tash,*

*It is <u>imperative</u> that we speak as soon as possible. I am not taking to the slopes today because of the <u>urgency</u> of this matter! Please call me on my mobile <u>as soon as</u> you receive this note or come and find me!! I am in Bar de la Galerie.*

*Jayne*

Tash smiled to herself. Jayne was a funny girl. The tone of the note was so dramatic. Tash had received four similar notes from her so far on this short break. The "urgent matter" was usually something so trivial that Tash had to employ all her self-restraint not to laugh in Jayne's face.

The other night it had been the "urgent" matter of whether the red velour Diesel top versus the classic DKNY sweatshirt was the most suitable for dinner. Before that she was called into Jayne's room "urgently" to discuss the choice of nail varnish for her toes. Toes that would be hidden in thick ski socks and boarding boots for the majority of the trip. It was very flattering that Jayne made such a big deal over the fact that Tash was a "style guru," as she had been dubbed, but Tash did wonder how Jayne had managed to get herself dressed for the past thirty years. Tash giggled as she read that it was "vital that they talk, more serious than a matter of life and death." You had to give it to Jayne, she had such a sense of humor. However, whatever the crisis—trendy O'Neil sunglasses versus classic Gucci, perhaps?—Tash didn't have time to go to Bar de la Galerie, she had to meet with the maître d' and the chef.

Tash had hoped that Rich would at least make it to this meeting, but he didn't, so he missed the complimentary lunch that they'd prepared as a rehearsal for the wedding breakfast. Tash lingered over her coffee, playing with discarded breadcrumbs from her roll. She piled the crumbs into a Thumbelina-sized mountain, then scattered them again.

It was five past four.

The restaurant walls were painted oxblood red, which Tash thought was extremely fitting; red was a hot, passionate color. She'd finalized the menu details and timing with the maître d' and the chef. A six-course meal for six now, not eight. Sitting down at 1 p.m.; no doubt not rising again until after sundown. There were to be red gladioli on the table and, although Rich didn't know it, Tash had bought a new boarding jacket in red. Well, every bride got a new outfit. The plan was to wake up early, be married at nine on the Pointe de Mossette overlooking the Portes du Soleil. Then they'd ski and board all morning, then change and have lunch at 1 p.m. Unconventional as far as wedding days went, but exactly what Tash and Rich wanted. Outdoors, energetic and individual.

Tash had drunk three glasses of wine with her complimentary lunch. She was supposed to be tasting them and then spitting them out, but it seemed such a waste, she couldn't bear it. And now a fourth glass, a dessert wine, had just been delivered to her table. Strictly speaking, she should have drunk this with the crème brioche, but she'd only taken a bite of the brioche and then demurred, pleading that every bride-to-be likes to watch her figure. The chef had nodded, understanding. He was French and therefore loved food, but loved slim women more.

Tash sighed contentedly. She was replete and ready. Replete from the delicious meal and ready for her delicious future. She wanted to hold her arms out wide and embrace it. She wanted to dive in and touch and feel, and see and smell and hear everything that life had in store for her and Rich. It had been a peculiar week. A roller-coaster ride. Mia's constant sniping and niggles had been wearing. It would have been nice if Mia had been like Jayne. Making friends with Jayne was like being a kid on a blistering hot summer day, dashing down a slide into a paddling pool of water—fun, thrilling and a giggle. Jayne would always have a special place in Tash's heart. Becoming friends with Mia had been closer to the experience of climbing up a greased pole but, although Tash still had some way to go, she believed it would be worth it. Everyone else seemed to like and respect Mia. It couldn't be that they were all mistaken. Besides, the more she'd got to know everyone, the better she liked them.

And best of all, since their talk yesterday, Tash felt that she and Rich had never been stronger. She had never felt as close to him as she did last night. She had felt entirely complete, entirely fulfilled. She said to herself, Bring it on. She and Rich were about to embark on a lifetime of love, respect and honesty. Life didn't get any better.

Tash swallowed back another slurp of dessert wine. She ought to go and find Mia and ask her if she would do a reading at the wedding. She'd go as soon as she finished this glass.

"Hi, I've been looking for you." Tash looked up and grinned as she saw Jayne. Perfect. Company.

"I know. I got your notes. I'm sorry I didn't call you. I've had such a busy day. Come on, pull up a chair, I'll tell you all about it. Do you fancy a glass of wine? Or maybe champagne? I fancy champagne." Tash giggled. "I cannot believe I'll be married this time tomorrow." Tash beamed at her friend. "It's kind of just hit me. With all the drama about Ted and Kate and the—let's face it—issues I've had with Mia, I'd almost forgotten why I'd come here." Tash rolled her eyes, paused, thought back to the night before, then beamed at Jayne. "But yesterday we boarded to Switzerland and we had the most romantic time." Jayne sat down opposite, bolt upright and unsmiling. She didn't look like someone who was about to start a party. Tash paused, and then asked, "Everything OK?"

"I have something very difficult to tell you, and I always think that with bad news it's best to get straight to the point, don't you?"

Jayne's eyes had changed. They were no longer smudgy, smiley and sincere, as Tash was sure they had been. They were flintlike and focused.

"What is it? Has there been an accident? My God, is it Rich?"

"No accident, but, yes, my bad news is about Rich."

Something didn't compute. Tash couldn't understand. Bad news. Her friend was about to tell her some bad news, so shouldn't she be trying to look more sympathetic? Shouldn't she be touching her arm or something? Good God, was this news so awful that it blasted apart common conventions? Tash didn't know what to think.

"Tash, I really am frightfully sorry, but your wedding is off." Jayne pronounced the sentence in tight, clipped tones. She used her poshest accent. The one that she knew terrified shop assistants.

"What?" laughed Tash. "What's the joke?" That's why Jayne had seemed unnatural. This wasn't *real* bad news; it was a joke, a poor-taste joke.

"No joke. Rich is having an affair." Jayne shrugged, surely that was explanation enough.

"I don't believe you," Tash said instantly.

She stared at Jayne, who stared right back. Tash searched her friend's face for some uncertainty, sympathy or sorrow, which surely ought to be the correct response if this ridiculous tale were true. She saw none. Jayne looked back with bored indifference.

"It is absolutely true."

"There's some mistake. Or an explanation," stumbled Tash.

Because, oh, God, this could not be true. Not Rich. Other men cheated on their girls and women, but her Rich would never do that to her, never. The waiter seemed to be lurching at her, then disappeared into the distance. The wine rack and the dessert cart were out of focus. The red walls pulsed like an exposed heart. Tash felt trapped in a semiconscious state, not dissimilar to going under anesthetic. She couldn't make sense of her world. Even as her heart and soul rejected the concept, her brain began to work overtime.

It could be true. Rich had a history of infidelity. What was so special about her, and her relationship, for her to imagine that she was immune? Why would Jayne make this up? She wouldn't, no one would. Besides, Rich *had* been acting peculiarly recently. And where was he today? Why didn't he want to meet the registrar? Had he sent Jayne to do his dirty work? Was it Mia? Had her fears been founded? Her brain scolded her immature heart and soul. Her brain said it did make sense and that her heart and soul were foolish for trusting him.

"How do you know?" asked Tash. Please, God, she prayed, let it be gossip. Let it be hearsay that is unsubstantiated and ultimately erroneous.

"Because it is me he is having an affair with." Jayne held Tash's gaze, she refused to falter or apologize.

"You?"

Tash gasped and reached for her glass of water. She glugged it back and tried to breathe. But she couldn't. Something as simple as breathing, which she'd been doing forever, was impossible. Tash could feel a debilitating pain in her gut. It throbbed with the same intensity that a stitch did. It felt like those undefined pains that kids suffer from between nine and fourteen—her mother used to call them growing pains. Where was her mum? She needed her mum to massage away this growing pain.

"We started sleeping together when I was sixteen and have been ever since."

"Ever since?" Tash repeated uselessly. She didn't understand.

"He didn't know how to tell you." Jayne stood up and walked out of the restaurant. She congratulated herself. She'd spent twenty-four hours perfecting that script and, really, she could not have delivered it better.

# 66

## *Jason's Reasoning*

"Christ, what a fucking mess," said Rich.

"Yours or mine?" asked Jase.

"Yours," said Rich, and then he added, "Well, mine, too, obviously. Fuck, who'd have thought it? Mia trying to get pregnant without telling you." Jase had filled Rich in on the events of the night before, but Rich was still struggling to compute the facts. "So, she wants a baby, yeah? With you?"

"No, not exactly with me. That's my point. She wants my baby, but not me."

"Fuck."

"Couldn't put it better myself, mate."

"She doesn't want your money?"

"I've told you, Rich, she wants nothing to do with me, not even my money."

Jason was finding Rich's inability to grasp the situation a little frustrating. Jase had been grappling with it all night, yet he'd hoped that his pal would be a step ahead of him and manage to offer some words of wisdom. "Do you want a beer?"

"No. I'll have an orange juice. I can't drink on top of this. It's too mad as it is." Jason opened the minibar and pulled out two cans of Fanta. It was sickly sweet stuff, but he figured they could both do with the sugar. Sugar was good for shock.

"I never knew she was lonely," Jase sighed.

"I never knew she was maternal," commented Rich.

"I never knew she rated me," added Jase.

"Oh, I knew that," said Rich, pleased that he had something over his pal. Even during moments such as this one, Rich's innate, testosterone-driven, competitive spirit was overwhelming.

"Did you?" Jason was thrilled and fearful at once.

"It's obvious, isn't it? You two were never happier than when you were together."

"It hasn't been obvious to me. She's always taking the piss out of me. She's always saying my job isn't a proper job and that I should use my talents to write a Booker Prize or something."

"She's very proud of you."

"If I had a pound for every time she's called me immature or objected to the company I keep, I'd be able to retire."

"I'd have thought the fact that she doesn't like whom you are screwing is evidence enough of her ardor, even to a numbskull like you."

Jason thought about it. Rich might have a point.

"But she doesn't want me, does she? She wants my sperm."

"I don't know, buddy, really I don't. Maybe she wants more."

Jason stared at his best friend, and the importance of his words zapped through him, hitting him with laser speed and precision. Could Rich be right? He'd like him to be right. He'd like there to be the slightest glimmer of a possibility that he and Mia had a real chance at being a real couple. Maybe he had always known that no other woman ever came up to scratch in comparison to Mia. None of them was as quick, or witty, or as sexy, or as demanding. Yes, he'd come across longer legs and firmer butts. He'd certainly come across more compliant, easygoing broads, but none of them excited him in the way Mia had, in the way Mia does. Was it possible that Rich was right? It seemed unlikely. He used to think Rich knew everything there was to know about women, but recently it was clear that Rich knew less than fuck-all.

"God, this is confusing."

Jason sat on his bed with his legs spread wide, and hung his head. Rich sat on a chair, but he held a similarly defeated stance. They had sat together for most of the day. The late afternoon light tumbled through the windows. The sky remained resolutely, beautifully blue, and the mountains were lit with sunshine, yet the air of depression in the bedroom hung so thickly the boys felt they could taste it. The stylish interior decor could do nothing to banish the gloom. Besides, Jason's mess made the luxurious room appear cramped and chaotic, like a slightly sordid YMCA. Wet clothes littered the backs of chairs, emitting steam and stench, and lone sneakers littered the floor looking for their partners. Jason breathed in, deeply. The only possible solution to this complex emotional issue was to ignore it. He turned his attention to Rich.

"So what's going on with you, the lovely Tash and the bunny boiler?"

"Well, I'd like to have stayed in Switzerland today. In fact, I wanted to get married in Switzerland, so that I could avoid Jayne until after the wedding," said Rich.

Jason stared at him, amazed and amused.

"And that's it, is it? That's your plan? You are thirty-three. You have a degree from one of the finest universities in the country. You have twelve years' experience as a management consultant at one of the biggest and most strategically demanding firms in the world and that's the best you can come up with. You're just going to avoid Jayne for the rest of your days."

"If at all possible, yes," said Rich. He was a little uncomfortable with Jason's mocking tone.

"And are you going to intercept Tash's mail? So that if Jayne writes to her—"

"Yes, if I have to."

"And her calls?"

"Yes."

STILL THINKING *of* YOU          425

"And are you going to keep her away from any social event where Jayne might be? Not to mention the possibility of stalking. I wouldn't put it past Jayne."

"Yes, yes," screamed Rich. He understood Jason's point.

"Mate, it's not going to work." Rich looked at Jason as though he had struck a fatal blow. "You are going to have to talk to Tash. By anyone's standards this is a big secret, but if you try to keep this from Tash and you are found out, which you will be, she'll never forgive you. Not with her one hundred percent honesty policy and all that."

"You said if I bluffed it out I'd be OK."

"That was before you went for a repeat performance and put your tongue down her throat and your hands down her bra."

"Thanks, mate, you're a real comfort," snarled Rich.

"I'm just telling you how it is. It's not me you're angry with." No, Rich was angry with himself. How had he allowed this situation to escalate out of control? "For what it's worth, I think Tash will forgive you."

"You do?" Rich looked at Jason hopefully.

"She's besotted with you. Just tell her. She'll be mad, but she'll forgive you eventually."

"You think so?"

"I'm sure. Go to her now, mate. Just get on with it. Don't be like me and Mia, don't let there be any crossed wires. Don't squander this opportunity. Go to her, before you're too late."

# 67

## *Tash Packs*

Rich turned the lock in the door and walked into their suite. Too late. He was already too late.

Tash had her back to him, and her suitcase lay wide open on the bed. Rich watched as Tash went to the wardrobe, took out some of her T-shirts, carefully folded them and put them in her case. Her actions were considered and precise. They were not the actions of a hysterical or rash woman. Rich knew that was worse for him.

"What are you doing?" he asked.

"Isn't it obvious? I'm packing," said Tash, without turning around to look at him. Rich didn't ask why she was packing. It would be insulting to do so. It was obvious why. Because he was a moron, that's why. Because he'd fucked up. Because he was incapable of sticking to one simple rule.

Tash didn't turn to Rich because he would see that she was crying. He would see hefty, ugly tears sliding down her cheeks and falling off her chin, splattering onto the clothes she was packing.

"I don't know what she's told you, but it isn't as bad as she's said. She's a liar."

"In that case, you are well suited because you talk some shit, too."

Rich paused. The truth of the statement floored him. He did, it was true.

"She said you are lovers." The word stuck in Tash's throat.

"We were."

His response stabbed her in the gut. "Since she was sixteen."

"Not ever since. I haven't slept with her since I met you. It's all over. As soon as I met you I knocked all that laddish stuff on the head, I swear to you," pleaded Rich.

Tash whipped around to face Rich. The tears and tension brimmed through her eyes, nose and mouth. She swiped her arm across her face, smearing snot, salty tears and saliva onto her sleeve. It was only in movies that parting scenes were ever beautiful.

"You swear to me? Ha! What does that mean? You are a liar."

"She's history. The kiss the other night, the grope, it didn't mean anything."

"What kiss? What grope?" Tash yelled, more confused, more furious. Hadn't he just said it was over?

Fuck, it looked as though Jayne had omitted that bit. Rich was making things worse. He didn't know what to say. He didn't know what not to say.

"I love you, Tash."

And the peculiar thing was that she knew he did love her, as much as he was capable of loving anyone. She knew that he could not have faked the intimacy that they had shared over the past nine months. But he'd still lied to her, misled and deceived her. The fact he loved her while doing so made this betrayal worse, not better.

"Did you send her to say the wedding was off? Did you get her to do your dirty work?" Tash couldn't quite decide which of the many betrayals was the most offensive.

"No. I didn't tell her to do any such thing. I didn't want you to know about us."

"So there is an 'us'?" she screamed angrily.

"No, no, there isn't. There never was." Rich tried to sound soothing. He sounded panicked. "Look, she was a fuck buddy. She didn't mean any more or less to me than the dozens of other girls I've been with."

"Other girls you've told me about or other secret fuck buddies?" asked Tash sarcastically.

Suddenly, after months of avoidance, Rich wanted to explain. He knew it wouldn't excuse, but he wanted the facts on the table. "She was the only person I failed to tell you about. It started years ago. I'd call her up from time to time. It went on longer than I expected. It didn't mean anything."

"Why didn't you tell me about her, then?" Tash took a guess. "Was she your backup? Were you planning on keeping her on the side, just in case things cooled down between us and you ever fancied a bit of extracurricular?"

"No, of course not."

Rich wanted to plead with Tash. He was prepared to beg. He wanted her to trust him again, to believe him. The problem was he didn't wear sincerity particularly well. No one ever did after they had been caught cheating.

"She's very beautiful," said Tash.

Rich stayed absolutely still. Any gesture he made would be interpreted incorrectly. Yes, of course, Jayne *was* very beautiful, but he wouldn't be helping himself by admitting as much to Tash.

"She's very sexy. Really extraordinarily so. And she's wealthy. Your friends like her. Even bloody Mia likes her. She's the perfect girl for you."

Jealousy stained the soul, blurred vision and threw judgment. This was not, thought Tash, the moment to be pointing out Jayne's good points. Tash had never known jealousy until this point. She had never felt the frenzied battle between good sense and evil imaginings. The brief fears she'd held that Rich might have something going on with Mia were nothing compared to the crazy, illogical terror that had seized her mind now.

Every time he'd tongued her tiny tits had he been longing for Jayne's voluptuous curves? Had he found her blondeness bland in comparison to Jayne's more exotic dark looks? Jayne worked in the same company. Had they been meeting for coffee, every day for a decade? Did he fuck her after hours, then take photos of her ass on the photocopying machine?

"No, no, Tash. You are the perfect girl for me."

Tash barely heard the interruption. Did he prefer her blow jobs? Did she make him laugh? Had they ever had a bath together? Did he blow in Jayne's ear? She wanted to hit Rich. She wanted to clobber him over and over again with her Jimmy Choos or, better still, with her huge snow boots—they'd do more damage. He had reduced her to inarticulate violence, such was her frustration, her disappointment, her foul anguish.

She had thought that she knew everything there was to know about the women in Rich's past. They'd had numerous conversations to exorcize any potential demons. She knew the pitch of their moans, their on-top-or-underneath preferences, their foibles about going out without makeup. She had processed and compartmentalized them all. She had steadily worked through his history, assessing it under a microscopic light to see if there were any latent threats or tantalizing unresolved issues. She'd thought she was in the clear and in control. She thought they knew one another. She thought they were honest with one another.

She hadn't held anything back. She'd told him everything. The things that put her in a good light and the things that left her looking shabby. He knew about her drunken lays and the time she'd tried (and failed) to seduce a married man. He knew that she'd sometimes treated hearts carelessly. Neither of them was a vestal virgin, but the thing they had going for them, the thing that set this relationship apart from all the others that they had both stumbled through, was that they had been honest with one another. They had started with a clean slate.

Or at least that's what she'd thought.

Rich moved toward Tash; she backed away. He stretched out to her, but she flinched, as though he were diseased. He wondered whether he ought to pull up a chair and sit down and try to go through the whole thing from the beginning. It might look too presumptive. She might be about to throw him out at any second. If he sat down and made himself comfortable—or at least less uncomfortable because right now, he was about as comfortable as a man who had endured an all-over body wax and was now being buggered by a giant hedgehog—then she might be further incensed. It worried him that, throughout this conversation, Tash had continued to pack her clothes. All that her case needed now was her toiletry bag.

"I am sorry I didn't tell you. I'd never told anyone."

"Why? I thought you and Jason got off on retelling one another's adventures?"

Rich was momentarily surprised. He hadn't realized Tash knew that. "I was ashamed, OK? I was sorry and ashamed. You saw the photos. She was a child."

"So were you. You were only three years older than her."

"I thought I was so mature."

"I can't imagine why."

"I felt to blame, as though I'd taken advantage of her. I didn't think Ted would be too pleased."

Tash fought with the humiliation. She felt such a fool. They'd been right. Everyone who raised an eyebrow and said that she and Rich were rushing things and that they didn't know each other well enough, they had all been right. She didn't know him. She'd been an idiot to trust him. Could she even trust what he was saying now? She went into the bathroom and reemerged with a bulging toiletry bag.

"Even if I accept why you kept it a secret from your mates all those moons ago, it doesn't explain why you didn't tell me. You were young in the photos, too. Young enough to make a mistake. I'd have understood."

"I don't think I treated her very well," admitted Rich.

"You're right about that, at least."

"I didn't want you to think badly of me."

"That doesn't wash. I know you did a stripper for a bet on a stag weekend. That was hardly your finest moment, but I didn't care. It was in your past. Oh, my God, she knew that, too."

"What?"

"Jayne. When she was talking about her ex, the one who had broken her heart, she mentioned he'd once screwed a stripper and that she'd been driven to distraction by the thought. Oh, God, all that time she was swapping confidences with me, they were about you. *My* fiancé." Tash needed to sit down. Or to run away. "I feel sick." Tash collapsed on the bed and covered her eyes with her hands. The room was swaying.

"I didn't want you to be friends. That's not my fault."

"It is your fault," she yelled. "It's entirely your fault."

Rich knelt on the floor next to the bed and carefully took hold of Tash's hands. He gently lowered them, moving slowly as though he were coaxing a timid animal, until her eyes were uncovered once again.

"It's you I love. You I want to marry. You have to believe me."

His breathing was heavy. It was an important sentence. Possibly the most important one he was ever going to utter. She had to believe him. Rich studied Tash's lovely face. He'd studied her big blue eyes, which at the moment were red and framed with smudged mascara. He stared at her beautiful mouth, her plump magenta lips. If he could have, he'd have sold his soul at that moment to see her broad smile radiate and to hear her happy laugh. He gaped at her cheekbones, the fine lines around her mouth and the tiny hairs on her ears. He tried to commit every detail about her to his memory. He was scaring himself by doing so because he was behaving like a man that was letting go. He'd lost her.

"I do believe that, Richard."

Hope?

Her face was still cold and closed.

No hope?

"Then what's the problem?" he asked.

Tash thought one of the problems was that he didn't see the problem, but she decided that line of argument would confuse him. She strove for clarity.

"Rich, I agreed to marry you after only two months because I thought we had a unique connection. I thought you understood what was important to me and that you had the same values. But it was all fake. You never believed in no secrets, no lies, just one hundred percent respect and honesty. You just told me what you thought I wanted to hear. The same as you've done with countless women before me. Just as you are probably doing now."

"I'm telling you the truth," insisted Rich, frustrated.

"I can't trust you. You've snuffed out the magic. I don't know you. It turns out I never did." Tash stood up, zipped up her suitcase and pulled it off the bed. She walked to the door, only pausing to take off her engagement ring and toss it into the ashtray on the dressing table.

# 68

## *Girlfriends*

Tash didn't really know where to go or what to do next. She had already rung the airport earlier on that afternoon, only to discover that there were no more flights that evening. She'd asked about booking herself onto a flight home the next day, but she'd been told that there was no availability. Her scheduled flight wasn't due for departure until Saturday. She had two nights and a day to kill. It was Rich she wanted to kill. She stood in the corridor and felt very alone. She needed a room and she needed a drink. She needed the drink first.

Tash dragged her suitcase to the lift and headed to the hotel bar.

"Going somewhere?"

Tash turned to see Mia sitting in front of the open fire in the bar. She had a bottle of wine open, half of which she'd already drunk. Tash couldn't imagine anyone she'd have less liked to bump into.

Except Rich.

Or Jayne.

Tash sighed. It was a small hotel, and it wasn't exactly brimming with her favorite people. She shrugged and sat down next to Mia, giving in to the inevitability and spite of fate.

"Yes, but only after I've had a drink."

"You can share this bottle with me, if you like."

Tash thought that any port in a storm had never seemed more pertinent. She did need a drink. Tash could almost taste the deep-red, fruity liquid. It was just too tempting. She nodded, reluctantly. Mia signaled for the waiter to bring another glass. When he had done so and discreetly disappeared back into the fabric of the hotel, Tash said, "The wedding is off."

"Oh." Mia paused, then added, "I'm sorry."

"You're not really," said Tash.

She no longer needed Mia to do a reading at the wedding, let alone to become a lifelong friend, and therefore no longer felt that she had to be diplomatic. "You weren't exactly overjoyed for us when we announced the engagement."

Mia sighed. She'd done a lot of thinking herself that day and a lot of drinking, too. One or the other made her explain herself.

"You seemed very young."

"I'm twenty-seven. I'm only six years younger than you."

"Yes, but you were full of the giddy confidence of a twenty-something, and I am stuffed full of the deadening cynicism of a thirty-something. We seemed light years apart."

"Well, at least the giddy confidence has been bashed out of me now," groaned Tash as she took a large gulp of wine. "So, do you now think I am officially grown up?"

"I think we're all old enough to know better, but do our worst anyway." Mia sighed. "It wasn't just your age. Rich had never introduced any of his women to the gang before. We didn't know what to expect."

"Something other than me, though, hey?"

Mia shrugged. "And the engagement was very quick. You were bound to come across a certain amount of reservation. It wasn't personal."

"It was."

"It wasn't meant to be."

The girls fell silent and together watched the open fire hiss and crackle, spitting out sizzling amber sparks that looked like tiny fireflies. Tash was too stressed to think about whether the silence was comfortable or uncomfortable. She felt too weary even to consider making polite small talk. She didn't care anymore.

Mia respected the stillness. She wished she had the courage to tell Tash that she'd had her own concerns, her own dramas, and therefore hadn't been as polite or welcoming as she ought. She could see that now. Mia kept quiet. Tash was bound to ask what the concerns and dramas were, and Mia wasn't prepared to share. Mia stole a sneaky, sidelong glance at Tash. Tash was correct, her self-righteous cockiness which Mia had rather charitably referred to as "giddy confidence" clearly had taken a beating. Tash looked frail. She didn't shine, and it surprised Mia that she felt sad that another light had been extinguished in the world. She thought she'd try her hand at being sympathetic.

"I was very surprised about Jayne."

"You knew?" Tash's fury at Rich was reignited. He'd even lied about that. The gang did know. Once again she felt peculiarly excluded. She imagined Mia and Rich cozied up, Mia offering an ear and advice as Rich confided in her that he was torn between two lovers. Mia would have loved that.

"I caught them kissing in the foyer of the cinema on Monday night."

"Oh." The relief that Rich hadn't been confiding in Mia was short-lived as Tash computed the info. "On Monday night? The bastard."

"Quite," said Mia, with what she hoped came across as the correct blend of compassion and understanding. She didn't want there to be a hint of "I told you so."

"I thought *you* were the problem," said Tash.

Mia should have seen it coming. What with Tash's famed honesty, she knew she was due a home truth or two.

"Me and Action Man? You've got to be kidding. It might come as a surprise to you, but not everyone finds Action Man as irresistible as you and Jayne clearly do."

Tash glared. "Will you stop with the bloody nicknames? No one uses them but you."

"Don't they?"

"No, Mia, they don't. Everyone else left them at college. Everyone else has moved on."

"That's because they all have something to move on to."

Tash wasn't really listening to Mia. She had a few things that she wanted to get off her chest and now, when she was awash with pain, insecurity and fury, seemed as good a time as any.

"I always saw the 'very private' nicknames for what they were, Mia—a way for you to constantly dredge up the past and continue to exclude me."

"Not true. I gave you a nickname, didn't I?"

"Calling me Barbie was unforgivable. Even Barbie Babe was tantamount to kicking my dog."

Mia knew that Tash was right. Barbie might have a great wardrobe. But even if Mattel did give her a white coat, glasses or even an astronaut costume, the Barbie doll was never going to be a feminist icon or a contestant on *Mastermind*. Mia searched around for something conciliatory.

"Barbie marries Action Man, doesn't she?"

"No. Barbie marries Ken, a eunuch, and they split after forty happy, costume-changing years. Action Man stays a confirmed old bachelor," said Tash crossly.

"Not when I played with mine," replied Mia.

Tash looked at Mia and searched her face for any hint of sarcasm or malice. She found none. The ludicrous nature of her situation hit her. It seemed pointless arguing with this woman about plastic dolls and things that had been said about a faithless, two-timing, bastard ex-fiancé. Tash started to giggle. She feared she was clinically hysterical.

"I'm exhausted, can we call a truce?" said Tash.

Mia had never wanted a friend more. Delighted, she beamed at Tash, and then stunned the breath out of her by leaning in and giving her an enormous hug. Just when Tash thought it was impossible for her to sustain any more shocks or surprises, Mia burst into tears.

"Jesus, Mia." Tash hugged Mia tightly and stroked her back, as Mia seemed to have no intention of loosening her grip. "What's wrong? Chill, girl. Take a deep breath, and tell me what the matter is."

"Everyone is always telling me to chill, to relax and to have more fun. But you know what? It's not as easy as that. It's almost impossible to have fun, or to be fun, for that matter, if you are unhappy."

"And are you?"

"Desperately," sobbed Mia.

Once again Tash found herself in a position where she didn't know what to do or say next. She was not a fan or a friend of

Mia's. She'd offered a truce; she had not expected full-on familiarity. She'd been longing for friendship for months, and there had been no sign that Mia was ever going to reciprocate the wish. But suddenly the ice maiden had melted, all over the settee.

Tash sighed. She had problems of her own. She knew what it was to feel alone and miserable. She had discovered that her fiancé was fooling around with a girl whom she had considered to be a good pal. She knew about hurt and betrayal and desperate unhappiness. So.

"Is this about Jason?"

"You know?" Mia was horrified. Had Jason been talking about them to Tash? She imagined Tash and Scaley cozied up. Tash offering an ear and advice as Jase confided in her that Mia had made a complete fool of herself trying to trick him into impregnating her. Tash would have loved that.

"I don't really know anything," said Tash, immediately dispelling Mia's fears. "It was just something Lloyd said about you two being a team, a couple, even though—"

"Even though we're not a couple."

"Exactly."

"We nearly were. Last night I snatched defeat away from the jaws of victory."

"Isn't that supposed to be the other way around?"

"I meant what I said."

Tash looked confused. Mia took a deep breath and weighed the risk. The chances were she wouldn't be seeing much of Tash after this evening, not now that Rich had messed everything up, so if she confided in her it didn't have to be a big deal. And even if she did see Tash in the future, say, they kept in touch—and at this moment (admittedly it could have been the alcohol she consumed), Mia could imagine stranger things than keeping in touch with Tash—say they kept in touch, despite Rich having been a prick, confiding in Tash didn't have to be a big deal.

Suddenly Mia saw Tash in a new light.

In fact, she saw everything in a new light. Tash's life wasn't perfect. Right now, it was pretty bloody miserable and through no
fault of her own. And poor Ted and Kate, their boat wasn't exactly
sailing fortune's seas at this precise juncture in time. Lloyd had
talked to Tash about her and Jase; that showed a level of concern.
A level of concern she hadn't extended to him when he was very
much in need of some mates. She had been very dismissive of all
of these people. She'd jealously resented any good luck and happiness that they'd enjoyed. She'd held the illogical notion that there
was only a limited supply of good things to go around—a limited
supply of soul mates, a restricted quantity of babies, a ration of
contentment, company and love. It was as though she believed
that every engagement or birth her friends and acquaintances announced diminished her opportunities of attaining similar bliss.
It was a ridiculous notion. Nonsense. Quite beneath the intelligence of a rational woman.

But, then, she hadn't been that intelligent or rational of late.
How rational was it to plan to have a baby with your best friend
and try to keep it from him? She'd been desperate and desolate.
She was only a short step away from bitter and a bit barmy.

She needed to talk to someone—anyone, really. Only half an
hour ago she would have thought that Tash was more anyone than
someone, but something had changed. Tash had just broken up
with her fiancé, but she wasn't weeping and wailing or acting like
a frantic shrew as Mia might have predicted from the young and
immature Tash of her imagination. Tash was behaving with composure and dignity. She was even finding it in her heart to dig up
some time and sympathy for Mia, although Mia knew she didn't
deserve it. Jase liked Tash. Kate, Ted and Lloyd liked Tash. Rich
loved Tash, despite his wandering dick. There had to be something
about her worth liking and, now the green scales of jealousy were

peeling from her eyes, Mia had the first clue as to what those qualities might be.

"I came here to seduce him," she started to explain.


# 69


## *Lloyd's Cavalry*


Tash and Mia were deep in conversation. It took until the end of the bottle of wine for Mia to explain exactly how much she longed for a child. It took another half bottle for Tash to pluck up the courage to suggest it wasn't a child per se that Mia wanted, but the whole shebang. She wanted a partner and a family. After another glass, Tash explicitly stated that, in her opinion, Mia wanted the partner to be Jason, and the whole pregnancy thing had been her subconscious trying to direct her.

Mia thought Tash was absolutely wrong—way off the mark—until they drained the second bottle. At that point Mia confessed that she'd had the same thought last night, but what should she do about it? Scaley *must* hate her now.

Tash and Mia were so deep in strategy and suggestion that they did not notice a new guest checking into the hotel, even though the tall, blond Austrian woman with gamine limbs and tightly cropped hair was extremely striking.

Greta declined the offer of help with her bag. It was only small; she was only planning on staying until Saturday. She asked for directions to Lloyd Carter's room and said, no, she'd rather they didn't inform him of her arrival, she wanted to surprise him. While, technically, this was a breach of hotel regulations, the receptionist was experienced enough to know this woman was not here to make trouble and she would be a welcome surprise guest.

Greta had had enough of sitting alone at home. Alone, it was too easy to feel hurt and vulnerable. It was her belief that the manufacturers of telephones put something in the handsets of mobiles and land phones which distorted conversations. Conversations that were supposed to be jovial and encouraging, or conciliatory and tender, somehow transformed into conversations which were pitted with snide jibes and hostile demands. Greta wanted to put a stop to it.

It was a mistake for Lloyd to have come away without her. He was inclined to the maudlin and the sentimental. She understood that. He'd given a lot up to be with her, she knew that. And it wasn't easy, not for anyone. Of course he lived with regrets, everyone did. But Greta did not believe that Lloyd ought to regret leaving his wife for her. Greta loved Lloyd. She loved him very, very much. And she would make him happy again, if only he would let her. If he ever stopped feeling guilty and allowed himself to be happy again, she'd be by his side. And even if he never stopped feeling guilty, she would still be by his side. Because that is what she wanted, and that is what Lloyd deserved.

Greta knew that there was a reasonable chance that Lloyd had called his ex-wife this week. He would have got drunk at some point (or, probably, at several points) and reasoned that it was a good idea to try to piece things back together with the mother of his child. He had said the same thing to her on a number of drunken occasions. That was the problem—when drink goes in, either truth or nonsense comes out, and it is sometimes hard to tell which is which. Greta knew that Lloyd wanting a reconciliation with Sophie was nonsense. Greta admitted that in a perfect world all marriages would be happy, enduring, fruitful marriages. The perfect world did not exist, not even in fairy tales. If it did, how come there were always so many stepparents in those old stories?

Logic would dictate that it would be easier the second time around, and it frustrated Greta, who had a supremely logical mind, that it was not. It was a lot harder. The blissfully ignorant are a recognized body; no one ever talks about the blissfully informed. Greta had hoped that once the divorce came through, Lloyd would believe that they had a clean slate, but he did not. He argued that the only way he could start again was to go back.

He was wrong.

It was impossible to turn back time or to push water back under the bridge. The English were so fond of their funny little idioms and sayings, yet they did not heed them. Greta walked purposefully into the lift and pressed the button for the second floor. She was here to tell Lloyd it was time to lay down his baggage and move on. While she was at it, she might mention that it was time for him to cut back on his alcohol units, too.

# 70

## *Tash's Advice*

When Mia first offered to share her room with Tash for the night, it struck Tash as bizarre. Only hours before she would have been surprised at Mia offering her a cup of coffee, let alone a lifeline. Tash briefly wondered whether she ought to feel

wary of sudden friendships. After all, she now understood that
Jayne's intimacy was calculated and had never been born of genuine
affection. Indeed, the opposite was true. Jayne had faked a friendship so as to be in a position to hurt Tash. It made her shudder.

However, Tash's embryonic friendship with Mia seemed very
different. For a start, it was born out of months of hostilities rather
than seconds of attraction. Tash did not know why that should be
a comfort, but it was. She did, at least, know something of Mia.
In fact, after several hours of talking she believed she knew an awful lot. Mia spoke with dignified honesty and a sometimes painful
but always indisputable clarity.

Throughout the evening Mia indulged herself. She dredged up
her and Jason's history and paraded it in front of Tash for inspec-
tion. She had never treated herself to such girlie comfort before.
She explained how they'd suddenly and almost inexplicably split
up at college. Their breakup was precipitated by a breakdown in
communication, more than anything else. Mia admitted that no
one had ever come close to satisfying her emotional, physical and
intellectual needs in the way that Jason had.

"Jason's never dated anyone seriously either, has he?" asked
Tash.

"No, he's a terrible tart."

"Or, it might be that he is also struggling to find someone who
comes up to scratch, after you," suggested Tash.

Both the girls were lying in bed, staring at the ceiling, which
was illuminated by moonlight. There was a long silence. Mia
weighed the potential of Tash being right.

"Do you think so?" asked Mia.

Tash turned on her side and propped herself up on her elbow.

"Go and ask him, Mia," she encouraged.

It was three in the morning. The girls had talked all night.
Hostilities had halted, and new allegiances had been formed.
They were behaving as though they were in a Cabinet room at a

time of great crisis. They had no concept of time and little concept of reality. Everything seemed to be topsy-turvy. That night,
opportunity had turned into probability. Love had turned sour.
Mistrust had turned to friendship. Anything was possible.

"What would I say to him?" Mia asked.

For the first time, for as long as she could remember, Mia
wanted advice. She was at sea and wanted to get to dry land. She
hoped and thought Tash had the skills to get her there.

"Just be honest, Mia. Tell him that the baby stuff was real, but
not absolutely considered. Tell him you want to give it a go. Tell
him you want to be a conventional couple. The way I see it you
have already wasted years, what more have you got to lose?"

"Precisely nothing," said Mia, as she climbed out of bed and
pulled on her clothes.

"Good luck," said Tash, as Mia quietly closed the door behind her.

# FRIDAY

# 71

## *Something Blue*

Tash was relieved to see Mia go. Not only did she believe that Mia and Jason had a genuine chance of making one another happy, but also, from a more selfish point of view, she needed the space. It had been useful to stumble across Mia's confusion and for Tash to dive into her problems rather than have to face her own terror. But now, at precisely three-fifteen on the morning of what ought to have been her wedding day, Tash wanted to think about her own situation.

She ought to have been asleep dreaming of the best day of her life. Or, if she was awake, it ought to have been because of giddy excitement, not the crucifying ache that throbbed in her gut which was keeping her awake now.

How could he have done it to her? How could he have lied and cheated? And exactly what had he done to her? Was he having an affair as Jayne claimed? Or was it something in his past, still terrible but perhaps not quite so insistent? What did he mean when he said the kiss and the grope meant nothing? How could a kiss and a grope mean nothing? Was he referring to the kiss in the cinema that Mia had seen? Or was there another kiss and grope? The questions fell in and out of her mind. They jostled one another, demanding consideration. Each question she answered only pushed another to the front. What sort of man had a ten-year fuck buddy? What was it about Jayne that made Rich go back and back? What was it about her that meant he never wanted to stay? Why hadn't he told her about Jayne? Was she his backup? Did he love Jayne? Did he love her? Did she love him? Did it matter either way?

Tash finally fell asleep at six in the morning, only to be awoken by Mia's alarm clock at seven. There was a split second when Tash's heart sang. It was her wedding day. Oh, my God, she was the happiest woman on the planet, and then almost in the same instant she remembered where she was sleeping and why, and her heart broke all over again.

She dragged herself out of bed and into the shower. She needed to eat breakfast. She didn't feel much that way inclined, but she had to call the registrar and cancel the wedding and she had to talk to the chef and the maître d'. Rich wouldn't think to cancel the arrangements; he'd had so little to do with making them. Too busy getting his end away. Bastard.

The shame and disappointment overwhelmed her. Tash started to weep, but there was no one to wipe her tears, so they washed down the drain with the soapy suds.


Lloyd was waiting for her in the breakfast room.

"I'm very sorry, Tash," he said, as he leaped up to hug her. Tash leaned into his chest, grateful for the hug and the warmth of another body.

"Does everyone know?"

"Rich is in a very bad way. He came to my room last night to look for you."

"I was with Mia."

"I guess he didn't think of that."

"No." Tash smiled. "I don't suppose it was expected."

"Sit down. I'll get your breakfast."

Lloyd scuttled to the buffet table and piled a number of pastries onto a plate. He grabbed a yogurt and ordered some toast and fried breakfast from the chef. He wanted to be a help and would have been mortified to realize that he was appearing insensitive as he whistled the tune of "Oh What a Beautiful Morning" under his breath. A song long banished to the deepest recesses of his mind, as long ago as junior high school.

"You seem very perky, Lloyd," said Tash, as she accepted the plate of pastries.

"Do I?" Lloyd was stricken. "I'm so sorry."

"Don't be." Tash grinned. "I'm not one for spreading misery. Hit me with it, what's going on in your life?"

Lloyd felt a little shamefaced in light of Tash's personal problems; on the other hand, he really, really wanted to tell someone. And Tash was the someone he wanted to tell.

"Greta flew in last night."

"Wow!"

"Exactly. She flew all this way to see me. She said she was missing me."

"And from the look on your face this morning, you've clearly missed her."

"Yes, I have. I was confused for a while. I knew I was missing something. Grieving over a lot of things, but I didn't know exactly how much I missed Greta, not until last night." Lloyd beamed. "I thought I wanted Sophie back."

"I've wondered whether that was the case."

"I just wanted a fresh start, but Sophie won't give me that."

"Or can't," pointed out Tash.

"Yes," conceded Lloyd. "But Greta can, and she wants to. It's not that I'm swapping one woman for another." Lloyd broke off and looked apologetically at Tash. He wanted her to understand the nuance of emotion.

"You're just trying to be happy, Lloyd. Good for you. Nothing would ever be fixed if you stayed unhappy and regretful forever."

"That's what Greta said." Lloyd beamed again.

Tash realized that this was the first time she'd seen him throw out a genuine smile. It was so wide you could have driven a truck through it.

"We had a 'big talk.'" Lloyd penciled quotation marks into the air with his fingers, clearly embarrassed.

"That is so great," said Tash. "I'm only sorry there won't be a wedding for her to join."

Lloyd's beam vanished. "You can't forgive him?"

"I can't bear him."

Tash thanked the waiter that had brought her toast and fried breakfast, and immediately picked up her fork. She started to pick up some scrambled egg, but then dropped the utensil. She didn't have it in her. You needed spirit to eat a hearty fried breakfast, and right now she was overwhelmed by just the toast and tiny pots of jam.

She hurt.

"He's so sorry. He really hasn't been having an affair."

"Why didn't he tell me about her, then?" demanded Tash.

She knew she was being unfair. How would Lloyd know? She didn't. Tash didn't understand it. It seemed that, for the majority, being honest with those they loved most was the hardest thing to be.

"Jayne's gone. She left by train."

"I wish I'd thought of that," muttered Tash.

"I talked to her last night. She's really screwed up, but she did admit to me that they aren't having an affair and that she'd wangled an invitation to the holiday just to split you up. She said that she's been making a play for Rich and that he has resisted."

"Except for the kiss and the grope, presumably," spat Tash.

Lloyd winced. Even he thought it was a shame that men couldn't treat women better and that they were so frequently ruled by their third eye. "He is so sorry," Lloyd repeated.

"Well, why isn't he here now, telling me himself?" challenged Tash. She hated herself for wanting this, but, quite simply, she did. She wanted to see Rich. She wished there was a way that he could satisfactorily explain his actions, but she knew there wasn't.

"He's gone to see the registrar and he talked to the chef and maître d'."

"He has?" Tash was stunned that Rich had behaved with even an iota of responsibility.

"He didn't want you to have to face that. Jase and I tried to persuade him not to be hasty. Not to cancel everything. We hoped you'd change your mind, but he said there was no chance of that."

"He was right."

"Are you sure? Are you absolutely sure you can't forgive him?" asked Lloyd.

He was speaking as a man who was newly coated with hope. Greta loved him. Greta loved him despite his mistakes and misgivings, and that made the world pretty damn fine as far as he was concerned. He wanted everyone to wear the same armor. He was also speaking as a man who had flushed chances away. A man who had broken a heart and a home, and he knew that was an incredible waste.

Lloyd knew that hope, and love, and trust could ebb and flow. The path of love wasn't a linear, progressive road. It was full of obstacles. Everyone encountered some bloody big boulders and deep, dark pitfalls. He thought Tash and Rich had what it took to scramble over and under, up and around any impediments. He didn't want to stand by and watch them waste their chances.

Tash sighed, "He's ruined everything. From now on, the world would always be that little bit worse."

"I understand what you mean, but it doesn't have to be that way."

"It does." Tash wanted to explain. "You know when you want a new top, say, something special to go with the skirt and boots and bag that you've already bought. And you search and search, and although you know exactly what you are looking for—you might have seen it in a magazine—you can't find it. And then you do. You find the perfect top. And you try it on. And it fits. And you look a million dollars, better than you've ever looked before. Better than you imagined you could look. Well, Rich was my top."

Tash grinned, sure she'd been lucid.

Understandably, Lloyd looked confused. He'd never hankered after a garment of clothing in his life. He bought the same shirts from M&S every year. Tash saw his confusion and wondered if she should have picked cars for her analogy. She rushed on, hoping she could make herself clear.

"And you wear that top every day because it suits you so perfectly and your friends say that you look fabulous in it. They're even a little bit envious. But then something gets spilled down your top. And you need to wash it, but you wash it in too hot a wash and it shrinks. Or when you iron it, it stretches in a funny way. You know what I'm saying, don't you?"

Lloyd wasn't sure he did.

"It never looks quite as good again, it no longer suits you properly and every time you wear it all you can think about is how perfect it *used* to be. All the top is fit for then is a yard sale."

Finally, Lloyd got it.

"No, Tash, you don't put that top in the jumble. It becomes your old favorite. It's worn in, not out." Lloyd paused. "I thought you loved him, Tash. I thought *you* knew about love."

"I do." Tash shook her head. "I don't think he deserves me anymore."

"Thank God, love has very little to do with deserving. Isn't loving someone about loving them even when they don't deserve it?"

Tash looked at Lloyd. He was full of hope and hesitancy. His eyes radiated determination, and there was no sign of the previously debilitating doubt.

"Since when were you so wise?" asked Tash.

"It's a very recent thing. I imagine it will only be temporary." Lloyd smiled. "More coffee?"

# 72

## *Fresh Tracks*

Tash put on her brand-new red snowboarding jacket. Even if there wasn't going to be a wedding, she could still wear her bridal outfit—that was an advantage to not having chosen a long, white, silk number. Not one she had foreseen, admittedly.

Tash needed to be in the mountains. She needed to board between the tall alpine trees bejeweled with fresh snow and morning sunshine. She needed to breathe in the clean air and dash across the powder bowls and easy wide flats. It was not a day for big cliff drops or tricks of any kind. She had had her fill of tricks. She wanted to be absorbed into the scene which on her arrival had appeared entirely make-believe. A world of marshmallow mountains, pretty, quaint chalets with chimneys and wooden shutters, and picturesque scenes that looked as though they had been designed by children. She wanted to luxuriate in the abundance of space, to find horizons that oozed serenity, so that she could succumb to the magic. She wanted to be alone.

She would ignore all the other skiers and boarders. She would not notice the laughing gangs of friends. She would disregard the snail trails of schoolchildren learning to weave their way down the slopes. And she would certainly not pay any attention to the smiling couples who darted through the snow together, laughing and cheering and generally making out, as though they were trying to personally insult her.

Tash planned to put Rich and Jayne completely out of her mind. She would not dwell on every conversation that she had ever had with Jayne. What was the point in examining them for clues as to why Jayne wanted to trick and betray her so completely? Wasn't it enough that Jayne was having sex with her boyfriend? Did she have to pretend to be Tash's friend, too, so that the betrayal was magnified? Tash tried not to think about the number of times when she had encouraged Rich to be nicer to Jayne. When she had told him to dance with her in the club and buy drinks for her in the bar. She felt an utter fool that she had, on at least two occasions, insisted that Rich sit next to Jayne at dinner so that they could get to know one another. To think she had been extolling Jayne's virtues when all along Rich was indecently familiar with everything Tash could highlight, and more.

She did not plan to board to Pointe de Mossette, the place where they were supposed to have gotten married, and sit and look out upon the Portes du Soleil. It just sort of happened.

Tash sat in the snow and wondered what she had done to deserve this. She checked her watch. It was ten o'clock. If everything had gone to plan, she would have been Mrs. Tyler by now. Tash knew what everyone back home would say. They'd tell her she'd had a lucky escape. That it was always better to find out about your partner's philandering ways before making the ultimate commitment. It was far harder to be left like Sophie, after several years of marriage. She knew that people would sensibly comment that she was lucky that they had not planned a huge, lavish wedding with a hundred guests. If that had been the case, the humiliation (not to mention the cost) would have been compounded. Imagine, she would have been returning toasters right now. She could almost hear her old aunties whispering such rational words of consolation.

So why didn't she feel lucky?

"Hello."

Tash knew that it was Rich without having to turn around. It wasn't that she recognized his voice. His voice was disguised with an embarrassed cough and an unnaturally high pitch, brought about by nerves. She just knew it would be Rich. She sensed him. She'd known he would find her. Perhaps that's why she had come to this point. After all, there were 650 kilometers of runs and 212 high-speed chairlifts in total in the five Portes. Les Portes du Soleil was one of the largest ski domains in the world. It was unlikely that they'd meet through coincidence. Tash had subconsciously given fate a nudge.

"I'm sorry," said Rich. He was prepared to say the words a million times if they helped. It appeared they didn't.

"You said," replied Tash, clearly unmoved.

It didn't stop him from saying them again. "I really am very sorry." He had never felt sorrier about anything in his life. The idea of Tash in pain was intolerable. The knowledge that he'd caused that pain was doubly so. "Can I sit down?"

"Does it matter how I answer that question? You pretty much do as you please, don't you, Richard?"

Rich sat down anyway. Tash stole a sly, sideways glance at him. He looked awful. He looked gray and drawn. It wasn't possible that he'd lost weight since yesterday, but it seemed that all his muscles had melted from his body. He didn't look like an Action Man; he looked frail and weak. This should have rendered him unattractive. Tash wondered why it didn't.

"I know I've fucked up."

"Yes."

Rich paused. It was clear that Tash was not going to help him in any way. This already unfeasibly daunting task would require gladiator-type courage if he was ever going to complete it, but complete it he must. He knew that the general consensus had been that he and Tash had rushed into their engagement; it didn't seem that way to him. Now that Rich had met Tash, he believed he'd been waiting all his life to meet her and that seemed a respectable length of time to him. He loved her. He'd messed up. He knew that. But he wasn't going to give up, not on the best thing that had ever happened to him.

"You were all 'Everyone makes mistakes' when Lloyd fucked up," said Rich. He was finding it hard to follow Tash's logic.

"Yes, and you were so condemning."

"Lloyd had an affair, I didn't," Rich pleaded. He thought he was being hung by a kangaroo court. "I made a mistake. I know and I'm sorry. But I am part of the great unwashed, Tash. I made a mistake, everyone does. Can't you imagine a day when you could forgive me? Not now, obviously, but sometime in the future?" Rich looked hopeful.

"No, I can't," deadpanned Tash. Tash wondered why it was easier to forgive someone you didn't love. It didn't make sense.

"No one would consider this the luckiest start to a marriage," he said tentatively.

"There isn't going to be a marriage," stated Tash.

"Tash, please give me a chance to explain. Jayne wasn't a backup plan."

Just hearing him say her name made Tash recoil in anguish. She didn't want to imagine him whispering to her in bed, calling out her name as he came. Over and over again for more than a decade!

"She was a grubby secret," said Rich.

"Oh, I'm sure she'd be thrilled to be described in such terms."

"Probably not. But right now I don't care. It was just sex to me. I thought it was the same for Jayne."

"You've hurt her, too. You know that, don't you? She's lost the plot because no one in their right mind would do the things she's done. She's clearly besotted by you."

"I think she has become obsessed with a notion of me," admitted Rich.

"Well, you must have encouraged that."

"I didn't."

Tash wondered if this was true. She didn't want to think that Rich was so dishonorable as to have led a girl on just for sex. She didn't want to think he was dishonorable or desperate, come to that. But was it possible that Jayne had developed such a strong attachment and Rich had remained entirely aloof?

"It was a crush. She didn't know me. It wasn't love. It was akin to what you felt for Prince Andrew when you were thirteen. I remember you telling me that you used to kiss his photo every night and that you persuaded your mum to travel all the way to London, to go to the Cenotaph one Remembrance Sunday, because you thought he might see you from his balcony and ask you to marry him."

Tash allowed herself a small grin at the memory and the fact that she'd shared such an embarrassing confession with Rich. "I was thirteen," she pointed out.

"Yes, but Jayne never grew out of her crush on me. Honestly, I was as oblivious as Prince Andrew was to you."

"Prince Andrew Albert Christian Edward wasn't screwing me," pointed out Tash.

Rich laughed, "You still remember his full name."

"I was very serious about him," said Tash. Half of her wished Rich couldn't always make her smile. The other half was eternally grateful that he could.

"I'm very serious about you," said Rich sensing, or at least hoping, that Tash might be thawing. "Deadly serious."

Rich reached out to take hold of Tash's hand. The action was comically clumsy because they were both wearing padded gloves. Yet, his touch tingled. His nearness seemed natural to her, despite her anger and hurt.

"Tash, I should have told you about Jayne. I see that now. Then she wouldn't have been able to cause all this confusion. I'm sorry I've made this mess, but is it possible that we could get through it?"

Rich was banking on Tash's optimism. Was it an unlimited supply? Or had the events of the past week depleted her supplies?

"I feel stupid for being so honest with you when you had secrets." Tash admitted the grimy truth about painful love affairs. The most intense pain is often the one you cause yourself.

"No, I was the stupid one," insisted Rich.

"And I feel stupid because despite the 'no secrets, no lies, just one hundred percent respect and honesty' rule, it wasn't just you who fucked up."

"It wasn't?" Rich was amazed and more than a little bit relieved.

"I thought I was immune to the petty and ugly aspects of love. But I'm not. I was still infected by jealousy. I am burning with jealousy."

"You have nothing to be jealous of."

"It seems that rationale has little to do with this."

"Maybe it doesn't. Maybe love is too magnificent to be controlled by a rationale or even a rule, however well intentioned that rule is. Maybe love is about the messy bits too. Jealousy might be part of love. It might be an essential part."

"Is this the bit when you tell me that lying is an essential part of love, too?" asked Tash impatiently.

"No. Lying has nothing to do with love. I am sorry, Tash." But he was thrilled to hear she was jealous. That had to be a good sign, didn't it? It showed she cared. "It's not possible to be in love one moment and then not the next," argued Rich. "And I know you were in love with me. I felt it, Tash."

Tash agreed with him. It was not possible to switch off love, like credit. Yet, it seemed her fortunes could still change in an instant like Ted and Kate's financial status. Tash looked at Rich and was at once furious and in love with him. As far as she was concerned, he was the most stupendous man on earth to have inspired such love in her and the most stupid man on earth to have thrown it away. She had never felt such an enormous sense of loss, waste and grief.

"I just don't think I know you anymore," Tash sighed. "Being with you would be too much of a risk." She wished she didn't believe it to be so.

"If I could, I'd sit here until the sun goes down, and overnight, all tomorrow and the next day, and tell you everything there is to know about me. Everything from the color of my exercise books in junior high school right through to my PIN. But it's not possible. There'd always be something I'd forgotten to tell you."

Tash shot Rich a look of disgust and distrust.

"Not anything else as big as Jayne, honestly," he rushed to clarify. "What I'm saying is that marriage is a *risk*. The couples that are in for trouble are the couples that don't know that. Even if we knew absolutely everything about one another now, there would still be discovery. In the future I might do something you don't like, or you might do something to offend me. There are no guarantees. But maybe, just maybe, we'd be OK. And you'd like the things you discovered about me. Maybe the discovery is the magical bit. The bit it's all about. I think we'd have a pretty good chance, Tash. I like everything I know about you. I love it all. Even the fact that you cut your toenails over the loo. And frankly, if anyone else ever had done such a thing in front of me, I'd have thought it disgusting."

Tash wanted to laugh. But could she? Should she?

"I love you, Tash. And if you'd just let me, I'll do my best to be as good a husband as I possibly can be. And I honestly don't think that would be a bad best. I know I broke our rule about no secrets, no lies, just one hundred percent respect and honesty. And I realize that ninety-five percent is not good enough for you. But I have learned by my mistake. Tash, please, will you marry me?"

Rich realized that he'd come to the end of what he wanted to say. It had been a long speech. Had it had any impact? When he'd chosen the words and practiced saying them last night, he'd had no idea what Tash's reaction would be. He didn't know if she would interrupt him with counterarguments or if she would just board off into the distance and out of his life. He'd hoped that she would fling her arms around him and insist that she'd love him forever, assure him that his mistake had not been insurmountable. But, true to form, Tash was surprising him. The one reaction he had not expected, or considered, was silence.

Tash looked out onto the beautiful vista in front of her. Was he making sense? Tash thought back to all she'd been through and all she'd seen in the past week. What had she learned from it?

She had seen love in many manifestations. Ted and Kate's love had allowed forgiveness, loyalty and hope. Their love did not allow room for blame, fickleness or despair, but did allow room for mistakes. Lloyd's love for Greta had cost dearly, way more than he'd expected to pay. But could he ever put a value on the happiness he'd felt last night when he opened the door and Greta had fallen into his arms and vowed to stay in his life? Mia and Jason's fear of the clout of their love had sent both of them chasing around the globe, in separate directions. They'd plunged themselves into lives of lonely, brief encounters. But even they, with their disproportionate amount of stubbornness, cynicism and pride, had eventually recognized that they were a team and that love isn't something to be afraid of.

It's something to be embraced.

Love allowed forgiveness, comfort, trust, compassion and new starts. Love was not a one-strike-and-you-are-out game. Like anything in life worth having, love demanded effort. Being in love—genuinely loving someone—meant you had to be brave and gracious, and well intentioned. Rich *was* talking sense. Tash took a deep breath and a chance.

"Is this the point where our friends and the registrar jump out from behind the trees and throw confetti?"

"No, babe. I didn't dare presume," said Rich. Did he dare now? Was she saying what he thought she was saying? "They are waiting for us back at the hotel," he added sheepishly.

"The rule about keeping it good, no secrets, no lies, just one hundred percent respect and honesty?"

"Reinstated, Tash. As of now." Rich stared into Tash's open face, and he willed her to take the plunge because he knew it was the right thing for them both. He knew that he would put every iota of his strength and soul into making her happy. Ever after. Tash smiled.

"OK." And then more firmly: "Yes, yes, I'll marry you, Rich."

# *Life is always a little sweeter with a book from Downtown Press!*